D0981615

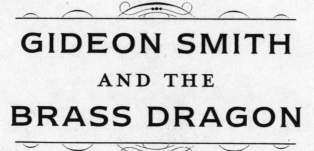

GIDEON SMITH
AND THE
BRASS DRAGON

David Barnett

TOR®

A TOM DOHERTY ASSOCIATES BOOK
New York

This is a work of fiction. All of the characters, organizations, and events portrayed in this novel are either products of the author's imagination or are used fictitiously.

GIDEON SMITH AND THE BRASS DRAGON

Copyright © 2014 by David Barnett

All rights reserved.

Maps by Jennifer Hanover

A Tor Book
Published by Tom Doherty Associates, LLC
175 Fifth Avenue
New York, NY 10010

www.tor-forge.com

Tor® is a registered trademark of Tom Doherty Associates, LLC.

Library of Congress Cataloging-in-Publication Data

Barnett, David.
 Gideon Smith and the Brass Dragon / David Barnett. — First edition.
  p. cm.
 "A Tom Doherty Associates Book"
 ISBN 978-0-7653-3425-1 (trade paperback)
 ISBN 978-1-4668-0909-3 (e-book)
 1. Alternative histories (Fiction) 2. Fantasy fiction. I. Title.
 PR6102.A7689G47 2014
 823'.92—dc23

                                             2014017604

Tor books may be purchased for educational, business, or promotional use. For information on bulk purchases, please contact Macmillan Corporate and Premium Sales Department at 1-800-221-7945, extension 5442, or write specialmarkets@macmillan.com.

First Edition: September 2014

Printed in the United States of America

0 9 8 7 6 5 4 3 2 1

Praise for David Barnett and
Gideon Smith and the Mechanical Girl

"A triumph of the modern pulp genre—funny, clever, and superbly executed. Barnett writes like a dream and I'm already anxious for the next book."

—George Mann, author of *The Immorality Engine*

"Steampunk adventure in the manner of the old penny dreadfuls . . . The narrative gets up a head of steam, and the characters, with their recognizable flaws, hold wide appeal."

—*Kirkus Reviews*

"Meet Gideon Smith, hero of the Empire . . . Vampires, villains, and vice, David Barnett happily hacks his way through nineteenth-century fiction to create Victorian England as it should have been—automatons, dirigibles, Egyptian mummies and all!"

—Jon Courtenay Grimwood

"Fiction meets history, meets steampunk, meets gothic horror in David Barnett's page-turning romp."

—*Historical Novel Society*

"A greathearted, rollicking romp through the many worlds of classic pulp—loads of fun."

—Nick Harkaway, author of *The Gone-Away World* and *Angelmaker*

"David Barnett makes the fantastic characters and industrial-age marvels decorating his delightful steampunk fantasy feel as real as London cutpurses and coal fog. . . . This funny, clever tale brings the thrills of penny-dreadful adventure to vivid life. Expect many sequels."

—*The Plain Dealer* (Cleveland)

"This ripping yarn is a colourful collision of steampunk, science fiction, and alternate history . . . discover it for yourself, preferably by torchlight under the bedclothes." —*The Sun*

"A rambunctious, captivating steampunk romp . . . Barnett is a superb storyteller and brings a refreshing verve, as well as a likeable hero, to the increasingly popular subgenre. And the good news is that this is the first volume in a trilogy."

—*The Guardian*

LAS VEGAS–CLARK COUNTY LIBRARY DISTRICT
7060 W. WINDMILL LN.
LAS VEGAS, NV 89113

ALSO BY DAVID BARNETT

Gideon Smith and the Mechanical Girl

To Charlie and Alice,
may you always be the heroes of your stories

ACKNOWLEDGMENTS

When this novel's predecessor, *Gideon Smith and the Mechanical Girl*, was published in September 2013, I had no idea what sort of reception it would receive. In retrospect, I couldn't have hoped for a better welcome for Gideon, Rowena, Maria, Aloysius, and all the rest.

The reviews have been wonderful, both from the major newspapers and magazines and from the army of book bloggers who seem to have taken Gideon & Co. to their hearts and who have written such lovely words about the first book. And thanks must go to those readers who picked up the book and enjoyed it—as a writer, nothing gladdens the heart more than getting an e-mail, message, or tweet from a complete stranger to say they sat up all night reading your book.

I must thank what I've come to think of as my Tor family for all their hard work in bringing these books to life—it's my name on the front of this book but it wouldn't exist without the determination and support of my wonderful editor, Claire Eddy, Bess Cozby, Patrick Nielsen Hayden, publicist extraordinaire Leah Withers, Irene Gallo, and everyone else through whose hands *Gideon* has passed on the journey to publication. And Emma Barnes at Snowbooks, publishers of the UK editions of the Gideon Smith series, is a marvel and a dynamo.

A special mention must go to Grant Balfour for the exhaustive (and exhausting) lessons on American history. Together with Claire Eddy, Grant was invaluable for teaching this Brit the minutiae of what went down, what it all meant, and what I could get away with riding roughshod over. Anything that rings true is probably down to them; anything that seems ridiculous is most likely all my own work.

My agent, John Jarrold, is friend, confidant, arse-kicker, and all-around good egg, without whom none of this would be happening.

And, as ever, my ultimate thanks must go to my wife, Claire, for her unwavering support, love, and selfless willingness to step in and kick my arse when my agent couldn't quite reach.

Finally, thanks for reading this far. I hope you read the rest of the book, and enjoy it. You can find me on Twitter at @davidmbarnett or online at www.davidbarnett.wordpress.com.

David Barnett
West Yorkshire
2014

In every cry of every Man,
In every Infant's cry of fear,
In every voice, in every ban,
The mind-forg'd manacles I hear.

—WILLIAM BLAKE,
"London"

1 CALIFORNIAN MEIJI
2 FREE STATES OF
   AMERICA
3 BRITISH AMERICA
4 NEW SPAIN
5 FRENCH LOUISIANA
6 THE CONFEDERACY
7 FREE FLORIDA
8 *Nyu Edo*
9 *Uvalde*
10 *San Antonio/Steamtown*
11 *New Jerusalem*
12 *Blackfoot land*
13 *Rooseville*
14 *Ciudad Cortes*
15 *New York*
16 *Fort York*

BRITISH
CANADA

MASON–DIXON
WALL

Atlantic

Ocean

Pacific

EQUATOR

Ocean

Atlantic

Ocean

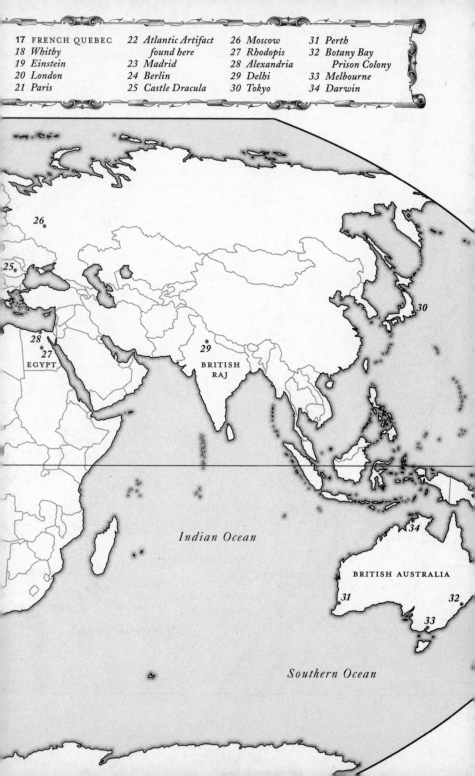

17 FRENCH QUEBEC   22 Atlantic Artifact   26 Moscow   31 Perth
18 Whitby   found here   27 Rhodopis   32 Botany Bay
19 Einstein   23 Madrid   28 Alexandria   Prison Colony
20 London   24 Berlin   29 Delhi   33 Melbourne
21 Paris   25 Castle Dracula   30 Tokyo   34 Darwin

26 Moscow

25 Castle Dracula

28 Alexandria
27 Rhodopis
EGYPT

29 Delhi
BRITISH RAJ

30 Tokyo

Indian Ocean

34 Darwin

BRITISH AUSTRALIA

31 Perth

32 Botany Bay

33 Melbourne

Southern Ocean

Nyu
Edo

To Sector 31
– the Lost World

Pacific Ocean

CAVALRY
GARRISON ■

OSWALD P. ACKROYD'S
■ FARM

YAQUI
CAMP
●
Steamtown
◎

Freedom   Uvalde
◎

Nuevo Laredo ◎

New York

Atlantic Ocean

New Orleans

Gulf of Mexico

N.

SCALE OF MILES

50   150   250

0   100   200   300

GIDEON SMITH
AND THE
BRASS DRAGON

1

The Lost World

Charles Darwin stood motionless at the mouth of the cave, his serge trousers pooled in a ragged heap around his ankles, as a shrieking pteranodon wheeled and soared in the blue morning sky.

"Good God, man!" said Stanford Rubicon, pushing away the crudely stitched-together palm fronds he had been using as a blanket. "How long have you been standing there like that?"

Kneading the sleep from his eyes, Rubicon clambered over the loose stones to where Darwin stood by the ashes of last night's fire, taking a moment to glance out from the lip of the cave to the steaming jungle below. The sun had risen over the jagged claws of the mountains to the east; it was shaping up to be another beautiful day in hell. The pteranodon, drifting on the rising warmth, cawed at Rubicon and glided out of sight. Darwin's rheumy eyes swiveled in their sockets toward Rubicon, filled with pain and humiliation. He tried to speak but succeeded only in dribbling down his long beard.

"There, there, old chap, don't fret," murmured Rubicon, pulling up Darwin's trousers without fuss or ceremony. "Soon have you mobile again."

Using the makeshift shovel, little more than a piece of curved bark tied with twine to a short stick, Rubicon gathered up a few pieces of their dwindling coal supply. There was only enough for three days, perhaps four, and that was if they didn't use it on their cooking fire. Rubicon blanched at the thought of getting more; the only seam they had found near enough to the surface to be extractable was, unfortunately, only a hundred yards upwind of a tyrannosaur nest. He considered the few black rocks on the shovel, then tipped a third back onto the small pile. Darwin would just have to not exert himself today, while they considered their next move.

Arranged at Darwin's stomach was the unwieldy yet vital furnace that kept him mobile and—though Rubicon was still mystified at the science behind it—alive. Beneath the aged botanist's torn shirt, now more gray than white through lack of starch and washing, copper pipes and iron pistons snaked over his body in a dull metal matrix, bulky with pistons and shunts at his major joints. Darwin must have gotten up to relieve himself in the middle of the night, and the amazing yet grotesque external skeleton that ensured his longevity must have seized up, as it was doing more and more frequently in the past month. Arranging the meager lumps of coal on a bed of kindling and pages torn from the books they had managed to rescue from the wreck that had stranded them there six months ago, Rubicon struck a match and, when he was sure the kindling was catching, shut the little metal door to the furnace. Then he cast around for the oilcan and applied a few drops to the joints of the skeleton, still unable to stop himself from blanching as he saw the pipes that were sunk into the flesh at Darwin's chest and at the base of his neck. The skeleton was the work of the eminent scientist Hermann Einstein, and it not only allowed the old man to move, albeit with a hissing, clanking, jerking motion, but also pumped his heart and did God knew what to his brain. Sometimes Rubicon wondered if he would ever understand the modern world, but looking out into the lush green jungle below, he wished beyond measure that he could see London again, its soaring spires, scientific mysteries, technological puzzles, and all.

As the furnace fired the tiny engines that powered the cage encasing Darwin's emaciated body, the old botanist creaked into life, the metal jaw that was stitched to the bone beneath his bearded chin yawning wide. He flexed his ropelike muscles with an exhalation of steam from his joints and turned his milky eyes on Rubicon.

"Stanford," he said softly. "I fear I cannot endure this purgatory another day."

Rubicon patted him on the shoulder, the ridges of pipes and tubes warm now beneath his hand. He looked out across the jungle. "Not long now, Charles," he said, though without conviction. "Help will come."

FROM THE JOURNAL OF CHARLES DARWIN, AUGUST ??, 1890

It is six months or thereabouts since the *HMS Beagle II* suffered its most woeful fate on the jagged rocks that lurk in the foaming seas around this lost world. Six months we have been stranded here, hidden from the outside world, barely surviving on our wits and hoping against hope to see the rescue mission that Professor Rubicon most wholeheartedly believes will arrive any day.

I confess that I do not share Rubicon's faith in the power of the Empire to effect such a rescue. We are many thousands of miles from land, in uncharted waters, and within the sphere of influence of the Japanese. We had to steal here in secrecy, avoiding the shipping lanes and telling no one of our progress or destination. It took Rubicon half a lifetime to find his lost world, and now he believes that Britain will simply chance upon it? For all his bluster and rugged enthusiasm, I fear that Rubicon is merely humoring me. He knows that my survival for so long is a miracle in itself, and he wishes merely to jolly me along when he knows full well that we shall both die in this tropical nightmare. In idle moments—and is there any other kind in this place?—I wonder how I shall meet my inevitable death. What creature, I wonder, shall end my life? Will it be the snapping jaws of the tyrannosaurs? The horns of a triceratops? A brace of predatory velociraptors? It would be a fitting end for Charles Darwin, my detractors might say. Natural selection? Evolution? Mammals supplanting the dinosaurs? The old fool was eaten by that which he claimed gave way for the ascent of man!

Or shall I, as I almost did last night, merely wind down, let my furnace go cold through lack of fuel, and quietly switch off as Professor Einstein's marvelous exoskeleton— surely both blessing and curse!—draws night's veil over my eyes for the final time?

I am, as I have opined before, too old for this. I was a young man, barely in my twenties, when I voyaged to the Galápagos. Now I am approaching my ninety-second birthday, and only Einstein's technology keeps me moving and living. I should never have let Rubicon talk me into this foolish venture. But the Professor of Adventure can be a persuasive chap, and even if he hadn't plied me with brandy in the Empirical Geographic Club that cold January evening, I confess I would probably still have agreed to his madcap scheme. To think, a lost world where the dinosaurs still roam! The Cretaceous period, frozen in time, trapped in amber like the flies I found in the Galápagos! If I had one wish before dying, it would be to see my darling Emma again. How she would thrill to my stories. I do hope the children are taking good care of her.

Darwin closed the notebook and placed his pencil in the elasticized strap that held it together. They had salvaged little from the wreckage of the *Beagle II*, and had taken only what they could carry through the warren of labyrinthine tunnels that led from the stony beach to the interior of the extinct volcano that hid the lost world behind its soaring, jagged peaks. If they had known that a seaquake would cause a landslide that blocked their return to the shore they might have taken more supplies, or not ventured deep into the catacombs at all. But, as Darwin had already noted, Rubicon had a persuasive nature. The Professor of Adventure! The toast of London! And he had doomed them all.

Of the six survivors of the wreck, only Darwin and Rubicon remained. The majority of the crew of the *Beagle II* had been lost in the storm-tossed waves that crushed the ship as though it were merely a child's toy in an overfilled bathtub. Rubicon had grasped Darwin's collar and struck out for the dark shore with strong strokes. The morning that rose over the uncharted island had revealed the flotsam of the wreckage drifting toward the beach, and four others alive: two seamen, the first mate, and the cabin boy. One of the sailors had died beneath the landslide as they ran through the black tunnels to the salvation of the jungles within the caldera of this unnamed volcano. The first mate had been torn apart by two battling spinosauri as the dwindling party looked on in horror and amazement at their first sightings of the impossible lizards that still ruled this unknown corner of the Earth. The cabin boy had fallen to his death from the high crags, trying to climb toward the freedom he believed must be over the horizon. He called horribly for his mother all the way down to the far jungle below, where Rubicon later found his bones picked clean by predators. The final crewman had lasted until just the previous month, when hunger and madness possessed his brittle mind and he stripped naked and ran screaming into the towering flora, never to be seen again. His final, distant screams, choked by whichever beast had taken him in the shadows of the jungle, haunted Darwin still.

Rubicon approached the rock where Darwin sat in melancholy reflection, wiping himself dry with a piece of the first mate's old coat. The professor was fastidiously clean, even in this abandoned hell, and he washed every morning in the cascade of water that ran from subterranean sources into a waterfall thirty feet below the lip of the cave. Rubicon was convinced that the salt waterfall must come from the outside sea, and he had formulated plans to follow the underground river through the impassable cliffs. But Darwin was not up to the journey and besides, Rubicon had not yet worked out how to pass through the raging torrent without drowning. Darwin wondered how long it would be before Rubicon abandoned him and sought freedom alone.

As Rubicon buttoned up the thick black cotton jumpsuit

he always wore on his adventures and finger-combed his beard into a manageable style, picking out ticks and fleas and crushing them beneath his square fingernails, he nodded to the distant peaks.

"I think I shall go and light the beacons again today."

Darwin nodded. Rubicon had spent days climbing as high as he could at each compass point of the caldera, assembling piles of dampened wood that smoked blackly and, he hoped, would attract the attention of passing ships or dirigibles. Not that they had seen even a hint of an airship since their incarceration; this corner of the Pacific was Japanese waters, but it seemed even they didn't pass over at all. At first the survivors had been afraid of attracting the attention of the Edo regime, or the breakaway Californian Meiji, but now they did not care. To be rescued by anyone, even enemies of the British Empire, would be preferable to this. The government in London could at least try to parlay with the Japanese for their release, even if they were arrested on suspicion of spying; the dinosaurs would not enter into any kind of dialogue with Whitehall, Darwin thought wryly, even if the authorities knew where to find them.

"If you think it will do any good, Stanford," said Darwin.

"I do," said Rubicon. "When men like us give up hope, Charles, then the very Empire is lost. I shall be back before dark."

※

Beneath the baking sun, Rubicon clambered swiftly up the eastern wall of the volcano, keen to reach the heights where the cooling breeze would dry the sweat pearling on his forehead. This was the least onerous of the climbs, apart from the final stretch of forty feet or so, which was a perilous vertical face with scant handholds, and he liked to tackle the eastern side first to limber up. That, and the unyielding sea beyond stretched toward the Americas; if there was any hope of rescue, it might well come from that direction. The Spaniards plied the waters between Mexico and the Californian Meiji, and the occasional

airship from the British-controlled Eastern Seaboard sometimes shuttled between New York or Boston and the Spanish territories. But six months had passed with no sign of life
elsewhere in the world; Rubicon tried to maintain a jolly,
hopeful facade for Darwin but his own optimism was fading
fast. If they were to die in this hellish lost land, he hoped
that Darwin went first. He couldn't bear the thought of the
old botanist slowly winding down, trapped by his steam-
driven exoskeleton and forced to watch, immobile, as death
approached—either on the lingering tiptoes of starvation or
with the snapping teeth of one of the beasts that roamed the
island.

This lost world had been everything that Rubicon had
dreamed of, everything he had devoted the last ten years to
finding. But his ambition to bring the rude beasts from before
the dawn of time to display in triumph at the London Zoo was
dashed, as surely as he would be on the rocks below if he lost
his footing negotiating the last segment of his climb. He allowed himself the fantasy of imagining that their mission had
been a success, and that they had returned to London with
the *Beagle II*'s hold groaning with breeding pairs of triceratops, pteranodons, ankylosauri, and even tyrannosaurs. He
would have been the toast of the Empire. He briefly wondered
what was being said of Darwin and himself now, how many
column inches were being devoted in the London papers to
their lost mission. Six months had passed . . . perhaps their
names were barely mentioned anymore. The great explorers,
missing in terra incognita. Presumed dead.

Rubicon hauled himself up onto the thin crest of the volcano's lip, barely three feet wide before it plunged in a sheer,
unscalable cliff to the angry surf that crashed on the jagged
rocks far below. There was no way of descending and no beach
or footing there if they did. Rubicon slung off his back the
sticks and vines he had bound together with twine and assembled them in the ring of rocks he had prepared there many
months ago, when he had first started lighting the bonfires.

Matches saved from the wreckage were kept in a leather wallet beneath the largest rock of the makeshift fireplace; only a dozen were left here now. He lit one and shielded it with his hand, holding it to the dry moss at the base of the small beacon and blowing it gently until the flames fanned out and the kindling caught.

The greenery burned reluctantly, sending thick black smoke pirouetting into the unbroken blue sky. Rubicon nodded with satisfaction. Three more beacons to light, then perhaps he might scoot by that tyrannosaur nest and see if he could scavenge a few lumps of coal for Darwin's furnace. Dusk was the safest time, when the beasts had eaten and lolled with full bellies around their nest—though "safety" in this place was a relative concept. He took a few sips of water from his canteen and prepared for the descent, scanning the horizon one last time with his hand shielding his eyes.

There was a ship.

Rubicon swore and rubbed his eyes. Surely it was a breaching whale, perhaps, or piece of driftwood. It was so very distant, merely a speck on the glittering blue waves. But as he peered and squinted he was sure he could make out an almost invisible thread of exhaust steam. It was a ship. And it was heading for the island, coming up from the south and the east.

Rubicon gathered up all the kindling and leaves he had and thrust them onto the bonfire, then turned and let himself over the edge. Slowly, slowly, he commanded. It would not do for you to fall to your death just as salvation is at hand.

※

"Charles! Charles!"

Darwin had been napping, and at the insistent calls from the unseen Rubicon he awoke sharply and stretched, his exoskeleton creaking and hissing at the joints. "Stanford?"

Darwin peered out beyond the lip of the cave. He could see the pillars of smoke from the eastern and southern walls of their prison, but not from the other walls. Had something terrible occurred to stop Rubicon lighting the other beacons?

The professor, his face red from exertion, appeared over the ledge, clambering madly into the cave.

"Stanford? Are you quite well?"

"A ship, Charles! A ship! We are saved!"

Darwin pursed his lips. "You are quite sure? Not a mirage, or—?"

"Quite sure!" said Rubicon happily. "I saw it from the east and then again from the south. It is closing in at a fair lick."

"British?" said Darwin, not daring to hope.

"I cannot tell," said Rubicon, shaking his head. "But it could be the *Flying Dutchman* itself for all that I care! Come on. I calculate it is heading for the place where the *Beagle II* was lost. We must make our way there at once."

Darwin frowned. "But the tunnels collapsed. And is that not close to the nest of those tyrannosaurs . . . ?"

Rubicon was filling his knapsack with their remaining dried meat and lumps of coal. "Pack just what you can carry," he said. "We must away directly."

Darwin nodded and tucked his journal into his own leather satchel. That was all he required: his notes, drawings, and observations of the fantastical flora and fauna on this lost island. Could it really be true? Was rescue really at hand?

Darwin staggered as the ground beneath his feet shook violently. He looked at Rubicon, who frowned and stared out to the jungle as another tremor rattled the cave.

"An earthquake?" asked Darwin.

Then there was another tremor, and another, and a column of smoke and dust rose from the mountainous caldera between the eastern and southern beacons. Rubicon shook his head. "No. A bombardment. They're shelling the rock face."

2

The Hero of the Effing Empire

Along one of the paths that Rubicon had cleared with stick and machete during their six-month incarceration on the island, the pair of them hurried toward the booming bombardment. The shelling had disturbed the island's occupants; the long necks of brontosaurs peeped inquisitively above the tree line, and pterosaurs shrieked and wheeled on the thermals rising from the hot jungle. On the periphery of his vision, Darwin, beset by buzzing flies that nipped at the beads of sweat on his forehead, saw shapes flit between the trees and bushes: raptors, no doubt. The carnivores were sufficiently startled by this incursion of the modern world to put their hunger to one side for the moment and let the two humans pass unmolested. Rubicon grabbed Darwin's arm and dragged him behind a thick tree trunk as three lumbering triceratops, their yellow eyes wide with uncomprehending panic, crossed the path and crashed into the jungle, flattening a copse of gigantic magnolia.

"We're coming up to the tyrannosaur nest," whispered Rubicon. "I suggest we give it a wide berth. I'm going to lead us through the undergrowth."

Darwin nodded. His legs felt heavy and unresponsive, a sure sign that his exoskeleton was seizing up again. He needed coal for the furnace, water for the pumps, and oil for the joints, none of which was in handy supply. Should this rescue of Rubicon's not occur, Darwin was suddenly sure that he would simply give up the ghost there and then. He could not bear this existence a moment longer.

They crept around the perimeter of the nest, a clearing in the forest that stank of ordure. Darwin could make out the shuffling shapes of the tyrannosaurs, disquieted by the bombardment but remaining fiercely territorial. Rubicon put a forefinger to his lips, met Darwin's gaze with a look that said *Don't ruin it now*, and led him quietly through the fig trees, palms, and unruly plane trees. Finally the nest was behind them and the trees thinned out to reveal the sheer rock face, the labyrinthine tunnels where the two men had entered the volcano lost beneath the mounds of massive rocks.

Another shell exploded on the far side of the wall, and there was a pregnant pause, then the rock face seemed to move like liquid, sliding in on itself and then rumbling down in an avalanche of huge boulders. Darwin and Rubicon stepped back to the jungle as the rock collapsed with a bellow, opening up a wedge of blue sky beyond. The wall was still sixty feet high, but Darwin could see the drifting steam of the ship that lay beyond, and he heard a roaring sound he at first thought was an attacking dinosaur . . . then realized was the first human voices apart from Rubicon's he had heard in months. It was men, and they were cheering.

Rubicon broke free of their cover and began to clamber up the rocks, Darwin struggling behind him. Before they had gotten halfway up, three figures appeared from the other side, then a phalanx of sailors carrying rifles. Darwin felt tears begin to fall uncontrollably down his face.

There was a broad man with a beard, wearing a white shirt and with the bearing of a sea captain. Beside him was a younger man, thin and tall with dark curls cascading down his shoulders. The third was a corpulent, huffing, pasty-faced figure, frowning into the sunlight and coughing with displeasure.

"Professors Stanford Rubicon and Charles Darwin, I presume?" called the younger man as the sailor began to descend to help the pair. Darwin sank to his knees on the rocks, all his strength having deserted him.

Rubicon called back, "You are most correct, sir! To whom do we have the utmost pleasure of addressing?"

The young man gestured to his right. "This is Captain

James Palmer, whose fine ship the *Lady Jane* has brought us to your aid. My companion is Mr. Aloysius Bent, a journalist currently attached to the periodical *World Marvels & Wonders*."

Even as Darwin's strength fled, Rubicon's seemed to return with renewed vigor. He closed the gap and grasped the young man's hands firmly. "And you, sir?"

The fat journalist who had been introduced as Bent spoke up. "This is Mr. Gideon Smith. He's only the Hero of the effing Empire."

"We are saved!" gasped Darwin, and collapsed in a faint on the piles of gently smoking rubble.

Darwin came to as one of the sailors put a canteen of glorious fresh water to his parched lips. He feared that when he opened his eyes it would all have been a dream, but there was Rubicon, talking to Captain Palmer, Mr. Smith, and Mr. Bent, as the crewmen with the rifles fanned out around them, their guns trained on the jungle.

"But how did you find us?" Rubicon was asking.

"A survivor from the wreck of the *Beagle II*," said Palmer. "He drifted for many days, clinging to a piece of timber. He was picked up by a Japanese whaler and languished in a prison near Osaka, accused of spying, for four months. He was freed as part of a diplomatic exchange with the British government, and when he returned to England he was able to pinpoint the *Beagle II*'s last position, give or take a couple of hundred miles. We sailed out of Tijuana at the bidding of the Spanish government two weeks ago. If it hadn't been for your beacon, I think we would have missed you completely."

"And did you find your lost world before you were wrecked, Rubicon?" asked Bent.

Darwin sat up with some effort. "You are standing in it, sir."

Gideon Smith looked around at the jungle rearing up before them. "You don't mean . . . prehistoric beasts? Here?"

Rubicon nodded. "Such as you have never imagined, Mr.

Smith. And half of 'em would have you for breakfast . . . some of 'em with one gulp!"

"But how did you survive?" asked Smith.

Darwin tapped his head. "With that which separates us from the monsters, sir. Intellect. Invention. The will to live. Survival of the fittest, you see."

The fat one, Bent, surveyed the jungle. "These beasts . . ."

"All around us," said Darwin. "Your ship is just over these rocks . . . ?"

Captain Palmer nodded. "Aye. We should be away." He turned to address one of the sailors. "Mr. Wilson, please go back to the *Lady Jane* and have the mate prepare us for sailing."

He turned to address Rubicon. "Sir, I understand your mission was to bring samples of these monsters back to London. I can tell you now that I will have no such business on my ship. We are here to rescue you, not transport a menagerie from under the noses of the Japanese."

"Understood," said Rubicon. He cast a glance back to the jungle. "Before we go . . . I would just like to collect something. . . ."

Darwin looked at him quizzically, but Rubicon promised he would be back within five minutes and jogged back into the dark trees.

"But how are they still alive, these dinosaurs?" asked Bent.

Darwin shook his head. "Whatever evolutionary occurrence or, perhaps, natural disaster that occurred toward the end of the Late Cretaceous epoch did not, seemingly, affect this island. It has remained untouched ever since, apart from the world, out of time. The creatures have thrived for more than sixty-five million years. It is a living museum!"

"And one we shan't be returning to," said Palmer, frowning. "We are right in Japanese waters here, gentlemen. If we get back to Tijuana without being seen it shall be a miracle. This could cause a major diplomatic incident."

Smith looked at the jungle. "Where is Professor Rubicon?"

Darwin tried to stand but fell again as the earth shook. He looked at Captain Palmer. "Your bombardment continues?"

Palmer narrowed his eyes. "No . . ."

The ground shook again, and again. There was a shout and Rubicon broke through the trees, running as fast as he could, waving at them. "Go!" he yelled. "Get out of here!"

"What the eff . . ." said Bent, and then there was a roar that made Darwin feel as though his eardrums had burst. The trees behind Rubicon splintered like matches and from the dark greenery burst a fluid brown streak, all yellow eyes and teeth like kitchen knives.

"Oh Lord," said Darwin. "A Tyrannosaurus rex!"

Smith and Palmer took hold of Darwin and hauled him up the rocks, as Bent scrabbled after them and Rubicon joined the climb. Darwin glanced at him but Rubicon kept his mind on scrambling over the blasted boulders as the seamen behind stood their ground and let loose a volley of bullets at the beast, forty feet from nose to whipping tail. It bent its head low and roared at them again. Darwin heard a scream, and Palmer cursed. He looked over his shoulder as they crested the boulders to see the beast shaking one of the sailors in its vast jaws.

"Pull back, men!" cried Palmer, leading them down the shale to a rowboat bobbing in the shallows. Ahead of them, anchored a hundred yards offshore, was the steamship the *Lady Jane.*

As they bundled into the rowboat, Darwin noticed the sun-bleached, seawater-bloated timbers of the wreck of the *Beagle II,* still caught in the savage rocks that surrounded the island. There was another scream: another lost sailor. After a further volley of shots the remaining crewmen skidded down to the small beach and piled into the boat, immediately pulling on the oars to take the men, painfully slowly, away from the island.

Then the tyrannosaur loomed into the jagged gap between the high walls, its claws scrabbling for purchase on the loose boulders. It sniffed at the unfamiliarly salty air, swiveling its blazing eyes to fix upon the frantically rowing sailors. Its brown tail, crested with black, whipped back and forth as it seemed to consider the vast, oceanic world that lay beyond its hidden lair.

"We are safe," said Darwin, as they closed half the gap to the *Lady Jane*. "I do not think the beasts can swim."

Bent puffed alarmingly beside him. "You don't *think*? Can't you be surer than that, Darwin? What the eff is that thing, anyway?"

"I told you," said Darwin. "Tyrannosaurus rex. The tyrant lizard. Dark master of the Cretaceous." He paused and glanced at Rubicon. "I wonder what made it attack us like that. What alerted it to our presence?"

The beast remained on the beach, stalking up and down and staring out at the *Lady Jane* as the crew helped the men aboard. Rubicon graciously declined help with his satchel, which he kept close to him as he climbed onto the deck.

"We'll make steam for Tijuana," said Captain Palmer. "As far away from that thing as humanly possible. We'll need to go swiftly and quietly, avoiding the shipping lanes until we get to Spanish-controlled waters." He looked at Darwin and Rubicon. "I dare say you gentlemen would like a bath and some good food, and a soft bed to sleep in."

Darwin began to weep. "I thought we would never be rescued. Thank you, kind sirs."

Palmer nodded toward Gideon Smith. "He's the one you want to thank. He's led the mission. Like our Mr. Bent said, Mr. Smith's the Hero of the Empire."

"I thought that particular appellation belonged to Captain Lucian Trigger," said Rubicon, "though I do not doubt that Mr. Smith is fully deserving of the title also."

"A lot has happened in the six months you have been missing," said Smith. "Let's go to Captain Palmer's quarters and I'll fill you both in."

"A favor, first, Captain," said Rubicon. "Could I put my bag in the furnace room, do you think? There's something in here that I would awfully like to keep warm."

Palmer narrowed his eyes, then shrugged and had one of the sailors take Rubicon into the bowels of the *Lady Jane*. Rubicon dismissed the sailor with his profuse thanks, and when he was alone he gingerly took his satchel and placed it securely between two crates, up against the hot steam boiler. Before he departed he opened the leather flap and glanced inside. There was an egg, as big as a man's head, mottled in purple and pale blue. Rubicon smiled and went to join the others for the promised food, bathing, and news, past the shadowy alcove where he failed to notice the figure of Aloysius Bent watching with interest.

As the ship began to disappear from view, she continued to stalk up and down the beach. She had been aware of them, of course, dimly, in her tiny brain. Creatures like none she had ever seen, like none that had ever lived in her world. They scurried around and hid in caves, nursing flames and harvesting fruits. They were food. Her mate had tasted one, many months ago, but the surviving two had always managed to evade her and her family.

But this was not about food. Food was plentiful, and were not she and her mate the rulers of all they surveyed? All they had surveyed, perhaps, until today. Until this jagged doorway was opened up and this strange, huge, wet world that stretched in all directions came into view. No, this was not about food.

This was about family.

Whatever they were, they were gone with others of their kind.

And they had stolen from her, stolen that which was most precious.

She raised her head to the dull sky and roared, and this time her roar was not reflected back at her by the rock walls of her home, but traveled out for who knew how long and how far? Out into infinity. Out where they had taken what was not theirs.

She dipped a claw into the lapping cold water and recoiled. She grunted, angry with herself. Then she stamped, hard, in the shallows, and left her huge foot there, in the water.

It wasn't so bad.

Taking a step, and then another, she waded out until she could no longer feel the rocky ground. Panicking, she thrashed her tail and reached her head up to the sky, her useless fore-arms paddling frantically. She pumped her legs and felt herself move forward. Her forearms, perhaps not so useless after all, allowed her to keep her head out of the water. And her tail, as it thrashed, steered her course between the tall, cruel rocks.

Out to the open sea. Out to where those who had stolen her unborn baby had gone.

With the single-minded ferocity of a wronged mother, she howled at the sky again and began to claw her way through the water, heading, though she didn't know it, south and east, in the all but dispersed wake of the *Lady Jane*.

3

The New World

More than two and a half thousand miles stretched between San Francisco and New York, and Jebediah Hart was going to have to cover every damn one of them, somehow. 'Course, they didn't call it San Fran anymore, not since the Japs had taken over back in 'sixty-eight. Nyu Edo, it was now. But Jeb was old enough to remember San Francisco, old enough to know this place where he sheltered from the sun near the South Fork River as Coloma, not Shinzui Hiru. Jeb had only been young when the Californian Meiji was founded, and he'd pulled up stakes with his family and headed back east. But while the British had taken a step back and allowed the Japs to take California without a fight—hell, it was the Spanish who rolled over in the first place, after all— the governors in Boston and New York were only keeping their powder dry. America was a big place, and there was a lot of it to civilize before the Japanese problem had to be dealt with head-on. In the meantime, folks like Jeb who knew California like the backs of their hands were something of a commodity, especially those who didn't mind trekking back and forth into the Meiji under cover of darkness, hiding in orange groves and sneaking through the deserts to keep an eye on what Emperor Mutsuhito was up to in Nyu Edo.

Truth to tell, Jeb had no great problem with the Japanese, save for the fact they'd expelled British-American families from California. They were clean and polite, and San Fran these days was a place of serene gardens and huge pagodas, temples and highways swept by quiet little men in pale robes. The invasion had put out the Spaniards more than anybody, but between their constant feuding with the French back in Europe and their tenuous hold on their territory right down south, not to mention the thorn in their side that was the growing Confederacy down below the Mason-Dixon Wall, there wasn't much they could do about it. So everybody was just biding their time, watching the Californian Meiji from afar, waiting to see what Mutsuhito would do.

'Course, all that was set to be blown right out of the water soon as Jeb got back to New York.

Jeb let his horse rest in the shade of a clutch of tall yellow pines. The bare short stumps that covered the hillside were testament to the speed and efficiency with which the Japanese had identified the natural resources in their new home and made use of them. When Jeb's family had packed up and left San Fran it had been little more than a collection of wooden shacks and dirt tracks; British-American families such as the Harts had been paid a pioneer supplement by the governors back east to settle on the West Coast with the tacit agreement of the Spanish who were struggling to keep a grip on California. It was a good plan, and more and more families would have arrived over time, eventually necessitating a garrison of cavalrymen to protect British interests in the West and eventually persuade the Spanish to give up California for good. Nobody was expecting the Japanese, though. The Spanish weren't strong enough to fend them off, and the British settlers didn't have enough of a claim on the land.

Jeb drank deeply from the canteen he filled in the shallows of the South Fork River, pouring the rest over his dusty head and refilling it for the next stage of his journey. He had to admit, the Japs had done a bang-up job on their Nyu Edo. It was remarkable what they'd achieved in a little over twenty years, turning that one-horse hick town into a thriving city that could, in time, match the British enclaves in the East.

Jeb spat into the sand and rubbed a handful of water over the back of his neck. Given time. After what he'd seen, the Japs might be living on *borrowed* time—provided he got back to New York in one piece, of course, and depending on who got to hear what he had to say, and how they acted on it. He allowed himself a cracked-toothed smile. No wonder the Meiji was so darned secretive, with what they were sitting on. They didn't like strangers, the Japanese, and from what Jeb understood, these guys, Mutsuhito's lot, were the *progressive* ones. The old guard they'd split away from back in Japan were supposed to be even worse. He'd had to prowl around at night, hiding between the quiet temples, skulking around the factories that dotted the dry hillsides, helping himself to oranges and killing squirrels and even black-tailed deer to eat. A guy like Jeb tended to stand out among the Japs, and he was glad to be getting back east with his hide intact. He shielded his eyes and looked back toward where the sun was sinking over Nyu Edo, and the Pacific Ocean beyond that. Another drink for the horse from the rushing South Fork, then time to make tracks.

Then he saw them. Seven black shapes, as still and silent as shadows, but ranged on the crest of a hill in broad sunlight, where shadows had no business. The silhouettes were bulky with armor and spiky with spears, bows, and blades. Jeb let the canteen fall from his hands into the dust.

Samurai.

The most venerable samurai families had stayed back in the old country, of course. It was only a handful of Japan's fearsome warrior clans that had made the journey east to the new world, those who had long-standing feuds with the old emperor, those who sniffed the opportunity for fresh battles to fight. There were those who said the samurai had grown soft in the Californian Meiji, grown fat on oranges and the sake they made from the vineyards on the southern slopes of the mountains.

Jeb knew there was no such thing as a samurai gone soft, and when the first wooden arrow fletched with goose feathers thunked into the tree behind him, he started saying his prayers. He wasn't going to get out of this alive.

The roar of the rifle just a yard from his left ear made him moan and drop to his knees. They had him surrounded. But one of the shadows on the hill crumpled and fell, raising a cloud of dust. Jeb blinked and looked around. There was a man there, a white man, who appeared to be hewn from the very landscape. He was dressed in a hodgepodge of brown leather and trail-battered furs, his boots reaching his knees, his blond hair straggling over his weathered face and caught in a ponytail at the back of his neck. In the crook of his arm he held a Winchester repeater, and pistols snug in a gun belt hung over his road-wearied, rough, dark denims.

"You might want to get up off the floor," said the stranger. " 'Tis not the best position from which to shoot."

Jeb arched an eyebrow at the stranger's speech, as much of a stew as his clothing, but there was no time to consider.

There was a holler, some kind of war cry from the samurai, and they began to pelt down the hill. The stranger let off two more shots with his rifle; two more samurai fell, their momentum rolling them over in the soft dust. Another shot; this time the stranger missed.

"Curses," the man muttered. "Come on, now, one shot, one kill. One shot, one kill." He grabbed Jeb by the scruff of his neck and pulled him to his feet. "Get behind the tree."

A volley of arrows whispered through the dry evening air as Jeb scuttled behind the trunk of the tree. The stranger pulled out a .45 from his left holster and let fly as he fired the Winchester single-handed. Two samurai fell. But the other two were feet away now, their katana drawn. They stopped, their black armor glinting in the dying light, their faces fierce beneath their helmets.

"This man is under my protection," said the stranger. "You leave him be."

One of the samurai growled something in Jap-speak. The other said, "He is a spy. He must face justice in Nyu Edo."

The stranger shrugged and his gun barked again. Six bullets from the rifle, reckoned Jeb. He hoped the man had a full chamber in his pistol. The warrior who had spoken Japanese took the bullet to the head and keeled over in a red mess. The stranger raised an eyebrow and said, "Bows and arrows won't win you this land; the Indians learned that. Nor cold steel either. Gunmetal and powder will unite America. You go. You tell them that."

Jeb peered around the tree. He'd never heard of a samurai running from battle before, but this one was, digging into the soft soil with his katana to haul him back up the ridge. When he'd become a shadow once more and disappeared, Jeb let out a whoop.

"Thank you, stranger," he said. "What's your name?"

The man reloaded his .45 and holstered it. "Well, there's a question," he said. "They call me many things. The Indians call me *Spirit*, in more ways than I can remember. The witches of New Orleans like to call me *Fantôme*. The Mormons in New Jerusalem think I'm Satan, and the civilized folk of New York don't believe in me at all!"

Jeb blinked. He'd heard tell . . . he never thought the stories were real, though. "It's you? The one they call the Nameless? It's really you?"

"'Tis not a name, as such, but one that will suffice." He looked at Jeb a long time. "And you are what they said you were? A spy? For the British back east?"

Jeb stared at him. He held out his hand and the man took it. Jeb said, "I might do a bit of . . . uh, mighty strong grip for a ghost." He paused and said tentatively, "Uh, why'd you save me? I was given to understand you ain't got much truck with the British."

The Nameless shrugged. "Perhaps I have less with the Japanese. The Spaniards have their own names for me, and I for them. I suppose I didn't much like the odds against you. . . ."

Jeb climbed on his horse, scrutinizing the other man. "If you don't like the Japanese, Spaniards, or British, who the hell *do* you like?"

"Americans," said the Nameless, smiling broadly. "I haven't found any yet. I'm still looking."

Jeb sank his spurs into his horse's sides, turning to wave at his savior as she broke out into a trot. As he'd half-expected, the man was gone.

Haruki Serizawa looked out across the bay from the window of his laboratory on the fourth floor of the squat brick building that occupied an elevated position in the hills above Nyu Edo. A thin ribbon of gray steam rose from the merchant ship from Kyoto that was unloading on the docks, bringing communications, lacquer-work knickknacks, and sides of beef. It would be loading up with oranges and nuts, pet lizards and cowhide leather. Japan and the Californian Meiji were in a state of diplomacy as chilled as the portions of beer-fed cattle that were being unloaded in trays of ice, but a polite trade was maintained. And the families separated by the wide, blue Pacific Ocean eagerly swapped news of the old country and the new world. Serizawa felt a sudden stab of longing for the Japan of his youth, for spring walks amid the falling blossoms, for the subtle turning of the seasons. Nyu Edo was a bastardized mess, in his opinion, the streets crazy with traditional pagodas jostling up against Western-style brick-and-stone edifices. An example of the . . . what was it the Germans called it? *Dementia praecox*. Schizophrenia. Serizawa had read about it in a journal from Europe. To be of split minds. That was Nyu Edo, clinging on to the traditions of Japan, embracing the mélange of the West. That, too, was Serizawa. He watched the stevedores, small as scorpions, finishing up unloading the steamer. He wondered if there was a letter for him among the crates of mail. A letter from his father.

Serizawa turned his attention back to the sheets of white paper on his work top, scrawled with formulas and sketches. He took off his black-rimmed spectacles and pinched his nose. Why could he not solve the problem with the temperature regulators in the lower joints? The devices worked perfectly

in the three pairs of upper joints, but the lower ones continued to stubbornly overheat. Perhaps it was that they were
carrying more weight. He put his spectacles back on his nose
and tapped his pencil on the paper. Perhaps . . . perhaps . . .
but his mind would not focus. The sun was sinking rapidly
over the bay. The screen whispered open behind him and he
glanced over his shoulder, shuffling quickly off of the stool at
the sight of the short, bald man in the white lab jacket.

"Science Officer Morioka," said Serizawa, bowing low.

"Serizawa." Morioka nodded. "How is your work proceed-
ing?"

"Very well," lied Serizawa. "I think I have solved the problem of the weight distribution on the lower pinions and
regulators."

Morioka nodded again, then said, "We have had a message
from Kyoto. The British have been sighted near, or in, sector
thirty-one."

Serizawa thought about this for what he believed to be a
respectable amount of time, then said, "What does that mean,
precisely, Science Officer?"

"Perhaps nothing." Morioka shrugged. "Perhaps everything.
But it adds a certain urgency to our work here."

Serizawa glanced back at the setting sun. It was funny; in
the West they called Japan the Land of the Rising Sun, but
from the Californian Meiji, the old country was where the sun
sank. He lived, ostensibly, in the West now. But he had had to
go East to find it. He said carefully, "I was rather hoping, Science Officer . . ."

"Urgency," said Morioka again. "Perhaps another hour this
evening, Serizawa. Perhaps two."

Serizawa bowed again. "Very good, Science Officer Morioka."

Serizawa walked along the street in the pools of white light
cast by the lanterns strung between poles, the warm, salty
breeze washing over him from the sea. He would be late for

his dinner. Again. He called in at the shrine and lit a candle, contemplating its flickering pale flame for a moment, wondering if those he had left behind had lit similar candles for him today. His mother, surely. His father . . . well.

Serizawa's home was situated halfway up a steep hill that ran upward from the central gardens. Nyu Edo was all hills, and his garden, though it had a pleasant, south-facing aspect, was inclined to such an extent that it made relaxing in the summer sun difficult. He let himself in and slid open the screens to the dining room, where his wife Akiko sat cross-legged before their ruined dinner.

There was a small cake.

"Happy birthday, Haruki," she said, smiling up at him.

"I'm sorry," he said. "Science Officer Morioka—"

"I know," she said. "Your work is very important."

"Michi?"

"Asleep. I said I would wake her when you came home. But first, eat. I have some Kobe beef, though it is probably spoiled."

He sat across from her and took a chunk of the cold beef with a pair of chopsticks. "It is perfect," he said. "You got it from the trade steamer today?"

She nodded.

"And was there anything else—?"

"No letters, Haruki."

He sighed and picked up another sliver of beef. "I was foolish to expect anything."

Anger darkened Akiko's tiny face. "You were not. It is your birthday and he is your father. He cannot carry on this ridiculous feud forever."

"He can, and he will. He has never forgiven us for leaving Japan."

Akiko poured two cups of sake. "It is his own fault we left. It is your father's technology that keeps Emperor Kōmei alive beyond his natural years. If the emperor had lived a normal life, Mutsuhito would not have been forced to flee here to establish the progressive government that Japan deserves. And we would not have had to come here with him."

"My father is a brilliant man," said Serizawa absently.

"As are you," said Akiko. "But you would not have flourished in Japan. And Kyoto would have been no place to raise our daughter. The world is changing at a pace far beyond what Japan can match, Haruki. Michi deserves that world, and all its wonders. We deserve it."

Serizawa stood and beckoned his wife to do the same. He embraced her warmly. "But I do not deserve you."

She kissed him, and he felt the smoothness of her kimono against his bare arms. He kissed her back, harder, until she pushed him gently away.

"No, Haruki Serizawa, you do not deserve me. Working until such late hours on your birthday. But go and wake Michi, as I promised you would. Then I shall show you how lucky you are to have me, and you can show me how grateful you can be."

The taste of the sake on Akiko's lips burning his own, he slid back the screens to their daughter's room, letting the gaslight from the dining room play on her peaceful, sleeping face. She was seven years old, a true child of the Californian Meiji. He and Akiko, they carried too much of their old lives from Japan. It was the generation born in this strange new world who would be the making—or not—of the displaced Mutsuhito Empire. He could never let go of Japan, not truly. But Michi . . . as Akiko had said, she was now a citizen of a much wider world. He wondered what she would make of it.

Serizawa crouched by her bed and stroked her forehead until it wrinkled and her eyes opened, puffy with sleep. She clutched the little wooden doll she had made at school. Kashira, she had called it, because it had no head. It wouldn't stand up properly, kept falling over, until Serizawa gave her a little lecture on center of gravity. She had pulled the head off and it had stood up fine. "Daddy!" she said, and gave him a hug that caused his heart to split in two.

"Hello, Prickly Pear," he said softly. Her name, Michi, meant "pathway"—Akiko had chosen it, felt it embodied the pioneer spirit of the Californian Meiji. Serizawa always called her Prickly Pear. She was of the Californian soil, beautiful and strong yet with a spiky will all her own.

"Happy birthday, Daddy," she said. "I have a present for you."

From beneath her sheet she withdrew a crudely wrapped ball, no bigger than a pebble. "We went on a trip with school to the hills."

"The hills?" Serizawa frowned. Although Nyu Edo was safe, the outskirts of the Meiji were still subject to the attentions of the Americans from the British enclaves back east and bandits from the wild country in between. Just that morning he had heard that Texan slavers had been seen far to the south.

"It was quite safe," said Michi, in that same tone her mother used on him when he was being silly. "I found this in the river and kept it for you."

He unwrapped the layers of tissue until a small, hard lump fell into his hand. He held it up to the light shafting between the screens, turning it between his thumb and forefinger.

"Isn't it pretty?" said Michi, settling back into the low bed, her eyelids drooping. "Doesn't it shine?"

"Yes," said Serizawa thoughtfully. It did shine indeed. It was a tiny nugget of what was unmistakably gold.

Michi snored lightly, and Serizawa kissed her on her freshly smooth forehead. He heard Akiko quietly clearing away the dinner things, and he slipped the nugget into his pocket. It was time for him to show his wife how grateful he could be.

4

A Visit from Mr. Walsingham

The door to 23 Grosvenor Square banged open and Aloysius Bent stepped into the cool, tiled hallway, agreeably sniffing at the smells of cooking wafting from the kitchens. "By effing Christ, it's good to be home!" he roared.

Mrs. Cadwallader, the housekeeper, emerged from the study and threw her hands into the air. "Land's sakes! Mr. Bent! And Mr. Smith!"

Gideon elbowed past Bent, who remained stock-still in the doorway, breathing deeply of the aromas of Mrs. Cadwallader's famous home cooking. He gave the housekeeper a warm embrace and she flapped her hands at him.

"One for me, too, Sally," said Bent, extending his fat arms around Mrs. Cadwallader, who wrinkled up her nose and pushed him away. "Come on, I might have a face like a stocking full of porridge, but I deserve a hug."

"Mr. Bent!" she cried. "Please don't be so familiar! It's Mrs. Cadwallader to you. And do let go. You smell as though you have been sleeping with horses!"

"The scent of good, honest work!" said Bent, sniffing the limp and blackened collar of his shirt. "Come on, Mrs. C, we've been saving the effing world again! Is that the best you've got?"

"Ignore him," said Gideon. "We landed at Highgate Aerodrome two hours ago and—"

"And we're famished," finished Bent. "What is that wonderful smell coming from the kitchens?"

Mrs. Cadwallader allowed herself a self-indulgent smile. "Pie and mash, Mr. Bent. Made with the very finest ingredients bought from the Tottenham Court Road just this morning. I take it you are ready to dine?"

"Not effing half," said Bent.

Gideon's stomach rumbled. For once, he was inclined to agree wholeheartedly with Mr. Aloysius Bent.

Bent sat back in his chair and farted as Mrs. Cadwallader began to clear the plates from the long mahogany table in the wood-paneled dining room. She wrinkled her nose and cast a pointed glance at Gideon, who said, "Mr. Bent, if you could try to remember your manners . . ."

Bent belched for good measure. "Left 'em in the East End, Gideon. They're not the sorts of manners that would be fit for high society in Mayfair, I'm afraid. Besides, breaking wind after a meal is considered a great compliment to the chef in some far-off lands. And after that bang-up spread from Mrs. C, she's lucky I didn't follow through as well."

Gideon shook his black-curled head. It had seemed a grand idea, at first, the suggestion that he take up residence in the former home of Captain Lucian Trigger, the erstwhile Hero of the Empire, following the events in London the previous month. And as Mr. Bent had been assigned to him as his official chronicler and companion, it was only natural that he be on hand. Bent had kept lodgings in some East End slum and readily agreed to give them up to move into the palatial apartments formerly owned by Trigger and his lover John Reed. It had a kind of symmetry, Mr. Walsingham had said. With both Trigger and Reed dead, Mrs. Cadwallader had been more than happy to have someone else to look after. The reality of living in close proximity to Aloysius Bent, however, had soon begun to pall.

Bent poured himself a generous measure of claret. "Think I'll finish off the piece for *World Marvels & Wonders* before I turn in, get it couriered over to them tomorrow. Then the day's my own. They'll be missing me in the Crown and Anchor. You didn't happen to see whether that cabbie brought my typewriter in from the steam-carriage, did you, Mrs. C?"

Mrs. Cadwallader brought the battered leather case from the hall. "Was it a terribly dangerous adventure, Mr. Smith?"

"Oh, like you wouldn't effing believe," Bent answered for him. "Dinosaurs, Mrs. Cadwallader. A . . . what was it, Gideon?"

"Tyrannosaurus rex."

"Tyrannosaurus rex, that's the effer." Bent nodded. "Tall as this house, teeth like the swords of the Iron Guard on the Queen's birthday parade. Nearly had us for breakfast."

Mrs. Cadwallader's hand flew to her mouth. Bent, warming to his tale, said, "Oh, yes, I didn't think we'd escape alive. Took one of the sailors in its vast jaws and cut him in two. Horrible."

"That's enough, Bent," said Gideon gently as Mrs. Cadwallader's complexion faded to a gray pallor.

"That's right," said Bent, pulling open the typewriter case. "You can read it in the next issue of the penny blood, like the rest of the sensation-hungry mob out there." He peered at the words he'd already battered out. "Think I'll call this one *The Lost World*. What do you think, Gideon?"

"Perfect," said Gideon, excusing himself and following Mrs. Cadwallader out of the dining room, as Bent began to hammer the keys.

Gideon found Mrs. Cadwallader in the study, amid all the trophies from the adventures of Dr. John Reed and Captain Trigger, who wrote up his international exploits in deathless prose for the penny bloods. The claw from the Exeter Werewolf, Lord Dexter's Top Hat, Markus Mesmer's Hypnowheel, the electric eyes of the Viennese Wardog . . . they were all there in glass cabinets, labeled and resting on velvet cushions. The housekeeper was standing before a portrait of Captain Trigger and Dr. Reed above the mantelpiece, her back to Gideon. He softly closed the door and walked over to her.

"You miss them, don't you?"

"Oh, terribly, Mr. Smith," she said tremulously, without turning around. "Do you know, before I came to work for them I would never have believed two men could be so in love. But their attachment was stronger than that of any married couple I have ever met."

"The memorial to them will open in Hyde Park on the first anniversary of their deaths, I believe."

Mrs. Cadwallader turned at last, tears in her eyes. "It's been a month now, Mr. Smith, but I still cry every day. Can it really be true, that Dr. Reed had gone bad?"

Gideon sighed. "I don't know, Mrs. Cadwallader. I never knew him before. But he had been trapped in that pyramid for a year. The loneliness he must have felt . . . only those horrible frog-faced mummies for company . . . who knows what that does to a man's mind?"

"But to come home with such . . . such vengeance in his heart! He was going to turn that brass dragon on Buckingham Palace! Kill Queen Victoria! If he had succeeded . . ."

"He didn't," said Gideon. "Lucian stopped him. I watched them fall from the dragon, Mrs. Cadwallader. They held each other all the way down. I truly believe that John had come back to Lucian at that moment."

She nodded, wiping away her tears with the corner of her apron. "It was how Captain Trigger would have wanted to go. He had become such a shadow of himself in that year that Dr. Reed was missing, Mr. Smith. If you hadn't come here, if you hadn't stopped Dr. Reed . . . I don't know what that would have done to Captain Trigger, if he had just watched from afar as Dr. Reed exacted such a mad revenge. It would have broken him. At least he died a whole man."

"He died a hero, Mrs. Cadwallader."

She smiled and cocked her head to one side. "And look at you, Mr. Smith. You were just a boy when you came knocking on this door. Now you're a man. The Hero of the Empire, no less."

It was Gideon's turn to smile. "It was only a month ago."

But much had changed in a month. From fisherman to . . . well, as Mrs. Cadwallader said. He had been appointed as the Hero of the Empire by Queen Victoria herself, to fill the gap left in the public consciousness by the death of Captain Trigger. He had been sent to Sandhurst for intensive training in firearms and hand-to-hand combat for an exhausting two-week period before being dispatched to rescue Professor Rubicon and Charles Darwin from that lost island in the Pacific. But already he was hungry for more. Hungry to pursue the turncoat Louis Cockayne and the purloined brass dragon Apep to America, hungry to rescue Maria from whatever fate to which Cockayne had delivered the beautiful automaton with a human brain.

As if reading his mind, Mrs. Cadwallader laid a hand on his forearm. "You will find Miss Maria, Mr. Smith. I am sure of it. Never was a thing more meant to be."

Gideon protested weakly, but his thoughts had been consumed by nothing else since the aerial battle over Hyde Park. The intervening month, as filled with activity as it had been, had done nothing to resolve his confusion regarding his feelings for the mysterious Maria. A clockwork-powered automaton with the pilfered, living brain of a dead London streetwalker, she was a scientific marvel, wrought by the genius of the missing scientist Hermann Einstein. But the effect she had on Gideon's heart could not be explained by a thousand scientists or a million formulas. He had denied what he felt for too long, and when he had finally reconciled his head with his heart, it had been too late. Louis Cockayne had betrayed them and stolen Maria away from him.

"Was there any news while we were away?" he said, by way of trying to force Maria from his thoughts.

"Another letter from the Grosvenor Square Residents' Committee," said Mrs. Cadwallader. "Complaining about Mr. Bent being . . . indisposed in the communal gardens on more than one occasion." She slapped her palm against her forehead. "Oh! Land's sakes! Your coming home has quite put me out of my mind! News! Of course! Mr. Bram Stoker!"

"They have recovered his body from the Rhodopis Pyramid?" said Gideon.

"His body? No, Mr. Smith! He is alive! He arrived home safe and well just after you departed for the Pacific!"

Gideon gaped at her. Stoker alive? It was impossible. The Irish writer had been crushed at the bottom of the collapsing pyramid. Elizabeth Bathory herself had seen him die— indeed, the noble vampire had taken his blood from his shattered body to enable her own escape from the ruined monument. There was a tinkle of bells from the hall. Mrs. Cadwallader said, "Tradesmen again. Or autograph hunters."

Gideon raised an eyebrow. "Autograph hunters?"

"They come with copies of *World Marvels & Wonders* for you to add your signature to. I shall get rid of them."

Gideon remembered the first time he had knocked at the door of the house on Grosvenor Square, the high hopes he had for Captain Lucian Trigger. He didn't know then, of course, that Trigger was merely the public front and that it was Dr. John Reed who was the true adventurer, doing the Crown's bidding in secret. "No, don't send them away," he said. "A signature costs nothing."

As Mrs. Cadwallader went to the door Gideon retreated back to the dining room, where Bent was rolling a cigarette in his meaty fingers. He saw Gideon and nodded toward that morning's *Illustrated London Argus*, on the table beside his typewriter.

"Seen this? Only another Jack the effing Ripper attack, two days ago." He shook his head. "Quality of reporting's gone right down the shitter since they shifted me to the penny blood."

Gideon turned as Mrs. Cadwallader coughed and showed in a familiar tall, thin man wearing his customary tails and carrying his topper in the crook of his arm. His cane tapped on the wooden floorboards and he arched one gray eyebrow, fixing Gideon with his unflinching stare.

"Mr. Walsingham," said Gideon.

Walsingham nodded. "Mr. Smith. Mr. Bent. I heard you had returned."

"Yes, that'll be the hour we spent being debriefed by your chaps at Highgate Aerodrome," said Bent.

"Quite so," said Walsingham, smoothing his mustache with white-gloved fingers. "A rather successful expedition, so I believe. You have returned one of our most eminent scientists and our beloved Professor of Adventure back home. Well done."

"All here," said Bent, tapping the sheaf of papers before him.

Walsingham held out his hand. "You have written your first fully-fledged Gideon Smith adventure for the penny dreadful? Excellent. I shall give it the once-over, Mr. Bent, and dispatch it to them myself."

Bent narrowed his eyes. "You'll censor it, you mean?"

Walsingham shrugged. "Merely edit out anything that might prove . . . damaging to the Empire."

Bent reluctantly handed over the manuscript, and Walsingham said, "What were your immediate plans, gentlemen?"

"Sleep, and lots of it," said Bent. "With ale and gin at regular intervals."

"We were going to go to the Stokers tomorrow," said Gideon, eyeing Bent. "I was just about to tell Mr. Bent . . . Bram has apparently returned alive from Egypt."

Bent goggled. "Alive? But he was crushed . . . Countess Bathory said so."

"I would not visit him in the mornings," said Walsingham mildly. "Mr. Stoker has become something of a . . . night owl since his return to London. Besides, you have another mission."

"But we've only just come back," protested Bent. "Where are you sending us this time?"

Walsingham looked Gideon in the eye. "America, Mr. Smith. We have had reports of a sighting of what we believe is the brass dragon, Apep."

Gideon stared at him. "Apep? Then I'm finally going for Maria?"

"Miss Rowena Fanshawe is cleared for takeoff from Highgate at noon," said Walsingham. "She will take you to New

York, where you will meet Governor Edward Lyle and be briefed on what we know so far."

Gideon swallowed drily. Maria. He was going to rescue Maria. At last.

Walsingham placed his topper on his head. "I shall see myself out. Godspeed, Mr. Smith, Mr. Bent. May you do the Empire proud once more."

5

Lighter Than Air

The steam-carriage deposited them on the stone apron outside the wooden, single-story building that was the headquarters of Fanshawe Aeronautical Endeavors just in time to see Rowena, her face smeared with black grease and carrying a foot-long wrench in her hand, chasing two boys in gray rags from the front door.

"And don't come back!" yelled Rowena, spotting Gideon and Bent unloading their luggage from the steam-cab and waving at them. She abandoned the chase and the two boys disappeared behind the piles of rusting gear wheels, cogs, and piston parts that were steadily growing beside Rowena's business premises.

"Autograph hunters?" asked Gideon, dropping his leather bag to embrace Rowena.

Bent paid the steam-driver, hovering a penny over his outstretched palm before changing his mind and exchanging it for a ha'penny. He ignored the man's baleful glare and said, "Knicker-nickers, more like. Trying to steal a pair of the Belle of the Airways' panties."

"It's good to see you, too, Aloysius," said Rowena, stretching her arms around his broad shoulders. She extracted herself from his pungent hug and cast a thumb back at the boundary fence of the Highgate Aerodrome, where the boys had fled. "Actually, they're after brass goggles. They've become quite the fashion accessory at high-class parties, by all accounts. These urchins can get a good price for the genuine article in some of the costume shops in Covent Garden."

"Who'd have thought?" said Bent, shaking his head. "I swear, since I've been hanging around with Smith here I've completely lost touch with what's going on in high society. I've more idea what they're wearing in Outer Mongolia than in Mayfair." He rubbed his chin thoughtfully. "Brass goggles, eh?"

Gideon shielded his eyes from the late summer sunlight and looked up at the *Skylady III*, tethered by steel cables as thick as his wrist to huge iron rings set into the stone-flagged apron. The first time he had seen the vast dirigible, it had been under the command of Louis Cockayne. He said, "She looks grand, Rowena."

Bent turned to appraise the dirigible, patting the pockets of his shapeless brown overcoat for his tobacco. "Don't rightly know if I should be even thinking about stepping an effing foot on that thing," he said sourly. "Not after that damn Louis Cockayne threatened to throw me off it. And then stole poor old Maria off Smith here."

"She was the *Yellow Rose* then," said Rowena, wiping the grease from her hands on a square of dirty cloth. "She's a whole different 'stat now, Aloysius. She's the *Skylady III*. That makes her mine, not Cockayne's. And you'll come to no harm under my command."

"As I recall, the *Skylady II* was blown to bits high above the Mediterranean," said Bent mildly. "Remind me what happened to the first one?"

"Shredded on the north face of the Eiger." Rowena smiled and ran a hand through her short, auburn hair. "Gideon, we've got an ascent slot at midday. She's wound and loaded; I just need to take a bath and get a few papers in order before we depart for New York. Which reminds me, Gideon . . . Walsingham left something for you."

"More effing problems, no doubt," said Bent.

"You don't have much faith in Mr. Walsingham," said Gideon as Rowena walked toward the offices. "He is the representative of the Crown, after all."

"Which is precisely why I don't trust him," said Bent. "Gideon . . . I've been around the block too many times. I know what they're capable of. Christ, you saw what happened to poor old Annie Crook."

But Gideon hadn't seen what had happened to Annie Crook—no one had, save for Mr. Walsingham and his most trusted advisers. Annie Crook had fallen in love with the wrong man, and Walsingham had been called in—or had taken it upon himself—to sort out the mess on behalf of his employer, the British Crown. Gideon didn't like to think about what they knew had happened—Annie Crook, a common shopgirl known to dabble in prostitution had been "seen to," her body dumped in the mud on the banks of the Thames, her brain transferred to Professor Hermann Einstein where the scientist implanted it into his automaton, Maria.

So yes, they knew what had happened to Annie Crook. And Mr. Walsingham would stop at nothing to protect the British Empire. But that was past history, and there was nothing Gideon could do about that. He had been tasked with a job by Queen Victoria herself, and if that meant taking orders from Walsingham . . .

"You must learn to trust more, Aloysius," said Gideon. "They pay our wages, after all."

"And you must learn to trust *less*, Gideon." Bent tapped the side of his nose. "They pay us, but they don't own us. Now, where did I put me pipe . . . ?"

Gideon left the other man trying to strike a match in the face of the crosswinds that tore across the wide apron of the aerodrome, following Rowena into the shadows of her offices. The gift of the former *Yellow Rose* from Cockayne and the recent fame from being honored by Queen Victoria herself for her part in defeating the crazed John Reed's plot to raze London had, by Rowena's own admission, done wonders for her business. But that had evidently not brought with it any improved organization skills. The office of Fanshawe Aeronautical Endeavors was piled high with yellowing documents, abandoned mugs of tea that had started to nurture cultures of blossoming blue mold, sections of clockwork, and steam-powered devices in various stages of being repaired or stripped down. One wall was dominated by a huge map of the world, into which colored pins had been stuck and connected with crisscrossing lengths of woolen yarn. Mandates, schedules, and handwritten notes were tacked up and down the sides of the massive chart.

"You are certain Mr. Walsingham trusted you with highly classified documents?" asked Gideon doubtfully, looking around for a space to sit down.

He ducked as Rowena aimed a lump of steel wool at his head. "Saucy. Admittedly, he did make me lock it in the safe first."

She yawned and stretched, the movement pulling apart the front of the oily brown overalls she wore. Gideon averted his eyes. Rowena Fanshawe was a beautiful young woman, and she had already made it quite clear she would . . . well. It had been a swift education for Gideon Smith, the fisherman from the wilds of the North Yorkshire coast who had been thrust center stage in the dramas he had always dreamed of experiencing. And while certain aspects of his new life— rampaging dinosaurs, international travel, the handling of heavy-duty weaponry—came quickly to him, affairs of the heart seemed to take longer to accommodate. The heart, and organs farther south. Bent had voiced on more than one occasion the opinion that Gideon and Rowena were a match made in heaven, and that were he ten, twenty, or thirty years younger (depending on the severity of his hangover when he made the observation) he would certainly make a go of it with the aerostat pilot himself.

But always, always his thoughts came back to Maria. Gideon cast his eyes to his feet, and Rowena, as though reading his mind, self-consciously pulled the gaping buttons of her overalls together. "Sorry," she said, stifling another yawn. "I only got back from Nepal two days ago, and Walsingham was waiting on my doorstep."

"You're sure you'll be all right to take us to New York?" asked Gideon.

Rowena nodded. "A quick bath and I'll be right as rain," she said. "It's the best part of two days to America, a day and a half if we've got the weather, but this 'stat practically flies herself; I can rest once we're aloft."

She began to haul aside a stack of hydraulic pistons leaning against the wall, revealing the door of a safe. She tapped a dirty fingernail on her lip for a moment, then snapped her fingers and began to spin the twin dials. Gideon held his breath then exhaled as the door clicked open, and she withdrew a thin black leather document folder, sealed with wax, and handed it to him.

Gideon examined the seal; it was imprinted with a letter "W" surrounded by thorny vines. Walsingham's mark, all right.

"Our orders, no doubt," said Rowena. She paused then added, "Gideon? The lock's broken on the bathroom door. Do you think you might . . . ?"

He smiled. "I'll stay here, make sure no one disturbs you."

Rowena smiled back as he stared thoughtfully at the seal on the document folder, then she let herself quietly into the bathroom, pulling the wooden door closed behind her.

"For eff's sake."

Gideon looked up. Bent was standing in the doorway, dumping his pipe ashes on the doorstep, the *Skylady III* bobbing behind him.

"What?" asked Gideon.

Bent shook his head. "You really are an effing idiot, aren't you? Carpe diem, Gideon."

"What does that mean?"

"Seize the day, lad. Carpe di-effing-em."

The lock on the bathroom door wasn't broken, of course, and Rowena chided herself even as she left it open and swiftly disrobed in the small, drafty room. The boiler above the bath shuddered and shook as she filled the bath with steaming water. She knew Gideon wouldn't follow her into the bathroom, though God knew she couldn't have telegraphed her invitation more obviously had a parade of music hall singers delivered it to Gideon in the popular tunes of the day. Easing herself into the hot water, Rowena shook her head, both amused and slightly saddened. She was very naughty, trying to tempt Gideon like that. He was a good man.

Too good for her, perhaps. Too honest and true, at any rate. It had been a month now, and still he pined for Maria, that funny little clockwork thing. *Now, now, Rowena, don't be so tart*, she thought as she soaped her legs. She had nothing against Maria, though she barely knew the automaton. Like any aerostat pilot, she'd seen more things than she could rightly explain in this strange old world. Even a flesh-and-blood boy in love with a mechanical girl lost its novelty after a while.

Still . . . Rowena Fanshawe had known many men, it was true, and would doubtless know many more. But as she held her breath and her eyes shut tight and submerged herself in the hot water, she wondered how fine a thing it would be, to love and be loved by a man like Gideon Smith.

From the bridge at the fore of the gondola slung beneath the huge balloon of the *Skylady III*, a freshly bathed Rowena Fanshawe touched two fingers to her forehead to acknowledge the aerodrome employee in bright orange overalls who waved two yellow flags at her, then banged on the wide panoramic window at the tether-monkeys to whom she paid a few pennies in the way of retainer, who swiftly unclipped the steel cables that held the 'stat earthbound. The *Skylady III* lurched and began to rise. They were bound for America.

Bent gripped the console, his knuckles whitening as they ascended. "Tell me again how this big effing thing stays in the air," he said, his voice tremulous.

Rowena shrugged. "Helium."

"I must have missed that science lesson at school. What, exactly, is helium?"

"It's a gas, Aloysius. A lifting gas. An entirely natural resource. It powers the Empire as much as coal; it gives us the mastery of the air. It's lighter than air, Aloysius. They're finding new deposits all the time, but it's still relatively scarce, which is why aerostats are the preserve of the richer nations."

Bent let loose a long fart. "Oh, God," he said. "Bit of natural gas of my own, there. Are the bathrooms still where I remember them?"

Rowena nodded as she held the wheel and said, "If it makes your airsickness feel any better, Aloysius, the galley is well-stocked with rum and sausages."

As the fat journalist clumsily let himself down the ladder from the bridge to the corridor below, Rowena looked around for Gideon. He was standing by the window at the starboard side, which opened out on to the observation deck where Louis Cockayne had taken them on board in an act of piracy as they were bound for Egypt. From that same deck, Rowena, Bent, and the others had watched as Gideon tackled John Reed aboard the brass dragon over London.

The *Skylady III* was a tripler—powered by a combination of clockwork, steam, and electricity. Rowena didn't understand the electricity much, and she didn't like relying on things she didn't understand, so she tended to make more use of the steam and clockwork. But steam meant coal, and coal was heavy and cost money, so she only used it when she was being paid well, like on this job, or when she needed to be somewhere fast, because when it had a full head of steam the *Skylady III* could certainly move.

She locked the 'stat into an ascending course holding due west, setting the electric bell—one of the innovations she had overcome her suspicion sufficiently to use—to sound when they reached the desired altitude. She looked back at Gideon and absently ran a forefinger along the line of her triceps, straining through the crisp white shirt she had changed into. A month of shoveling coal and winding the *Skylady III*'s clockwork mechanisms (she was not yet making enough money out of her royal honor to employ more staff at Fanshawe Aeronautical Endeavors) had toughened up her already lithe and strong body. She felt a wave of something she couldn't quite identify as she regarded Gideon, something a little maternal, perhaps, that made her want to take him protectively in her strong arms. Perhaps it was something else, something lighter than air that fluttered behind her breasts, that ached between her legs. Something that made her happy and sad all at once. She was glad to be taking Gideon to find Maria. She smiled. Of course she was.

Gideon never tired of watching London unravel below him as an aerostat carried him to his next adventure. For so long he had dreamed of such a life, earthbound in Sandsend, only his regular escape into his favorite penny blood, *World Marvels & Wonders*, breaking the monotony of fishing the seas every day on his father's gearship, the *Cold Drake*.

Be careful what you wish for. That was what they said, wasn't it? Funny how you only ever heard that advice after you'd *gotten* what you wished for. As thin fingers of cloud began to draw a white veil over the huge sprawl of London falling slowly away beneath them, Gideon thought of the life he had now, living in opulence in Mayfair and flying off to New York at the drop of a hat when the Crown required it. He thought of the intensive training he had undertaken, how he could now strip down and rebuild a repeating rifle nearly without thinking, how he knew seven ways to kill a man without his target uttering a sound.

And he thought of what he had lost to be here.

He thought of his father, Arthur Smith.

Arthur Smith, who had died by the claws of the foul frog-faced creature, which either worked for John Reed or controlled his mind—Gideon still couldn't decide which. Arthur Smith, who had worked his fingers to the bone to make a good life for Gideon, especially after the death of his wife and his other two boys. Arthur Smith, who had indulgently shared—or pretended to, Gideon realized suddenly—his only living son's passion for the unlikely adventures of Captain Lucian Trigger, the Hero of the Empire.

What would old Arthur make of all this? There'd be sadness, of course, that the business he inherited from his own father and built up into a solid foundation for his family—until death began to claim them—wasn't going to continue in the hands of his son. But he would have known that Gideon's heart was never in fishing, that his mind and heart were forever given to the slipstreams of the dirigibles that floated high overhead. Arthur would have been happy for Gideon, would have burst with pride when his only surviving son received the Victoria Cross, the highest honor for bravery in the land, from the Queen herself.

Gideon blinked; London was lost beneath the clouds. He stroked the black leather of the document folder in his hands, then used his thumbnail to break Walsingham's seal. Orders. He had just begun to read when a small bell sounded and Rowena announced they had reached their cruising altitude. While Gideon had dreamed, she had crossed the bridge and stood alongside him; her unique scent of Pear's soap and gear oil filled his nose. Rowena laid a hand on his forearm.

"Were you thinking about Maria?"

Gideon smiled at her. "No. I was thinking about my dad. It's been so busy since . . . since it happened. I feel I've barely had time to mourn him properly."

Rowena gazed past him at the stringy threads of cloud skidding over the glass window. "I know how you feel. I lost my father when I was very young, too."

She still had her hand on his arm. Awkwardly, Gideon placed his own hand over hers. "I'm sorry. I didn't know."

She smiled. "It was a long time ago."

They stood together in silence for a moment, connected by loss and by touch, his palm across the back of her hand, until Bent hauled himself up the ladders, two bottles tucked under one arm and balancing a plate of gently steaming sausages in the other.

"I've just flushed my breakfast out over Greenwich," he cackled. "Time to refill the tanks with rum and vittles. And I've a pack of cards to pass the time; they're in my front trouser pocket. Be a darling, Rowena, and fish 'em out, would you? Just mind you don't grab the old chap by mistake."

6

THE EMPIRE STATE

The sun sank far behind New York, lighting up the roofs and towers of Manhattan with golden fire as the *Skylady III* soared over the glittering Atlantic toward the vast, jumbled city. Gideon held his breath as Rowena began to bring the 'stat down lower. He had never dared hope he would see the fabled city at the heart of the Empire State, the living testimony to Queen Victoria's mastery of the Earth. He had read of it, of course, many, many times in the pages of *World Marvels & Wonders*. Gideon's recent adventures had taken him to Egypt, to the New Spain territory of Tijuana, and to the Lost World, an unmapped dot in the great swell of the Pacific Ocean. But as the *Skylady III* gingerly nosed over Manhattan, the grasping towers of the great city casting long shadows over the gridlike streets below, Gideon felt the hairs on the back of his arms prickle and stand on end.

New York! Now he felt like a real adventurer. Manhattan was like a black insect that clung to the Atlantic coast, soot-darkened towers in the Gothic style thrusting upward, scraping at the underside of heaven. Whereas London had enjoyed a brief flirtation with the architecture of the lost civilizations of South America, erecting ziggurats with tumbling foliage flowing down their terraces all over the capital, New York seemed to have embraced the legacy of old Europe: a forest of pointed towers, jagged arches, and ribbed vaults.

"Rowena," said Bent, standing beside Gideon on the bridge, looking out the panoramic window that curved around the front end of the gondola as the city opened up like a rich child's model plaything, "should we, strictly speaking, be actually *lower* than some of these effing towers?"

"Just following Walsingham's orders," said Rowena through gritted teeth. Gideon could tell she wasn't entirely comfortable with steering the massive 'stat between the soaring spires.

Bent held on to the console, his suit and overcoat even more crumpled, if that were possible, after the transatlantic journey, and peered through the window. "There's some effer in that window, waving at us."

Rowena jabbed her finger at the map from Walsingham's leather folder. "Apparently the Governor of New York has a private aerodrome, here." Gideon looked at the map over her shoulder. The Governor's Residence was situated in the Albert Gardens, a huge, rectangular swathe of greenery at the center of Manhattan. "We've been granted landing privileges. Unfortunately, this is the only way to get there."

Gideon looked up at the towers. "It's like London . . . but different. I swear some of these buildings are taller than the Lady of Liberty flood barrier at Greenwich."

Bent sniffed. As Gideon gazed upward, Bent risked a look down. "In my experience, the higher a city's rich raise themselves up, the deeper its poor sink in the shit."

Rowena didn't take her eyes from the course ahead, her hands moving blindly but unerringly over the instrument panel in front of her, as though she could sense the readings on the dials and clocks through strange osmosis alone, but she said, "And your experience of the world's cities is vast, is it, Aloysius?"

Bent sniffed. "Lived all my life in London. That's as much experience as a man needs, in my humble opinion. Greatest city in the world."

"I think New York might have designs on that claim," said Gideon, blinking as the *Skylady III* emerged from the manmade canyon of towers into an open space, the red rays of the sinking sun flooding the bridge. The Albert Gardens was an oasis in the center of the city, a green pause amid the teeming life of Manhattan, a long, sculpted park surrounded on all sides by teetering towers and spires, an elevated steam-train track threading among them.

Beside him, Rowena visibly relaxed. "We're through. I don't see why they couldn't have had us land at North Beach Aerodrome and steam-bussed us in, though."

Terra firma within his grasp, Bent seemed more jovial, too. He nudged Gideon in the ribs. "That's because we're vee eye effing pees, ain't it? Very Important Personages, that's us. The Hero of the Effing Empire and his faithful chronicler."

Gideon said nothing. As Rowena studied the orders from Walsingham and began to swing the *Skylady III* around and down toward the grand Governor's Residence on the east side of the Albert Gardens, his head and heart still danced high in the thin air far above them.

The Governor of New York, Edward Lyle, was a rotund man whose finely cut purple velvet jacket and black breeches proudly showed off his portly physique like a badge of office. He had thick, bushy eyebrows, one of which seemed permanently arched as though he questioned everything, and his mop of unruly dark hair was partially hidden beneath a stovepipe hat, taller than the current London fashion dictated.

"The Yanks try to do everything bigger than the Brits, even their effing hats," murmured Bent to Gideon as they descended from the gondola to the stone apron adjacent to the Governor's Residence. Bent nodded to the opulent building. "Very grand. Ruskinian Gothic, if I'm not mistaken. Not a bad pile."

Lyle was accompanied by half a dozen soldiers in dusky blue livery, each one flint-eyed and mustachioed, their wide-brimmed hats bearing the crossed-sabers insignia of the American Cavalry. Each shouldered a modern slide-action twenty-four-inch octagonal-barrel Winchester. Gideon smiled inwardly; he was getting quite adept in the recognition of arms.

The governor stepped forward to greet the arrivals. He was a full head shorter than Gideon, and he pushed back the stovepipe on his head to properly look at the adventurer, his eyebrow arching even more sharply as the setting sun slid over the balloon of the *Skylady III*.

"Mr. Gideon Smith!" declared Lyle, holding out his hand. "It is a great honor to have the Hero of the Empire here in New York."

"It's an honor to be here," said Gideon, shaking the governor's hand. He thrilled slightly at the lilt of Lyle's American accent.

Lyle turned and took Rowena's hand, kissing it softly, and said, "Miss Fanshawe, the Belle of the Airways. And Mr. Aloysius Bent, esteemed man of letters."

"You've done your homework, Governor," said Bent, though Gideon could tell he was more than satisfied with Lyle's appellation.

Lyle inclined his head. "No need for mugging up, Mr. Bent. Your exploits have thrilled America as much as Britain, I dare say." He clapped his hands together. "Now, you must be exhausted after your long journey. There are rooms for you all in my humble residence yonder, and doubtless you'll be glad of a good night's sleep. If I might be so bold, however, to suggest you might freshen up and then join me for a spot of dinner? We have much to discuss."

"Dinner?" said Bent. "I like the cut of your jib, Lyle." He wiped a dark stain off his waistcoat and sniffed suspiciously at the shoulder of his black jacket. "Shall we skip the freshening up, though, and cut straight to the chase?"

Gideon bowed his head. "Your hospitality is most welcome, Governor. We would be delighted to join you."

As Lyle and his soldiers led the way across the apron toward the huge residence, Gideon looked up at the soaring towers where gas and oil lamps were flickering into life against the encroaching darkness.

Bent poked with a carving knife at the carcass at the center of the oval mahogany table as he suppressed a belch. "Damn fine bird you served up there, Lyle. What do you call it?"

Lyle sat back in his chair, deftly unfastening the top button on his breeches. "That's a turkey, sir. We generally have it for Thanksgiving, in November, and at Christmastime. I thought I'd have one cooked early, for my important visitors."

"Can't beat a plump goose at Christmas," said Bent, holding up his glass for the waiter to refill with wine. "But that wasn't a bad spread at all."

Lyle smiled. "I am gratified it met with your approval, Mr. Bent."

The wood-paneled room, brightly lit with gas sconces on the walls, had a large window looking out into the dark gardens of the Governor's Residence. Beyond, pinpricks of light picked out the black pillars that rose into the deepening violet sky. Lyle caught Rowena gazing out at the towers.

"Skyscrapers, we call 'em, Miss Fanshawe. They say New York is the city that never sleeps. Those lights will burn all night in some quarters."

"Why do you build upward, Mr. Lyle?" asked Rowena. "One thing you're not short of in America is space."

Bent chuckled and quoted, "*'And they said, Go to, let us build a city and a tower, whose top may reach unto heaven.'*"

Lyle smiled. "Is your knowledge of history and geography as broad as your grasp of Scripture, sir?"

Bent waved his glass. "I get by. I daresay Mr. Smith here would benefit from a recap. You know young'uns today; don't know what they teach them in schools."

Lyle pushed back his chair and hauled himself up. Behind him on the wood paneling a furled Union Flag and a portrait of Queen Victoria flanked a large chart of the American territories. He took up a cane and pointed at the East Coast.

"New York, also known as the Empire State ever since Queen Victoria graced us with her presence back in 'sixty-six." He tapped a little way to the north. "Of course, Boston is the official capital of British America, but down here in Manhattan is where the real work is done, where you'll find the real America. They come from all over the world to New York.

Italians we have, and Bohemians. Irish. Germans. They come here looking for a new life. They get to New York and stop. So we build upward, to accommodate them all. We even have a few French." He smiled. "The Frenchies backed the wrong horse back in 1775, of course. Had the rebels won, America would look a very different place today, I daresay."

"But they didn't win, of course," said Gideon. "America remains British."

Lyle tapped a forefinger on his full lips. "Are you named for Gideon, the great American mystery man?"

"I don't think so. My mother was a churchgoer."

"Quite. But it was Gideon, I'm sure you'll remember from school, Mr. Smith, who foiled the rebels. He took down the terrorist Paul Revere, stopped him alerting the revolutionaries to the arrival of the British forces. April 18, 1775—British troops marched into Lexington and Concord and arrested the ringleaders of the rebellion. You can go to Boston if you wish and see the pickled heads of Samuel Adams and John Hancock."

"Think we'll give that a miss," said Bent.

Lyle said, "And America, as you say, remains British. At least here on the East Coast."

Lyle swept the cane across the broad expanse of the map. "Over here, on the West Coast, that's Japanese territory. Or rather, the Californian Meiji. The son of the old emperor, tired of waiting for his old man to die, set up shop here in 'sixty-eight. The Spanish used to hold it, but not very well. We were making inroads into settling when the Japs turned up. We'd a small town, San Francisco, which we'd taken from the Spaniards. The Japs took it from us. Nyu Edo they call it now."

He circled the middle of the map. "This? Empty land. Up for the taking. The land of the free, you might say. We have settlers out there, pioneering families trying to establish British American interests in the wilds, but it's a dangerous life."

"I'd been given to understand there were already people there," said Bent. "The Indians?"

"Well, yes." Lyle coughed. "But I'm talking about *civilized* peoples, Mr. Bent."

"And do the Japanese have designs on this free land?" asked Gideon.

"We *all* have designs on expansion, Mr. Smith," said Lyle. He pointed the cane to the far south. "Except for New Spain, maybe. Their perpetual war with the French back in Europe means they're pulling resources out of the Americas, not putting them in." The cane danced northward. "Up here is Canada, where we're making small gains. But it's an unforgiving territory that'll take a lot of taming. Which is why we're concentrating on expanding our borders westward."

Lyle tapped the eastern coastline far below New York and ran the cane across the map to just below Nyu Edo. "And this is British America's greatest feat of engineering. The Mason-Dixon Wall. Two thousand miles of brick, stone, and mortar, stretching clear across the continent. Back in 1833 when the Slavery Abolition Act was passed, the southern states didn't like it, not one bit. So they seceded and formed the Confederacy. At first London wanted us to take the land back, it being cotton-rich country. But advances in air travel meant we could get cotton from India, so we let 'em be. Besides, London wouldn't send us more troops and resources, and we just couldn't get embroiled in a war that could last decades. So we cleared out good, decent folk from points south, and brought them into British America properly. And Queen Victoria decided in 1838 that if British America couldn't reclaim the southern lands, then we'd build a wall to keep them out."

The cane swept westward. "And over here, we have French Louisiana. Louis the Sixteenth fled here after the British punished the French for their part in the failed American Revolution. They say he fell in with witches. They say he's still alive, presiding over a hellish city-state of black magic and fornication."

"Sounds right up my street," said Bent, chuckling.

Lyle leveled a serious stare at him. "I doubt you'd say that if you had the misfortune to find yourself in New Orleans, sir. The spies we've sent down . . . well, they never came back."

"Can't say I blame 'em—all that effing fornication."

Lyle moved on. "And then we have Texas. It was always wild country down there. The warlords started off as British governors, but a few of them got together after the Wall was built, decided they didn't want to pay their taxes and didn't want to be beholden to a London that had cut them off with the Confederacy and French Louisiana. Neither did they like being told they couldn't keep slaves. They didn't want any part of the Confederacy, though; they wanted to live their own way. They're godless, violent slavers, Mr. Smith, who will stop at nothing to ensure their anarchic, lawless way of life is preserved. They're killers, ravishers. They make their own rules, and they aren't the rules of civilized men. They take what they want and murder anyone who tries to stop them."

Lyle fell silent, and Gideon asked, "Mr. Lyle, how much do you know about our mission?"

Lyle looked around the table. "You all have the necessary *clearances?*"

"Of course. You can speak freely here. I would trust Mr. Bent and Rowena with my life. Have done, many times."

Lyle nodded, though he still seemed cautious. "I received a full briefing, of course, about what you're doing here. From the highest authority."

"Oh, get on with it, Lyle," said Bent. "You can say his name. He won't magically appear behind you. Walsingham gave you the full rundown, did he?"

Lyle appeared to relax. "Yes, Mr. Walsingham. He told me that you had secured from Egypt an ancient weapon, a fabulous brass dragon that flies and shoots fireballs, powered by unknown machinery." Lyle shook his head. "What a marvel. What a thing. Imagine what uses such an infernal device could be put to."

"That's the problem, Mr. Lyle," said Gideon. "We do

imagine what it could be used for. That's why we have to get it back. And, more than that, Maria . . ."

Lyle nodded. "The automaton." He had been thoroughly briefed, then. "The thing that flies the dragon."

Gideon narrowed his eyes. "Maria isn't a *thing*, Mr. Lyle."

Lyle met his gaze. "Yes, Walsingham briefed me on that, as well." He shrugged. "To each his own, Mr. Smith."

Bent jabbed at a rogue potato with his fork. "Do you have a wife yourself, Lyle? Or are you one of those who's married to the job?"

Lyle glanced down at his plate. "Everything I do, Mr. Bent, I do for my wife, Clara, and my son, Alfie." He looked up to meet Bent's eyes. "*Everything*, Mr. Bent."

"Then you'll know that love is blind, Lyle, and not be so judgmental," admonished Bent sharply. "I daresay that as much as you love 'em, your wife and kid aren't actually *perfect*."

Lyle's eyes flashed, and Gideon murmured, "Aloysius . . ."

The governor sighed. "No. Mr. Bent is right. Who is perfect? Let he who is without sin cast the first stone, and all." He gazed into the distance—into the far-off past, it seemed to Gideon. "No, they are not perfect." He shook his head and pulled himself back to the room. "Mr. Walsingham also tells me that one Louis Cockayne made off with your brass dragon and your automaton."

"Effing pirate," said Bent.

"Cockayne is known to me." Lyle nodded. "He is somewhat famous in America. A master gunman, an adventurer—and yes, Mr. Bent, a pirate. Louis Cockayne goes where the money is, buys low, sells high, and gets out of town fast."

"So where is the money?" asked Gideon. "Here in New York? Boston? Perhaps the Japanese settlements in the West, or New Spain?"

Lyle gave a humorless smile. "Possibly, and Louis Cockayne's done business in all of those places. But something like your brass dragon, that's going to be difficult to sell. If he goes to Nyu Edo, or Ciudad Cortes, he risks stirring up a diplomatic incident once the new masters of the dragon unveil their prize. No, he knows his markets, Louis Cockayne, and he's going to take the dragon to people who have pots of money and don't much care for the provenance of what they're buying."

Bent said, "Well, I don't know about anyone else, but I can see what's coming next."

Lyle smiled thinly again. "I'm afraid Mr. Bent is quite correct." He turned back to the map and tapped the region below the Mason-Dixon Wall with the cane. "Mr. Smith, Texas is where you will need to go to find your dragon and your mechanical girl."

After dinner, Rowena excused herself and retired, the stresses of the flight having finally caught up with her. Lyle told Gideon and Bent that he often took a cigar in the gardens after his meal, inviting them to join him.

"America is more . . . complicated than I thought," said Gideon as they walked around the walled garden, steering a course between the pools of pale light thrown by the gas lamps strung along the gravel path.

"It doesn't sound like a lot of fun being Governor of New York," added Bent, puffing on one of Lyle's huge cigars.

The governor paused for a long moment, and Gideon listened with him to the sounds of the darkness: close up, the gentle song of night birds, and farther away, the constant hum of the city, a symphony of steam exhalations, clanking machinery, distant shouts, and snatches of music on the breeze that spoke of the approaching change of season.

"The things that delight and dismay are often one and the same," Lyle said eventually. "There are one and a half million souls crammed into these five boroughs, living alongside and above and below one another, but without them I would feel so very, very alone. Mr. Bent, over dinner you quoted from Genesis, did you not? You alluded to the tower of Babel? All the scattered diaspora of humanity is here on one island, a

babbling cacophony of voices . . . but it is the differences between us that highlight our *oneness*. We are surrounded on all
sides by hostile territory, hostile people, but that only serves
to unite us in the pursuit of survival and happiness. To answer
your question, Mr. Bent—no, being Governor of New York is
not often *fun*. But it is the most rewarding position I could
ever hope for on this vast earth, and I am privileged to curate
this most wonderful of cities."

Gideon noticed that Bent was scribbling rapidly with the
worn stub of a pencil in a notebook he had pulled from one of
the many pockets of his crumpled but voluminous overcoat.
"Smashing stuff, this," said Bent. "It'll make great copy when
I write this up."

Lyle raised an amused eyebrow. "However . . ."

Gideon invited the governor to continue.

He said, "I know you gentlemen are agents of the Crown,
but may I be presumptuous enough to hope we can speak
freely, as friends?"

"Speak away, Lyle," said Bent, pocketing his notebook.
"You're off the record, as it were."

Lyle nodded and looked out into the darkness. "London is
so very far away, gentlemen. It is difficult convincing some
parties here that it is in our best interests to remain so closely
tied to the Empire."

"There are those who counsel rebellion?" said Gideon.

"No, no, of course not," said Lyle. "But you must understand . . . the taxes here are greater than those you pay in London;
they have to be. The lion's share is sent back to Britain, with a
small portion retained for municipal spending. From that, city
governors such as myself must pay the army to keep order, the
public works department, teachers, hospital workers, the sanita-
tion sector . . . why, if I told you how much it cost to build and
maintain the Mason-Dixon Wall alone, it would make your eyes
water, sirs! But Queen Victoria desired a defense greater than
the Great Wall of China, a structure that could be seen from
the very moon, should mankind ever set foot upon it."

"It was taxes that caused the last revolution," said Bent. "You think that could happen again?"

"Not on my watch," said Lyle. "But there are those who wonder whether America could not survive—indeed, thrive—away from the influence of the Empire. We have all the resources we require here. All we need is the money to get to them, and to keep the Japanese, the Texans, and the Spanish at bay. The Frenchies keep themselves to themselves, thank God. There are enough people eyeing up the unclaimed lands, and you wouldn't believe how much coal a city like New York runs on."

"Where do you get it?" asked Bent.

Lyle shrugged. "We have coalfields to the south, in Pennsylvania. But it's hard, dangerous work getting it out. Much of it we import. We have to keep the machine moving. If we stop, we die."

As Gideon digested Lyle's words, something flickered at the corner of his eye. He turned around and peered into the darkness beyond the gas lamps, at the edges of the walled garden where tall trees softened the border. He relaxed. A bird, nothing more. But then he heard the lightest of thumps from the other side of the garden and a skittering in the gravel.

Bent had heard it, too, and he murmured something just as Gideon saw what seemed to be a shadow detaching itself from the tree ahead of him.

Lyle swore.

"What is it?" asked Gideon, turning around to see another black shadow, and another, dropping from the trees before and behind them. He circled on the spot; there were three figures, dressed from head to toe in black, save for slits in their hoods that showed narrow eyes glinting in the moonlight.

"Ninja," said Lyle softly. "Japanese assassins."

"Where are those effing soldiers?" Bent demanded, then hollered, "Help! Help in the garden!"

Gideon slid his hand inside his jacket, where his Webley & Scott British Bulldog revolver sat snugly in its leather pouch.

"Back," he hissed, stepping in front of Lyle and Bent. Two of the ninja were approaching, crouched, from the north and west, thin blades glinting in their hands. Gideon sensed that the third must be behind him, and he whirled quickly, throwing his gun arm over Bent's shoulder.

"Stop, or I shoot!"

"Just effing get on with it," said Bent. "Didn't you hear him? They're effing assassins."

Despite his training, Gideon had yet to kill a man in cold blood. He could feel his hands shaking, as they had never done on the shooting range. But there he had fired at wooden targets; here were living, breathing, flesh-and-blood men approaching.

"Governor?"

The appearance of a young soldier at the French windows broke the spell. The ninja approaching from the rear whirled around, his hand suddenly extended, his fingers splayed. The soldier's eyes widened as a sharpened star thudded into his windpipe, and then he crumpled to the ground, gasping and spraying blood in red-black gouts. Gideon let loose the first of his bullets, hitting the ninja in the chest, the impact spinning the assassin around and into the trunk of a young cypress tree.

"Gideon . . ." said Bent.

He turned to see the two ninja running silently across the gravel toward them, and he fired again, throwing the one to the right off his feet. But Gideon had only winged the ninja's arm, and he rose again, the glint of one of those deadly throwing stars in the palm of his gloved hand. Gideon unleashed the Bulldog again, this time aiming for the assassin's head. His earlier hesitation cost him, though, because the final ninja was upon them, his long, thin blade slashing at Gideon's gun hand.

Gideon pushed Bent backward, knocking his friend off his feet and landing on top of him; he could hear the breath knocked out of Bent as he absorbed Gideon's weight. Lyle staggered and the ninja seeped over him like a shadowy ghost, pulling the governor's arm behind his back and holding the blade across his throat.

Stalemate. Gideon got carefully to his feet, just as three more soldiers appeared at the French doors. He held up his hand. "Wait! Stay back!" he shouted. To the assassin he said more calmly, "What do you want?"

The man's eyes were wide behind his mask, swiveling between Gideon, the soldiers in the doorway, and the corpses of his compatriots. Something felt . . . not right. For a trained assassin, the man seemed very nervous, almost terrified. Gideon said again, softly, "What do you want?"

The man muttered something in a language utterly foreign to Gideon, and Lyle said through gritted teeth, "Isn't it obvious? He wants to kill the Governor of New York."

Lyle's words seemed to galvanize the ninja, and he stood a little straighter, steadying his blade at Lyle's neck. "Do something," pleaded the governor.

"Put down the weapon or I shoot," said Gideon.

The ninja pressed his blade into the folds of fat at Lyle's throat.

Behind him, Gideon was aware of more movement in the doors of the building. He didn't dare take his eyes off the ninja, but sensed Rowena's presence all the same; the commotion had woken her.

"Stay back, all of you," said Gideon quietly. "You, too, Rowena."

"Gideon . . ." he heard her say.

"Back," he ordered. The ninja's eyes were swiveling beneath his mask. He was panicking. Lyle's eyes bulged as the blade tightened at his throat.

"You don't want to do this," said Gideon.

Lyle closed his eyes. "He's right. You don't want to do this."

The attacker didn't seem to know *what* he wanted, anymore. He was a skittish thing, for an assassin, thought Gideon. The man muttered something, presumably in Japanese, and Gideon saw a thin line of dark blood appear at Lyle's throat.

Before Gideon knew what he was doing, the Bulldog barked in his hands. For a moment, nothing happened. Then the ninja went slack, a curtain of red blood fell across his eyes, and he slumped backward onto the gravel path.

Lyle stepped forward, rubbing the blood away from what Gideon saw was only the slightest scratch on his neck, as the soldiers ran into the garden and approached the fallen assassins. "Mr. Smith," Lyle said. "You have saved my life."

A cavalry officer pulled the mask from the face of the first assassin Gideon had felled. He was swarthy, with narrowed eyes, and a tattoo crawled up his neck—what Gideon supposed was some Japanese symbol or script. Bent appeared at his shoulder, his notepad in his hand.

"Jap all right," said the soldier, pulling the mask back down.

Lyle laid a hand on Gideon's shoulder. "Mr. Smith, I am forever in your debt. I think a calming brandy is called for."

Gideon stared dumbly at the fallen bodies as Rowena rushed to his side. She embraced him, tangling her fingers in his hair. He felt suddenly sick.

"Ssh," she whispered. "I know. I know what it's like. You had to do it."

"Yes," he said, numb. "I had to do it."

In the dining room, their dinner things cleared away, Lyle poured each of them a generous measure. Gideon said, "Is this a regular occurrence? Attacks by assassins?"

"Thankfully, no," said the governor. He had been cleaned up, a bandage applied to the slight wound on his neck. "This is the first time the Japanese have been so bold." He paused, staring into the swirling, golden heart of his brandy. "I wonder what made them carry out such a direct attack, at the heart of British America. What has forced their hand? Why have they become so bold?"

"Anybody'd think they *wanted* an effing war," said Bent.

"The Californian Meiji will deny this attack, of course,

but nevertheless this is a most disturbing development. If the Japanese really do want war, Mr. Bent, we can ill afford it."

Gideon stood before the large map, drinking in the unfamiliar names. The distance those assassins must have had to cross, from Nyu Edo to New York, made his head spin. "But why would they want war? Isn't America big enough for everyone?"

Lyle laughed. "The *world* isn't big enough for everyone, Mr. Smith, though it might seem a vast and often uncharted place. The desire of the human race to own and control should never be underestimated."

"Bloody good job we were here," said Bent.

Gideon turned from the map as Rowena said, "Yes, wasn't it? I must say, Mr. Lyle, I'd have thought you'd have been . . . better protected."

Bent slapped the table. "She's right, Lyle. Your cavalry were about as much use as an effing butter fireguard! But for Gideon here they'd have cooked your goose." He paused. "Or your turkey, I suppose."

"I am indeed lucky." Lyle nodded. "And I shall forever be in your debt, Mr. Smith. As to my security, Mr. Bent, you can rest assured that under normal circumstances the men under my command are exemplary soldiers. But the world's changing, and we are facing threats we never anticipated. Black-clad assassins armed with swords and knives, as silent and invisible as the wind? We couldn't legislate for that, Mr. Bent. But, as they say, everything that does not kill us makes us stronger. We shall not be caught out in that way again. Of course, the Japanese will probably have more tricks up their sleeves. . . ." Lyle bit his lip. "I probably shouldn't say too much, but . . . well, I've had information that they've got a *weapon*, the Japs. Something that could destroy New York in a day." He sat back and shook his head. "Secret weapons. Brass dragons. Silent assassins. I swear to God, what a world we live in."

Gideon turned back to the map, his finger trailing down from New York to the vast emptiness beneath the thick line of the Mason-Dixon Wall. And somewhere down there was Maria, and the dragon, and Louis Cockayne.

As if reading his thoughts, Edward Lyle appeared at his elbow and pointed to a dot on the map, just below the Wall. "If I were a gambling man, I'd put money that your Mr. Cockayne is there."

Gideon leaned forward and read the name. "San Antonio."

Lyle grunted. "That's the name the Spaniards gave it. These days it's mostly known south of the Wall as Steamtown."

7

THE KING OF STEAMTOWN

Thaddeus Pinch liked to boast that he was more machine than man, which was only fitting for the self-styled King of Steamtown. Louis Cockayne had once asked him if that included his dick. That had been at a card game very much like the one he was embroiled in now, late at night in a spit-and-sawdust saloon bar in San Antonio, as Cockayne faced off against the grotesque figure of Pinch. The King of Steamtown's assembled cronies had collectively gasped; no one spoke to Thaddeus Pinch like that. No one, that was, except for Louis Cockayne. Charm and—yes, pun intended—a pair of brass balls went a long way with a man like Pinch, and he'd guffawed long and hard, steam hissing from the pistons and valves around his steel jaw.

That time, Cockayne had been playing for a stack of chips that bought him three nights in the company of the best whores in the best whorehouse in the whole of Steamtown.

Now, though, his charm seemed to have failed him. He hoped his fabled luck didn't do the same.

Because this time, Louis Cockayne was playing for his life.

Pinch's left arm, a thick brass cylinder snaking with thin pipes and hydraulic pistons, reached out for the glass of whisky on the worn green baize table between him and Cockayne. With his fleshy right hand he slapped the toggles on his metal forearm and his jointed fingers, mottled with verdigris, closed around the glass with a sigh of escaping steam. He raised the whisky to his mouth and sucked hard on the wooden straw, rivulets of golden liquid dribbling down the square, steel lower jaw, fixed with huge bolts through the festering, swollen flesh of his drawn cheeks.

The King of Steamtown liked to tell how he lost each limb, each body part, and how Steamtown's scientists—some of whom had come to San Antonio of their own free will, drawn by the freedom of the Texan warlord's burgeoning city-state, others who had been kidnapped and set to work for Thaddeus Pinch whether they liked it or not—had replaced and repaired them. Cockayne had heard the stories many, many times before. Pinch's jaw had been blown off by a gun-slinger who came to San Antonio to try to earn the bounty the governors back east had put on Pinch's head. The sun-bleached bones of the would-be assassin still swung in a rust-ing gibbet in the town square. Pinch's left arm had been bitten off by a coyote. His right leg had to be amputated below the knee after Pinch, loaded on whisky and peyote, had crashed one of Jim Bowie's Steamcrawlers into a cactus while racing around the desert one full-mooned night. If Pinch really had lost his dick, it would doubtless have been to the clap. The only women in Steamtown were the whores who were forced to work the city's many brothels, and ex-whores who had been bought out of their enforced service by San Antonio's menfolk who decided that their days of paying for sex were over, and they wanted to take a wife.

Not many of those men and their unshackled wives started families. Steamtown was no place to raise children. Besides, when Thaddeus Pinch decided he needed to boost the popu-lation of San Antonio, he simply sent his slavers out to get more people: men to work the coal mines and ranches, and women for the brothels.

It was a big old world, and there was no shortage of bodies. And no shortage of those who made their own way to Steam-town, drawn by the lure of the only truly free city in America, probably even the world.

Of course, Louis Cockayne wished he were just about

anywhere else on the globe rather than sitting in front of Thaddeus Pinch playing poker.

"It's time to put up or shut up, Cockayne," lisped Pinch through his steel maw. His new teeth were cruel, jagged spikes, at shiny odds with the tobacco-browned stumps of his top row. He took another dribbling sip of whisky through his wooden straw and with his good hand laid his cards down on the table.

Six of hearts. Seven of clubs. Eight of hearts. Nine of spades. Ten of diamonds.

"Straight," said Pinch.

Cockayne chewed on the cheap cigar Pinch had gifted him and finished off his own whisky quickly. Pinch's mob was behind the King of Steamtown, his trusted lieutenants and cronies; a more unlikeable bunch of rapists, thieves, and murderers you never hoped to meet down a dark alley. Closest to Pinch was Inkerman, a fat, pug-nosed, rat-eyed bastard with appetites that apparently ran the gamut from children to grandmas, and all points in between. Word was, a ride didn't actually have to be alive for Inkerman to saddle up. Word was, that was how he liked it best.

Cockayne didn't like Inkerman at all, never had. Now that the fat bastard was wearing Cockayne's best leather gun belt, complete with his pearl-handled revolvers, he liked the man even less.

"I'm waiting," said Pinch.

Cockayne laid down his cards. Two, four, five, eight, queen. Of spades.

"Flush," he said, breathing a silent prayer to lady luck.

Pinch banged his brass arm on the table, roaring a spittle-flecked laugh. His hangers-on quickly joined in. Cockayne allowed himself a crooked smile.

"You're one lucky bastard, Cockayne," said Pinch when he recovered. His eyes narrowed. "Fourteen straight wins. You're not holding out on me, are you, Louis? Not cheating?"

Cockayne stood slowly, his hands flat on the table, never taking his eyes off Pinch, even when a volley of clicks accompanied the swift drawing of pistols and rifles, all pointed in Cockayne's direction, from the King of Steamtown's unruly court.

"I may be a thief, I may be a killer, I may be a wanted man on three continents," said Cockayne levelly. "But I never in my life cheated at cards."

Pinch appraised him for a moment. "You're one cool motherfucker, Cockayne," he said. "You could do well in Steamtown. I've always got an opening for a man like you. A real good opening, right by my side."

Cockayne cast an eye at Inkerman, who grunted uncomfortably. Cockayne tipped him a wink as Pinch continued, "All you have to do is talk, Louis. Talk to me."

"I've told you all I can, Thaddeus."

Pinch sighed. "Take him back to the pen."

Inkerman and three of the thugs waved their guns at Cockayne, and he moved ahead of them to the swing doors that let out on to the dusty street, illuminated by oil lamps and ringing with the sounds of the coal mines that surrounded the center of San Antonio working into the night.

Pinch said, "Same time tomorrow. If you lose, I will kill you, you know."

Cockayne shrugged. "No you won't. Not while you think I know something."

Pinch turned away from him. "Don't be too sure, Louis. Just tell me everything you know about that goddamn dragon before it's too late."

The pen was a single-story stone building on the edge of town, nestled between two strip-mining sites where slaves toiled day and night to bring up the coal that powered Steamtown. It was one big cell, windowless, with iron bars dividing it from a thin office. Inkerman was the nominal sheriff of San Antonio, but since the former governor had driven Steamtown's secession from British America along with the other Texas townships back in 'fifty, law in the town had been a brutal, ad hoc affair. Justice was delivered swiftly and mostly without ceremony, at the end of a gun or a rope, and often at the whim of Pinch (who'd taken over the family business from his daddy), Inkerman, or one of the revolving cadre of deputies. As a result, the pen was rarely in use—imprisonment not often being a sentence passed down by Steamtown's law enforcers—and Louis Cockayne was currently its sole guest.

Inkerman chewed on a strip of beef jerky and regarded Cockayne with his little rat eyes, leaning his fat ass on the corner of the desk in the office. The door leading outside was tantalizingly open, the sounds of the Steamtown night drifting in on the warm breeze, but the cell gates were locked resolutely tight. As if to drive home the fact, Inkerman twirled the metal ring jangling with half a dozen keys around his pinky, then clipped it to his gun belt—from which Cockayne's revolvers hung.

"I have a very long shit-list these days, Inkerman, and you're right at the top of it," said Cockayne quietly, glaring through the bars.

The sheriff snorted. "Pinch'll get your dragon to fly with or without you, Cockayne. The best you can hope for is a quick death." He stroked his battered holsters. "Might even use your own guns on you."

Cockayne patted his pockets—not for weapons, since he'd been summarily stripped of anything he might use against Pinch or his men—but for his cigarillos. He located one and beckoned to Inkerman. "Light?"

Inkerman grunted, but Cockayne had heard full well Pinch telling the fat idiot that Cockayne might be a prisoner, but he was an old friend of Steamtown, and had to be treated with a bit of respect . . . as long as he was alive. Inkerman pulled out a box of matches and said, "You know the drill."

Cockayne raised an eyebrow then pushed his face, the

cheroot between his teeth, into the gap between the bars. He raised his hands backward, fingers splayed, so Inkerman could see he wasn't hiding anything. Inkerman struck a match and held it at arm's length while Cockayne puffed on the cigarillo, then backed off again.

"You're still scared of me," said Cockayne through a cloud of bluish smoke.

"I ain't a cretin." Inkerman shrugged.

Cockayne watched him through narrowed eyes for a moment then turned away. Inkerman said, "I'm going back to the saloon. There are three boys outside who would love to blow your nuts off. Best just go to sleep, Cockayne, and think of how you're going to make your dragon fly."

The dragon flew, all right. From London to the Gulf of Mexico it flew, in one seamless journey. It was faster than a dirigible, but the trip was still a long one. Cockayne had forced himself to stay awake because he didn't know whether his control over the dragon's strange pilot would hold if he fell asleep, and he didn't fancy waking up to find himself falling down to the dark Atlantic far below.

How the damned thing flew, well, that was quite a different matter. Cockayne had watched from the banks of the Nile as the Rhodopis Pyramid had collapsed and the magnificent brass dragon, its wings glowing in the Egyptian sun, rose from the ruins. He'd pursued it in the *Yellow Rose* to London, where mad old John Reed planned to blow Queen Victoria and all in Buckingham Palace to kingdom come. He'd watched Gideon Smith, that spunky hick from the sticks, try to clean Reed's clock for him . . . and nearly get his ass handed to him on a plate until Lucian Trigger took matters into his own hands.

And he'd spotted an opportunity—he was Louis Cockayne, after all! That was what he did!—to take control of the brass dragon they called Apep and ride off into the sunset, sitting on what he knew was a winged, fire-breathing gold mine.

He just didn't have a clue how the goddamn thing stayed up in the air. Within the head of the dragon was a cockpit, fashioned by the hands of ancient Egyptian craftsmen two millennia ago. The cockpit contained one seat in age-faded cowhide before an instrument panel with five recesses. As far as Cockayne understood it, the thing had remained dormant until John Reed and his undead guardians obtained the five lost artifacts that fit those holes: a roughly hewn figure from ancient Egypt called a *shabti*; a ruby ring that had sat in the coffers of the British Royal Family for who knew how long; a small box inlaid with jewels and gems that had been buried by smugglers on the North Yorkshire coast; a golden scarab, latterly in the vaults of Castle Dracula in Transylvania; and an amulet that Reed had discovered (and which had set him on the path toward his damnation) around the neck of a mummy being studied in Boston. These were the things that somehow powered the dragon.

All that was needed to fly it was Maria.

Cockayne had to admit that even he had felt a pang of doubt right at the moment he'd stolen Apep from under the noses of the others. Maria was integral to the flying of the thing—an automaton, but damn near a real woman. Beautiful, too. She was a clockwork girl with the living brain of a murdered prostitute, but that wasn't all that was in her head, by all accounts. The key to the whole mess that had left Reed and Trigger dead was the Atlantic Artifact, a doohickey from God knew where that was somehow connected to Maria's brain by the scientist Hermann Einstein and was responsible for bringing both Maria and Apep to life.

He'd felt a pang of doubt, because that kid Gideon Smith was obviously in love with Maria, clockwork girl or not. Cockayne had seen stranger things—but not by much. He could hear the wail from Smith as he'd absconded with Maria, once he'd figured out that the only way to communicate with her was with that golden apple John Reed had stolen from the lost valley of Shangri-La up in the Himalayas. Once she was plugged into Apep, Maria somehow *was* the brass dragon—all she needed was her long-dead pharaoh Amasis to command her, and Cockayne was happy to step into that role. Thing was, it also meant that Maria spoke only ancient Egyptian, which Cockayne was a bit rusty on. Good thing the golden apple allowed the holder to speak and understand any language. Nice, useful bit of equipment, that.

Pity he'd lost it.

Cockayne had driven Maria across the Atlantic, coming in low over the coast of New Spain and up into the Texan lands below the Wall. He'd had Maria do a couple of victory rolls over San Antonio, then ordered her east, into the lower peaks of the heavily forested Appalachian Mountains. It was one thing to show off the merchandise to men like Thaddeus Pinch, but it was quite another to go flying straight into Steamtown with the goods. There was careful negotiation to be carried out first.

Cockayne had been worried about what would happen when Apep landed—Maria's clockwork body packed a mean punch. But it turned out that as long as she was plugged into the dragon, her real personality was subsumed beneath the overriding Apep identity, so he'd just left her sitting in the head of the dragon while he went to make arrangements.

They'd landed the dragon in darkness, in one of the wilder regions of the mountains. There was a one-horse town ten miles away, and he'd hidden Apep beneath some foliage and trekked there for supplies. There was no Pony Express office there, and the mail service wouldn't go within a hundred miles of San Antonio anyway. But he'd managed to buy the services of a young gun to take a message to Steamtown, offering Apep for sale to Thaddeus Pinch for the cool sum of five hundred thousand pounds.

It took two weeks for the rider to return with an answer. Cockayne had no idea how Pinch would respond—after all, he still owed the King of Steamtown a pile of money, and the one time he'd been given the opportunity to pay off his debts (by taking charge of a slaving expedition to Africa) Gideon god-damn Smith had scuppered his plan and freed his cargo in Al-exandria. Thaddeus had every right to be pissed at Cockayne, but Cockayne also knew that the boss of Steamtown's interest would be piqued. Pinch had seen his little aerial display, of course, and the response he sent back with the rider was brief and to the point: *Bring me your dragon.*

So Cockayne, glad he could stop living rough like some backwoodsman, had saddled up Apep and headed west.

Which was when everything went south.

If Cockayne had no knowledge of how Apep flew, he had even less idea as to why the bastard thing fell out of the sky like that. One minute they were flying into the setting sun, Maria's hands playing over the control panel, pulling the invis-ible strings that maneuvered the brass dragon through the sky; the next she was sitting bolt upright, her pretty little fea-tures contorted in pain.

"What the hell's going on?" demanded Cockayne, then re-membered he'd stowed the golden apple in his leather satchel. He retrieved it as Maria began to babble in ancient Egyptian.

"Charging complete . . . initiating fusion . . . preparing sche-matic download . . ."

Cockayne swore and rubbed the apple with his sleeve, as though it were some kind of lamp with a genie in it. "I thought this damn thing was supposed to make us speak the same language."

". . . commencing fusion . . ." said Maria. "Oh!"

Apep bucked wildly, throwing Cockayne off his feet. He landed hard in the brass cabin—not made for passenger comfort—and the apple rolled away from him. Maria contin-ued to speak in a low monotone, but he could no longer under-stand the tongue. Not that it mattered; he had other things on his mind. The brass dragon spiraled upward and then began to dive, and the golden desert rushing toward them was the last thing Cockayne saw.

Until he woke up in Steamtown. They'd crashed fifteen miles northeast of San Antonio, by all accounts. Cockayne was beaten up, but alive. He was in a bed in a whorehouse, with Pinch standing over him, when he woke.

"I got your dragon," said Pinch. "How about you show me how it flies, then I'll show you my money?"

The dragon had been brought in on the back of a trailer pulled by three of Jim Bowie's Steamcrawlers, which Pinch had taken possession of following Bowie's death. Cockayne didn't mention that he and John Reed had had a hand in that. Louis Cockayne had done business with Steamtown many times, but that didn't mean he was one of Pinch's cronies. He followed the money, and in the matter of Bowie, the British Crown had been paying very well indeed.

Pinch had soon enough hauled Cockayne out of his sickbed and taken him to the dragon. Louis had tapped brass plates here, twisted on joints there, rubbed his chin and hummed and *ahh*ed. But it hadn't taken Pinch long to realize that Louis was playing for time.

"What the hell's up, Cockayne?" Pinch had demanded. "You busted the goddamn thing? This is exactly as we found it."

Cockayne touched his bandaged head. "Think I took a bad knock, Thaddeus. I'm having trouble remembering right."

What Cockayne was really having trouble with, though, was the fact that while Apep seemed in good order, it was lacking one or two things. Namely, all the artifacts in the instrument panel and the Golden Apple of Shangri-La.

Oh, and Maria.

That was two weeks ago, and Thaddeus Pinch was losing patience, fast. He knew Cockayne was holding out on him, but couldn't for the life of him see why. He'd even shown Cockayne four tea chests stuffed with British pound notes. All he had to do was show Pinch how the dragon flew.

Cockayne sighed and lay down on the bunk in the cell, listening to the ever more raucous sounds of Steamtown. Without Maria, Cockayne couldn't make Apep fly. And if Apep didn't fly, Cockayne's days were numbered. Pinch might like him, but even the King of Steamtown had his limits, no matter how lucky at cards Louis Cockayne was.

He pulled his hat down over his eyes, but sleep wouldn't come.

"Oh, Maria," he murmured. "Where the hell are you?"

8

OF MONSTERS AND MEN

Gideon smiled absently as the maid poured him tea from a silver pot, trying to tune out Bent's retelling to no one in particular of the previous evening's events in the garden.

"It was effing amazing," said Bent, spraying the white tablecloth with pieces of half-chewed egg. "Blam! Down went one. Blam! Another. But the third had a blade at Lyle's throat . . . I thought he was done for. I mean, Gideon's not a bad shot and all that, but he'd not picked a gun up until month ago. Still, I should have had faith in the Hero of the Empire. . . ."

Bent shook his head and reached for another bread roll. With his other hand he dug into one of the seemingly endless, bottomless pockets in his shabby raincoat and withdrew his notebook.

Rowena chewed her toast thoughtfully and kept her eyes on Gideon across the table from her. She said quietly, "Are you all right?"

He glanced up, suddenly aware of her speaking to him. "What? Sorry . . . ? Yes, yes, I'm fine."

"Gideon, like I told you last night, I know what it's like, the first time you kill a man in cold blood. It's not as it is in the penny dreadfuls. It's not *clean*."

"No," he said slowly, the image of that last ninja refusing to fade from his mind's eye. He remembered the narrow eyes that slowly widened as Gideon's intent became apparent, the color draining from the man's skin just before he fired, the mess that exploded over Edward Lyle's shoulder as Gideon's bullet slammed home in the ninja's forehead. "No, not *clean*."

He gave Rowena a reassuring smile as Bent thrust his note-pad under Gideon's nose. "What do you make of this, then?"

The journalist had sketched a series of interconnecting lines on the page.

龙

"This was the tattoo on that Japanese feller's neck, the first one you shot," said Bent thoughtfully. "Ring any bells for you?"

Gideon shook his head. Bent said, "Looks familiar to me, but I can't quite place it." He flipped the notebook shut and pointed at Gideon's barely touched plate of ham and eggs. "You not eating that? Don't mind if I help myself, do you? We're supposed to be meeting Lyle in ten minutes."

Governor Lyle's office had expansive views of the Albert Gardens, and in the sunshine of the morning they looked magnificent against the skyline of Manhattan, rising from a sea of smog just beyond the tree line. Lyle had a fresh bandage on his neck, but otherwise looked none the worse for his tribulations the previous evening. He had with him a thin, rangy man in faded denim trousers, a red shirt, and a leather waistcoat. The man carried a wide-brimmed hat in his hands, and with his piercing blue eyes set into his weather-beaten face he kept casting glances at Rowena, but he stayed silent. Gideon looked sidelong at Rowena to see if she was returning the interest. But Lyle was already stepping around his wide desk, shaking Gideon's hand warmly.

"Mr. Smith. I hope you slept well after last night's excitement."

Gideon shrugged. In truth, he hadn't slept well at all, despite the comfortable bed in the west wing of the Governor's Residence. Killing those three men must have affected him more than he had realized. Perhaps he wasn't cut out to be the Hero of the Empire after all.

Bent picked up a small, framed photograph from the desk:
a smiling, pretty woman with a small, serious-faced boy on
her knee.

"This your wife and kid, Lyle? She's a looker, and the kid
takes after her, thank effing Christ." Bent replaced the frame.
"Did the rumpus last night not wake 'em?"

Gideon saw the slightest look pass between Lyle and the
stranger before the governor said, "Don't you be worrying
yourself about my family, Mr. Bent. I'd have thought you'd
be wanting to get on with your mission as soon as possible."
Lyle picked up a sheaf of papers from his desk. "Here's what
we know, and what we told Whitehall two weeks ago." Gideon
took the papers from him. Lyle said, "In essence, we have a
garrison located on the Mason-Dixon Wall perhaps fifty miles
northeast of San Antonio. A month ago they filed a report
saying that there had been unusual activity in the air above
Steamtown. More than one of the men reported seeing what
they described as some kind of winged serpent, or dragon, in
the skies."

"A month ago?" Gideon frowned. "Why weren't we told
immediately?"

Lyle smiled apologetically. "For one thing, we didn't even
know anyone had a missing dragon they were looking for. No
one saw fit to tell us to be on the lookout for one. For another . . . Mr. Smith, you must understand . . . these soldiers,
they're away from home for long periods, and it's a lonely life
manning the garrisons. San Antonio's just a short ride away,
with its saloons and cathouses—excuse me, Miss Fanshawe—
but of course it's off-limits. They get a little . . . stir-crazy. Besides, we thought if there was something unusual in the air, it
was more than likely some outlandish machine or experiment
of Thaddeus Pinch's."

"Thaddeus Pinch?"

"It's all in my report, Mr. Smith. But Thaddeus Pinch is a
lunatic. His father was the former British Governor of San
Antonio, until he decided he wanted to run things himself

instead of reporting back to London. He was crazy when he died, and he passed the governorship on to his son, like it was some kind of hereditary title. If anything, the son is even crazier than the father. Now Pinch likes folks to call him the King of Steamtown. He has all manner of madcap schemes in his head. And some of the best scientists in America are either in his pay or under lock and key, unfortunately. Pinch has a lot of history with Louis Cockayne. If Cockayne sells your dragon to anyone, Mr. Smith, it's more than likely going to be Thaddeus Pinch."

"Sell the dragon . . . ?" said Gideon. It hadn't occurred to him to wonder why, exactly, Cockayne had stolen Apep. If it was for base profit, then Maria must have been part of the deal. Gideon suddenly felt sick to his stomach. "We need to get down there immediately. Rowena, how long will it take us in the *Skylady III*?"

But Lyle held up his hands. "Whoa, Mr. Smith. I'm very much afraid it isn't going to be anywhere like as easy as that. For one thing, no dirigibles fly over Steamtown. Pinch has an arsenal of steam-cannons there that the Fleet Air Arm would kill for. He's brought all kinds of cargo 'stats down—from here, from New Spain, from the Meiji. Passenger 'stats, too; survivors ended up in the slave markets. Now, nobody risks flying within a hundred miles of San Antonio." Lyle smiled ingratiatingly at Rowena. "Secondly—and I hope Miss Fanshawe forgives me here—but Steamtown is no sort of place for a fine-looking lady."

"I can look after myself," said Rowena, but Gideon shot her a raised eyebrow. She didn't sound convinced.

"Rowena?"

She sighed. "I've heard plenty of tales of Steamtown, Gideon. Women there . . . they're either whores or wives. Which basically amounts to the same thing in San Antonio, except one you get paid for and one you don't."

The stranger rolled up the brim of his hat and said in a thick accent, "Hope you don't mind me saying, Miss, but a handsome woman like you . . . I shouldn't like to think what might happen in Steamtown."

Gideon felt his cheeks burning. "I can look after her," he said.

The stranger suppressed a smile. "You might be able to shoot three Japs in a garden, Mr. Smith, but if you get blown out of the sky over Texas, you sure you're going to hold Pinch's army off Miss Fanshawe with that itty-bitty peashooter I heard you're packing?"

"I am *here*," said Rowena, "when you've both quite finished talking about me as though I'm a virgin locked in a tower."

The man held up his hands in apology, and Lyle said, "Forgive me, I should have introduced you all earlier. Mr. Smith, Miss Fanshawe, Mr. Bent, this is Jebediah Hart."

He bowed. "My friends call me Jeb."

"Nice to meet you, Jeb," said Bent cheerfully.

"Why exactly is *Mr. Hart* here?" asked Gideon, less so.

Lyle grinned. "Jeb knows Texas like the back of his hand. Hell, Jeb knows everywhere like the back of his hand. If anyone can get you into Steamtown, it's him."

Jeb sat on the corner of Lyle's desk. "There's a military transport dirigible making a scheduled supply drop at the Texas garrison, today. Pinch will be expecting it; he knows the timetable of every official 'stat service around his territory. He won't touch it, of course; bringing down a military 'stat is more trouble than even a crazy old bastard like Thaddeus Pinch can handle."

"If this Pinch is such a pain in the effing arse, why don't you just go and kick his backside for him?" said Bent.

Lyle shrugged. "Because Pinch and the other Texan warlords have officially seceded from British America. If we clear them out—as much as we'd love to—that's an act of war. We can't be sure that they're not cozying up with the Spaniards or even the Japs. And unless London is going to finance a war, Mr. Bent, then I'm certainly not in a position to go poking a hornet's nest."

"So you're going to help us just walk into this Steamtown, Mr. Hart?" said Gideon.

Jeb smirked. "Walking in won't be a problem, Mr. Smith. It's in the getting out you might need some help."

"I've already prepared some letters of authority so you can get whatever help you need from the garrison . . . short of an actual escort into San Antonio, of course," said Lyle. "Miss Fanshawe, you're more than welcome to stay here at the Governor's Residence as long as you wish."

Rowena nodded tightly. Gideon could tell she was still smarting over being told to stay out of Steamtown, even though she seemed to accept that going there was a bad idea. "Thank you, Governor. I would like to be here in case Gideon and Mr. Bent need any assistance."

"I won't stop you, Rowena," said Gideon quietly. "You can do exactly what you wish."

She sighed. "The governor's right, Gideon. I should perhaps stay on alert here in New York, ready to attend should I be required."

He thought again of Rowena's embrace in the gardens last night, the gladness he had felt at her relief and concern. She was a good friend, Rowena Fanshawe, a vital ally. He glanced at her as she looked out the wide window. He felt somewhat disappointed that she wasn't coming with them, though he understood the dangers she would be facing if she did. He would miss her bravery and her strong right arm, he told himself. That was it. He would miss her bravery.

While Lyle sorted the paperwork into order, Jeb nodded at Gideon. "Let's see this gun of yours, Mr. Smith. I like to know what kind of firepower I'm taking into Texas."

Gideon withdrew the Webley Bulldog and handed it to him. Jeb grinned, showing his missing teeth, and pulled from his holster his own gun, holding it up to overshadow the Bulldog.

"Colt Buntline Special," said Jeb, winking at Rowena in

a manner that Gideon thought was most inappropriate. "Twelve-inch barrel."

Bent sighed and began to unbutton his trousers. He reached inside and pulled out his own weapon, stock first, from his trouser leg.

"Winchester Model 1886," he said, slapping it on the desk with a dull clang, startling Lyle into looking up. Rowena snickered to herself. She had seen Bent sliding the gun down his shapeless trousers outside the office. "Now, if this effing contest is well and truly won, I wanted to pick our new friend Jeb's brain about something he said earlier. As I understand it, this San Antonio's in the arse-end of nowhere. I take it that when you said we'd be *walking in*, it was a figure of speech?"

Jeb put his hat on his head. "That it was, Mr. Bent. We'll be riding in."

Bent's jaw dropped. "Not on effing horses?"

"It's the only way to travel, out west."

Bent sighed heavily. "Yee-effing-hah," he said, without very much conviction at all.

New York to the Texas garrison was only half the distance of London to Manhattan, and it was nightfall when the gray military 'stat touched down on the dusty airfield set out beside a stone-built fort lit by oil lamps. Even in the dark it was hot, the warm breeze carrying the unfamiliar sounds of insects and distant howls.

"Why is everywhere we go so effing hot?" complained Bent as they disembarked. The military 'stat had been cramped and uncomfortable with no real passenger cabin. They'd sat amid boxes of supplies and bags of mail for the frontier ranches, Bent feeling every swing and dip of the dirigible. "Can't our next adventure be at the effing North Pole or something?"

Gideon could feel the sweat running down his back. Jeb had snoozed practically the whole journey, and alit from the 'stat looking as fresh as he had when he'd climbed aboard. Gideon felt crumpled and aching and grumpy.

"What's with him?" asked Jeb. "All the *effing* this, *effing* that?"

"Mr. Bent met with an unfortunate accident," said Gideon, stretching in the night as a team of blue-uniformed soldiers emerged from the fort to unload the 'stat. "He was hit on the head by a falling pyramid block. Now he can't say . . . a certain word."

"Effing effrontery, is what it is," said Bent.

Jeb grinned. "Let's see if eight hours on horseback can't improve your vocabulary, Mr. Bent."

The early dawn brought more heat, and after helping himself to coffee in the cool of the mess hall, ignoring the curious stares of the fifty or so cavalry officers enjoying breakfast, Gideon stepped outside to find Bent hugging the narrowing shadows in the lee of the fort. Gideon had dressed in a white shirt and tight fawn trousers shoved into black boots. Bent, it seemed, was wearing the same suit he had been in since they'd left London—the waistcoat displaying the vast bulge of his belly, the jacket and trousers stained and shapeless. It was a new suit, Gideon knew, purchased just a couple of weeks before. "It's not the suit that's creased, it's my body." Bent had laughed.

The bright daylight brought a surprise for Gideon: seemingly unending desert in every direction, bisected at either side of the garrison by the famous Mason-Dixon Wall. Strange rock formations sat darkly on the horizon, and loose balls of dried vegetation, propelled by the merest breath of hot wind, rolled between the almost comical cactus figures.

"Bit disappointing, innit?" said Bent, nodding at the wall.

Gideon had to admit it was. He'd understood the Mason-Dixon Wall was a vast engineering triumph, a signal of Queen Victoria's intent to conquer the whole of the Americas. The wall here was barely six feet high, an occasionally tumble-down structure of loose stone and faded brickwork that snaked off into the vanishing point of the horizon. He doubted it could keep a group of particularly single-minded rabbits out, let alone the rampaging hordes of Steamtown or the gray-clad soldiers of the Confederacy.

Jeb Hart joined them, swilling coffee around a tin mug. Bent said, "Just talking about your wall, Hart. Not as grand as we'd been led to believe."

Jeb shrugged and spat a stream of coffee into the dust. "It's not so much a defense, it's a . . . whatchamacallit."

"It's a symbol, sir, is what it is," said a deep voice. It belonged to a veteran soldier, evidently some kind of officer at the garrison, who stepped out of the fort, towering over them all. His wide handlebar mustache twitched as his stone-gray eyes set deep in his lined, tanned face regarded each of them in turn. "Bricks and mortar don't keep the peace in Texas. It's guns and blood, sir. Guns and blood."

Jeb drained his coffee then said, "This is Captain Humbert. He's in charge of the garrison. Captain, Mr. Aloysius Bent and Gideon Smith, the Hero of the Empire."

The tiniest of smiles played about Humbert's thin line of a mouth. "Ah, yes. The Hero of the Empire."

Gideon shifted uncomfortably, suddenly feeling a little silly. Bent seemed to sense his mood, and he puffed his chest out. "That he is, Captain. Things he's seen'd make your mustache effing curl."

"I doubt that," said Humbert, keeping his gaze on Gideon.

"Vampires!" said Bent. "Mummies, mark you! And not just any mummies. Mummies with teeth like nails. Effing dinosaurs!"

"Mr. Bent," murmured Gideon. "I'm sure Captain Humbert—"

"Oh, don't worry," said Humbert. "I'm impressed, Smith. Fighting monsters is all well and good. But down in San Antonio you're dealing with *men*. The sorts of men who make your monsters look like toothless jackalopes."

There was silence for a moment, punctuated by the sounds of the cavalrymen inside finishing up their breakfast. Captain Humbert pulled from within his tunic a folded sheet of paper. "Requisition order from your Governor Lyle back in New York," he said. "We can't directly aid you in your mission, gentlemen, but we can provide horses and weapons, so long as they can't be traced to this garrison." He handed the paper to Jeb. "Mr. Hart, go to the stables and get yourself three ponies." Humbert paused, appraising Bent. "Actually, better make that two ponies and a heavy. I think Tucker, our old draft horse, might be up for one last journey."

Bent scowled. "Is he having a go at me?"

Jeb laughed. "Come on, we need to make tracks if we're going to hit Steamtown before dark."

Captain Humbert saluted them as Jeb led them to the stables. Bent cast a glance over his shoulder and nudged Gideon hard in the ribs. "And what the eff is a jackalope, anyway?"

9

El Chupacabras

The boundary between New Spain and Texas ebbed and flowed, depending on who could be bothered to draw the borders. The loose conglomeration of warlords who controlled the land south of the Mason-Dixon Wall never bothered too much about where their control began and ended. The biggest Texan settlement was San Antonio, and their quest for coal had driven expansion north and east, with sporadic raids on points due south every couple of months. They didn't range too far west for fear of attracting too much interest from the hitherto insular Californian Meiji.

New Spain, however, had maintained a town on what it liked to think of as its northern border for almost three centuries. Uvalde was more than eight hundred miles from the New Spanish capital, Ciudad Cortes; that might as well have been the *five thousand* miles that separated the dusty border town from Madrid itself, for all the notice the New Spanish viceroy took of Uvalde.

Inez Batiste Palomo tethered her chestnut mare to the brittle branch of a twisted acacia. The tree clung to the shadowed side of the dilapidated stone building that squatted, roofless, a hundred yards from the abandoned mine. This part of the countryside was littered with such mines: half-dug exploration shafts that the Texans had sunk while looking for coal. This looked like it had once been a working mine; perhaps the Texans had discovered a seam that looked promising, but petered out after they had sunk the shaft. Perhaps the New Spanish had driven them away from the edge of this canyon, two hours' ride from Uvalde. If so, that would have been back before Don Sergio de la Garcia had been summoned back to Madrid. Back when Uvalde was a safe place to live.

Inez retied the bun at the back of her jet-black hair and brushed the trail dust from her long skirts. The roof of the stone building had long since collapsed, and she pushed gingerly past the broken timbers of the door, treading carefully and watching for coyotes or worse that might be sheltering within the cool walls. The building had perhaps been a home for the miners or a way station to process the coal; whatever the reason for abandoning the mine, this building had been forgotten along with it.

Inez had made good progress and arrived early, with just enough time to reapply her blood-red lipstick using the small compact mirror she carried in her cloth bag. She glanced at her pocket watch; she hoped Chantico would arrive soon. It was another two hours' ride back to Uvalde, and she wanted to be cleaned up and waiting in Casa Batiste when her father returned at nightfall from his visit to Nuevo Laredo, none the wiser about her sojourn so far from Uvalde.

The old mine was in quite a pleasant location, thought Inez as she carefully picked her way through the empty rooms. It was on high ground, where the air was fresh, and a creek ran by a hundred yards away. There was doubtless fishing to be had, and the ground looked arable enough. In the distance the flat, sculpted mesas heralded the drier, more arid territories to the east. The men of San Antonio would not have appreciated the land in the same way that Inez did. The creek would merely have been a useful source of water had the mine proven viable, not the thing of beauty that she saw. The verdant plains grasses that hinted at a workable soil would have been an annoyance to clear, perhaps to make way for rail tracks to transport the coal back to Steamtown. Inez listened to the warm breeze sighing through the grasses, and it made her happy. Thankfully, the Texans had seen fit to abandon the mine, and now its lost buildings were hers. And Chantico's. She tapped a painted fingernail against her chin. Where *was* he?

There was a scuffling sound from the outside of the collapsed building. At last. Inez stood and smoothed her skirts again, stealing one last glance in her compact. She was ready for him. She was ready for her forbidden love.

Inez frowned. Was that the sound of voices? Had Chantico not come alone? That was most unlike him. Suddenly, she felt afraid. What if it was not Chantico at all?

Three figures stepped into the doorway, and Inez's heart skipped a beat. Texans. Men, rough, leering.

"I *told* you it was a woman." The first, a small, rangy man with straw-blond hair, grinned.

"Damned pretty one, too," said the second, taller one.

The third, older than the other two, his belly hanging over his gun belt, spat into the dust. "We gonna get us a bonus from Mr. Pinch for bringing this chickadee back."

Inez finally found her voice, though she could not keep it from trembling. "You are making a mistake. I am the daughter of Don Juan Batiste, the Governor of Uvalde, under the protection of the Viceroy of New Spain in Ciudad Cortes," she said in flawless English.

"She's even prettier when she's frightened," said the second man.

"What say we break her in before we take her back to Steamtown?" said the first excitedly. "Hank? Huh, Hank? What say?"

The third simply spat again then began to unfasten his gun belt.

Inez stepped backward until she came up against the solid stone wall. She thought she was going to vomit. This wasn't supposed to happen. She wanted her father, wanted to be in the relative safety of Casa Batiste. She suddenly missed her mother, dead for seven years, so very, very much. Where in God's name was Chantico?

"Stop right there!"

The three Texans turned around to look at the figure

framed in the broken doorway. He wore tight black breeches tucked into leather riding boots and a loose black shirt open at the chest. His face was cowled by a large black bandana with holes for the eyes, and he held out a rapier at arm's length, his body poised.

Inez felt her head swim. It wasn't possible. No one had reported a sighting for months. Two years, even. And most people said he was merely a myth anyway.

Yet here he was.

"My name is El Chupacabras," said the masked man in heavily accented English. "This girl is under my protection. Leave this place now, or prepare to die."

❖

Oh, Chantico, what in the name of God are you doing? Inez had passed through fear to wonder to hope to the unwavering certainty that she was now about to be brutally molested and shipped off to San Antonio's brothels, never to be seen again. She had thought, for a moment, that the figure in the shadows was truly El Chupacabras, reputed to be the greatest swordsman in all of New Spain, the champion of the underdog and the put-upon, the protector of the border people from both the marauding Texan hordes and the greed of the Spanish nobility. But no. As soon as he had opened his mouth, she had seen the ragged eyeholes on his badly stitched cowl, the faded black cotton of his ill-fitting shirt, the rapier that was no more than three lengths of sharpened fence wire, bound together and stuck into an unconvincing hilt. As soon as he had opened his mouth and his struggling English emerged, she had known. Besides . . . El Chupacabras was named for the mythical goatsucker of the night. The creature didn't exist. And the man hadn't been heard from in more than two years, not even a whisper, as if he had never existed, either.

Oh, Chantico. You are going to get us both killed . . . if we are lucky.

The three Texans had turned to face him, their guns

drawn. The fat one slowly raised his hands in surrender, and Inez saw Chantico's eyes widen behind his crude mask before he gripped his makeshift sword with greater resolve.

"El Chupacabras?" said the fat one. "Oh, well, that changes things. Boys, put your guns down."

The blond one, whom Inez thought of as *no es ninguna lumbrera*—certainly not the brightest star in the sky—looked dumbfounded, his hands still gripping his gaping trouser fly. "You serious?"

"Nah," said the fat one, swiftly training his revolver on Chantico. "Take your hood off, boy."

Chantico did as he was told, pulling the mask—little more than a cotton bag—from his head, his black hair springing up, his eyes narrowed. His sword wavered until he put it down.

"Injun," said the fat one, a little surprised. He cocked the chamber of his gun and glanced at the others. "What d'you reckon? Take him back for the mines?"

"I don't care," said the blond. "I had my fill of Injuns today. I'm riding this señorita before we go back to Steamtown. Blow his fucking head off for all it matters to me."

He turned back to Inez with a lascivious grin and began to pull down his dusty denims.

The fat one shrugged and leveled his gun at Chantico. "Can't say I can be bothered dragging him all the way back. Get ready to meet your ancestors in the happy hunting ground, boy."

As the blond advanced on Inez, there was the loud report of a single gunshot that echoed around the tumbledown stone building and resounded into the sky, sending a flock of mockingbirds rising up from the grasses by the creek. She closed her eyes and began to pray.

A second later she opened them again. The blond had his back to her, fumbling for his guns. The fat one was lying dead on the stone floor, blood pooling around his head. Standing on the sill of the shutterless window was another figure, in a worn, haphazardly stitched leather jacket lined with matted furs, his boots thick with dust. His rifle spat again and the taller of the Texans jerked backward, blood spraying from his face. Inez and Chantico's eyes locked. Was this a savior, or an even greater danger?

"You would do well to dress appropriately, to face death," said the newcomer to the blond. "In other words, pull up your trousers." The sun briefly illuminated a face equally handsome and grizzled, thought Inez. The blond, clutching his button-fly with one hand, trained his shaking revolver on the man with the other.

The man put one boot on a chunk of fallen masonry and regarded the blond coolly. "You really think so? It is in you to go up against me?"

The blond—little more than a boy, Inez saw now—blanched and lowered his gun. "It's really you? Are you going to kill me?"

"Yes, it's really me," said the man, chewing his cigar. "And I shall kill you, yes, unless you do precisely as I say. You are going to mount your steed and make haste to Steamtown. You are going to tell Thaddeus Pinch that this territory is under my protection now, and his presence here will be looked upon badly. You understand that?"

The boy nodded vigorously. The man raised one eyebrow. "Well?"

"Yes, sir!" said the boy, pushing roughly past Chantico and out of the stone building, where he paused only momentarily to puzzle over the strange cargo on the back of the newcomer's horse before untethering his dead compadres' mounts and hightailing it east toward San Antonio with the two riderless horses galloping behind his own.

"Thank you," said Inez. Chantico had moved to her side, stepping gingerly over the dead bodies of the two Texans. Inez didn't know if she was furious with him or if she wanted to take him in her arms and never let him go. Both, she thought. But she still wasn't entirely sure the danger had passed. "Who are you?"

He looked at each of them in turn. "Who are *you*?"

"Inez Batiste Palomo, of Uvalde," she said.

"The governor's daughter?"

Inez blinked. "Why, yes. Yes I am."

"Chantico," said Chantico, his eyes on the floor.

"You're Yaqui?" asked the man. "From the settlement on the north side of the canyon?"

Chantico nodded. The man said, "You've been there awhile now, more than a year. Your people don't usually stay in one place so long."

"The Spanish kept moving us on," said Chantico, glancing at Inez. "The hunting's good where we are now, and the fishing."

"And I'll warrant that the place of power in the big cavern has proved both useful and fruitful," said the man, his eyes twinkling.

Now it was Chantico's turn to be surprised. "How did you . . . ?"

He glanced again at Inez, who scowled back. Place of power? Chantico had never mentioned that to her. She said to the man, "Now it is your turn. Who are you?"

The man nodded to Chantico. "The Yaqui know me."

Chantico looked at Inez and licked his dry lips. "My people call him Chichijal, which is like . . . the spirit. The ghost."

Inez looked at the dead bodies of the Texans. "His bullets looked pretty solid to me." She turned back to him. "What is your name in English? Or Spanish?"

"I have no name." He gazed thoughtfully at the pair of them. "But suppose you tell me what *you* are doing here? The daughter of a Spanish governor and a Yaqui boy." He raised an eyebrow. "And why is the Yaqui boy dressed like *that*?"

Inez folded her arms. "Yes, Chantico, can you explain this?"

Chantico sighed and sat heavily on a broken piece of roof timber. "You are always going on, El Chupacabras *this*, El Chupacabras *that*. The savior of New Spain's downtrodden. I made the costume . . . I thought . . ."

Inez laughed, the tension flooding from her. "You thought to fool me that El Chupacabras, the great cowled hero of the dusty plains, was not missing or dead after all, but had been *you*, Chantico of the Yaqui, all along?"

Chantico scowled. Inez went on, "With your mask made from . . . what is this? An old flour bag? Dyed with . . . ?"

"The juice of juniper berries," muttered Chantico.

"Juniper berries! And a rapier made of old fence wire! Oh, Chantico."

"You're lovers," said the man without a name.

Inez glared at him. He held up his hands and smiled. "I have traveled the length and breadth of this land and the only time I heard a boy and a girl speak to each other thus, with such honeyed barbs, was when they were sweethearts."

"It is none of your damned business, sir!" said Inez.

Chantico laid a hand on her arm. "Inez," he said softly. "You cannot speak to him like that. He is Chichijal. The Texans, they call him the Nameless."

"Very original," said Inez sourly. She brushed down her skirts. "Well, *Señor Sin Nombre*, I suppose I should thank you for rescuing us. If in fact you have. You are not planning to take us to San Antonio yourself, for profit?"

The Nameless shook his head. "No, ma'am, I'm not. The Texans are no friends of mine. They abuse the land as much as the British, or the Japanese." He looked pointedly at her. "Or the Spanish."

Inez drew herself to her full height, her nostrils flaring. "What do you mean, sir?"

The Nameless shrugged. "This land . . . something's not right here. It's not meant to be carved up and fought over by folks from far away. This isn't how it is meant to be."

"I am Yaqui," said Chantico. "I was born here."

"So was I!" said Inez.

"True," said the Nameless thoughtfully. "You were both born here. That's right." He stared ahead, as though studying something that neither Inez nor Chantico could see. He blinked and said, "Both born here . . . but still. How do a Yaqui boy and the daughter of the Governor of Uvalde find each other?"

Inez folded her arms and stared out the window. Chantico smiled. "My people, we move around a lot. We used to go into what the Spanish call Uvalde on market days, selling leather and cactus juice. Every market day, I feel like someone is watching me. Eventually I see Inez, looking from a window in her big house. She cannot take her eyes off me."

Inez snorted and aimed the toe of her riding boot at Chantico. "You lie. You were like a puppy dog, mooning about outside my window."

"So why did you throw me the note? Asking to meet me after dark?"

"I pitied you!" roared Inez, her cheeks flushing. She paused. "Besides, I like puppy dogs."

The Nameless was smirking at them. "You might be just what I've been looking for, these long years."

Inez turned to him. "Looking? For what?"

The Nameless seemed lost in thought for a moment then said, "Looking for America. Follow me. I have something to show you."

They stood in a row outside the abandoned mine shaft, the old winding gear partially collapsed, the square hole shored up with rotting timbers. The Nameless took a clay pipe from one of the crazily stitched pockets of his jacket and struck a match, puffing until it began to smoke, then tossed the match into the shaft.

Even Inez knew this was foolhardy, and she pulled Chantico back sharply. She glared at the Nameless. "Don't you know there are gases in there that can explode?"

He gazed into the black pit. "Usually, there are. There must have been no coal in there, or maybe just a little. That's why this place is deserted."

Inez put her fists on her hips. "So . . . ?"

"So . . ." said the Nameless eventually. "So, there is some kind of gas. I can see it."

Inez screwed up her eyes and peered at the pit. "I see nothing."

"It's like . . . sunshine," said the Nameless, a little uncertainly. "I have seen it before, on occasion, though I have no idea what it is."

"I still see nothing. Do you, Chantico?"

Chantico shrugged. "No."

The Nameless puffed thoughtfully on his small white pipe. "I see things that most men can't," he said shortly. "And there's a gas like sunshine coming out of that pit. I think it's important. I just don't know why, or how. Not yet."

"So you brought us out here to show us something we cannot see?" said Inez.

"No," said the Nameless. He turned and led them to the far side of the building, where his horse, a gray stallion, was tethered alongside Inez's mare. "I brought you out here to show you this."

On the back of the stallion was a woman, still, facedown. Something stuck out of her back—something that looked like a giant key.

"Is she dead?" whispered Chantico.

"I don't think she was ever alive," said the Nameless.

The woman wore long skirts and a small jacket that was torn, as was her white shirt. Blond hair cascaded over her face, and Inez moved it gently to one side. She was quite beautiful, with pale skin. She appeared to be sleeping. Inez laid a hand on her cheek. It was cool, but not cold. There was the faintest *thrum* of movement deep within the woman, but not like a heartbeat, not like breathing. Inez touched the key. "She has been stabbed with this thing?"

"No," said the Nameless, hauling her down from the horse and laying her on her side in the shadows. "I put that there."

"You killed her?" said Chantico.

"No. I found her, in the desert." He took from his saddle-bag a cloth sack. "She had these with her."

Chantico peeked inside the bag. There were all kinds of strange things: a little fat man made of stone, a box that shone with precious stones, a ruby amulet. He asked, "Is that apple made of *gold*?"

"What do you mean, you *found* her?" asked Inez. "You don't just find women like this. And why did you stick a key in her back?"

"Did you see the dragon?" asked the Nameless.

"I did," said Chantico quietly.

"I heard of it," said Inez. "My father said it was a new kind of airship, maybe something the Japanese were testing."

"It was made of brass," said the Nameless. "She was with it. I took her away before the Texans came for the dragon." He bent down and lifted up the back of her shirt. There was no blood where the key stuck into her back, as Inez expected. The Nameless tugged it out. There was a small, metal-ringed aperture there. "The key fits her. I wound her up, but nothing happened. But the key fits." He looked up at Inez. "I think she's made from clockwork. I don't think she's a real woman."

Inez crouched beside the Nameless. There was something about her . . . almost as if she was actually too flawless to be real. Her skin felt smooth, like the softest, most expensive kid leather. Putting a hand to the woman's breast, Inez could feel the faint hum of machinery, but no heart pumping.

"But I think she is, somehow, alive," said the Nameless. "I don't know how or why, but I feel it."

"Like you can see the sun gas?" said Chantico.

He nodded. Inez said, "So what are you going to do with her?"

"Leave her here," said the Nameless. "This is a safe place now. You are going to look after her for me."

Inez stood. "But I have to be back at Uvalde before night-fall! And Chantico at the encampment! We can't stay here and babysit your . . . your clockwork woman!"

The Nameless stood also. "I'll get rid of those dead Texans, bury 'em away from here. I'll fix up the roof, bring you some water. Then I've got errands to run."

"But I need to get home!" said Inez.

The Nameless looked into the middle distance again. "I know. But something's coming."

Chantico frowned at the blue sky. "A storm?"

"Maybe," said the Nameless. "Maybe."

While the Nameless was inside, Chantico and Inez embraced by their horses. She pushed him away as she felt the lump in his groin press against her.

"Please, Inez," he moaned. "I will be quick."

"No," she said firmly. "And I don't like you being *quick*, Chantico. When will you learn? Besides, I'm quite not in the mood anymore. What do you make of him? Is he crazy?"

"He is the spirit, Inez. The one with no name. You can't say he's crazy."

Inez mounted her horse. "I will come back tomorrow. I will make some excuse. See you here?"

Chantico nodded as he untethered her mare.

Inez turned the horse toward Uvalde and looked down at Chantico. "I do love you, you know. And I think you were very sweet, with that El Chupacabras business." The costume and Chantico's makeshift sword were in Inez's saddlebag. The fabric smelled of Chantico, and she wanted it with her in bed that night.

"I love you, too, darling Inez."

She looked thoughtfully at the house. "Everyone is someone, Chantico. He must have a name, a history. He must come from somewhere."

As Inez spurred her horse into movement, Chantico blew her a kiss. "I think he does come from somewhere," he said, almost to himself. "I think he comes from America."

10

Aubrey's Bar & Grill

 After Gideon, Bent, and Hart had departed for the military airfield in Newark, Rowena mooched around the Albert Gardens, following its meandering paths, resting in its meadows. She sat in contemplative silence in Sheep Meadow, watching the rising smog of the city that, by lunchtime every day, had obliterated the view of the higher skyscrapers from the street level. The elevated steam stilt-trains thundered between the towers, ferrying commuters to their jobs and goods from the airfields and docks to the big stores downtown and the communities of the five boroughs that came under Edward Lyle's governorship.

It was peaceful in the Albert Gardens, though the clamor of Manhattan was never too distant, only a shout on the breeze or an exhalation of steam away. The trees of the Gardens fought valiantly against the encroaching smog to keep the air clean, but New York was a lost cause once the mighty engine of American business was cranked up.

As the day wore on, Rowena picked at the packed lunch the servants had prepared for her in the kitchens of the governor's mansion. She was already bored. Rowena understood the need for Gideon and Bent to travel south of the Wall by covert means, understood they could not go flying in on the *Skylady III*. And she was no fool; she had heard enough of Steamtown to steer well clear of it all her adult life. Hell, most male 'stat pilots gave Steamtown a wide berth. Some places, you just didn't go.

Still, she felt uncommonly like she was missing out on something. She chided herself; she had been engaged for a

job, one that had paid handsomely. She had fulfilled the assigned task, brought Gideon and Bent to New York. Should
she wish, she could fly away now—she looked over to where
the top of the *Skylady III*'s balloon could be seen, bobbing
above the trees that bordered the Governor's Residence. There
was more money on offer, to take Gideon and Bent back to
London should they complete their mission, but she was under no obligation to do so. There were any number of passenger 'stats or military dirigibles that could transfer them back
to England.

It was good business to wait; if she was going to return to
London anyway then she might as well stay put for a few days
and earn money for piloting the return trip as well. That was
what she told herself, at any rate. But she wasn't only Rowena
Fanshawe, proprietor and sole employee of Fanshawe Aeronautical Endeavors, established 1883, Highgate Aerodrome,
London. She was also Rowena Fanshawe, holder of the Conspicuous Gallantry Medal, the adventuress who had played
her part in saving Queen Victoria from the deluded machina-
tions of Dr. John Reed.

And, goddammit, she cared about Gideon Smith, cared
enough to worry that he was off on some foolish mission in the
most hostile territory in America. A few weeks ago he'd been a
wet-behind-the-ears fisherman. Now he was expected to be
the Hero of the Empire.

She bit into her apple in frustration, chewing thoughtfully
as New Yorkers escaped from the rising temperature of the
smog-bound city to the shadowy oasis of the Albert Gardens.
The space had been modeled on Hyde Park, with its own version of the Serpentine glittering at its center. Rowena watched
nannies pushing baby carriages, sneaking looks at her from
beneath their bonnets; she saw office clerks in brown derbies
and the waxed mustaches the Manhattanites so loved, casting
surreptitious glances at her; a crowd of Bowery boys in lace-
less boots and patched trousers climbed over each other like

puppies, whistling at her and running away, laughing. Two gentlemen doffed their tall stovepipe hats at her, beating out tattoos on the path with their gold-tipped canes. New York had burst out of the expectations laid upon it as a mere colony of Britain long ago; it was as if the rebel spirit had not been crushed by the redcoats but merely molded into the haughty self-confidence that earned New Yorkers their unfathomable reputation among London's chattering classes. It seemed to Rowena that peering out beneath every bonnet, stovepipe, and derby was a look that said, *All right, you won. We're British. But don't expect us to be like any British you've ever seen before.* . . .

Of course, Rowena was hardly like any British woman the New Yorkers had ever seen or heard of, either. Her flying trousers were scandalously close-fitting, her hair cropped defiantly short. She had opened two buttons on her crisp white cotton shirt against the heat; young Manhattan women might show more ankle than their counterparts in Mayfair, but they were still a conservative lot. Conservative, that was, outside the negro clubs in Harlem, where former slaves freed long ago danced to the beat of drum music throughout the night; or the pubs in the Bronx, where the Irish sipped porter and played fiddles; or the trattorias on Mulberry Street, where Roman passions were played out after dark. It was the white, British American women who were laced up tight as any Londoner Rowena had ever seen. As another brace of nannies scowled at her she leaned forward and recklessly unfastened another button on her shirt, smiling at them.

Rowena cast another glance at her distant 'stat. She hated earthbound mores and despised the judgment others held her in, the shackles and bounds society felt should be placed upon her. Only in the sky, above the smog, above the clouds, did Rowena feel really, truly free. She was tempted, there and then, to flee. But she held herself back. She had made a promise that she would wait awhile, in case Gideon needed her. But that didn't mean she had to hang around the stuffy Governor's Residence. If she couldn't fly, she could do the next best thing.

She could go to Aubrey's Bar & Grill.

❧

Rowena walked into Aubrey's just as darkness was falling; she had agreed to an early dinner with Lyle then told him she was going to see the sights. Which she was; there were few sights more worth seeing than the ones at Aubrey's after dark.

It was, to give it its full name, the Union Hall of the New York Chapter of the Esteemed Brethren of International Airshipmen, located in a squat building among the sheds and hangars of the North Beach Aerodrome. The members' bar was in the hands of one Aubrey Flanagan, a Cork man who, in '45, had built his own airship and carried families devastated by the potato blight over to new lives in America. After three years of ferrying his countrymen to New York, Aubrey had settled in Manhattan and acquired the license to run the bar in the Union Hall, and after that everyone just called it Aubrey's Bar & Grill. Aubrey was, in his own words, "built like a brick shithouse, with hair like a bog-brush," and he could generally be found behind his bar, serving up porter and rum and supervising a constant flow of sausages from the kitchens. Every 'stat pilot worth the name found their way to Aubrey's sooner or later, and Rowena was no exception. Pushing open the double doors to the warmth, shrill conversation, and frantic accordion music within, she felt like she was coming home.

Life in the air was not subject to the same rules as that on the ground, but female 'stat pilots were still enough of a novelty for all eyes to turn toward Rowena as she walked across the crowded hall. Those who she knew nodded, waved, or raised an eyebrow in greeting. Those she didn't laid the weight of their appreciative gaze upon her, until a neighbor or friend nudged and whispered, "That's Rowena Fanshawe."

She changed course on her way to the bar and stepped into the cool, shadowy chapel. 'Stat pilots weren't known for being religious, as such; more spiritual. She'd known airshipmen to hang around their necks crosses and Stars of David and every-thing in between, every totem or symbol they picked up on their journeys to the far corners of the Earth. They relied on their wits and their expertise, 'stat pilots, but there was noth-ing wrong with hedging your bets. The chapel, lit by church candles on tall metal stands, was dominated by a long cork-board on one wall, onto which were pinned grainy photographs of lost Brethren or, where there were no photographs avail-able, sketches or even just scrawled names. A yellowed roll of paper above the corkboard was inscribed in flowing script, MY SOUL IS IN THE SKY. How many pilots would recognize it, as Ro-wena did, from Shakespeare's *A Midsummer Night's Dream* she neither knew nor cared. It was written across the roll call of the lost in every chapel in every Union Hall across the Em-pire, and on every corkboard was the photograph, or sketch, or handwritten name that always drew her.

Charles Collier. She found him, near the middle of the board, a ragged-edged photograph of a man with sandy hair, his mustache waxed proud, the line of his mouth slightly up-turned at the corners, echoing the crease lines at the corners of his eyes that betrayed good humor. He wore a pair of brass goggles on his head, the shearling collar of his leather jacket pulled up. Rowena stroked the photograph, then took up a flat votive candle from the wicker basket beneath the corkboard and borrowed a flame from the nearest lit candle. She placed it in the rack below the corkboard and stayed silent, head bowed, in mute contemplation for a moment.

Rowena raised her head and looked at the photograph of Charles Collier once more. It was time for a drink.

Aubrey leaned across the bar and threw his huge arms around Rowena, scattering empty glasses and full ashtrays.

"Rowena Fanshawe!" he exclaimed. "By the bulging sac of Jean-Pierre Blanchard, what sends you flying our way?"

Rowena extricated herself from his bearlike hug. "Bit of business, Aubrey. How are you?"

"As good as the Lord and as fit as the devil." He laughed then paused. "Or is it the other way around? Anyhow, let me get you a drink. Porter?"

Rowena shook her head. "Rum. As usual."

He roared again. "I'll get you on some fine Irish porter one of these days, Rowena Fanshawe. Put hairs on your chest!"

"That's what I'm afraid of," she said, accepting the generous measure of dark, spiced rum that Aubrey poured for her. She reached into her satchel for her wallet but he waved his meaty fist at her.

"Your money's no good here tonight, Rowena. Tonight you drink on Aubrey Flanagan." He picked up a glass of his own and banged on the bar for silence. "Shut it, you balloon-rats! We have a proper heroine in the house! Raise your glasses to Rowena Fanshawe."

There was a chorus of cheers that Rowena waved away. She drained the glass and Aubrey poured another. He said, "We all read about what happened, that Battle of London. You did mighty fine there, Rowena. Mighty fine indeed. We're awful proud of you."

"How's Fanny?" asked Rowena.

"Fit as a fiddle! She's in the back, cooking up her sausages. They're a fine body of men, these Brethren, but greedy! You never saw the like. They'll eat 'til sausages come out of their arses. They're like dogs. Don't know when to stop."

Rowena spent an easy hour catching up with Brethren gossip, until Aubrey had to take up his shillelagh from the shelf behind him and go and sort out a fight in the far corner that was threatening to turn into a brawl. She rose unsteadily from her stool—damn Aubrey's generous measures—and weaved through the throng toward the Union Hall proper, where one or two airshipmen browsed the contracts that had been pinned to the walls. This was where most 'stat pilots picked up their jobs when they were at loose ends, and Rowena scrutinized the nearest. She was itching to get back in the air, even if it was just a short cargo hop to Boston.

Behind the desk was the hirer, a thin man in a suit that had
seen better days. She saw him hail the two men who were in
the Union Hall ahead of her, and an urgent, low conversation
took place. The two men shook their heads and walked away.
Intrigued, Rowena wandered over.

"Any jobs going?"

The hirer looked her up and down. "You Brethren?"

The rum had emboldened her. She jabbed her thumb at
her chest. "I'm Rowena Fanshawe."

The hirer clicked his tongue. "I do have a job, but it's not for
you."

She placed her hands on the table and leaned forward.
"Any job is for me."

"It's for a big 'stat. What you flying?"

"Tripler, out of the Gefa-Flug factory in Aachen. She's called
the *Skylady III*. Used to fly under the name the *Yellow Rose*."

The hirer sat back and whistled. "Louis Cockayne's 'stat?
And how did you get your hands on that? I'd say you must have
won it off him, but Louis Cockayne doesn't lose at cards."

Rowena smiled. "No, but sometimes he bites off more than
he can chew."

The hirer rubbed his chin. "We-e-ell . . . you could handle
the cargo, certainly. But it's the destination, Miss Fanshawe.
It's south of the Wall."

Rowena raised an eyebrow, but didn't react further. "The
Mason-Dixon Wall?"

"That's the only Wall we talk about 'round here. Specifically . . . San Antonio."

"Steamtown?" said Rowena. "Who's doing business with
Steamtown? And what's the cargo?"

"The contractor is classified," said the hirer. "And the
cargo is classified as well. All you got to know is that you load
up here at dawn, get down to Steamtown, and stay the hell in
your 'stat while they unload. There'll be a cargo to bring back,
as well. The contract states that your hold has to be locked

throughout and you don't even think about looking in there."
He rubbed his chin again. "I don't know . . . a woman like you
in Steamtown . . ."

"I can look after myself," said Rowena. She was getting
tired of having to point that out. "Besides . . ."

He shrugged. "Besides, as a chartered 'stat pilot and paid-
up member of the Esteemed Brethren of International Airshipmen, even those barbarians would know better than to try
any funny business. You stay put on your bridge and keep a
gun to hand, and you won't come to any harm."

"So the contract's mine?"

The hirer tapped his chin then held out two manila enve-
lopes. "This here's your manifest. It won't tell you anything
about the cargo, but it will tell you what you do when you get
to Steamtown." He held the other out but pulled it back as
Rowena reached for it. "This here's classified documents, to be
handed over at Steamtown air ground. They're secured with
the Brethren seal, and if that's broken . . . well, I can't guaran-
tee anything when you get to Steamtown."

"All very mysterious," muttered Rowena, taking both en-
velopes. "But legal?"

The hirer shrugged. "It came through formal channels,
but with the rules I just told you."

"It could be anything," said Rowena.

"You know the Brethren code," said the hirer. "*Periculo tuo*
and all that."

Periculo tuo. At your own risk. The Brethren would fix you
up with work, lend you money if you needed it, get you out of
somewhere fast if you were in trouble. But you were responsible for the jobs you took on. If a cargo turned out to be unsavory or worse . . . then you knew the risks.

The hirer raised an eyebrow. "You still want it?"

Whatever was in there, she had to take the job if she wanted
to go down to Steamtown. It went against the grain to take on
a cargo without knowing what it was, but . . . she nodded.

"You got it. Be here with your 'stat at dawn. And fair winds, Miss Fanshawe. Fair winds."

Rowena told Governor Lyle that she was going away for a few days, to "see friends." Which, she hoped, would prove true. He looked doubtful, though.

"You're not thinking of heading down to Texas, Miss Fanshawe? Remember what we said, this has to be a covert operation. . . ."

"I don't go anywhere I'm not paid to," said Rowena sweetly.

She took to her bed early and was awake and alert in the small hours, accepting breakfast from the kitchen and finally feeling her earthbound anxieties fall away as she nosed the *Skylady III* into the gradually lightening sky and toward North Beach Aerodrome.

Never in the trading history of Fanshawe Aeronautical Endeavors had Rowena taken a cargo on board without knowing its provenance, not since she started the business with the *Skylady I*, a Thompson Flashman blimp that had lifting power for only two passengers and a long hundredweight of cargo. But as the instructions stated, she sat on the bridge of the 'stat staring grimly ahead at the pale approach of dawn while representatives of the mysterious contract holder loaded up the cargo bay from the ground. Even more galling, she had to allow them access to the gondola—without even seeing them!—so they could chain up the interior door down to the cargo bay. Eventually, a groundsman from the Aerodrome climbed up the rope ladder to tell her they were done.

"What's in there?" she asked.

He shrugged. "Don't know. They loaded up from covered wagons."

"And who exactly are they?"

He hesitated. "You don't want to know."

As her slot arrived and she was waved into the air, the groundsmen casting off the cables, Rowena quickly brought the *Skylady III* up to a cruising height. New York rumbled into life and the ever-present smog began to creep up from street-level, the heat and the churning of ten thousand steam engines creating a rising tide of insidious, impenetrable gray that would engulf the tops of the skyscrapers by nightfall. She charted a course south and west, and then she only needed to glance over the instructions one more time (ten miles out of San Antonio she was to signal a preset sequence with the heliograph, to allow her access to Steamtown and stop the Texans blowing her out of the sky with their steam-cannons) then sit tight while her bay was unloaded and filled up with the return cargo.

She had the best of intentions, she really did. But once she was airborne, with few distractions in the largely 'stat-free skies on her course, she couldn't stop herself staring at the manila envelope she was meant to hand over to the Steamtown groundsmen. She went to make a pot of coffee and toast some bread in the galley, but as she sat back in the leather chair on the bridge, her eyes kept gazing toward the envelope.

She picked it up and inspected the wax seal. It was imprinted with the gothic "B" symbol of the Brethren. She plucked the union pin from the lapel of her flying jacket, which was embossed with the same ornate feature. A bit of candle wax, pressed with the pin . . . they'd never know the difference between that and the original seal in Steamtown, where they didn't get much Brethren traffic, surely.

"To hell with it," she muttered, and slid her thumb under the envelope's flap, breaking the Brethren seal. She slid out a single sheet of paper, which bore no company masthead or other identifying marks. It detailed the return cargo only: an eye-watering five hundred tons of coal. Rowena had never lifted anything approaching that and hoped it didn't leave her grounded in San Antonio or crashed in the desert. At the bottom of the manifest were the words "payment as agreed" and a scrawled signature she couldn't decipher.

So someone in Manhattan was doing business with Steamtown. What had Governor Lyle said? *You wouldn't believe how*

much coal a city like New York runs on. . . . Much of it, we buy in.
Governor Lyle would be very interested to know that the coal
his city ran on was being bought from Steamtown, she
thought. And it wasn't money that someone was paying
with . . . but just what had been loaded up in her hold that
Steamtown would take as payment in kind for coal?

For another half an hour, Rowena sat on the bridge, watching the vast empty prairies unfold before her. Then she made
a decision, and went to get a hefty crowbar from the stores.
The men had chained up the handles of the door down to the
cargo bay, but after a moment's hesitation it was the work of
two minutes to pry the chain and padlock off with a sharp
snap.

She hauled open the door and peered down into the cargo
bay.

"Oh," she said eventually. "Oh, shit."

11

DAMN STEAMTOWN TO A HUNDRED HELLS

"Mr. Bent, I am presuming you haven't done much in the way of riding before," called Jeb Hart, his words echoing around the rust-colored walls of the steep-sided canyon he was leading them through.

"I am renowned . . . ," panted Bent from the rear, ". . . as something . . . of a . . . chevalier in the brothels of White-chapel . . . you cheeky effer. . . ."

"He means horses, not whores," said Gideon from the middle of the short column.

"Well, I wouldn't be expected to be a horseman, chap of my girth and sensibilities," shouted Bent. "I'm an effing journalist, not some kind of country gent or . . . or cattle wrangler!"

They had been riding for half a day, the pace slow due to Bent's steed, an old workhorse from the barracks, plodding at its own pace and requiring frequent stops to drink water and to piss—"not unlike Mr. Bent himself," Jeb Hart had observed. Gideon was on nodding terms with horses, having ridden a bit in his youth, though not over any great distance. He was enjoying the feel of freedom that riding afforded him, the sensation that he could dig his heels into the pony and bolt off into the wide-open spaces, and not see another man for days. Even in the wilds of the Yorkshire Moors there was only so far you could go before you chanced upon a village or trading post. Here the world seemed infinite in both breadth and possibilities.

Their route had taken them along the Mason-Dixon Wall for the first three hours, then Hart had led them on a meandering path north, ducking into valleys and around hills until the Wall was lost from sight, and finally he brought them in an arc back westward. "They're a suspicious bunch in Steamtown," he'd said. "We need to make them think we've been out on the plains for a matter of weeks, not just flown in on a military dirigible."

At the next stop, where a cool spring ran down the wall of the canyon just as it opened out into a wide, yellow prairie dotted with the shapes of dark cacti, Hart rubbed dust into the trouser legs of Gideon and Bent, and tore at their sleeves with a length of thorny bush.

"That's my best coat," Bent protested.

"All part of the deception," said Jeb. The horses were allowed to drink deep from the small pool that gathered where the spring flowed down the orange rocks. Jeb filled the canteens and squinted into the west.

"I figure we've time for some food. Might just get us to Steamtown before dark."

"Food, thank God, thought you were never going to effing mention food," said Bent, walking up and down with a rolling, simian gait. "Christ, my poor old effing arse is like a pound of tripe that's been set to with a carpet beater. I don't think I'll ever shit right again."

Gideon, too, was feeling saddle-sore from the journey. He was keen to get to their destination, but wary, too. "What's the plan when we get to San Antonio?"

Hart looked up from where he was fanning the campfire embers with his hat. "I was hoping you was going to tell me, Mr. Smith. I'm merely your guide."

Gideon looked to the sun as it proceeded toward the line of mountains out west. "What will this Thaddeus Pinch's reaction to us walking into his town be?"

Hart piled some dry twigs onto the leaping flames amid the brushwood. "Well, it's true to say that Steamtown don't get many tourists, as such. But people do go to visit. Men, of course, with what you might call appetites."

Gideon frowned and Bent sighed. "He means them as fancy a roll in the hay with the hookers. And the whorehouses are that special, are they, Hart? That men would travel thousands of miles to visit them?"

Hart shrugged. "It's not so much the women, Mr. Bent, as the rules. There are none. Anything goes in Steamtown, and frequently does. There are no boundaries, no one telling you you've gone too far." He blew softly at the heart of the fire. "I guess some men likes that freedom."

"Then we'll be two . . . two gentlemen from London, perhaps unsavory types, touring the Americas and eager to see this Steamtown we've heard so much about," said Gideon. "And you'll be the guide whose services we have secured."

"Sounds reasonable to me," said Hart. "They know my face in Steamtown, know that's the sort of thing I might be apt to do."

Bent nudged him. " 'Course, what they don't know is that you work for the Governor of New York," he said with a wink.

Hart didn't smile. "No, Mr. Bent, and I'd rather they didn't, no more than you'd want them to know you was agents of the British Crown. That wouldn't be very good at all, not for any of us."

While Hart warmed up some beans, Gideon sat on a rock and watched Bent flicking through his notebook. When he came to the sketch he'd made of the tattoo, Bent said, "Here, you been around Nyu Edo and all that. You read that Japanese stuff?"

"Enough to get me by." Hart nodded, taking the notebook from Bent. He stared at it and frowned just long enough for Gideon to catch his expression, then said, "Mr. Bent, I don't think this is actually . . . um, where did you say you saw it?"

"On the neck of that dead ninja who attacked Lyle," said Bent.

Hart shook his head. "No. Like I said, I just about get by. No idea what that is at all."

Gideon caught the swift glance Bent shot at him. "Maybe you'd like a longer look?"

Hart shook his head. "No, thank you, Mr. Bent. Not one I

recognize. Now I think our beans are ready; we should eat up
if we want to get to Steamtown before dark."

They made good time after their meal, or so it seemed to
Gideon. Even Bent managed to pick up the pace, though his
incessant complaining about the tenderness of his rump continued unabated and with increasingly imaginative language.

Hart slowed to allow Gideon to come alongside as they
passed by a ridge of rock topped with tufts of desert grass. He
shielded a match from the wind to light a cigar and appraised
Gideon from beneath the shadow of his hat.

"So you're the best the Empire has, then?"

Gideon shifted uncomfortably in his saddle. "I wouldn't say
that."

Hart spat in the dry dust. "So if this job's so important,
why send you if you're not the best?"

Gideon fixed his eyes on the horizon. "As Governor Lyle
said, this is a necessarily secret endeavor."

Hart nodded. "But the British government doesn't have
more experienced operatives at its disposal than a fisherman
and a scribbler?"

Gideon glanced at him. Mr. Hart certainly seemed to know
more than he let on. He said, "If you know so much about me,
you'll know that this is also something of a personal mission."

"You should never mix business and pleasure, Mr. Smith,"
said Hart. He peered forward. "You see that?"

Gideon followed his outstretched hand to where a column
of black smoke bisected the blue sky beyond the ridge. "Steamtown?" he said.

"Not yet," said Hart. "I'll take a look."

As he spurred his horse forward into a canter, Bent eventually caught up with Gideon. He said, "He's just trying to needle you. Ignore him."

"He's right though, isn't he?" said Gideon. "Why has Mr.
Walsingham sent the two of us to rescue Maria and bring back
Apep?"

Bent sighed. "Look, you know my feelings on the whole shooting match. Walsingham and his crew, they're not to be trusted. But sometimes what they want and what you want can rub up, fit together for a while. Let's get through this little soiree in one piece and maybe we can start asking a few questions, eh?"

Gideon looked ahead to where Hart had stopped at the edge of the ridge. "Come on," he said. "Let's see what this is all about."

Oswald P. Ackroyd had just about had enough. It was a tough enough life, overseeing a ranch with fifteen hundred head of cattle in the middle of nowhere, a hundred miles from the nearest collection of wooden houses that you might call a town. He had to work his fingers to the bone from dawn to past dark every single day—not even a rest on the Lord's day, because there wasn't a church he could get to and back on a Sunday. He had only his sister's feckless son Albert to help out, because despite his best efforts he'd only been able to fill his sweet wife Caroline with daughters. Not that he could have loved those four girls more, because he couldn't. But being the father of girls had its own troubles, especially with a young man in the house who was getting to that age when he was randy as a dog day and night. Also, the girls now wanted pretty things, dresses and combs and mirrors, so when he did eventually get to drive some beef over to Nixontown or Redcreek Gorge or, once a year, to the big markets at Randolph City, then he had to take them with him or come back laden with trinkets and white cloth . . . either way, several guineas lighter than he should have been.

But all that he could cope with, because Oswald P. Ackroyd was a loving, generous, hardworking man who just wanted the best for his family, and if that meant taking the pioneer shilling and coming out here to one of the few patches of arable land so close to the Mason-Dixon Wall, then so be it. So long as he could take Caroline back to New York once a year or so to see her folks, and keep young Albert's trousers tightly buckled, then everyone was relatively happy. Everyone got by.

What really pissed him off were these Steamtown bastards who thought they could waltz on to his ranch and start calling the shots.

There were four of them, and the ringleader was sitting on the porch—in Oswald's favorite rocking chair, chewing tobacco. He spat a brown stream onto the stoop and didn't apologize. Oswald gripped the barrel of his shotgun tighter with his sweating palm.

"Now, then, pappy," drawled the Steamtown punk, his hat pushed back over his black hair. "Suppose you just put that peashooter down before someone gets hurt."

"Suppose you just get the hell off my land," said Oswald.

The man tutted. "Nasty mouth you got there, pappy. And you with four such pretty daughters as well."

Oswald glanced over his shoulder at Caroline and the girls, huddled in the kitchen behind him. "You don't even look at my girls, mister." God*damn* Albert for being away getting supplies at Nixontown today. The one day he might have come in useful. Goddamn him.

The man sat forward. His three boys were lounging around the porch, two with Winchester repeaters, the other making a show of polishing the barrels of a pair of Colts with his ragged shirtsleeve. "Look here, pappy. All we want is two . . . make that three hundred head of beef. We gotta eat in Steamtown, same as regular folks. Think of it as *insurance*."

"Insurance against what?"

The man took out his own pistol from its holster and waved it in the general direction of the kitchen. "Insurance against you waking up one morning with your throat slit and your wife and daughters turning tricks in Madame Choo-Choo's down in Steamtown. Three hundred head of beef. Got to be worth that for peace of mind, eh, pappy?"

Oswald lifted the shotgun and clicked off the safety. "I'll

give you a piece of my mind, boy. Get the hell off my land. And stop calling me pappy."

The man spat again, unfazed. "Sorry to hear that, pappy. 'Cause now we're gonna take all your beef, and your daughters, too. Boys."

◈

"Cattle ranch," said Hart, shielding his eyes against the sun.

"It's on fire!" said Gideon. "Someone might be hurt. We need to get down there."

"Whoa, Smith," said Hart. "Not our problem. We need to get to Steamtown."

Bent put a hand out and grasped Gideon's shoulder. "He's right, Gideon. We should stay focused on what we're here to do. Representing the Crown and all that, eh?"

A gunshot reported around the canyon. Gideon shrugged Bent off. "There are people in trouble, Aloysius. They need help." He dug his heels into his horse's flanks, and it whinnied and headed down the trail that wound from the ridge down to the verdant valley where the main building of the ranch spewed flames and black smoke into the sky.

Hart sighed. "Is he always like this?"

Bent nodded.

"I guess that's what makes him a hero, then," said Hart. "Come on, Mr. Bent, we'd better go and keep Mr. Smith out of trouble."

◈

Oswald had managed to shoot one of the men, which had only made the others angrier. He shouted for Caroline to take the girls up to the bedroom and lock them in.

"Bad move, asshole," spat the ringleader, who took one of the oil lamps hanging from the porch and smashed it against the wooden wall of the house. Too late, Oswald realized he had consigned his family to a horrible death.

"Can't we ride the girls before we roast 'em?" whined one of the other men as he filled his pockets with the belongings of his dead compadre.

"Shut it," hissed the boss. He struck a match on his gun belt and held it cupped in his hand for a moment. "Say adios to the old homestead, pappy." He touched the flame to the oil-damp wall and it caught with a roar, grabbing hold of the timbers and spreading down to the porch and up to the second story.

"We're gonna take all your goddamn cattle now," said the man. "First we're gonna kill you, though. And the worst thing is? You're gonna die not knowing whether we got your wife and girls out of that house and rode them into the dust or whether we sat back and watched 'em burn. How about that, pappy?"

Oswald felt the strength sap from him. He turned to force his way into the house, already filling with acrid, black smoke. He heard the distinct sound of a gun cocking behind him.

"No you don't, pappy."

"Get the hell off my land," said Oswald weakly, and kicked open the door. Behind him a gun barked. It took him the blink of an eye to realize that it was more distant than he'd thought it would be. And that he was still standing.

"Fuck." That was from one of the punks.

He turned to see the ringleader crumpled in a heap on the porch, the other two turning to face three men on horseback who were pounding along the dirt drive. The newcomers' guns barked again and one of the other men fell. Oswald tossed his rifle to one side and shouldered his way to the kitchen, the smoke clawing at his eyes and throat. He closed his eyes and felt his way to the stairs, almost bumping into Caroline as she inched down.

"The girls?" he said, his eyes streaming.

"Here," she said. "Oswald, what in the name of—?"

"Out," he croaked, leading them back through the kitchen, just as the timbers in the ceiling cracked and a beam fell across the path, the four girls screaming in unison. Oswald was suddenly disoriented in the black smoke, didn't know if he was making for the door or back into the heart of his burning, ruined home. He put out a hand and brought it back sharply as he made contact with burning wood. He gripped on to Caroline with his other hand and managed to say, "Hold on to your mother, girls."

If they were going to die, at least they would all die together.

"Hello? Hello?"

The voice came from ahead of him, and he fumbled toward it. Whether it belonged to the Steamtown bastards or his mysterious saviors, he didn't care. He reached out a hand and it was taken in a firm grip, which began to haul him swiftly through the smoke until his streaming eyes were flooded with sunlight, not smoke, and he fell, coughing, to the smoldering timbers of the porch, Caroline and the girls staggering out around him.

"Better get you away from here," said the voice again. British? Oswald felt himself lifted by strong hands and pulled forward, away from the smoke and heat, until he could gasp for fresh air and turn to see the conflagration that was reducing the home he had built with his bare hands to ash and embers.

Caroline embraced him and he hugged his four girls in turn before turning to the three men who had saved them. One was American; he introduced himself as Jeb Hart, and the others as two gentlemen from London, Mr. Gideon Smith and Mr. Aloysius Bent. Even their near-death experience did not stop the girls giggling as the strapping young Gideon Smith kissed each of their hands in turn.

"Who were they?" asked Smith.

"Steamtown," said Oswald. "After my cattle. I should have handed them over; I might still have a home."

"What will you do?" asked Smith.

Oswald shrugged. "I still have the beef. Did you get them all? There were four. I shot one."

"We got two, certainly," said the American, Hart. "I didn't see the other go; maybe we did get three."

"Thank you," said Oswald, shaking each of their hands. "Thank you."

Mr. Hart said, "There's a garrison maybe three-quarters of a day's ride north from here; if you go and tell them that Mr. Jeb Hart and Mr. Gideon Smith sent you, they can arrange for passage back to New York, if you wish."

"What about the cattle?" asked Oswald.

Hart shrugged and looked at the sun. "We'd best be on our way."

Oswald watched them go, then put his arms around his wife and daughters and watched the last of their home fall in on itself, consumed by the fire. Damn Steamtown. Damn them all to a hundred hells.

Night was falling when he became aware of another rider. The fire had abated and they managed to rescue a few items—singed blankets, a cook pot, some odds and ends—from the smoldering wreckage. They'd taken a piece of still-burning timber and made a campfire from it to boil water and cook what little food they could scavenge. From the light of the fire he saw the shape of the rider trotting up. Was it someone from Steamtown, sent to find their lost bastards? He didn't even have his guns. Caroline and the girls huddled behind him as the man brought his horse to a halt.

The man wore leathers and skins, his trousers cut with rough tassels like the Indians wore them, a rough white shirt beneath a leather jerkin lined with haphazardly stitched animal furs. The man stopped alongside the campfire and touched his fingers to his forehead.

"Greetings."

Oswald looked him over. "Greetings yourself. What do you want? We're not rightly tolerant of strangers at the moment, so you might find our hospitality lacking."

The man leaned forward on his saddle pommel and regarded the house. Then he asked, "You have somewhere to go?"

Oswald shook his head. The man ruminated for a moment, then said, "There's a little community I know, could probably benefit from you and your beef."

Oswald glanced at Caroline, who gave him the briefest of nods. He said to the stranger, "Tell me more. And what's your name?"

The man slid off his horse. "Don't really have one, sir. Now, let me tell you about this place. There's a creek and some fine grazing land . . ."

12

Two Gentlemen of London

Louis Cockayne's luck had just run out.

Thaddeus Pinch laid down a royal flush with as much of a flourish as his steam-powered limb could summon, and his metal jaw pulled up in a grotesque parody of a grin; the action caused the suppurating sores where the device was bolted to his skull to open like miniature wet smiles, weeping blood and viscous fluid down his jawline. Louis felt like throwing up, for more reasons than one. Pinch was a freak, sure enough, a disgusting tinker-toy of a half-man. But he was also a disgusting tinker-toy of a half-man of his word. And he had pledged that when Louis Cockayne lost at cards, then it was time to die.

Inkerman guffawed and applauded like a loon when Cockayne laid down his hand. Jesus, the cretin practically had a hard-on at the thought of what Pinch was going to do to Cockayne. Louis was pretty sure that it wasn't going to be a bullet in the head there and then, though. Pinch still needed to find out how to fly the brass dragon.

Which was *good*, because it meant Pinch would probably keep Cockayne alive a little while longer.

But it was also *bad*, because it probably meant there was going to be pain in Louis Cockayne's immediate future. Lots and lots of pain.

Thaddeus Pinch sat back in his chair, his flinty eyes on Cockayne. He took a dribbling slurp of whisky through his straw, then said, "Well, well, well. The famed Cockayne luck seems to have deserted him."

"Deserted him!" chuckled Inkerman, nudging the five or

six other cronies in Pinch's inner circle who were gathered around their boss in the oil-lit saloon. "Deserted him!"

"Fuck off," muttered Cockayne. His repertoire of snappy comebacks seemed to have deserted him as well. He was beginning to rue the day he'd ever clapped eyes on that goddamn brass dragon. Or maybe . . . maybe he should have just left well enough alone. Perhaps he could have picked up a nice fat reward for his work in defeating John Reed. Perhaps he could have been a free man, right now, with fewer enemies after his blood.

You're just too goddamn greedy, Louis, he thought. *Sometimes you just oughta cut your losses, play on the side of the angels for a while.*

"I'll fuck you off," growled Inkerman back. "Boss, let me kill him."

There was an exhalation of steam as Pinch raised his metal arm. "No, not yet. First he's got to talk. Inkerman, take him over to the smithy. Make him comfortable. I got some business to attend to. Send someone to find Billy-Joe and have him come over here."

Pinch waved for another bottle of whisky, his brow creased with annoyance. He liked Louis Cockayne, he really did. He didn't want to have to kill him. But he couldn't be seen to be going soft. He touched the sores at his jaw. As if. Thaddeus Pinch lived with unimaginable pain every day. No man could accuse him of being *soft.* But it was worth the pain. Would be, at any rate. Because one day Thaddeus Pinch would be perfect. His flesh was weak, but his spirit was oh so very willing. He would transcend the weakness of the flesh. Thaddeus Pinch would embrace the future, and the future was machines. He would cut away all that was soft and undesirable, all that weak flesh that made him just like other men. Thaddeus Pinch would be superior. Flesh began to decay and die from the moment you were born. That wasn't for Thaddeus Pinch, to end his days stooped over and gray, waiting for some punk to come and blow his head off and take over Steamtown. No, that wasn't for Thaddeus Pinch.

Thaddeus Pinch was going to live forever.

Unlike Louis Cockayne. Pinch chided himself for his weakness. So he liked Cockayne. So the hell what? Cockayne had crossed him. So he had to die. Pinch would give him one last chance to talk . . . suitably loosened up, of course. But if he didn't, then who cared? Some of the finest minds in America were here in Steamtown. That bastard dragon would fly eventually; the law of averages said so. Pinch would get every goddamn man of science he had on the thing, and it would fly. He was Thaddeus Pinch, and he always got what he wanted.

And Louis Cockayne's head would be on a spike at the gates of Steamtown as a warning to anybody else who thought to take Thaddeus Pinch for a fool.

The door to the saloon swung open and the boy, Billy-Joe, stumbled in, wringing his hat in his hands, three saddlebags slung over his shoulders. Pinch regarded him levelly for a moment then said, "Don't worry, son, I'm not going to bawl you out. I already heard what happened. Was it really him?"

Billy-Joe nodded vigorously. "I swear to God, Mr. Pinch, sir. It was him. The Nameless."

Pinch ruminated for a while. "And he said those kids were under his protection?"

"The whole area, Mr. Pinch, sir. Said we was to leave the place well alone. And there was something else . . . the Nameless had this girl over the back of his horse. She looked dead. Had a giant key sticking out of her back."

"A key?" Pinch said absently. The Nameless. This could get bad.

"That's what it looked like, sir, I swear."

Pinch stood with effort and clanked over to the grimy window. He wasn't soft, but he also wasn't stupid. Nobody in Steamtown would expect him to go up against the Nameless.

That would be just the same as signing your own death warrant. Some things couldn't be explained, and some things just weren't fucked with. That was how it was.

He turned to Billy-Joe. "Anyway . . . was the tip-off good? Did you find the Indian trading party?"

Billy-Joe smiled, relieved to have good news. "Sure was, Mr. Pinch. Exactly where you said they'd be. I brought all the horses back." He shucked the saddlebags onto the floor and bent to open them. "Leather, some carvings, but some gold nuggets as well."

Pinch nodded. "Good work. Our informant earned his money this time." He paused. "This Spaniard . . . she said she was the daughter of the Governor of Uvalde?"

Billy-Joe nodded.

"All right," said Pinch. "Find Inkerman in the smithy. Tell him I want five men to go with you to Uvalde. Rough the place up a bit, just send 'em a little warning. Don't bother bringing anyone back, and don't kill anyone if you don't have to. But let's let Uvalde know we're not to be trifled with."

"Now, Mr. Pinch, sir?"

"No time like the present, son." Pinch smiled. "There'll be a bottle of whisky and the whore of your choice waiting for you when you get back."

They heard Steamtown before they saw it. Jeb Hart led them through a wide gap in the Mason-Dixon Wall—battered through, he said, by Thaddeus Pinch's Steamcrawlers to allow the men of San Antonio unfettered access to the prairies beyond.

"I thought the Wall was supposed to keep them out," said Bent.

Jeb poked his thumb over his shoulder. "You seen how far back the garrison is. There ain't another one along the Wall for twice as far in that direction. Like Humbert said, it's a symbol rather than anything useful, especially so far from the British-controlled territories."

"What *is* that noise?" asked Gideon.

They saw the source soon enough in the gathering gloom. Tall towers topped with winding gears that clanked and banged in an endless, insidious rhythm; the burr of steel cables being wound onto immense turning barrels; the exhalation of steam from small, unlovely trains that tugged wheeled bins between the scattered workings. The whole landscape was blighted by the coal mines sunk deep into the Texas earth, and beneath the constant rattle and hum was another, more sonorous sound that Gideon realized was singing.

From the bowels of the nearest mine a vast cage was being winched up to ground level, and emerging from it was a line of men, their shapeless clothing ragged. They were predominantly negroes, though scattered coal-dusted white men were among their number. It was the colored men who were singing, a low yet sweet lament.

"Steal away, steal away! Steal away to Jesus! Steal away, steal away home! I ain't got long to stay here!"

Bent spat into the dry dust. "Slaves. I thought Wilberforce had done away with this sort of shit long ago."

"Across the Empire, maybe," said Hart. "You're not in the Empire anymore, Mr. Bent."

Gideon slowed his pace as the men fell into pairs and began to trudge forward. One of them glanced at Gideon then looked away.

"My Lord calls me! He calls me by the thunder! The trumpet sounds in my soul! I ain't got long to stay here!"

"It's barbaric," said Gideon. The first time he had met Louis Cockayne, the Yankee had been in Africa, rounding up men to bring back to Texas. Now Gideon, who had freed Cockayne's captives, knew where they had been bound.

"At least they're optimistic," said Bent, sounding unconvinced. "All this talk of going home."

Around the mines were men with rifles who squinted at the newcomers. Hart raised a hand and nodded onward, in the direction the slaves were being marched. He turned to Gideon and said, "They're not going anywhere, leastways alive. They're singing for death."

"My Lord, he calls me! He calls me by the lightning! The trumpet sounds it in my soul! I ain't got long to stay here!"

Through the clamor and dust eddies of the mine Gideon could see lights ahead and the outline of wooden buildings.

"Steamtown," said Hart.

"I thought we'd have more trouble getting in," said Gideon.

"As I said, it's not getting in we have to worry about," said Hart. "It's getting out."

Bent moaned. "Jesus effing Christ. I'm a journalist. I shouldn't be partaking in these madcap escapades."

Hart turned to Gideon. "Mr. Smith, if I might offer a word of advice. . . . You're going to see some things in Steamtown that won't be to your liking, not least of which is Thaddeus Pinch. My counsel is that you keep your opinions private until our mission is complete. We're a long way from London, Mr. Smith. A very long way."

Ahead of them, the column of slaves was passing through a large gate. At either side of the gate tall coils of barbed wire rolled along the periphery of what he could now see was the main thoroughfare of a large town, lined with wooden houses and stores. Beyond he could see rickety tenements through wood smoke and steam mingled in the air. Coming the other way were more men, driven on by horsemen armed with rifles.

"The night shift," said Hart. "Steamtown's mines work all day, all night."

"But Pinch can't do this," hissed Gideon. "Why isn't Whitehall doing something?"

"He can, and he does," said Hart. "Rightly speaking, Pinch doesn't call what he does slavery. He says the folks he brings down here—men for the mines, women for the brothels—are *indentured*."

"So why don't they just walk away?" asked Bent.

Hart shrugged. "They try, some of them. Those that don't get a bullet in the back find they've nowhere to go. The desert is littered with the bleached bones of those who've tried to flee Steamtown."

"What do you mean by indentured?" asked Gideon as they approached the big gate. There were two men, one on either side, looking intently at them with raised Winchesters.

"Pinch says they can work off their indentures, become free men. He reckons that takes ten years."

"Ten years!" said Bent. "I wouldn't last five minutes down those mines."

"Me neither," said Gideon. As a child he'd been terrified of enclosed, subterranean places ever since an ill-planned adventure in the caves near his home. He'd had to overcome his fears in Egypt, to save the day, but he had only just managed to conquer the terror he now felt crawling up his spine again at the thought of spending so much time underground.

Hart smiled humorlessly. "Pinch works them so hard, only the strongest last long enough to earn their freedom. Average life expectancy down those mines? I'd say about five years."

They pulled up their horses at the gate. One of the armed men stepped forward and said, "What's your business in Steamtown?"

Hart said, "You know me. Tell Thaddeus Pinch I'm here. Tell him I've got with me two gentlemen from London to see him."

"You know," said Pinch, "folks like to believe that down here in Steamtown we're little better than animals. That we are somehow inferior to other men. That we're less cultured, less knowledgeable."

"My heart bleeds," said Louis Cockayne. He was having trouble speaking, due to the fattened lip and at least two broken teeth he'd suffered in the beating Inkerman had taken great delight in inflicting on him in the dark, hot confines of the Steamtown smithy. Not Inkerman alone, of course, because the big ape was too cowardly for that. Inkerman and three others had punched and kicked Cockayne, setting about him with leather straps. One of them had fixed a cruel-looking set of brass knuckles to his hand, and Cockayne wasn't wholly sure his jaw wasn't broken. Now he was pushed forward over the wide anvil, a goon on each arm, looking forward over the blazing forge, beyond which Pinch ruminated. It had been bad. He was afraid it was going to get a lot worse.

"We're not barbarians, Louis," continued Pinch. "I got some of the finest minds in the country down here, working on my designs, my engines. And some of us are very well-read indeed."

Cockayne said nothing, waiting for him to get to the point.

When Pinch reached down and took the wooden handle of a long poker from the forge, Cockayne wished he'd used a different turn of phrase to himself.

"I like reading about kings, Louis. Only fitting, for the King of Steamtown, that I should know my brethren down the long tail of history, no? Boys, take down his trousers."

Cockayne's struggle earned a punch to the head that had him seeing stars. "Thaddeus . . . ," he said. "What the hell are you doing?"

Pinch stared at the glowing orange tip of the length of forged steel. "Oh yes, I like to read about the kings and queens of old, Louis. You know Edward the Second? Sixth Plantagenet king, direct descendant of Henry the Second. Born in 1284, died 1327. Do you know how he met his end?"

Cockayne shook his head. Pinch held the glowing tip close to Cockayne's eyes, so close he could feel the heat prickling his bloodied and bruised flesh.

"They shoved a red-hot poker up his ass."

"Pinch . . . ," began Cockayne, but the King of Steamtown had already moved out of his sight line. Cockayne's head was gripped, facing him forward. He felt the heat on his buttocks. He roared, "Pinch!"

"Last chance, Louis," called Pinch behind him. "You know how much it's gotta hurt, having a red-hot poker stuck up your ass? You're gonna die, Louis. Talk to me."

Cockayne screwed his eyes tight shut and spat in the glowing forge in front of him. "Fuck. Fuck, fuck, fuck. Okay, Thaddeus. I guess my memory's coming back."

Pinch didn't move from his position at Cockayne's rear. He said, "I'm listening, Louis."

Cockayne took a deep breath then said, "The dragon? It's Egyptian. Ancient Egyptian. Impossibly old technology. No one knows how the hell it works."

"You do, Louis," said Pinch encouragingly. "You made it fly."

"Not really," said Cockayne. "I was little more than a passenger. The dragon needs . . . it needs a girl."

There was a pause, then Pinch reappeared in front of Cockayne. "A girl? You pulling my dick, Louis?"

"Not just any girl. She's called . . ." Cockayne felt his heart thud into his stomach. "She's called Maria. She's a clockwork girl. With a human brain. Don't ask me how the hell that works, Thaddeus, because I haven't got a fucking clue. But it does work, and she flies the goddamn dragon."

Pinch slowly put the poker back in the forge, his eyes staring into the middle distance. He brought up his metal arm with an exhalation of steam and scratched his iron jaw. "A clockwork girl?"

"Some shit to do with an artifact in her head," said Cockayne. "Thaddeus? Can I pull my goddamn trousers up?"

Pinch waved absently and the goons released Cockayne. He shrugged their hands off him and pulled up his trousers, glaring through a blackened, half-closed eye at Inkerman. Pinch seemed off in a world of his own.

"A clockwork girl," he said again. "Imagine that. She's what I've been looking for all my life." His gaze snapped toward Cockayne. "Where is she, this Maria?"

Cockayne shook his head. "I don't know, and that's the God's honest truth, Thaddeus. Something went wrong up there and we crashed. I woke up here. I haven't got a clue where she is."

"Take him back to the pen," said Pinch absently.

"We aren't going to kill him?" said Inkerman, sounding disappointed.

"No, not yet," said Pinch. "Inkerman, did you speak to Billy-Joe after he ran into the Nameless?"

Cockayne raised an eyebrow. It hurt like hell. But the Nameless? What was *he* doing around these parts?

Inkerman nodded. Pinch asked, "He mention this girl he saw, over the Nameless's horse? The girl with the key in her back?"

Cockayne felt suddenly sick. He'd saved his own hide, but at what cost? Maybe it would have been better to die with his secret. He spat out blood and half a tooth and asked, "What're you going to do, Thaddeus?"

Pinch clanked around in front of him. "Do, Louis? Why, I'm gonna find this Maria. She's going to make my dragon fly, and then . . . well, the King of Steamtown needs a queen, don't you think?"

As the punks started to drag Cockayne out of the smithy, a burly man with a Winchester pushed past them, nodding nervously at Pinch. "Sir, I need to speak to you. You know the party we sent out to get those heads of beef, up north of the Wall?"

Pinch shrugged. "They back?"

"Only one, sir. Rest of 'em are dead."

Pinch frowned. "That rat-ass little cattle farmer has killed three of my boys?"

The man screwed his hat up into a ball in his fists. "That's not all, sir. You know Jeb Hart? The scout guy?"

"Sure," said Pinch. "What's he got to do with anything?"

"He's at the gate, sir. With two gentlemen from London."

Pinch cast the briefest of looks at Cockayne. "Get him back to the pen," he said. "And go tell Jeb Hart to bring his visitors to me. I'll be at Madame Choo-Choo's."

13

Myths and Legends

Her father was already back from Nuevo Laredo when Inez returned to Uvalde. She found him in his study in their casa, a bottle of *jerez* half done in already. He was poring over papers on his desk and didn't see her standing in the doorway. Suddenly he roared, making her jump, and cast the papers over his shoulder.

"Father?"

He turned unsteadily, scraping his wooden chair around on the polished floorboards, and regarded her with a heavy-lidded stare. "Where have you been?"

"Out," she said. "Riding."

He turned back to the bottle and poured himself another measure. "You're late. You have missed dinner. I saw Father Eduardo when I got back. He said you weren't at church on Sunday. He said you haven't been to church for several Sundays."

"Neither have you," she said.

His eyes blazed at her. "I am busy. What is your excuse?"

She looked at her feet. Telling him that she had spent her Sunday mornings in the arms of Chantico would not be wise. It was all right for the Governor of Uvalde to be a lapsed Catholic, but not his daughter.

"Father?" she said hesitantly. "Was there bad news at Nuevo Laredo?"

"There is always bad news at Nuevo Laredo," he said, slurring. "Bastards."

Inez was shocked. She had never heard him speak like that. He gestured toward the papers scattered across the floor. "They are raising our taxes. They are reducing their supply runs to us to once every two weeks. The garrison they have been promising for a whole year now will not materialize at all. Ciudad Cortes is increasing *their* taxes and cutting *their* supplies, so they do the same to us. Madrid wages war with France, so Ciudad Cortes feels abandoned. It goes right down the chain until it stops with us, and there is no one for us to raise taxes or abandon. They wish to forget about Uvalde. They wish us to disappear from their concern forever." He pinched his nose. "When places feel abandoned, they draw in their borders, wish to feel more protected. I heard at Nuevo Laredo that some Indian trading party was slaughtered by Texan raiders just a few miles from the garrison."

Inez gasped, and before she could stop herself, she had already murmured, "They would not have done this to Don de la Garcia." As the words left her lips she tried to reel them in, but it was of course useless.

Her father's red eyes blazed. "Don de la Garcia! Don de la Garcia! I am sick to high heaven of hearing of Don de la Garcia! Let his name never be uttered in this house again!"

Then, so shockingly that Inez could barely believe she had heard it: "Bitch."

She gaped at him. "Father?"

"You heard me," he said. "You think Don de la Garcia cared so much for Uvalde? Then why is he sunning himself in luxury in Madrid, hmm? Answer me that!"

Inez's head swam with the insult. But she rallied and said, "You know he was summoned back. He had no say in the matter."

Even as she spoke, her father's venomous words tolled in her head. *Bitch. Bitch. Bitch.*

"Did I want the job? Did I want to step into Don de la Garcia's oh-so-polished boots? No, I did not. But someone has to run the affairs of Uvalde. Someone has to keep this place from disappearing beneath the sands."

"Why did you call me . . . that word?" she asked quietly. "What would Mother say?"

Don Juan Batiste stood unsteadily and weaved toward her. He sneered. "She would say, like mother, like daughter."

Inez felt the blood pound in her ears. "How dare you! How dare you speak of her in those words! She was my mother. Your wife."

"Your mother, my wife," he echoed. "But that does not make you my daughter. You are old enough to know the truth now, Inez. You are not mine. That . . . that *whore* got herself caught out after spreading her legs for the ever-so-perfect Don Sergio de la Garcia. And I rescued her from penury and shame, took her little bastard on as my own."

Batiste brought his hand back and swiped it across Inez's face. She was smaller, faster, and lither than her father. She could have dodged the blow. But shock kept her rooted to the spot. As the sting of his palm reddened her cheek, she vowed to herself that no man would ever touch her in that way again.

"What do you think to that, hmm?" spat Batiste. "Don de la Garcia didn't just abandon Uvalde. He abandoned his daughter, too."

But Inez had already clamped her hands to her ears and fled.

Inez sat on the flat roof of the casa, her refuge since she was a small child. Now her childhood hung off her in tatters. The man she had thought of as *father* had never been close to her, never loving, but she had convinced herself that that was merely his character. Don Juan Batiste had been the Deputy Governor of Uvalde since before she was born, and now she knew that every day he must have looked upon his superior, Don de la Garcia, with his own wife and two daughters, knowing that his own child was really the governor's.

Inez's mother had died six years ago of cholera, and she had taken the secret with her to the grave. Inez truly did not know how to feel. On the one hand, it all explained—and perhaps allowed her to forgive—Batiste's aloofness toward her over the years. A part of her felt almost sorry for him. On the other . . . he had taken in Inez's mother, heavy with child. It would have cost him nothing more than it already had to love them both unconditionally, rather than nursing the resentment that had suddenly burst forth. A bigger part of her, she decided, hated him.

And she could not shake a tiny thrill at the thought that the handsome, dashing, courageous Don de la Garcia was actually her very own father.

Night had fallen over Uvalde, and the lanterns brightly lit the town square beneath the casa. She had brought three oil lamps to illuminate the roof, and from within her cocoon of pale light she watched the market stalls being packed away, the cafés and tapas bars opening up. Cicadas chirruped in the darkness, and she closed her eyes and inhaled the faint aroma of pine from the plane trees in the dusty streets around the square.

Pecan, and the scent of Chantico. She didn't know why, but after fleeing her father's study she had riffled through her bag for the stupid El Chupacabras costume he had made, and slipped into the tight trousers and black shirt. She hadn't bothered retrieving his makeshift blade, instead grabbing a rapier from her father's cabinet in the hallway. She really must teach Chantico some proper blade work, the true art of *La Destreza*. Stepping back from the raised edge of the roof, she hefted the rapier and assumed the guard position, giving her imaginary opponent the courtesy of a brief nod before dancing forward into the line of his invisible blade, *stesso tempo*, parrying his thrust and fluidly transforming her defense into an attack that swiftly finished off her enemy. Since the age of seven she had been a fencing expert. Perhaps she also had something of El Chupacabras—wherever *he* had gone—within her, as well as Don Sergio de la Garcia.

A commotion in the town square suddenly brought her back to her body, and the gunshots that rang out had her ducking low behind the rooftop ledge. There were half a dozen horsemen galloping around the square, the stallholders scattering with yells and screams. She peered over the ledge at the men.

They were Texans.

She cursed herself for giving her name to those Steamtown *banditos* at the abandoned mine. The one the Nameless had sent back to his bosses had evidently delivered his message . . . and Steamtown had decided to retaliate against Uvalde if it couldn't touch the Nameless directly. Shock caused her to stumble forward as she recognized the lead horseman in the dancing lamplight: the one who had thought to assault her.

The rider took up an oil lantern from one stall and smashed it against the canopy of another, the flames quickly taking hold and spreading. This was why her fath—Don Batiste was a weak man. He left Uvalde open to the attacks and bullying of others. He had failed to secure a garrison from Nuevo Laredo, and once word got out, the town would be at the mercy of thugs like these forever. Nuevo Laredo, and Ciudad Cortes, did not care about this little border outpost. They would probably rather it wasn't here at all. A few more raids like this, and they might get their wish.

The Texans didn't look as though they were on a kidnapping mission, thank God. And they were firing their guns into the air, not at the townsfolk. It was a message, then, that Uvalde had better watch out.

Anger boiled Inez's blood.

Why weren't the townsfolk fighting back? Why were they fleeing like rats? There were only six of the Texans. Was this what Uvalde had become? New Spain's dirty little secret, a nest of cowards led by a weak-willed man who was only comfortable bullying young girls?

Where was Don Sergio de la Garcia? Where was El Chupacabras?

Inez looked down in fury at her leather-gloved hands, at the sword in her right, the silly little flour-bag mask dyed with juniper berries in her left. Where was El Chupacabras? Why had the masked hero of the prairies deserted them?

Perhaps he hadn't.

Before she knew what she was doing, Inez had pulled on the mask. She leaped to the ledge and held her sword aloft. Then she cried, "Uvalde!"

The Texans looked up and paused, pulling up their horses. The townsfolk slowed then stopped, looking up at her, bathed in lamplight and the dancing shadows from the burning market. The bandits glanced at each other, uncertain. A child, hiding beneath an upturned fruit stall, crawled out onto the cobbles and pointed at her.

"El Chupacabras!"

The name rolled like white horses on the crests of waves around the suddenly still town square. *El Chupacabras. El Chupacabras. El Chupacabras.*

Then, as one man, a huddled group skulking in the shadows of the tapas bar surged forward, causing the nearest Texan's horse to whinny and kick up on its hind legs, shedding its rider. They fell upon him with punches and kicks, and the crowd reversed its flow away from the square and back into it, taking up chairs and sticks, unsheathing swords and guns, and taking up the cry "El Chupacabras! El Chupacabras! El Chupacabras!" as they launched themselves at the remaining invaders.

Inez watched them for a long moment, the fire below reflecting in her shining eyes, then stole away from the rooftop and back into the casa.

⁂

Early the next morning she found Batiste still in his study. He had not been to bed. He looked at her with red-rimmed eyes and croaked, "I am sorry. Can you forgive me?"

Inez shrugged. "In time, perhaps."

He looked at the three heavy carpetbags she carried. "Where are you going?"

"I am leaving. There is nothing for me here."

Batiste fell to his knees and began to weep. "Please, Inez, I am sorry."

She gave him a tight smile. "Me, too. Take care of the town, yes? El Chupacabras won't be here every time you need saving."

Then she saddled up her horse and took to the trail, and with every step her horse took her closer to Chantico, she felt her heart might take flight.

He rolled up his papers and took a small cup of tea from the pot on his countertop that had long since gone cold. He would sleep on it. Perhaps the mistake was in trying to ape the human form too closely. That might be it. He would sleep on it and come back fresh tomorrow.

Haruki Serizawa pinched his nose tightly. His eyes felt tight, and his back hurt from hunching over the roll of paper on which he had been scribbling formulas and calculations for eight solid hours. It was getting dark outside; he should think about finishing and getting home to Akiko and Michi. Those leg servers just would not hold, though. He thought he might have found a way to strengthen the joints, and during testing at the warehouse yesterday they had seemed to hold, but he could see that there were stresses forming in the long brass plates that simply did not show up in his calculations. Perhaps the thing was just too tall after all. Perhaps there was only so big you could go.

He rolled up his papers and took a small cup of tea from the pot on his countertop that had long since gone cold. He would sleep on it. Perhaps the mistake was in trying to ape the human form too closely. That might be it. He would sleep on it and come back fresh tomorrow.

The screen to the laboratory slid back, and Science Officer Morioka stepped in. Serizawa bowed, wincing as his stiff back pinched him.

"Come with me," said Morioka without ceremony.

Serizawa followed him down the corridor to Morioka's office. A clean table holding just a single bonsai tree and a thick envelope awaited them. Morioka sat down in his chair and invited Serizawa to take the other seat.

"I have had an idea for building up the supports on the upper legs," began Serizawa, but Morioka cut him off with an impatient wave.

"The time for ideas is past. Now only action. Swift action."

Serizawa sighed; he could see where this was going.

Morioka tapped the envelope with his fingers. "I told you that the British had been sighted in sector thirty-one."

Serizawa nodded.

"Our investigations have proved that they did, in fact, breach the defenses. With the worst possible consequences."

Morioka opened the envelope and withdrew a stack of photographs. "These were taken yesterday in sector twelve. There is an observatory and watch base there. It is only a hundred miles from Nyu Edo."

He pushed the photographs across the desk and Serizawa took them. The first showed the observatory; it was wrecked, the dome smashed, the large telescope lying on the ground like a felled tree. The second was of the dormitories in which the soldiers who manned the watch base presumably slept; they too were smashed, the bedrolls and clothing strewn on the rocky ground.

"A typhoon? A tsunami?" said Serizawa.

Morioka smiled tightly. "Continue."

Serizawa turned to the third photograph and blanched. He had not eaten all day, and he had been looking forward to noodles and beef when he got home. Now his appetite fled. "Is that a . . . man?"

"It was," said Morioka. "Look at the next."

Serizawa flicked through the remaining photographs then placed them facedown on the desk. He could look no more. Those poor men . . .

He asked, "How many dead?"

"All of them," said Morioka. "Twenty-seven. We lost touch with the base on sector twelve two days ago. They were due to send a boat with the month's reports. We sent a gunboat out to investigate. This is what they found. Every building smashed, every man dead. This was no typhoon, Serizawa. No tsunami." He leaned forward. "This is what we have been waiting for. This is what we have been preparing for."

Serizawa felt sick again, but not just because of the

photographs. He felt sick because his work was nowhere near ready. Morioka said, "So, no ideas. Action. Swift action. I want us to be ready by the day after next."

"But, Science Officer Morioka . . ."

"No buts," said Morioka. He gestured at the photographs. "You want this for Nyu Edo? You want this for the people of the Californian Meiji? Your own wife and child?"

"Of course not!" said Serizawa, shocked. "But . . . it might not come here. Sector twelve is a little to the south . . . it might make landfall elsewhere."

"And it might not. We must be prepared for all eventualities. That is our task, Serizawa. If we fail . . . then honor will have to be satisfied. Do you understand me?"

He did. He said, "I suppose I shall go back to the laboratory, work a while longer on those leg pistons. . . ."

Morioka smiled. "Take as long as you need to, Serizawa." He inclined his head. "The Meiji shall be indebted to you for your work."

He worked until he fell forward on his worktop and slept for fifteen fitful minutes, before waking sharply from dreams that were drenched in men's blood. The whole building was deserted, and Serizawa decided he was no use to anyone exhausted. He wound his way quickly home along the empty streets, peering out between the buildings at the dark sea and the terror that every wave brought closer to Nyu Edo.

He tried to slip quietly into bed but Akiko said coldly, "I am not asleep. Why are you so late?"

"Science Officer Morioka," he said helplessly.

Akiko turned toward him. "Haruki, you have to tell that man you are not a slave. You have a family. You are not paid to work every hour of the day."

"My work—"

"Yes, I know," she sighed. "Your work is very important. Your child is also very important, Haruki. Your wife is very important. Is this about your father? He might be hailed as the finest scientist in all of Japan, the man who has kept the emperor alive beyond his years. Let them say that, Haruki! You do not have to compete with your father! You do not have to drive yourself into a grave trying to . . . to trump him! Is that what you want? To be a better man than your father, or die trying?"

He sat up in bed, suddenly gripped by a fear that rolled in like fog off the sea. He took his wife by her shoulders. "Tomorrow, you and Michi must come and stay with me."

Akiko shrugged him off and sat up. "Stay with you? What are you talking about?"

"In the laboratory. There are rooms where no one ever goes. You can stay there."

"Do not be ridiculous." Akiko pouted. "Why would we want to do that when we have a perfectly good home here?"

"Nyu Edo isn't safe," he said. Panic was rising within him. "It isn't safe."

The screen to the bedroom slid back and Michi stood in the doorway, rubbing her eyes. "What are you shouting about?"

"We're not shouting, Prickly Pear," said Serizawa softly. "Go back to bed."

Michi ignored him and wriggled in between her parents. Akiko smoothed her hair and whispered, "What do you mean, *not safe*? Do you know something? The British, or the Spanish . . . ?"

He shook his head. "There is a place . . . an island. It is called sector thirty-one."

"A lovely name," said Akiko. "Why does this matter to us?"

"They keep . . . *things* there. One has gotten loose. It is headed this way."

Akiko snuggled down beside the gently snoring Michi. "I think you have been drinking sake with Science Officer Morioka, Haruki, not working hard. What kind of *things*?"

He looked at the pale outline of the moon shining through

the paper blind over the window and waited a long time before answering. Akiko had fallen back asleep, her breathing in
rhythm with Michi's. He felt flooded with love for them, and
fear. He whispered, "Monsters."

14

The Lord of the Star of the Dawn

 A group of children was playing with an inflated pig's bladder in the shadow of the hills that sheltered the Yaqui village from the sun and the winds that could tear through the canyon, especially in the colder months. They kicked the makeshift ball among themselves, the older ones showing off their skills at passing it from foot to knee to head to foot again before kicking it on to their neighbor. Chantico watched them for a while. He had always enjoyed playing kickball, at least when he was still considered a youth. He was a man now, and he was expected to put such things behind him. He had completed the journey into manhood, had undergone the five tasks, one for each of the five worlds that made up the *ania* where they all lived. He had ventured out into the desert wilderness world, and he had run ceaselessly for a day and a night. He had embraced the tallest cactus in the valley and in pain found the doorway into the flower world. He had found in the night world his totem animal, which was *Wo'i* the coyote, like his father's had been and his father's before him. He had gone to sleep and woken with full knowledge of the deer song, imparted to him in the dreamworld. And in the mystical world . . . in the mystical world he had passed through the unbreakable rock into the place of power, deep within the bowels of the sandstone mesa that loomed over the village. There he had passed fully into manhood, and into the embrace of secrets.

The pig's bladder came rolling over to him. Chantico deftly flicked it up with the toe of his slipper, keeping it aloft with his knee, then volleyed it back to the children, who applauded and whistled and begged him to stay and join their game.

But Chantico, who had just left the abandoned mine and its eventful day of spirits and clockwork women and Texans and not even a tumble in the shadows with beautiful Inez, was a man now, and he had to put away childish things. He needed to organize a meeting of the *kopolai*. But first, he could see his mother and father outside their tent, and even at this distance the frowns on their faces were evident.

The settlement was largely composed of the wigwams belonging to the tribe's main family groups, with the smaller tents of older children who had started families of their own dotted around the grand filial tents. There had also been a move to create more permanent wooden huts, a sign that the Yaqui thought this spot was particularly blessed. The hunting and fishing were certainly good, and the camp was well situated for defending. But the advantage was not just its location. The camp had once, centuries before, been a town or even a rudimentary city. There were stonework buildings, or at least the footprints of them, one of which had been built up again to form the meetinghouse of the tribal elders. The Spanish, back in the days when they were seeking to conquer and tame all this land, must have wiped out the settlement. That, according to *Yoemyo'otui*, the Old Man, meant the place was drenched in spirits. It was the Old Man who had found the place of power in the caves, and even Chantico and the others had felt the emanations rising from its rocks, felt the lives that still reverberated through the five worlds from the black stains on the flat rock that the Old Man said could be nothing other than an altar, for nothing else but sacrifice.

"Chantico!" His father, Noshi, was standing with his arms folded in front of their wigwam, Chantico's mother behind him. He had told them he was going with the trading party to the Spanish towns to the south; he had evidently timed his return badly. The trading party must have returned already, or were not back yet. Either way, his lie was exposed.

"Father, Mother," he said, bowing to both of them. He was

shocked when his mother broke ranks and ran to him, hitching up her skirt, and embraced him tightly.

"Oh, Chantico, thank the spirits," she said. "You are alive."

"Of course I am," he said. Had word reached the camp about the Texans who had tried to ravish Inez and kill him? But how? Chichijal? But that was impossible.

"We had word from a scout of the tribe that inhabits the valley between the three mesas," said Noshi grimly. "Our trading party . . . they have been slaughtered. All dead. Or so we thought."

"Texan raiders?" asked Chantico. All dead. His friend Ecatzin usually went out with the traders, with the moccasins his wife made. Chantico felt suddenly sick.

His father said, "Why don't you tell us? You were with them, correct? You will know if it was Steamtown boys. Or maybe you weren't with the traders after all, hmm, Chantico?"

"Thank the spirits he wasn't!"

"Hush, woman," murmured Noshi. "He has lied to us." He looked back to Chantico. "You have been spending time with *Yoemyo'otui*, haven't you? The Old Man? He is wicked, Chantico. He is what the Spanish call *brujo*, yes? A witch-man. I do not want you wasting your time with him."

"He is not wicked!" Chantico pouted. "He is of the old people! He will save our tribe."

Chantico's father waved his arm around the camp, at the protective wall of the cliffs, at the tall grasses in which deer grazed and rabbits burrowed, at the cold stream in which spawning salmon leapt. "Save us from *what*, Chantico?"

"From those who would cause us harm," he said. "Steamtown."

"Speaking of the dead, perhaps you had better go and pay your respects to Ecatzin's mother, and the others," said his father. "Then you can do some chores, perhaps atone for your lies and deceit."

Instead, Chantico went straight to find the Old Man.

No one knew his name anymore. They simply called him *Yoemyo'otui*, or the Old Man. And the Old Man didn't give his name out. Names were power, he said, and if your enemy knew your name you might as well have put your balls in his hand and given him your knife. He pointed at each of them in turn in the circle around the pale fire deep in the caves, and he recited their names, giving their imaginary balls a twist with his gnarled hand.

The Old Man was supposed to be able to remember Cortez taking Tenochtitlán, but Chantico had once pointed out that that would make the Old Man hundreds of years old. The Old Man had shrugged and said, "What of it?" He was Aztec, he said, purebred and, yes, if that was what people wanted to say, *brujo*. Witch-man. He had rattled bones and torn still-beating hearts out of living chests. No one really knew when or why the Old Man had attached himself to the tribe. He once said that it was because the Yaqui were the only people the Spanish had never properly conquered, and that the Yaqui would save the Americas from the invaders. He spoke a lot of nonsense, but he did it in an insistent, seductive manner. No one really took the Old Man seriously.

Until Quetzalcoatl came.

After a hurried conversation outside the Old Man's wigwam, Chantico was dispatched to spread the word that a meeting would take place in the caves within the half hour. A year ago, their gatherings had attracted only half a dozen people; now those who stole away from the camp to make their way to the place of power numbered twenty; Chantico could only imagine the puzzled expressions on the faces of his parents as they scratched their heads and wondered where all the young people had gone. Soon the time would be right for the Old Man to assume his rightful position as chief of the tribe, and then Ecatzin and all those who had died at Texan hands would be properly avenged.

The cave was lit with torches and a large fire in front of the altar stone. Beneath, in a natural bowl, the Yaqui gathered in silence; the Old Man stood between the fire and the altar, swaying, his eyes rolled back in his head, feathers and beads dangling from his jet-black hair. He had a sense of the dramatic, did the Old Man. He liked to play to the crowd. He muttered in Nahuatl, splaying his bony fingers and extending his hands over the crowd. He played them like that music box with ivory keys the traveling carny man had once shown Chantico when the carnival had passed close to the Yaqui camp.

Chantico stood to one side of the front row. He had been with the secret group since the Old Man had started it up, since he had first brought them to this spirit-haunted place of power. Chantico liked to think of himself as part of the inner circle. Had not the Old Man immediately called this meeting after he'd imparted his news? With consummate showmanship, the Old Man cast a handful of dust and seeds into the fire, making it leap and sparkle and eliciting gasps from the gathering in the cavern. His eyes snapped open.

"You know him, eh, the Lord of the Star of the Dawn?" said the Old Man, his voice strong, his eyes black and twinkling in a face as brown and ridged as the canyon-scored landscape. "The one who draws the line between the world and the sky, the plumed serpent, eh?"

The crowd nodded and murmured. The Old Man said, "Quetzalcoatl, that's who I'm talking about, eh? You seen him, Chaske, am I not right, eh? You watched him swooping out of the sun, as bold as you like. And you, Chetan, with your eyes of a hawk, you watched him looping over the desert. We all saw him, eh? We all knew him. I heard him called by a hundred different names in my time, heard him called Kukulcan and Gukumatz, Ce Acatl and Naxcitl, Topiltzin, too. But we all know him as Quetzalcoatl, eh?"

"What does it mean?" called a voice from the crowd. Someone else shouted, "And where has Quetzalcoatl been since then? It's been weeks!"

The Old Man beckoned for Chantico to join him at the

altar. Burning with pride, Chantico stepped to his side. The Old Man said, "The boy here, he's heard something about Quetzalcoatl."

Someone laughed. "Chantico? What can he have heard?"

Chantico's face burned. The Old Man said, "Tell them who you heard it off, boy, eh?"

"Chichijal," said Chantico quietly, then again, more loudly. "Chichijal. The one they call the Nameless. He told me himself."

There was more than one gasp from the assembly. The Old Man said, "Tell them what he told you, eh?"

Chantico nodded. "The Nameless, he spoke of a dragon. He said it had crashed in the desert. He said the dragon was made of *brass*."

Someone shouted, "Brass? So it could just be one of the machines they put in the sky, not Quetzalcoatl at all?"

The Old Man waved his arms. "Was it not Quetzalcoatl who created the world? Is he not the god of intelligence? Of self-reflection? Does he not hold up a mirror to the world he created, eh, with his own blood? You do not know. You have not traveled in *ania* as I have. You have not seen the world beyond. The white man, he takes the fruit of the bowels of the earth and he burns it and he creates steam and fuss and noise, and he drives forth his engines across the face of the earth and through the thin, cold sky. The white man, he has lost touch with nature. He has lost his link with the Earth. That is what Quetzalcoatl is trying to tell us.

"He appears to us in brass and cogs, pistons and steel, belching fire as gears grind against gears. He is telling us that what the white man does is an affront to nature, to the entire five worlds! The white man has taken the earth and wrung it dry to fuel his endless death machine. That is why Quetzalcoatl has appeared to us now. It is a test. To see if we are worthy."

Chantico coughed. He didn't know how much he was meant to tell the Old Man, whether he was to mention the clockwork woman at all. But there was something important the Nameless had told him that he hadn't yet imparted to the crowd. The Old Man looked at him. "Chantico?"

"The Texans . . . the place they call Steamtown. The Nameless said . . . he said they have Quetzalcoatl."

There was a collective gasp. The Old Man's words had galvanized and awed the group. Now they were affronted and incensed. It would take but a word, thought Chantico, and they would go and grasp their axes and bows and fall upon Steamtown, even if it meant every one of them was slaughtered.

The Old Man was nodding enthusiastically. "The message is clear. Quetzalcoatl has delivered himself unto the mercy of the white man, eh? He awaits to see if our actions will free him."

"But what must we do?" asked Chantico. "They have guns . . . cannons . . . surely Quetzalcoatl would not expect us to throw ourselves to our deaths."

"Just as Quetzalcoatl gave his blood to create the world, so he demands blood to replenish himself, eh?" said the Old Man. "But perhaps not ours." He paused, stroking his chin with his long fingers, staring into the fire. "Perhaps the conquistadores who murdered the Yaqui sons today ought to pay, eh?"

There was a murmur of general agreement. Chantico began to feel uncomfortable, as though he had not thought this through very well. The Old Man turned to him. "Perhaps . . . perhaps that little daughter of Cortes you have been meeting with in secret, Chantico?"

"W-what do you mean?" whispered Chantico, the blood draining from his face. "What do you mean?"

The Old Man closed his eyes. "Inez Batiste Palomo. The daughter of the Governor of Uvalde. You and her, you are *waata*, eh, Chantico? In love."

Someone called, "A Spanish girl?" Chantico could not tell whether the voice was dripping with disgust or envy.

The Old Man placed a gnarled hand on Chantico's head; he flinched away. "It is all right. Quetzalcoatl has brought you together, to test you. To test all of us. She must be brought here, to our place of power. She must be sacrificed to empower Quetzalcoatl, to allow him to shed the carapace of brass and steel in which the modern world has imprisoned him, so that the plumed serpent can fly once more and wreak vengeance on behalf of the Yaqui and all the peoples of the Americas."

Chantico reeled away from the Old Man and the fire, which fizzed and sparkled with his poisonous words. No. No, no, no. How could it all have gone so very badly wrong? He had condemned Inez to death at the hands of these . . . these madmen. His impulse was to flee, to warn her. But they would only follow him, overpower Inez, and bring her back here to the most horrible of fates. Chantico looked to the Yaqui, but the Old Man's hold over them was complete; they were swaying and holding out their arms to him in supplication as he stood with the flames of the sparkling fire licking at his robes. He mimed putting his fist to his chest and tearing his ribs away, holding up an imaginary dripping heart to the chanting crowd. And soon it would be no imaginary heart, but that of his true love. When Inez said she had given her heart to him, he did not think she intended it so literally. His head swam. What would the Nameless say? What of . . .

Wait.

Chantico's crazy, rambling mind had been about to ask what would become of the clockwork girl whom the Nameless had tasked them with protecting. But there, of course, lay Inez's salvation, and Chantico's redemption.

"Wait," he said, this time aloud. He took the Old Man by the sleeve and shook him violently. "Wait. There is another way. A better way."

The Old Man invited him to continue, holding a hand out to silence the chanting assembly. Chantico cleared his throat and said, "Chichijal, the Nameless, spirit of the prairies, he brought someone to me. A girl . . . alive but not alive."

The Old Man frowned. "How can this be?"

Chantico shook his head. "I don't know. But clockwork drives her, and pistons power her heart. She is somehow *of*

Quetzalcoatl. She was with the great plumed god when he committed himself to the embrace of the desert and was captured by the Texans."

The Old Man squinted at him. "And you know where to find this girl who is alive but not alive?"

After but a moment's hesitation, Chantico nodded.

The Old Man clapped his hands together. "Then bring her to us, eh? Let us see if the girl who is alive yet not alive can give her clockwork heart in sacrifice to the rebirth of great Quetzalcoatl and avenge the Yaqui people. Bring her to us by tomorrow."

Chantico nodded. The Old Man placed a hand on his shoulder. "And Chantico? If you fail, or if this does not work . . . then it's back to what the white man calls *plan A*, eh?"

Chantico swallowed and stole away from the hot darkness of the cave.

15

ALIAS SMITH AND JONES

Gideon Smith felt like anything but a hero as he rode down the dusty main street of San Antonio, flanked by Jeb Hart and Aloysius Bent. All eyes were on them, staring from the verandas of the clapboard buildings and the shadowy doorways of the white stone and redbrick structures that together created a jumbled, haphazard township of no discernible style. The night was illuminated by oil lamps swinging from the stoops, strings of fizzing electrical bulbs, and ornate columns of gas-powered lights. The buildings seemed to stretch off in tight warrens beyond the main street, and tall pit towers worked dully against the darkening sky, their ever-present hum and clank a counterpoint to the shouts, piano music, and occasional distant gunshot.

Gideon felt farther from home than he ever had before, even when he was in the deserts of Egypt, even in the lost world where they had rescued Rubicon and Darwin. Something sick and heavy thudded in his stomach, a nausea that made him long for the bustle of Mayfair, the warmth of Grosvenor Square, and the smells wafting in from Mrs. Cadwallader's kitchen. Even more so, he pined for the gentle wash of the tide on the Sandsend shore and the cozy lights from the fishermen's cottages. Perhaps that was it. Perhaps he had never been so far from the sea before. Perhaps he was landlocked and dusty, desperate for the currents of air and water to chime with the thudding of the blood in his head, quieting it.

Or perhaps he was just deathly afraid. There was a ruckus to their left, coming from a brightly lit wooden building with a hand-painted sign that said CASINO over the door. A fat man came tumbling through the swinging doors, pursued by two others who set about him with fists and the handles of their pistols. No one stopped to help. A thin, rangy dog yelped at the melee and an onlooker gave it a casual kick, so it skidded away as though scalded. From a dark alley, a woman screamed and screamed, then sobbed.

Gideon felt Jeb Hart's hand on his forearm, reaching over from his horse. "I know what you're thinking, Smith," he murmured. "Don't. Leave it, if you want to walk out of here alive."

Gideon gestured helplessly toward the alley as they passed. Hart shook his head. "You've got a job to do, Smith. Don't get distracted."

Yes, Gideon Smith, the Hero of the Empire, was afraid. On all his previous escapades, he'd had someone else to rely on: Captain Trigger, Rowena Fanshawe, Bram Stoker, or Countess Bathory. Even Louis Cockayne. Now it was just himself and Bent. And the journalist, for all his bluster, was well out of his depth; he looked even more terrified than Gideon felt. Hart was just a guide, leading them, it felt like, into the lion's den. Hart's words came back to him. *So you're the best the Empire has, then?*

He knew, in his heart, that he wasn't.

He also knew that, somehow, he would have to be.

"We're here," said Hart. They pulled up outside a large, two-story wooden building. A sign proclaimed it to be MADAME CHOO-CHOO's. The accompanying painted image of a lady of the night, her vastly overexaggerated attributes falling out of her dress, left no doubt as to what the place was.

"A whorehouse," said Bent with forced jollity. "Things are looking up."

"I'm going to stable our horses, maybe get us some rooms at the hotel," said Hart, sliding off his mount.

Gideon raised an eyebrow. "Aren't you coming in with us? And a hotel? How long do you think we'll be here?"

Hart shrugged. "That's up to you, Smith. It's your mission, not mine. I said I'd get you here, and that I've done."

Bent raised his hand. "Erm, wasn't there something about getting us effing out of here, as well?"

Hart smiled. "Again, that's up to you. Good luck in there. You'll need it."

Gideon dismounted and helped Bent do the same, with less grace and more swearing. "Jesus effing Christ, I'm going to be walking like I've got a barrel up my arse for the next week."

They stood before the frosted glass windows of Madame Choo-Choo's and glanced at each other. Bent said softly, "You know what you're doing here, Gideon? Tell me you do. I don't want to spent the rest of my days down one of these bastard mines."

Gideon touched his arm. "Trust me," he said, though without conviction. "I'm a hero."

✺

Madame Choo-Choo turned out to be a mannequin, like the ones they had in the expensive frock shops in Mayfair, with grotesquely made-up features and a blond wig. She sat behind a desk, shuddering and shaking from the hidden pumps and pistons that powered her, making her head turn jerkily from one side to the other and causing her stiff hands to move up and down in a manner that managed to be lascivious and rather unpleasant at the same time. Beyond the small entrance hall, through thick, heavy drapes, could be heard tinkling laughter, low voices, and the occasional slap of flesh upon flesh.

"Good evening, sir," the mannequin hissed. "Come and take the weight off, kick off your boots, and find a little loving at Madame Choo-Choo's."

Her voice was a sickening parody of what someone—some man—imagined a French lady's voice to be like, high-pitched and giggly, evidently recorded on a wax cylinder that rotated within the dummy's breast. Gideon jumped as Madame Choo-Choo suddenly spewed a little paper chit from her over-rouged lips. Gideon caught it. There was a number printed on it, eight.

As he glanced at it she started up again, the scratchy recording welcoming Bent to the brothel and spitting out his ticket.

"Twenty-three," he read. "My lucky number."

"You boys go right through," said Madame Choo-Choo. "Please don't be abusing the girlsgirlsgirlsgirlsgirlsgirlsgi—"

The dummy fell silent as a meaty hand slapped it around the back of its head. Gideon looked up at the man who stood there, his other hand resting on his gun belt. He had rotten teeth in a fat face, a tarnished sheriff's badge pinned to his leather waistcoat.

"She talks too much," said the man. "Needs a slap now'n again." He bared his stumpy teeth. "Like all women. You'll be the gentlemen from London?"

Gideon held out his hand. "Mr. . . . Smith."

Bent was glaring at him. Perhaps he should have been more creative. The journalist stepped forward, standing deliberately on Gideon's foot, and held out his own hand. "Mr. Jones."

"Smith and Jones," said the sheriff. "Okay. I'm Inkerman, the law around these parts. Mr. Pinch is expecting you. Come on in."

Inkerman pushed aside the thick drapes and nodded for Gideon and Bent to go through. When his eyes became accustomed to the dark, Gideon found himself in a wide room with a long bar on one wall and a shadowed staircase heading up. There were half a dozen tables and couches arranged along the other walls. Arranged on them were half-dressed women, some of them in clinches with men, some moaning, some whispering. At least one was weeping.

The only light came from an oil lamp on the biggest table, around which three or four men sat. Inkerman pointed to it and Gideon nodded, heading forward. Then he saw the figure that could only be Thaddeus Pinch. Even in Hermann Einstein's madcap house, where he had found Maria, Gideon had never seen anything as grotesque as Pinch. The King of Steamtown seemed to revel in the pain his modifications caused him, bearing the suppurating sores where metal met flesh as though they were medals. Pinch looked like a man whose body was a weak inconvenience that needed to be improved, replaced. He looked like a man whose humanity was something to be cut away, excised. He looked like a man whom Gideon Smith was right to fear.

"This is Mr. Smith and Mr. Jones, from London," said Inkerman, pointing to two chairs facing Pinch. As Gideon and Bent sat down Inkerman took his place by Pinch, remaining standing, his hands resting on the butts of his guns.

"Mr. Smith and Mr. Jones," said Pinch, his voice hissing through his metal jaw, saliva dribbling from his teeth in stringy webs. "You're a long way from home, sirs. What brings you to Steamtown?"

"Nice place you got here, Pinch," said Bent, looking around. He brandished his ticket. "What's this all about, though?"

Pinch's jaw wobbled alarmingly, pulsing blood from the bolts at his neck. Gideon realized he was smiling, or trying to. He said, "Choo-Choo's is a popular spot, gentlemen. Sometimes it gets oversubscribed. Impatient, horny men don't make for peaceful times. To make things fair, we give out chits. The number you get equals the girl you get. Saves arguments." He twisted his head to look at the tickets. "Twenty-three. That's Consuela. Fiery little Spanish thing. You'll enjoy her. And Mr. Smith has . . . number eight. Ah, I think that's a fresh little filly we got, still needs a bit of breaking in. You'll have to be firm with her, Mr. Smith. She needs showing who's boss. Still going on about her rights, how we got no call holding her here." He sat back, lifting up his steam-powered arm to reach for his glass of whisky. "She'll learn. They always do, eventually."

"Well, when in Rome . . . ," said Bent. "Though, any chance of a glass of that firewater you're sipping there, Pinch?"

Gideon watched with horrid fascination as Pinch, with a grinding of gears and a whisper of boiling steam, raised his arm. A moment later, a woman appeared at the table bearing a tray with two glasses and a bottle of whisky. She wore a corset in which her breasts barely hid themselves, and a scandalous display of pale flesh between her stocking tops and her bloomers. No skirt of any description. Bent made a happy sound and gave the girl's rump a light slap. Gideon looked at him, aghast. Was this all an act to help ingratiate them with Pinch, or had the journalist so quickly and easily regressed to the base level of the Steamtowners once away from the civilizing influence of the Empire?

Pinch poured Gideon and Bent a glass each of whisky with what Gideon had started to think of as his "good" arm. There was a piano in the far, dark corner that Gideon hadn't noticed before. A man staggered to it, sat down, and began to plonk tunelessly at the keys. Pinch nudged one of his boys and said, "Have him stop or have him shot." Then he turned to Gideon and fixed him with his dark eyes. "Does my appearance disturb you, Mr. Smith?"

Gideon considered for a moment. "Yes."

Pinch laughed. "You're honest. Direct. I like that. Nine men out of ten, fuck, ninety-nine out of a hundred asked that question, they'd say 'No, Mr. Pinch, whatever do you mean? You look as purty as a bitch, Mr. Pinch.' I know what I look like, Mr. Smith. I want to look this way." With effort, Pinch stood and walked to the frosted glass window. "Some folks, they say it ain't natural." He turned to Gideon. "And I say, what the fuck's natural, then? What's natural about this world? Is it natural to wear fancy suits cut from dyed cloth? Is it natural to roast your meat before you eat it? Is it natural for a woman to cover her body just so's a man can rip the clothes from her? Is it natural to fly through the fucking air on balloons, Mr. Smith?"

Gideon could feel Bent's eyes on him, willing him to say the right thing. He said, "No, those things aren't natural, Mr. Pinch. But they're what elevates us from the animals. They're what make us human."

Gideon jumped as Pinch strode over with a clank and a cloud of steam emanating from his leg, pushing his face close to Gideon's. "Yes, Mr. Smith! Oh, yes, Mr. Smith!"

Pinch stood up and glared at his cronies. "Would any of you have the fucking brains to say that? Or would you just stick my cock in your mouths and nod? Jesus, maybe I should get rid of you all and surround myself with people like Mr. Smith here." He sat down again heavily, rubbing the sores at the edges of his jaw. "Yes, Mr. Smith. Those things are what make us human. But what if I want to be better than human? Is that so hard to understand? We fly, Mr. Smith. It's been the dream of man since time immemorial, and now we fly. It is only the flesh that binds us to the natural world, and inch by inch, sinew by sinew, drop of blood by drop of blood, I am replacing the flesh, Mr. Smith. I am becoming as a fucking god."

There was silence in the bar. Pinch's men shifted uncomfortably and directed hooded glares at the Englishmen. Gideon stared at Pinch. He wasn't just strange, he was insane. The sort of insane that chilled the blood. Pinch leaned forward. "Which raises the question, Mr. Smith, me being as a fucking god and all . . . just why are you treating me like I'm some kind of shit-kicking asshole?"

Bent laughed nervously. "Bloody fine hooch you brew up down here, Pinch. Bloody fine. Anyway, what say we have a look around town? See, me and Mr. Smith, we might be in the market for . . . investing in Steamtown. Yes, investing, isn't that right, Smith?" Bent kicked him under the table. "I said, investing, we should have a look around—"

"Shut the fuck up," snarled Pinch.

"Yes," said Gideon quietly. There was no point in lying now, he could see that. Pinch was clearly insane, but he held all the cards. "Best be quiet."

Pinch snapped the fingers on his good hand impatiently and Inkerman, after some fumbling, placed what looked like a rolled-up newspaper or pamphlet in his hand. Gideon's heart sank as he unfurled it on the table. It was a copy of *World Marvels & Wonders*.

"The Battle of London," said Pinch. "I must say, it's a

good likeness of you, Mr. Gideon Smith." He squinted at the penny blood, then at Bent. "Of you, sir, maybe not so much."

"Ah," said Bent. "Looks like the game's up, then." He paused for a moment then said, "Run."

Gideon stood as Bent made a dash for the door, but a volley of clicks brought the journalist to a halt. Ten guns were trained on them. Pinch slammed the penny dreadful on the table. "Did you think we were savages down here, Mr. Smith? Did you think that we didn't thrill to the adventures of the Hero of the Empire? You might be out of the Empire, Smith, but you haven't fallen off the edge of the world." He shook his head. "Jesus H. Christ, the sheer audacity of you English never fails to amaze me. That's why my daddy seceded from your control, why he decided to take his chances alone in this hostile territory rather than get taxed into his grave by some shriveled old bitch of a queen thousands of miles away."

"Mr. Pinch," said Gideon levelly, "I'll thank you not to speak that way about Queen Victoria."

"Are you going to kill us?" asked Bent.

"Probably," said Pinch. "But not yet, and maybe not at all if you give me what I want."

"Which is?" asked Gideon.

Pinch rolled up the copy of *World Marvels & Wonders* and tapped his metal jaw with it. "I found this story very energizing. All this thrilling talk of brass dragons. Funny, then, you should show up when you do. Especially after a certain Mr. Louis Cockayne of my acquaintance tried to sell me a brass dragon not more'n two weeks back."

Gideon kept his face neutral. Cockayne had been written out of the official version of the events that had come to be known as the Battle of London; there was no reason for Pinch to suspect they knew each other at all. He said, "Cockayne stole the dragon from the Crown. We've been sent to get it back."

Pinch nodded. "Then you might do better—and live longer—than Cockayne. You know how the thing flies?"

Gideon shrugged noncommittally.

"Okay, what do you know about this Maria chickadee who flies the dragon?"

Gideon's eyes narrowed. "What do *you* know of Maria?"

"Only that I want her, Smith. I want her to fly the dragon, and I want her to be my queen."

Bent gaped at him. "Your queen?"

Pinch nodded. "The King and Queen of Steamtown. You could say we were made for each other." He began to laugh unpleasantly. He waved at Inkerman. "These fuckers know more than they're telling. Stick 'em in the pen until they're ready to talk. And find that sneaky bastard Hart."

The punks closed in on Gideon and Bent. Inkerman said, "Frisk 'em for weapons, boys."

They took Gideon's Bulldog, and the Colt he had secreted inside his jacket, as well as the hunting knife strapped to his leg. Bent handed over his notebook. "That's all I got," he said. "Pen is mightier than the sword, and all that."

"Frisk him anyway," said Inkerman.

Bent shrugged and held up his arms. "Careful down the trousers, though; there's a couple of open sores on my old feller." He cupped his hand conspiratorially around his mouth. "Touch of the clap. It's very catching, apparently."

The crony held up his own hands and backed off, glancing at Inkerman, who sighed. "Oh, he don't look like he knows one end of a gun from the other anyway. Let's get 'em to the pen."

Gideon held Pinch's gaze as they began to hustle him toward the door. "You're making a big mistake. We're agents of the Crown."

Pinch grimaced, or smiled. Gideon wasn't sure which. "Like I said, you're a long way from home, Mr. Smith. There's only one law in Steamtown, and you're looking at it. We'll have another chat tomorrow morning."

Outside, Jeb Hart silently watched the shapes that moved behind the frosted glass. He couldn't see for sure, but it seemed pretty obvious that Smith and Bent had been found out already. He stole back the way he'd come, back to the stables. He wasn't sure if this was a disaster, or exactly what was expected to happen. He didn't really care. All that he knew was that he was now supposed to get his ass the hell out of Steamtown at the earliest opportunity. He didn't need telling twice.

"That went well," said Bent as Inkerman and his thugs pushed him and Gideon into a dark cell in the squat pen on the edge of the main street. Inkerman locked the iron bars that ran the length of the pen and grinned at them.

"I'm going for something to eat. There are a couple of boys outside, so think on that. You want to piss, there's a bucket in the corner. You want to eat, you wait until I get back, and I'll bring you some vittles. You want to talk, you start hollering. We'll get you to Mr. Pinch."

"What if we just want to agree that this has been a terrible mistake and go home?" suggested Bent hopefully.

Inkerman grinned again. "I'll be back in an hour or so. You boys play nice until then."

When he'd left, Gideon immediately began to shake the bars, but they didn't so much as budge. Bent said, "I wonder what happened to Hart."

"If he has any sense he got out of Steamtown as soon as we were rumbled," said Gideon.

Bent watched him attacking the bars for a moment then asked, "What's the plan?"

"I don't have one," said Gideon. "Do you?"

They both jumped at the voice that came from the shadows they'd thought empty behind them. "Didn't I tell you to always be prepared, Smith? And if you can't be prepared, be lucky?"

Gideon turned slowly, his eyes wide, his jaw dropping. And

there he was, the brim of his hat pulled low over his eyes in the darkness at the back of the pen.

Louis Cockayne.

The Yankee gave a lopsided grin. "And here we are, cell mates. I guess it's your lucky day after all, Smith."

Gideon pulled back his fist, let fly, and knocked Louis Cockayne flat on his backside.

16

JAILBREAK

 "Hey, you don't hit like a lady anymore," said Cockayne, rubbing his jaw. "You been taking lessons?"

"Get up," said Gideon through gritted teeth. "Get up so I can knock you down again."

Bent put a hand on his arm. "Gideon . . . either you're suddenly punching like a pile driver, or someone got to Cockayne before us. Look at his face."

The strength ebbed out of Gideon as he realized Bent was right. Somebody had done a real number on Cockayne, and it wasn't him. He still kept his guard up, though—both his fists and his resolve not to let Cockayne get away with what he had done. He said, "Get up. I won't hit you again."

"My lucky day," said Cockayne, struggling to his feet.

Bent said, "What happened to you? Thaddeus Pinch?"

Cockayne nodded, rubbing the patch of his chin where a fresh bruise courtesy of Gideon was blossoming amid the cuts and swelling. "How'd you guess?"

"Just lucky, I suppose," said Gideon. "Unlike you. Perhaps the next time you steal something that isn't yours you might be a little more choosy who you try to sell it to."

Cockayne raised an eyebrow at Bent. "He been taking lessons in smart-mouthing as well as hitting?"

"He's come a long way since he got his clock cleaned by John Reed on top of that dragon," conceded Bent. "He's doing better than anyone expected, in truth."

Gideon coughed loudly. This was getting away from him. He said, "I am actually here, you know. And I'm less concerned with your . . . your assessment of my progress, Mr. Bent, than I am with where exactly Apep and Maria are."

"That's easy," said Cockayne, sitting down on one of four hinged bunks that folded up flat against the wall. "Little way north of here there's an old mission called the Alamo. That's where Pinch is keeping the dragon, under tarpaulins and very heavy armed guard."

"So you did sell it to him," said Gideon, raising his arm almost involuntarily, ready to deliver another punch.

Cockayne held up his hands. "Well, that's a pretty loose definition of what happened. I came here to sell Apep to Pinch, that's true. And he does actually have possession of it. But no actual money changed hands." Cockayne pinched his nose gingerly, grimacing at the pain. "Think it's broken. In other words, you could say I was ripped off."

"No honor among thieves," pointed out Bent.

"He doesn't seem to have Maria, though," said Gideon. "Unless he's lying. Is he?"

Cockayne shrugged. "Look, maybe I should tell you what happened, from me leaving London to ending up here in Steamtown."

"A poker up your effing arse?" said Bent. "Hell's teeth. He doesn't eff about, this Pinch geezer, does he?"

"No," said Cockayne. "He ain't renowned for effing about." He looked at Gideon and stood up to face him square on. "Look, Smith . . . Gideon. I don't say this very often, but . . . I'm sorry. I got it wrong. I shouldn't have done what I did. I guess I was seduced by the idea of the money."

"You're a pirate, Cockayne. A thief. A kidnapper. I shouldn't expect any better from you."

Cockayne opened his mouth to say something, but Gideon silenced him with a raised hand and a glint in his eye that the American had never seen before. "But I did trust you, Louis. I thought you were on our side. I thought you were helping us."

"I was," said Cockayne quietly. "Swear to God. But something inside me just kind of . . . snapped, soon as I realized I had Maria and Apep in the palm of my hand, soon as I realized what that apple did, what power I had."

"And the first thing you think to do when you get something so powerful, so wonderful, so beautiful in your hands? Sell it to the highest bidder."

Cockayne shrugged. "We all try to be better humans, Smith, but sometimes we can't help but give in to our baser urges. It's what keeps guys like me out of heaven, or nirvana, or whatever the hell you want, I guess. Do you know what I mean, about giving in to your urges?"

Gideon hit him again, sending Cockayne sprawling to the floor. "Yes," said Gideon with some satisfaction. "That was me giving in to mine."

Cockayne sat on the bunk, his head tipped back, holding his nose. "Smiff, cad I ast you just how benny tibes you're gonna hid me?"

"That's it, for now," said Gideon.

Cockayne pinched the bridge of his nose and blew out a glob of blood and snot at Gideon's feet. Sniffing, he said, "That's better." He glanced at Bent. "They ain't sent Gideon to sense-of-humor school yet, then?"

Bent chortled. Gideon shot him a look. "Whose side are you on?"

"Smith, Smith, we're all on the same side now," said Cockayne warmly. "You came looking for me, right?"

"We came looking for Maria and Apep," said Gideon. "You're only useful for telling us where to find them."

"And as soon as we get out of here I'll take you to where we crashed." Cockayne nodded enthusiastically. "We can start the search there. So, what's the plan?"

There was a moment of silence. Gideon looked at his hands. Bent began to whistle tunelessly. "Come on, Inkerman will be back soon," said Cockayne urgently. "What's the plan? You rode into Steamtown, got yourself thrown into the same cell . . ." He paused. "You did know I was in the pen, right?"

Bent wrinkled his nose.

"Getting yourself arrested wasn't part of the plan?"

Gideon gave the minutest of shrugs.

Cockayne slapped his hand against his forehead, which hurt so much he swore violently, took off his hat, and stamped on it several times. "Jesus shit, Smith! You haven't got a plan at all? Haven't you learned anything?"

"We were sort of playing it by ear. . . ." said Gideon quietly.

Cockayne picked up his hat and screwed it into a ball, pushing his bruised and battered face into Gideon's. Gideon flinched away. "I'll give you playing by ear . . . Jesus shit, Smith!" He unrolled his hat and slammed it back onto his head. He began to stalk up and down the cell. "Okay, we're going to have to improvise. What weapons have you got on you?"

Gideon held his hands wide helplessly. He'd had the upper hand, and Louis Cockayne had turned everything on its head, like he always did in those card games. Now Gideon was on the defensive. He said, "Uh, nothing. They frisked us and took it all."

"And you didn't save anything? You haven't even got a stiletto knife up your ass?"

Gideon winced and Cockayne turned away. "I don't believe it. Not only am I going to die, I'm going to spend my last days with you two." He looked up at Bent. "I suppose there's no point asking you."

"Well, actually," said Bent, unbuttoning his fly, "I did manage to keep a little something back. . . ."

Cockayne's eyes lit up. "Knife? Gun? Dynamite?"

Bent glanced around conspiratorially and delved into the folds of his trousers, emerging with a small hip flask. "Nicked it from Governor Lyle's drinks cabinet. Spirytus, it said on the label. Polish, I think. Don't know what the eff it is, but it's ninety-six percent proof." He chuckled. "Should make the long nights fly by."

Gideon groaned. "Alcohol, Bent? For a minute there I thought you had something useful."

"Maybe he has," said Cockayne thoughtfully. "Give that here."

"Hey," said Bent as Cockayne snatched the hip flask from his hands. Cockayne flipped the top and sniffed it. "Jesus." He forced the stopper back in. "Okay, Inkerman's on his way back. Here's what you've got to do."

Inkerman strolled back into the pen after holding a half-audible exchange with whoever was guarding the cell outside and, surmised Gideon, relieving them of their watch. The fat sheriff—though his office probably had more to do with the privileges it afforded him in this godforsaken place than any innate sense of justice—sauntered into the pen, chewing on a strip of jerky, and regarded them with his ratty little eyes.

"Well, well, well, ain't this cozy," he said through a mouth-ful of beef. "Three little piggies. Maybe I'll huff and I'll puff . . ."

"And maybe I'll blow your head off," muttered Cockayne. He winked at Gideon, who nudged Bent in the ribs.

The journalist stepped forward, clicking his fingers through the bars. " 'Ere, Inkerman. Cockayne says you can be relied on for a light. I'm dying for a ciggie."

"You got any?" said Inkerman. "I ain't standing you a smoke. And did laughing boy tell you the drill?"

He nodded at Cockayne, who was glaring at him. Bent produced a flat tin of rolled cigarettes and held it through the bars. "Have one of mine, if you like."

Inkerman grinned and took one, which he slid behind his ear. "Very good of you. I gotta say, you're one helluva more amenable houseguest than Mr. Cockayne." He paused. "Still gotta insist on the drill, though."

Bent nodded and stuck a cigarette in his mouth, pushing his face into the space between two bars and holding his hands out as far as they would go behind him. Inkerman struck a match and held it out toward Bent, who maneuvered the end of his cigarette into it and sucked hard. When it was lit, Bent backed off and Inkerman held up the match to Gideon. "You having one?"

Gideon shook his head but said, "I think Cockayne will."

Cockayne had already pushed his face against the bars, holding his hands out behind him. Inkerman looked at him, then at the match. He let it fall from his fingers, and it burned itself out on the dirt floor.

"Aw, look at that. It was my last match, as well."

Cockayne said nothing, simply stared impassively through the bars. Inkerman shrugged and dug in his waistcoat pocket for another match. "Cat got your tongue, Cockayne? Aw, you're no fun when you won't get riled." He struck the match and held it out. "Suit yourself. Your smokes are numbered, anyhow."

The match hovered around the end of Cockayne's cigarette, Inkerman guffawing as he kept the flickering flame just out of reach. Cockayne raised one eyebrow and grinned back, the cigarette falling from his lips. Then he spat a spray of the colorless spirit Bent had filched from the governor's cabinet, enveloping the match and expanding the flame with a *whump* into a fireball that engulfed Inkerman before he had time to even scream.

"Quick, before he falls backward!" yelled Cockayne, and Gideon, having the longest reach of any of them, stretched through the bars and grabbed hold of Inkerman's belt. The fat sheriff's head was a blackening ball at the center of the yellow flames, and Inkerman was slapping at his face. Gideon grimaced as he pulled Inkerman hard into the bars, and Cockayne hit him once in the face, pulling his fist back and shaking it.

"Goddamn! I don't know what hurts most, the burning in my hand or the burning in my throat. What the hell did you say that stuff was called, Bent?"

"Spirytus," said Bent, gazing in horrified fascination at Inkerman as he slid down the bars. "Do you think we should put him out?"

"You got the keys?" said Cockayne.

Gideon jangled the bunch he'd extricated from Inkerman's belt. "Bent's right . . . we should do something."

"You get the bars open before this whole place goes up," said Cockayne. Inkerman had flailed backward, spreading the fire to the papers on his desk. Cockayne unbuttoned his fly and Gideon gaped at him.

"Is he getting the old chap out?" asked Bent. "He is! He's going to—"

Cockayne let loose a stream of piss that hit Inkerman in his head and sent clouds of acrid steam rising to mingle with the black smoke filling the pen. Gideon shook his head and fumbled with the keys until he found the right one and the cage doors swung open.

"Wait there," said Cockayne. "I need to check that the coast is clear."

He dipped into the smoke and reappeared a moment later. He winked at Gideon and kicked the cage shut, neatly whipping out the bunch of keys. He said, "You never do learn, do you, Smith."

"You effer!" shouted Bent, rattling the bars. The door was stuck fast.

Gideon glared at him. "Like a dog to its vomit."

Cockayne grinned. "I'm doing this to prove something, Smith."

"That you're a bastard?" said Bent.

"No. That you can trust me." He reached down and unlocked the cage. Behind him, Inkerman moaned. "Just remember, I could have left you in there. But I trust you, Smith, so you gotta trust me."

"When hell freezes over," said Gideon, dragging Bent out of the cage. "But for now . . . come on, let's get out of here."

"One minute," said Cockayne. He bent down and retrieved

his pearl-handled guns from the shuddering body of Inkerman. Gideon gagged at the smell of roasting flesh. Inkerman's head was a blackened thing running with its own juices. Cockayne whispered, "Told you that you were at the top of my shit-list, Inkerman." He put the barrel of one gun against the man's head. Even in the smoke-filled pen, Gideon could read his pain-filled eyes. *Do it. Please.*

"The old Louis Cockayne was a real bastard who'd leave you to burn," said Cockayne. "Count yourself lucky I'm a reformed character, and you can thank Gideon Smith for that."

Gideon turned away as the gun reported with a loud echo. Cockayne emerged from the smoke, his face grim. He held open the door. "Now for the hard part, Smith. We have to get out of Steamtown alive."

※

Cockayne led them into the dusty, dark alleys off the main drag, taking them between the clapboard houses and edging along the shadowed verandas on the largely unlit streets into an area that was dominated by single-story whitewashed stone buildings.

"The old Spanish quarter," whispered Cockayne, holding up his hand as a horse-drawn wagon, a tank of water sloshing on the back, rumbled past in the direction they'd come from.

"Eff to the tour, Cockayne," gasped Bent, leaning against the wall, a hand on the stitch in his side. "Just get us out of here."

"I'm trying to," he said. He looked at Gideon. "I'm going to take us west, thread through some of the coal mines and the slave quarters. They'll be expecting us to be making for the Wall."

There was shouting from the edge of town where the pen was located, and when he looked back Gideon could see the underside of the black clouds painted a dull orange. Cockayne squinted into the night sky and frowned. "The fire's spreading," he said. "Should keep them busy for a while."

Cockayne paused between two buildings, at a wide road

that was better lit than any of them would have liked. He held up his hand, glanced around the edge of the dark house in both directions, then led them softly out on to the dust track.

And right into a sudden pool of light that erupted from a dozen strongly focused oil lamps that were abruptly exposed. There were six men on horseback flanking a trio of grumbling crablike vehicles that were spewing steam and coal dust from their exhausts. Their steel-plate armor casings were mounted above a series of wheels covered in what looked to Gideon to be hinged metal belts, creating snug tracks on which the wheels could mount almost any low-lying obstacle and negotiate any terrain. Suddenly he plucked a memory from an old issue of *World Marvels & Wonders*, a Lucian Trigger adventure that he recalled also featured Louis Cockayne . . . in the theater of lies and half-truths that Gideon now knew the penny blood stories were. That wasn't to say everything in the adventures was false—Lucian Trigger might have embellished the escapades of his lover, Dr. John Reed, for public consumption, but Gideon had to assume that much of it, the menaces included, were based on fact.

Menaces such as these. Gideon sensed Cockayne whipping out his pearl-handled revolvers, hefting their familiar weight now that they were free from Inkerman. Unfortunately, the relief Gideon felt at Cockayne's keen eye beside him was drowned out by the volley of clicks from the rifles held by the men on the horses and clinging to the growling vehicles. Cockayne muttered, "Great. The Bowie Steamcrawlers."

"No point running, Louis," rasped a voice from behind the bright lights. It was Thaddeus Pinch. "Might as well just come quietly now."

"So you can torture me?" shouted Cockayne. "No thanks, Pinch."

"What about you, Mr. Smith? Mr. Bent? What say we talk about this like adults, huh? I'm hardly going to cause harm to two agents of the Crown, am I?"

Bent murmured, "He's got a point, Gideon."

"Yeah," said Cockayne. "A red-hot one he nearly rammed up my mark, back the way we came, right?"

"What's the signal?" hissed Gideon.

"This."

Cockayne's guns spat twin explosions again and again, each bullet unerringly finding an oil lamp. Some flared and died, and some sprayed their unfortunate holders with blazing oil. As the street was plunged into darkness filled with the shouts of the men and the roar of the Steamcrawlers, Cockayne pushed Gideon and Bent back, taking the lead and winding through the narrow spaces between the stone buildings until the houses thinned out and the pit towers reared up ahead in the darkness. The rumbling of the Steamcrawlers was replaced by the clanking of the mine gear.

"There's a quarry beyond the mines," said Cockayne, glancing behind them. "We should be able to slip down into that and leave the Steamcrawlers standing. Then we've just got to get out the other side before Pinch summons the wherewithal to get a posse around the quarry."

"I'm effed," said Bent. "We need to rest."

"No time," said Gideon. "We have to keep moving."

Behind them, the shouts grew louder. Gideon grabbed the panting journalist by the sleeves and dragged him onward, between two tall wire fences that bordered two adjacent mines. A group of negroes sharing a bucket of water with a long-handled ladle in the dull light of one of the mines watched impassively as they ran past. Gideon wanted to stop and tell them that he would free them, somehow. Then he felt wretched and naïve. It wasn't his mission to wage war on Texas, to free its slaves. What would he tell these dull-eyed men who watched him rushing by? That he could do nothing to help them right now, but he would write a letter in the strongest possible terms to the authorities when he returned to England?

"Smith, quit daydreaming. We got a problem."

Gideon blinked as Cockayne put out an arm and stopped his progress. He felt stones and loose earth crumble at his feet, and he realized he was on the edge of a yawning chasm, its far side in darkness and its bottom hidden by shadows far below.

"I thought you said this was an effing quarry, Cockayne, not a canyon."

"They must've done a bit of work since the last time I was here," said Cockayne apologetically. "Shit. I'm out of bullets as well."

Gideon turned slowly as Pinch, sitting on top of the lead Steamcrawler, rolled inexorably toward them between the mines. His bizarre vehicle stopped, juddering and exhaling steam, the barrels of three guns fixed on Gideon from dark slits in the Steamcrawler's armor.

"Nice, huh?" said Pinch, patting the Steamcrawler. "Jim Bowie left 'em to me after he got himself iced in the desert. I said to Bowie, you got to know your limits, your boundaries. He was always off in places that didn't concern him, having adventures and getting the British and Spanish royally pissed. Me, I know my place. Steamtown." A match flared, igniting the end of his cigar, reflecting in his dark eyes in a way that spelled pure crazy to Gideon. "And I'm the fucking King of Steamtown, gentlemen, and I will have my due tribute."

Pinch picked up a rifle and trained it on Gideon, his deputies locking Bent and Cockayne in their sights. He said, "We've been blasting the shit out of this quarry with dynamite for a year now. It's two hundred and fifty feet to the bottom. Either you jump or you get a bullet in your heads. Don't rightly give a shit which you do, myself. But I thought I'd give you a choice." His metal jaw wobbled, his blackened teeth bared. "I'm good like that."

17

Payment in Kind

Carefully following the instructions that had been left with her, Rowena stood on the observation deck of the *Skylady III* and aimed her Lime Light Signaling Lamp in the direction of the cluster of distant lights around the black shape that crouched on the pale horizon. San Antonio. Steamtown. She was half an hour away, and they would have sighted her long ago, readying their defenses against the incoming 'stat. Only transmitting the coded message—it seemed to be a string of numbers broken up by words such as "blackbird" and "eagle," "bugle" and "spoon," utter nonsense—would cause Steamtown to hold its fire and allow her to land in the airfield the manifest told her was on the east side of the town. Rowena flashed the signal three times, hoping that someone at the other end had a signaling telescope trained upon her and was transcribing the message that would enable her to approach unmolested.

Flashing the code left her just her enough time to get the QF three-pounder Hotchkiss from the armory out to the observation deck. According to the helpful notes, the airfield was adjacent to several warehouses containing—Rowena surmised—coal. Which meant she would need help retrieving the Hotchkiss and her collection of incendiaries. Coal burned very nicely, and the Hotchkiss would be the flame she put to the touch paper of Steamtown.

Rowena strode from the observation deck into the bridge and surveyed what she'd found when she burst the lock and chain off the hold. There were fifty-four of them, evidently payment for the cargo of coal she had been hired to take back to New York. She'd felt sick when she first opened up the hold, sick to her stomach that she'd been involved, no matter how unwittingly, in this. Then she had reconsidered. Better that it was Rowena Fanshawe who had taken the contract than someone who would have followed the orders to the letter.

"I need some help," she announced. The fifty-four faces turned to her. "I need to bring some equipment—artillery and ammunition, mostly—from the armory up to the observation deck. I need strong arms and, more importantly, steady hands."

There were five or six hesitant hands raised, then more, until eventually all of her passengers were volunteering. Even the children. That someone had quite happily sold children into slavery for a 'stat's hold full of coal . . . she didn't feel sick anymore. She felt angry.

When Rowena had first jimmied the lock off and opened the door the fifty-four pairs of eyes regarded her with a mixture of slight interest, fear, and hatred. And why not? As far as they were concerned, she was just another link in the chain that was dragging them from one wretched life to another. Half of them were black, and after she'd unchained them all and taken them up to the galley (a Frenchman with them had rustled up the most marvelous stew from ingredients Rowena, a self-confessed terrible cook, kept in the larder) she did a quick census. The blacks were mainly the descendants of slaves from the South who had moved to the British territories when the Mason-Dixon Wall was being built. In British America they had been free, true, but by no means as liberated as the whites in New York, especially when it came to finding work and places to live. Black people tended to congregate in the Harlem district, and these families reported that slaver gangs who haunted the shadows were a regular and well-known hazard. While nightsticks and knives had been used to cajole many of the people in Rowena's 'stat to the North Beach Aerodrome, the slavers also used more subtle means.

"I applied for a situation on the docks," said a broad, shaven-headed man named Oscar, hugging in his protective arms a wife with downcast eyes and three small girls with rags tied in their hair. "The pay was good. They said they'd like to meet the family, make sure I wasn't some union plant. I brought us all down to the warehouse." He shook his head, tears welling up in his eyes. "They took us all at gunpoint to the airfield. Told us we'd all be getting a new situation, all right, me down the mines and Catherine here . . ." He hugged her tighter still.

"No one's going down the mines, and no woman is working . . . working anywhere in that horrible place. Not while you are under my protection."

"And who are you, if you don't mind me asking?" The accent was Scottish, from a young man who must have been one of the British citizens of little or no resources who had taken cheap passage to America to help build the Empire State. They were of the masses, the great unwashed, those unwanted, unloved, and unmissed by the upper classes. And in America they had found not the promised land, but others like them. Among the other captives Rowena had noticed down-at-the-heel Italians, a pair of German brothers, a contingent of homegrown Americans with no stable income or proper roots. The Empire had diffused many wonderful concepts and inventions around the world, reflected Rowena. Unfortunately, many not-so-great ideas had also followed the British colossus that bestrode the world, and the class system was one of them.

"Me? I'm Rowena Fanshawe of Fa—"

"Of the Captain Trigger adventures?"

She had been about to say "of Fanshawe Aeronautical Endeavors" when the young Scot interrupted her. Something in his shining eyes reminded her of Gideon, and her stomach churned unexpectedly. Was he down there, ahead of them in the gathering darkness, in that pit of vipers? Was he hurt? Was he even alive? And did she care, beyond their friendship, beyond the sense of brotherhood they shared from adventuring high in the airways and beyond?

She smiled. "Yes, of the adventures."

As the young Scot began to relate, in hushed whispers, a précis of Rowena's greatest moments (or, in the case of some of the accounts by Lucian Trigger that had appeared in *World Marvels & Wonders*, most outrageous lies) she turned her attention to what would happen when they finally reached Steamtown.

※

They were still bound for Steamtown despite Rowena's discovery. Her first thought on facing her motley and unexpected group of passengers had been *what the hell am I going to do with you lot?*

"I have enough fuel for the return trip," she'd said. "Do you want to go back to New York?"

A few hands had raised, but Oscar had snorted. "Back there? Where they sold us into slavery? Land of opportunity indeed."

Those hesitant hands had sunk down. Rowena looked at the prairie passing below them. "I could find a cavalry garrison, let you off there . . . ?"

The passengers looked at each other and shrugged. They had no homes to go to. They had come to America looking for a new life, and found only betrayal. Rowena drummed her fingers on her chin. "I suppose I could make for Free Florida . . . or even New Orleans. . . ."

Despite Governor Lyle's brief rundown back in New York of the geography of America, there was much more to it than the major colonies of Britain, Japan, and Spain, Rowena knew. There were any number of places she could take the freed slaves. Free Florida was a community of runaway slaves from the Confederate States and Texas, its northern border always in danger from raiding parties and vengeful lynch mobs. Between the Confederacy and Steamtown squatted Louisiana's dark, haunted swamps and wide, sluggish rivers. New Orleans was witch haunted and redolent with legend, but at least free.

These people might even find a home in the Free States

of America, a growing territory north of the Wall, unrecognized as a nation-state by the British but home to those rebels who had shipped out of the East Coast after the failed revolution in 1775.

Rowena would have to stop somewhere to take on more fuel, but maybe she could even get them to Rooseville or New Jerusalem, or any one of the independent little communities springing up across the plains between British America and the Californian Meiji.

But, of course, all of those options meant abandoning what she had come down here to do in the first place.

"What do you want to do?" Oscar had asked. "Where do you think we should go?"

Rowena shook her head. "I can't make that decision for you."

"Were you planning to go back to New York after delivering your cargo?"

Rowena bit her lip. "Not quite. I only took the job as cover. . . . I'm on something of a mission of my own. My friends are in Steamtown. I think they're in trouble."

The others had gravitated toward Oscar and his easy authority. Rowena withdrew, letting them speak in hushed tones and the occasional raised voice, while she fussed over the instruments and maps.

Eventually Oscar said, "Miss Fanshawe?"

She returned to the crowd. "What's it going to be, then?"

Oscar looked around at the other expectant faces. "Miss Fanshawe, we can make a decision as to the rest of our lives later. For now, we are agreed that we have much to thank you for. Without you, we would be sold into slavery. If you have friends in trouble in Steamtown, then that is where we should go." He swept his hands around the bridge. "But what when we get there? I hear they have terrible weapons in Steamtown."

Rowena smiled broadly. "So do I, Oscar. You want to see 'em?"

In the armory Rowena put Oscar and two others on the three-pounder Hotchkiss and gave another two men each a crate of shells. She said, "Don't trip, don't slip, and for God's sake don't drop them, or we're all going up in flames."

When the Hotchkiss was bolted to its mooring on the observation deck, she asked, "I don't suppose anyone has any experience of flying a 'stat?" Steamtown was looming closer, and she needed to put the *Skylady III* into what looked from the ground like a landing pattern.

Naturally, no one had, so she picked the two who seemed the most levelheaded—the young Scot and a dependable-looking Dutchman—and took them to the control panel. She put the *Skylady III* in a gentle descent and locked the course, giving her two new copilots the briefest of introductions to the wheel and meters so that they could at least get the 'stat up into the air and possibly even bring her down safely should something happen to Rowena out on the deck.

Outside, the warm wind was picking up as they nosed gradually downward toward the now-visible lit strip of a main drag, surrounded by labyrinthine streets of wooden houses and stone buildings. Over the town loomed the tall mining towers, winking oil lamps at their peaks. Ahead of the 'stat was the airfield, picked out in swinging lamps, with the space between the airfield and the town taken up by low warehouses and barns.

Oscar handed Rowena one of the incendiary shells and she carefully loaded it into the Hotchkiss. She said, "As soon as we're close enough I'm going to let fly. You keep handing me those shells until I say stop. You others, keep those crates steady, don't let them slide about."

Oscar nodded, and Rowena lined up the sights on the tall airfield tower. She was getting close enough to see activity on the ground now; there were no other 'stats in sight, but several figures milled about at the base of the tower. She felt a sudden pang then pushed it away. There may well be innocents down there, but she had to assume that anyone who had their liberty in Steamtown was at the very least complicit in the town's crimes.

"Who's behind this?" she asked Oscar. Slaver gangs hiding in the shadows she could understand; even elaborate confidence tricks to hook in whole families. But someone must be coordinating the slavers, negotiating human lives for coal, contracting 'stat pilots. From what she'd heard of Steamtown it was a raucous, lawless stew of forced labor in mines and brothels. The smarts to organize an exchange of resources must be coming from New York.

Oscar shrugged. "My grandfather was a slave in the fields of Alabama. He won his freedom and came north. I remember my grandfather, though I was only small when he died. But I remember him talking about the British, about how they freed the slaves." Oscar laid a hand on the crate of shells. "I suppose as long as someone is willing to buy men, women, and children, someone else is always willing to sell them."

Rowena put her eye to the sights again. Someone in the wooden tower was signaling to them with a lamp; Rowena should be checking the Morse code against the notes in the manifest, and probably preparing a response. Instead she ran her final checks over the Hotchkiss.

"Time to send Steamtown a message," she said. "Stand back, boys. This is going to make one hell of a racket."

⁂

"Thaddeus," said Cockayne. "Be reasonable. We can talk about this."

Pinch's men trained their lanterns on the three of them, and Pinch said, "Time for talking's long past, Louis. You had your chance. Now's the time for shooting, or jumping."

Gideon took a step back and felt the edge of the quarry crumble beneath his heel. He couldn't see the bottom of it. Perhaps if they jumped, there might be a ledge or vines or . . . but no. That sort of thing happened in *World Marvels & Wonders*, in the Lucian Trigger adventures he'd devoured as a boy. Such chance salvation just didn't happen in real life. He'd been given an unreasonable worldview by Captain Trigger's breathless prose, and he had learned the hard way that fortune and plot devices don't shape stories; people do.

"Pinch," he said. "Need I remind you that I am the appointed representative of Her Majesty's Government and—"

"And I'm his official chronicler," interrupted Bent, glaring at Gideon. "So I'm just as important as he is."

The crablike Steamcrawler edged forward with a shudder and a sudden exhalation of exhaust gases. Pinch leaned forward, his jaw glinting in the lamplight. "Don't fuck with me, Smith. If this was any kind of *official* mission they wouldn't have sent a greenhorn and a lard-ass."

"I object!" said Bent. "Gideon's not fat."

"You need us," cut in Gideon. "You need us to tell you how to fly Apep."

"Apep?" said Pinch. "That's what the dragon's called?" He turned to one of his deputies. "Any of you bastards read and write? Jesus, Cockayne, I can't believe you fried Inkerman. He wasn't much to look at, I know, but at least he knew his letters." One of the cowboys raised a tentative arm. "Write that down on something. Apep. We'll go raid a library somewhere, bring some books back."

"We can tell you all you need to know," said Gideon carefully.

Pinch laughed. "Like I said, Smith, you all had your chance to talk. I got enough from Louis; there's a clockwork chick called Maria who flies the thing. All I have to do is find her. After that, it shouldn't be too difficult. I can be very persuasive, after all."

There was a distant noise that seemed at odds with the clamor of Steamtown. Gideon glanced at Cockayne and Bent, who were looking up; they'd heard it, too.

"Er, Mister Pinch, sir . . ." said one of his cronies.

"Enough yapping," said Pinch. He cocked his pistol. "What's it going to be, Smith? You taking a dive over the edge, or do you want a bullet in your head? I ain't got all night."

"Mister Pinch . . ."

"What?" said Pinch irritably, turning to the cowboy, just as the night was illuminated by a blossom of pale fire far behind them.

"Holy Jesus shit," spat Pinch after a stunned moment. "Steamtown's under attack."

"You seem to be enjoying this," said Oscar as he passed Rowena another shell with his large, steady hands.

She loaded it swiftly into the Hotchkiss, the observation deck of the *Skylady III* illuminated by the flames from the blazing warehouse below them. "I would be lying if I said I didn't find it somewhat liberating," said Rowena, as she took sight along the gun and discharged the shell with a thunderous roar. She straightened and peered into the smoke-threaded gloom, nodding in satisfaction as another squat building exploded into flames.

"I do not like being told where I can and cannot go," she told Oscar. "And I certainly do not like men who trade in human lives as though they were cattle. Now, what do you say we take some of those mines out next?"

"I would advise caution," said Oscar. "Weren't the men on this dirigible bound for those mines? There might be slaves down there, even at this late hour."

"Yes," she said, resting a hand on the Hotchkiss. "You're right, of course. I—"

Rowena jumped as something whistled past the observation deck with force and speed. She leaned over the balustrade. "Damn. Steam-cannon."

"The gas that keeps us aloft will burn if we are hit?" Oscar frowned.

Rowena shook her head. "Helium won't burn at all. But a hit from one of those iron balls they're tossing with compressed steam muscles could certainly bring us down. Playtime's over, I think. Oscar, can you take good care of these

incendiary shells? I don't want them rolling all over the place.
It's time I took the helm of my 'stat."

Rowena fought through the crowded bridge and took the
wheel. She gave the *Skylady III* more power and began to bring
her higher. They'd done a good deal of damage to the eastern side of Steamtown; she felt satisfied with that. The question was, what now? She needed to get her cargo out of here
and to safety. She wondered where Gideon and Bent had gotten to. Squinting through the smoke ahead of her, she picked
out the main drag of Steamtown and, over to the west, a lot of
activity clustered around the base of two tall pit towers: bright
lamplight and the scurrying shadows of men. Rowena raised an
eyebrow. She could pick out trouble like more refined women
could pick out the scent of a posy of flowers. A little look
wouldn't hurt, as they were in the neighborhood.

The young Scot was standing by her like a devoted puppy.
As she neared the commotion she saw a wide, black space
dropping away, a canyon or quarry. And what were those
things? Not Jim Bowie's Steamcrawlers? They were! In a
circle around . . . oh. She looked at her admirer. "All right,
Hamish, stop staring down my shirt and listen carefully. Find
Oscar out on the observation deck. There are two rope ladders coiled on the hull of the gondola. Here's what I need you
to do."

Cockayne punched Gideon in the arm. "Well bloody done,
Smith. I knew you must have something up your sleeve."

Gideon stared wordlessly at the flames licking the black
sky on the far side of town. "This isn't my doing," he said.

"Shut the eff up," said Bent. "Take credit where you can."
He looked at Cockayne and rolled his eyes. "You really need
to give this boy some lessons in being a bastard, Cockayne."

Pinch had his back to them, staring at the sky and shaking
with undisguised fury. *If I only had a gun*, thought Gideon.
Or even a knife. Once he might have blanched at the thought

of shooting a man in the back. That was before he came to Steamtown.

"This is an act of war," seethed Pinch. He turned around on top of the Steamcrawler and pointed his metal hand at Gideon. "You have done this! There will be retribution! Your government will pay!"

"Nothing to do with me," said Gideon. "How would a greenhorn and a lard-ass bust up half your town, Pinch?"

His eyes burning, Pinch raised the gun again. "I just made your decision for you, Smith. Say your prayers."

Gideon smiled. "I already have. And I think they've just been answered."

He heard Bent gasp as the familiar balloon of the *Skylady III* emerged from the smoke-filled sky above them. Cockayne gave Gideon a quizzical look. "Rowena?"

He nodded. Pinch looked up, his metal jaw hanging slack, his gun arm falling to his side, as the dirigible soared over-head, and two rope ladders swung out of the night sky.

"Grab on," said Gideon, taking Bent's arms and locking him onto the nearest ladder as it trailed across the dust. Cock-ayne didn't need telling twice, leaping onto the other ladder. A bullet whistled past Gideon's head, and he turned to see Pinch boiling with anger, trying to hold his gun steady.

"This ain't over, Smith," he rasped.

"No," said Gideon. "I wouldn't imagine it is." Then he took a running jump off the edge of the canyon and into the darkness, his hands grasping the wooden slats of the rope lad-der that Bent clung to with his eyes shut tight.

※

"I could kiss you," said Bent as he was hauled over the edge of the observation deck. He blinked in surprise at the multi-tude of smiling faces and the hands that dragged at his jacket. "Blimey, Rowena, picked up a few friends?"

"I'll explain later," she said, helping Gideon on to the deck. She embraced him tightly.

"I thought you were told to stay out of Steamtown," he said.

She kissed him on the cheek. "I never was any good at obeying orders from men."

She turned as another figure clambered over the railing and gave her a lopsided grin. "Hey, Rowena, do I get a smacker as well?"

"Louis Cockayne," she said. "You sure do." Then she punched him as hard as she could in his already black-and-blue face.

He picked himself up onto his elbows. "Jesus, Rowena. You hit harder'n Smith here. You're still a sight for sore eyes, though."

Then the sky was rent by a piercing whistle, and the observation deck bucked and swung wildly as something hit the *Skylady III* with force and speed.

18

SOMEWHERE BETTER TO GO

"We're hit," said Rowena above the screaming from the packed bridge. "Steam-cannon. Shit."

The *Skylady III* lurched alarmingly to port as Rowena wrestled with the wheel. She tapped the pressure gauge with her fingernail. "We're losing gas from the aft-starboard cell."

Gideon struggled to her side. "Are we going to crash?"

She tugged at the wheel, pulling their nose upward, as another cannonball whistled perilously close alongside the 'stat. "What's below us?"

"A quarry," said Gideon. "Pinch said it was two hundred and fifty feet down."

Rowena swore again, hauling on the wheel as a crunch sounded from the rear of the gondola. "Got us again. Missed the balloon, though."

"What can I do?" asked Gideon, holding on to the instrument panel as the 'stat rocked violently.

"Are you religious?"

"Not really."

She leaned forward and kissed him hard on the lips. "Then no use in praying. I'll take that for luck instead. Get everybody down on the deck and tell them to cover their heads. I'll get us the hell out of Steamtown."

Gideon did as he was told, trying to calm the fifty-odd strangers who were crammed on to the bridge. He looked back as Rowena wrestled with the wheel, and the yawning fear in his stomach subsided somewhat as the *Skylady III* steadied. They were in good hands with Rowena, he knew. Bent crawled across the bridge toward him, panic in his eyes.

"Is this it, Gideon? Are we going to die?" He swiveled his

broad head in alarm. "And among strangers, too. Who the hell are this lot?"

"I think we're rising," said Gideon, climbing to his feet. Rowena was leaning forward over the wheel, breathing heavily. He called, "Rowena?"

"Steadied her," she said, looking back at him. "That was some good-luck kiss."

"I think we're out of range of their cannons," called Cockayne from where he was perched in the doorway to the observation deck. "My, Steamtown looks lovely when she burns."

"The aft-starboard cell is completely gone," said Rowena, studying the instruments. "And the port side's losing gas, too." She looked at Gideon. "I can keep us aloft, but not for long, and not for very far. Any ideas?"

"There's a British army garrison to the east, along the Wall," he said.

She shook her head. "I passed that on the way down. No chance we'll make that."

"What about that farm?" said Bent, steadying himself on the hull. "Just north of the Wall. Plenty of space there. And that farmer owes us one, by my reckoning."

Rowena shrugged. "Sounds like as good an idea as any." She began to turn the 'stat. To their left, dawn was paling the sky in the far east. "Mr. Bent? One of my guests is a rather accomplished chef, from France. Perhaps you could take him down to the galley, see what can be rustled up? Perhaps everyone can be accommodated in the stateroom."

Bent sniffed. "He'll have to go a long way to beat my famous rum-and-sausage breakfast. But I'm willing to give it a go." Bent turned to the crowd, slowly picking themselves up from the deck. "Don't panic, ladies and gentlemen, I'm a member of Her Majesty's Press, and a bona fide, medal-wearing hero to boot. If you'll all follow me, we'll get some grub and then you can form an orderly queue and tell me all your lovely stories."

As the *Skylady III* limped into the lightening sky, the prairie ahead of them turning from deep red to golden brown, Rowena told Gideon and Cockayne of the strange cargo she had brought to Steamtown.

"And you have no idea who contracted you?" said Cockayne.

She glared at him. "If you're going to say something smart, Louis, then don't. Just don't. Of course I would never have taken on such a job ordinarily, but I wanted an excuse to get to Steamtown."

Cockayne held up his hands in mock surrender. "Hey, don't hit me. I was just asking."

Gideon nursed a tin cup of coffee from the pot that Bent had sent up. He stared at the unfolding landscape, the 'stat flying low and slow, seemingly just skimming the eerie rock formations that rose up from the desert. "Trading people for coal." He shook his head. "I'll have to do something about it."

Rowena laid a hand on his arm. "Gideon, you can't save the world single-handedly," she said softly.

"She's right, Smith," said Cockayne. "We need to focus on the matter at hand. Though I bet you'd damn well give it a go if you could."

Rowena raised an eyebrow. "You know, Louis, someone who didn't know you might think you actually like Gideon Smith."

Gideon felt his cheeks burning despite himself. Cockayne laughed. "Smith? He knocked me flat on my back. What's not to like? He actually hits like a man these days."

Gideon looked at him. "Why did you do it, Cockayne? Why did you steal Maria from me?"

"Do you love her?" asked Cockayne. "That clockwork thing with a dead woman's brain?"

Gideon narrowed his eyes then looked away. Cockayne said, "Why can't you admit it, Smith? What's holding you back? You've been halfway around the world chasing this little chicky, and you can't come out and say you love her?"

"Leave it, Louis," murmured Rowena.

Cockayne shook his head. "Uh-uh. Smith here's a great one for passing judgment on the rest of us. 'Why'd you do it, Louis?' Or 'Must you keep farting, Bent?' And 'Don't touch my pecker, Rowena.'"

"Shut it," said Gideon quietly.

Cockayne put his battered face against Gideon's. "Just fucking admit it, Smith," he hissed through his broken teeth. "You're hot for a pile of gears and pistons with a whore's brain. Just fucking admit it, fisherman."

"All right, I admit it!" roared Gideon. "I love her! Is that so fucking difficult for you to understand?"

Rowena touched his arm again, and he looked to where an ashen-faced Bent was leading the others up the ladder to the bridge. They were all stock-still, staring at him.

Cockayne laughed. "No," he said quietly. "No, it's not too difficult to understand. What I didn't understand was why you wouldn't give in and say it, Gideon. It's one of the things that make you what it says on your wage packet. It's what separates you and me and Rowena and even our friend Bent from them." He cocked his head slightly to the passengers. "Being a hero isn't always about shooting guns and spouting platitudes. Sometimes bravery's just about having the gonads to stick your head above the parapet and say, 'Hey, I'm different. And I don't give a rat's ass.'"

Gideon felt the anger drain from him. Cockayne winked and Rowena sighed. "You and your little heroes' club," she said, but Gideon caught her giving Cockayne a small smile. Bent approached and said, "I have no effing idea what all that was about, but . . . ain't that the farm?"

Gideon looked ahead. "Yes, I think it is."

"Then we'd better get a wriggle on. Looks like Farmer Giles is up and leaving."

"You're spooking the goddamn cattle!" shouted Oswald P. Ackroyd, holding fast to the reins of his horse as it whinnied and stamped its hooves on the dry earth. He'd waved Albert on to try to keep the thousand-strong herd moving, and Caroline was driving the covered wagon, from which the girls peered out in awe at the thing that cast its long shadow over them.

"Mr. Ackroyd," called Gideon, cupping his hands around his mouth. The *Skylady III* was barely fifty feet off the ground now, Rowena holding their course steady as the crippled 'stat continued to lose altitude and power. "It's me, Gideon Smith. And Mr. Bent. Do you remember us?"

"I remember you," shouted Ackroyd. "What the hell are you doing?"

"We need somewhere to land, so we can try to repair our ship. Are you leaving the farm?"

Ackroyd shielded his eyes against the rising sun and nodded. "We got somewhere better to go. You ever hear of the Nameless?"

Cockayne, at Gideon's side, nudged him. "Tell him yeah, we've heard of the Nameless. Tell him we want to see him."

Gideon looked at him. "Do we? Why? Who is he?"

"Tell you later," said Cockayne. "Heard his name mentioned back in Steamtown."

"Where did the Nameless tell you to go?" called Gideon.

"Follow the Wall west and then take a bearing southwest in ten miles. Keep going until you see an abandoned mine."

Gideon looked at Cockayne. "That sounds uncomfortably close to Steamtown for my liking." He turned back to the bridge. "Rowena? Think we can make that?"

She bit her lip as she looked at the instrument panel. "We'll have to."

As the *Skylady III* began to jerkily wheel away from the cattle drive, Gideon waved. "Thank you, Mr. Ackroyd. We'll see you there."

*   *   *

"Where the *fuck* is Billy-Joe?" seethed Thaddeus Pinch. Inkerman might have been an ugly cuss, but he had enough smarts to keep his boss informed. These ass-hats Pinch had surrounded himself with didn't know their cocks from their noses half the time.

"I think you sent him across to Uvalde," said one of the ass-hats, scratching his ass-hat head.

Pinch cuffed him upside his cauliflower ear. "I know that. But he should be back by now. Where is he?"

They all scuffed their boots in the dust. "Don't think they came back, Mr. Pinch, sir."

Goddamn it all. He was surrounded by cretins. Which was all he could expect, them being fleshly and weak. And all around him, his beloved Steamtown burned. Most of the coal stores had gone up in flames. He'd heard that indentured men from three of the dormitories had fled east during the confusion. That was damn near a hundred men. Someone told him that in one of the brothels on the north side of town the women had up and knifed all the men in their beds, and gone into the night as well.

But he still had the dragon. He'd made sure of that, tripling the guard on the Alamo. Gideon goddamn Smith wasn't going to get his hands on it anytime soon. Besides, no one knew where this Maria was. Pinch shook his head at the thought of it. A clockwork toy that looked like a living, breathing woman, with all that power at her fingertips. It had given him a hard-on just to picture her in his mind's eye, even as he stood in the chaos, watching the crippled airship banking into the night sky. But where the hell would you find such a thing, lost in the deserts of Texas?

It was then that he'd remembered what Billy-Joe had told him in the saloon. He'd been too fixated on the Nameless, too worried that the spooky fucker was going to come and give him shit in Steamtown. Not that it mattered now. Steamtown was all but gone. Let the Nameless come and walk down the main street with his stupid patchwork clothes like some crazy frontiersman. Let him go up against Thaddeus Pinch. Some stupid prairie legend against a man who was practically a machine god? Let the fucker try.

Yes, he'd been too focused on the Nameless to listen to what Billy-Joe had been trying to tell him. *And there was something else. . . . The Nameless had this girl over the back of his horse. She looked dead. Had a giant key sticking out of her back.* Hellfire and damnation. A girl with a key in her back. Maria.

"You," said Pinch. "Do you know where Billy-Joe and the others went yesterday? When they ran up against the Nameless?"

One of the other cretins raised his hand hesitantly. "I do, Mr. Pinch, sir. They were over at one of the old abandoned mines, maybe twenty miles west. Close to where the Yaqui have their camp."

Pinch clapped him on the shoulder with his metal arm. The man didn't flinch. He was either smart or too stupid to be afraid. Either way, Pinch could make use of him. "What's your name again?"

"Larry, Mr. Pinch, sir."

Pinch dug in his pocket and flipped the burnt sheriff's badge he'd plucked from Inkerman's charred corpse at him. "You've just been promoted, Larry. Now get me every available gun who isn't guarding the dragon, get every Steamcrawler still in working order fired up, and have them at the gates in an hour."

"Where are we going, Mr. Pinch?" asked Larry.

Pinch cuffed him in the head. "Don't ask questions. Just do it."

He looked out into the dawn. He was going to get his queen, she was going to fly his dragon, and then Gideon Smith, Louis Cockayne, and any other bastard who had ever crossed Thaddeus Pinch were going to get the wrath of Steamtown down on their sorry asses.

※

Someone had been busy—either Chantico or the mysterious gringo who had no name. Inez suspected the latter. She loved Chantico dearly, but he didn't strike her as the type to be able to do so much work on the old house. Much of the roof had been repaired already, and several of the rooms had been cleared of rubble. Thankfully, the bodies of the dead Texans had also disappeared without a trace. The house was almost pleasant now, and in the kitchen area there was a big barrel of water, cold and fresh. The Nameless must have done all this, must have filled that up from the creek. Six skinned rabbits hung from a hook in the kitchen, and there were yams and berries piled up on the stone work surface.

Almost like home. But where was Chantico? The Nameless had patched up a lean-to behind the house where the horses could be tethered, with a water trough and piles of dried grass. Inez's horse, exhausted after the long early-morning ride from Uvalde, was the only one there. She had thought Chantico would be here to meet her.

She went to the interior room where they had put the clockwork woman—she was so heavy!—and secured the door with a padlock they had found amid the bits and pieces scattered around the building. There were no windows, so there was no chance of anyone finding her there. Inez cursed herself for letting Chantico keep the key. Where *was* he? Hung on a nail on the door was a small leather pouch of Yaqui design, and a note scrawled in Chantico's spidery hand. He was rare among his tribe for the ability to read and write both Spanish and English so well, and she was proud of him. His letter to her was no great literary achievement, however. It simply said *Lo siento*. Sorry.

Inez rattled the door handle. What was he sorry for? Not being here? She tipped the pouch into her cupped hand and gasped. There was a red stone in there, as big as the top of her thumb, which seemed to glow with its own internal life. Its setting looked like gold, and it was tangled in a golden chain. It must have been obtained by Chantico on one of the many Yaqui trading expeditions. It was quite beautiful. She searched through the warren of rooms (whoever set up this place really must have thought the mine was going to bear fruit, because there were rooms for a score of men here) and found a wash-room with a big stone sink and even a tarnished tin bath. There was a cracked mirror, mottled with blossoms of mold, on the wall, and Inez fastened the gold chain at the back of her neck, admiring the red stone at her breast. She looked herself in the eyes, moving a thread of hair from across her eyes, and suddenly her stomach lurched. Her room in the casa at Uvalde, the hot running water, her dresses and boots and nice things . . . she had left them all behind. For a Yaqui boy and, it seemed, a tumbledown house in the middle of bandito country. Had she any idea what she had done?

Inez tucked the pendant away within her shirt and smoothed down her skirts. The Nameless had made a fine start, but there was plenty to do before this place was livable, and no better time to start. She had some matches in her sidesaddle and could get a fire going in the kitchen; perhaps a rabbit stew could be on the hob for whenever Chantico decided to show his face. She touched the lump of the amulet at her breast. Just so long as he didn't get the idea that she would do all the cooking and cleaning while he swanned around on tribe business, so long as he threw her the odd trinket now and again. She had given up her old life and was not about to embrace a new one that was just as restrictive. This was a new world, and Chantico had better get used to it.

After she had diced the rabbits and got a big pot of water boiling on the stove, Inez found a long stick and tied a few lengths of dry brush to one end to fashion a passable broom. The house really was coming along nicely. A few rooms still had no roof, and the shutters on all windows but the one in the room that Inez had mentally marked out as her and Chantico's bedroom needed repair, but her vigorous brushing had worked yet more wonders in the large rooms. There was a distinct lack of furniture, of course. Either they would have to think of a way to trade, or Chantico would have to get busy with chisel and wood saw. Inez paused to take a drink of water from her hip flask. It was barely daylight, and she had achieved so much. But where was that blasted Chantico? She took his note from the pocket of her skirts and read it again.

Lo siento.

A sharp pain suddenly stabbed her heart. What, exactly, was he saying sorry for? What if his own heart had gone cold; what if he had deserted her? She bit her lip, just as something caught her eye on the horizon, a billowing cloud of dust rising up before the ascending white-hot orb of the sun. Riders? Steamtown riders?

No. The swirls of sand were being dragged into the air by something else, something huge and unwieldy that charted an erratic course toward her, *close* to the ground but unmistakably *above* it. Inez's makeshift broom fell to the dust and her jaw slowly dropped.

It was an airship.

19

La Chupacabras!

"So . . . your cover was blown, you were thrown in jail, half of Steamtown has been blasted to smithereens, and you've whisked fifty slaves from under Thaddeus Pinch's nose," said Cockayne over a pot of hot coffee on the bridge. "And you've still failed to get back the brass dragon or locate Maria. You did say this was a *secret* mission, Smith?"

"One we wouldn't have to undertake at all but for your rank criminality, Cockayne." Gideon scowled.

"Seconds out, round two." Bent chuckled. "'Ere, Rowena, you should have seen Gideon lay Cockayne out in that cell with one punch."

Cockayne put his shoulders back. "Only because Pinch's goons had tortured me half to death. Anytime you want to try again, Smith . . ."

Rowena put her head in her hands. "For God's sake. You're like a bunch of schoolboys."

Cockayne raised an eyebrow. "Says the woman who got trigger-happy with a QF Three-Pounder Hotchkiss. Jesus Christ, Rowena, you don't do things by half, do you? You know Pinch ain't gonna rest until he's had his pound of flesh now. He'll be madder'n a scorpion."

"Which might work in our favor," said Gideon. "If he's angry he might make mistakes."

"You got a plan?" asked Bent.

"If it's as good as your last one, we can all expect to be getting intimate with red-hot pokers real soon," said Cockayne.

"Strictly speaking, Mr. Cockayne, you're in my custody for the theft of property of the British Crown and abduction of one of its subjects. I removed you from that jail—"

Cockayne blinked. "*You* removed *me* from jail?"

"—from that jail in San Antonio for the express purpose of allowing you to redeem your earlier crimes by helping in our mission to locate and liberate Maria and the brass dragon Apep," finished Gideon, his eyes locked on Cockayne's. "If you want, I can hand you over to the custody of the nearest British garrison and arrange for you to be transported back to London to stand trial."

"Jesus," breathed Cockayne. "Pinch'd never get a poker up your ass. You already got a stick jammed up there."

Gideon scowled. Was even Rowena trying hard to hide an involuntary smile at that? He said, "So yes, I do have a plan. We're going to land the *Skylady III* at this settlement Mr. Ackroyd told us about, then we're going to effect whatever repairs are necessary."

"Then?" asked Cockayne.

"I'll tell you when we get there," finished Gideon lamely. He knew the others knew he didn't have any idea at all. But he couldn't show how weak and useless he was. They were relying on him.

Cockayne pointed through the glass. "Good. I'll look forward to it, because I think the place is coming up right now."

Inez watched from the shadows of the house as the airship—impressively huge, though listing badly—limped in and cast down its anchors, which dragged in the sand until they snagged on rocks and tree stumps, bringing the vast dirigible to a bobbing halt. Winding gears brought the gondola down to just a few feet off the ground, and then the occupants began to disembark down a wooden stairway that unfolded from an observation deck. A woman first, in white shirt and khaki breeches, followed by three men, one of them fat and in most unsuitable clothing for the prairie, and then a veritable flood of people—children, too. They certainly didn't look like Steamtown rabble, so she ventured out of the cool stone building and watched them from the sun-kissed veranda, which had also been patched up remarkably well by the Nameless. The woman and three men who had dropped to the ground first seemed to be the most assured and in charge, and they immediately began scouting around, inspecting the abandoned mine shaft and turning their attention to the house, where they eventually sighted Inez. She raised a hand in greeting, and they began to approach. Just to make sure, she cocked her rifle's safety and laid it out in plain sight on the wooden rail running around the veranda.

"I am guessing you are a long way off course," she called in English.

The woman, who had very short hair but was strikingly beautiful, smiled at her. "In a way. We're far from any aerodrome, true, but we were heading here." She pulled off a leather glove when the four of them arrived and held out her hand. "I'm Rowena Fanshawe, and that's my 'stat—sorry, airship— the *Skylady III*. She's in a pretty bad way, I'm afraid."

Rowena turned and introduced the others. "Mr. Gideon Smith," she said of the handsome young man with curly black hair. Then she pointed toward the older, fat man, squinting at the sun and sweating already. "Mr. Aloysius Bent, a journalist."

"Charmed," said Bent, mopping his brow with a dirty handkerchief. "Christ, it's effing hot."

The tallest of them touched the brim of his hat, his mustache twitching. "And I'm Louis Cockayne."

Rowena, Smith, and Bent were English, Cockayne American. Inez nodded and said, "I am Inez Batiste Palomo."

"Is this your home?" said Smith.

She glanced back at it. She supposed it was, now. "Yes, in a way." She frowned. "You said you were making for here? But why?"

"Long story," said Smith. "We had a little . . . trouble in a place called San Antonio. You know it?"

Inez spat in the dust. "Steamtown."

"She knows it." Bent chuckled. "Some chap called Ackroyd, runs a ranch north of the Wall, he told us to come here.

He's on his way with a thousand head of cattle. Those Steamtown thugs burned his farm down. Said he was told there was a new community here." He turned to Cockayne. "Who did he say told him to come?"

Cockayne was watching Inez closely. "The Nameless. You ever heard of him?"

She nodded. "New community? And this farmer is coming here?" She looked at the crowd that had gathered around the gondola of the airship. "And these people . . . ?"

"They were on their way to Steamtown, sold into slavery," said Rowena. "They have no home. . . ."

Inez chewed her lip for a moment then said, "You had better all come inside. I have water, and there is a rabbit stew on the stove." She clicked her tongue. "Although I wasn't expecting so many for dinner . . ."

After the stew—vastly bulked out by an impromptu rabbit-hunting session on the prairie—was gone, Inez and Rowena organized the passengers into small parties to clean up the rooms and to go and get fresh water from the creek, as well as to gather bundles of reeds to form makeshift beds. Bent and Cockayne stood on the veranda, smoking, while Gideon stalked up and down in the dust. Bent had his notebook out and showed it to Cockayne.

"You know Japanese, Cockayne? You ever seen this symbol?"

Cockayne glanced at it. "Can't say I have. Where's it from?"

"On the neck of a ninja tried to assassinate the New York governor. Something about it's been getting my goat."

Cockayne took another look and shrugged. "Japanese, Chinese . . . I can never tell their writing apart, I'm afraid."

Bent put the end of his pencil thoughtfully in his mouth, then looked up, annoyed, as Gideon kicked up a cloud of dust. "Sit down, for eff's sake, I'm trying to concentrate."

"I can't," said Gideon. "I need to be doing *something*."

"Listen to him, Smith. You're just expending energy."

Rowena and Inez came back from where they had been inspecting the 'stat. Bent murmured, "Pretty little thing, the Spanish girl."

Cockayne raised an amused eyebrow. "You noticed?"

"Well?" asked Gideon. "What's the verdict?"

"She isn't going to fly again anytime soon," said Rowena, wiping grease from her hands with an old rag. "Two cells completely deflated."

"She needs special gas to fly?" asked Inez.

"Helium." Rowena nodded. "I need an aerodrome or a big city. What's the nearest major settlement in New Spain?"

"I was made to learn the classics back in Uvalde, where I lived before . . . before," said Inez thoughtfully. "Helium is from *helios*, yes? The sun?"

"Yes," said Rowena absently. "It was named because it has a yellow signature on the spectrum. . . . How big is this Uvalde? Does it have an airfield?"

"No." Inez pointed toward the abandoned mine. "But the Nameless, he said that he could see a gas coming from the pit. He said it looked like sunshine."

Rowena frowned. "Helium is invisible to the human eye."

Inez shrugged. "He said he could see all kinds of things."

Rowena was tapping a finger on her chin. "It's possible . . . it's naturally occurring underground. . . ."

"There's a portable helium gauge on the *Yellow Rose*," said Cockayne excitedly. "And a small liquefaction engine. For emergency extraction."

"I know," said Rowena, glaring at him. "And she's the *Sky-lady III*, not the *Yellow Rose*. I'll check it out."

"I'll help," said Cockayne, flicking his cigarette into the dust.

"No need," said Rowena tightly. "I can do it."

Gideon turned to Cockayne. "Wait. You said you'd heard of this Nameless. Who is he?"

Cockayne shrugged as Rowena walked back to the 'stat.

"There's lots to tell, but it's all hearsay and legend. I've heard tales of the Nameless for years. They say he was born in 'seventy-five—"

Bent laughed. "He's a boy?"

Cockayne gave him a withering look. "*Seventeen* seventy-five."

"But that would make him more than a hundred years old," said Bent.

"Seventeen seventy-five," said Gideon. "The year of the failed rebellion."

"Some say he's walked the land ever since, trying to put things right," mused Cockayne. "According to some stories, he's no longer human. Others, they say he never was. I never saw him, and never met anyone I trusted who said they did."

"I have met him," said Inez. "He was here. He saved us from the Steamtown rabble."

"Us?" said Cockayne.

"Chantico is my . . . my lover. He is Yaqui Indian. We were meeting here when we were ambushed. The Nameless saved us. I had a . . . a disagreement with my father in Uvalde, and I have come to live here with Chantico. The Nameless said things were wrong, that the land should not be split up between the great powers, Britain and Spain and Japan. He thought he had found what he was looking for with us, with this place."

"And what was that?" asked Gideon.

"America," she said softly. She looked around at the small knots of people who had been bound for slavery in Steamtown. People with nowhere to go. Nowhere but here. "I didn't know what he meant, but now . . ."

She blinked and looked up. "There is something else. He wanted us to look after . . . well, I was going to say a woman. But she's made of clockwork."

"Maria!"

Inez jumped as Gideon grabbed her by the arms. "A clockwork woman? Maria? He had her? Where is she?"

"You're hurting me," she said.

Cockayne pulled him off. "Smith, calm down for God's sake."

"I'm sorry," said Gideon, taking a deep breath. "But that is why we're here. We're looking for Maria . . . she looks like an ordinary woman. Very beautiful."

"Very beautiful," agreed Inez. "Apart from the key in her back."

Gideon felt his legs buckle, and Bent put out a hand to steady him. "Is she well? Did she say anything?"

Inez shrugged. "She is unconscious. Wound down. I don't know what you would say. You want to see her?"

Gideon gaped at her. "She's here?"

Inez led them into the house, along the dusty corridors to the inner room where she and Chantico had laid Maria. The door was locked, and Inez rattled the handle irritably.

"That idiot Chantico has the key," said Inez. "I thought he would be here now."

"No problem," said Cockayne. "Stand back."

He put his boot against the padlock, braced himself on Gideon and Bent, and kicked hard, twice, until the wood splintered. Inez pushed open the door. "She is in—oh."

The room was empty.

Gideon made a muted roaring sound and punched the stone wall.

"Calm down, Smith," ordered Cockayne. "This Indian must know where she is, if he's got the key. We just need to wait until he gets here."

"Where does he live?" asked Gideon. "We should go there now."

Cockayne held up his hands. "Whoa, Gideon. You don't just go riding into Yaqui camps shouting your head off." He gripped his shoulder. "We've waited this long, another hour or two won't kill us. Besides, you're beat. We're all beat. We've been up all night. We need some rest or we're no use to anyone."

"Amen to that," said Bent, yawning. "Where can I lay my throbbing head?"

"We have collected reeds. You will just have to make a rough bed," said Inez.

"I'm so knackered you could hang me on a clothesline and I'd sleep for a day," he said.

"I'm going to turn in as well," said Cockayne. Bent farted, sighed, and departed. "Though not in the same room as him. Wake me if there's any trouble. Smith, I suggest you get some sleep, too."

"I'll go and see if Rowena needs any help," said Gideon as Cockayne went to find a quiet room. He looked at Inez. "Thank you. For taking care of Maria."

"We haven't done a very good job," she said.

He smiled. "Cockayne is right. We'll find her when Chantico comes back. I'm sorry if I hurt you before."

Inez said, "This Maria, she is your . . . you are . . . ?"

Gideon nodded. "I know. It's difficult to understand."

She shook her head. "I know what it is like to love someone different from yourself." She smiled. "Though maybe not *so* different."

"You are going to rest, too?"

"No," she said tightly. "I have just remembered something I have to do."

Inez felt like crying tears of anger. *Chantico, you* idiot! She stared at the note in his feathery scrawl. *Lo siento*. Presumably he had been too cowardly or too *idiotic* to write what he really meant. Sorry for stealing the clockwork girl. She stalked up and down the room she had assigned to them—to them! He was going to have to swim a sea of horseshit if he wanted to share her bed again!—and kicked at her saddlebags on the cold stone floor. The question was, where had he taken her—where had he taken Maria? She remembered his look of guilt and reproach when the Nameless had mentioned the *place of power* near the Yaqui camp. Why had Chantico never mentioned that? Could he have taken Maria there? If so, presumably he had done this in secret. The Nameless would hardly abet Chantico in taking Maria away when he had expressly said that they should keep her safe here. Perhaps the Nameless somehow knew, in his grim prairie spirit way, that someone would come looking for Maria. She kicked the saddlebag again, and the rapier she had taken from the casa skittered along the floor.

Inez had never been to the Yaqui settlement, but she knew it was just over the far side of the canyon, beyond the hills. Not far at all. She rummaged in the saddlebag and pulled out Chantico's black shirt and trousers, the silly mask. Back in Uvalde . . . the people, they had truly thought she was El Chupacabras. The Texans had been scared of her, and the townsfolk had been inspired. Perhaps . . . she swiftly unbuttoned her blouse. Perhaps El Chupacabras would ride again, put right whatever idiocy Chantico was *lo siento* for. But no. Not El Chupacabras. El Chupacabras had gone. Like Sergio de la Garcia. Like Chantico. Like the Nameless. Men went away, or were weak, or idiotic, or all three.

She pulled on the black shirt, buttoned up the trousers, and fastened the cowl tight around her head. No, not El Chupacabras at all. She took up the rapier, hefted it in her gloved hand.

La Chupacabras!

"Can you fix it?" asked Gideon.

Rowena laughed lightly. "I love the faith you have in people, Gideon. But yes, I think I can. The gauge is showing that there is indeed helium down that mine. Whoever started digging for coal must have fractured the rock and released it." She looked out across the prairie. "This whole landscape could be full of it, just below the surface. Anyway, without boring you, there's a long, laborious process of liquefaction to extract it and turn it into usable lifting gas, and this"—she patted the large, square device on wheels, as big as a steam-cab with twice as many pipes, pistons, and valves across its back—"is going to do the job. In the meantime, I'm going to get the balloon patched up. Are you any good with a needle and thread?"

But Gideon was looking into the distance, where a wide dust cloud was approaching. "What now?" he said.

Rowena climbed on top of the liquefaction engine and peered through a brass extendable telescope. "Don't panic," she said. "It's our friend with the cattle."

Gideon glanced back at the house. "Have you spoken to those people who were bound for Steamtown? What do they want to do?"

"Unsurprisingly, not many of them are keen to return to New York. They've been betrayed by whichever company or organization was rounding up immigrants and packing them off to trade for coal. And, by extension, they've been betrayed by the British government itself."

"Do you think they'll stay here?" he wondered. "The rancher talked about a new community. . . ."

Ahead of the approaching herd, two figures on horseback emerged from the swirling cloud. Oswald P. Ackroyd and his nephew, their chaps yellow with trail dust, hailed Gideon and brought their horses to a halt near the *Skylady III*.

"Howdy, Mr. Smith. You beat us here, then?"

Gideon nodded at the 'stat. "Only just."

Ackroyd let himself down from his horse and stretched, looking around. "The Nameless was right. This is a nice spot. And that's good grazing land over yonder." He frowned at the stone building, at the people sitting around in the morning sun. "These folks all live here? We're gonna need a bigger homestead. Good thing Albert's handy with a saw and hammer."

Gideon followed his gaze and frowned. There was a figure all in black creeping away from the house, leading by the reins the only horse there—Inez's. While Rowena pointed out the creek and the arable land to Ackroyd, Gideon picked up her telescope and put it to his eye, taking a moment to focus on the figure—which, it turned out, was masked as well. Even so, that fan of black hair, the voluptuous shape . . . it could only be Inez herself. But where was she going, and why was she dressed so outlandishly?

Gideon turned to Ackroyd. "A fine horse you have."

Ackroyd patted the mare. "Strong as an ox, this one. She could do that journey twice over without breaking a sweat, there and back."

Gideon smiled. "In that case, do you mind awfully if I borrow her?"

20

MARIA

++VERNACULAR ASSIMILATION: TRUE++

++HOST BRAIN TO BODY-MASS RATIO 1:40++

++BRAIN: ORGANIC MATERIAL. NONORGANIC MAKEUP:
GLASS, COPPER, BRASS, DRIED ANIMAL SKIN++

++AUTOMOTIVE FORCE: MAINSPRING-POWERED MECHA-
NISM ACHIEVING VARIOUS LEVELS OF TORQUE. COLLO-
QUIAL: CLOCKWORK++

++FUSION OF BRAIN/CLOCKWORK COMPONENTS TO
ACHIEVE INDEPENDENT AUTOMOTIVE FORCE: 96
PERCENT COMPLETE. HOST REMAINS IN STASIS++

++READYING SIGNAL++

++DOPAMINE LEVELS: INSUFFICIENT++

++SEROTONIN LEVELS: INSUFFICIENT++

++OXYTOCIN LEVELS: INSUFFICIENT++

++SIGNAL TRANSMISSION: FALSE++

++AWAITING FURTHER DEVELOPMENTS++

Chantico hung back in the dancing shadows cast on the lime-
stone walls by the torches, the bag containing the diverse and
mysterious treasures that had been found with the clockwork
girl hanging from his hand. He had made a terrible, terrible
mistake.

Inez was going to be furious with him.

He had been to the abandoned mine at dawn and man-
handled the clockwork girl—so heavy!—on to the back of his
horse. The Old Man had been delighted with his work, but
Chantico felt sick to his stomach. Still . . . what was a bunch
of cogs and gears, no matter how much like a living woman it
looked, when balanced against the life of his beloved?

He hoped Inez would see it that way, too.

The clockwork woman was stretched out on the altar, the Old Man standing at her head, presiding over the gathering. There were more people than he had ever seen in the cave, perhaps thirty. Word had spread like wildfire that the Old Man was going to do something special, that he was going to bring Quetzalcoatl to save the Yaqui people.

So why did Chantico feel so bad?

The Old Man was swaying, his eyelids fluttering, his gnarled hands on either side of the clockwork girl's head. In the basin below, the gathering swayed along with him. Someone was banging a drum in rhythm with Chantico's pounding heart, and the people began to hum, low and steady, like an approaching swarm of insects. Chantico's blood roared in his ears, and he redoubled his grip on the bag.

The drumming stopped.

The Old Man opened his eyes.

He licked his lips and rasped, "Life is because of the gods; with their sacrifice they gave us life, eh? They produce our sustenance, which nourishes life. In return, we make our own offerings."

He raised his hands in supplication.

"Quetzalcoatl is a just god and does not demand the spilling of human blood. It was Tezcatlipoca, angered by what he saw as Quetzalcoatl's weakness in this regard, who imprisoned the great feathered serpent in brass and metal and sent him crashing in flames to Earth, eh?"

Chantico frowned; this was new. The Old Man was embellishing the story. Chantico took a step forward, out of the shadows. Despite himself, he was intrigued to see how a thing that was not alive could be sacrificed, and just what effect it would have.

"Thus," said the Old Man, "a suitable sacrifice must be found. And we have been delivered this mockery of a woman, a thing neither alive nor dead, with which to parlay for Quetzalcoatl's return to grace."

The Old Man looked around the crowd, their faces hidden in shadow. He put his hands together and steepled his fingers in front of his dry lips. Then he whispered, "Quetzalcoatl appeared to me in a vision last night, eh? I took the fruit of the peyote into myself and asked for guidance in the desert. And guidance came."

The crowd gasped. Chantico frowned even deeper. Something was terribly, terribly wrong about all of this.

The Old Man nodded vigorously. "Quetzalcoatl told me that his captor is a man who is half human, half machine. They call him Pinch, but he is in truth the earthly visage of Tezcatlipoca himself!"

Several of the Yaqui fell to their knees, moaning.

"But Tezcatlipoca has struck a deal with Quetzalcoatl. He said he would free him if Quetzalcoatl could bring him a wife who was less human than he. Quetzalcoatl asked how this was possible, as he was a prisoner. Tezcatlipoca told him that his worshippers would rise to help the lord of the morning."

The Old Man held out his arms. "Behold! We have in our hands the key to Quetzalcoatl's liberation! And will the Yaqui not forever be the favored children of the Lord of the Star of the Dawn?"

A roar went up from those in the cavern. Chantico thought his heart might burst, but whether it was from pride or fear he could not really tell.

"We must take the bride to Tezcatlipoca, eh?" declared the Old Man. "Come, now! Let us lift her and carry her off! To Steamtown, to parlay the release of the great god Quetzalcoatl!"

Steamtown? Chantico looked at the others, but their eyes were shining with fervor; they moved forward, reaching for the clockwork girl. Steamtown? They would be slaughtered.

"Stop right there!"

Chantico looked up, across the cave to the tunnel that led to the outside. The crowd fell silent, the flickering flames from the torches casting their orange glow on a black-clad figure, masked and holding a shining rapier high.

"That girl is under the protection of La Chupacabras!"

Oh, Inez, thought Chantico furiously. *What in the name of the gods are you doing?*

⁕

Inez Batiste Palomo had never felt so alive. Her heart hammered fit to burst, but it gave wings to her feet. She leaped from the rock to the sloping ground, dancing on her toes, spinning around and bringing her rapier down—*movimiento natural!*—in a fluid slashing motion, causing the surging crowd to halt and fall backward. Every lesson she had learned seemed burned upon her head, so that she barely had to think of an action, and she was already fulfilling it. *Tajo!* She cut in a sweeping movement across the Indians. *Estocada!* She thrust her weapon at the nearest, forcing him back into the natural basin at the center of the torch-lit cave. She twirled almost within the arms of a grasping Indian—*medio de proporcion!*—and pirouetted away, casting around to take in the situation. About thirty Yaqui, in an agitated mood. A stone slab, some kind of altar, on which lay Maria. An incredibly ancient Indian, in faded, stiff robes, his scrawny neck garlanded with strings of beads and leather thongs, glaring at her with shining eyes.

And there, skulking in the shadows like the thief in the night that he was, stood Chantico.

Idiot, she mouthed at him.

Lo siento, he mimed back.

She stood straight, breathing hard, and held out her sword arm straight, the rapier extended toward the old man.

"You. Release the girl."

He raised his head, looking down his crooked nose at her. "It is not a girl, eh? It is a machine."

He reached into his robes and withdrew a gun. Colt .45, if Inez identified it correctly. Not the usual Yaqui weapon of choice. He smiled and said, "You, on the other hand, are a girl. Young Chantico's Spanish whore, I believe. And you will bleed. It appears Quetzalcoatl will have his sacrifice this day after all."

Gideon groaned. A cave. Why was it always a cave? He was a child again, on his ill-planned venture into the tunnels that marbled the Lythe Bank near his home of Sandsend, lost in the darkness, feeling the weight of the rock pressing down on him, squeezing the life out of him, until his father, Arthur, had come to get him, carrying him out into the precious sunlit day. He had thought he had conquered his fear when he was forced to enter the underwater passageway that led to the Rhodopis Pyramid in Egypt, spurred on by Louis Cockayne's assertion that his fear was merely a lie. But Gideon knew, deep down, that such a terror could never be truly dispelled, only buried. And the yawning mouth of the cave ahead of him suddenly and clearly excavated his fear once more.

But much had changed. Then, he had been a small boy. Then, he had been a mere fisherman's son. Now he was the Hero of the Empire. Or so they kept telling him.

Gideon slid off Ackroyd's horse and tethered it in the shadow of a flowering tree. Inez's own horse was tied to a rock by the cave entrance. Whatever her reason for donning that strange outfit, she had come here and gone into the depths of the rocky hill. He could only guess that it had to do with her lover, Chantico, and that it was in some way connected to Maria.

He swallowed hard. He had come so far looking for Maria. He could not fail now. Checking the revolver he had taken from the armory onboard the *Skylady III,* he ventured forward and allowed himself to be swallowed by the darkness.

The black was not total, however. The dim echo of torch-light illuminated a path through the rocks and into a wide, tall tunnel leading off from the cave entrance. He could hear voices, too. Slowly, he picked his way along the passageway, the flickering light brightening as he advanced, until the tunnel opened out into a large interior cavern. Gideon crouched down beside a rocky outcrop, assessing the scene before him. There was a mass of people, mainly young, with shining eyes and dark faces. Indians, congregating in a basin, facing a raised dais around which he could see Inez—masked, with a rapier held out straight, but unmistakably Inez—with a young Indian at her side. Her weapon was pointed at a thin, elderly Indian, who clutched a gun in his clawed hand. Between them was a rough stone altar.

His heart leaped.

Maria.

"And you will bleed," said the old man, his rasping voice echoing around the torch-lit cave. "It appears Quetzalcoatl will have his sacrifice this day after all."

"Not if I have anything to do with it," said Gideon, standing up straight. He reached to the stone wall and plucked a flaming torch from where it had been driven into a fissure, and he held it high, making sure they could see his gun.

"Who are you?" growled the old man, keeping his gun trained on Inez.

"Señor Smith!" she exclaimed.

"That's right. I'm Gideon Smith. The Hero of the Empire. I don't know what is going on here, but Maria is coming with me."

The old man laughed, which was not the reaction Gideon was hoping for. "The dust runs red with the blood of a thousand heroes, eh? Your empire means nothing here, Gideon Smith. You are simply another dead man."

The old man moved with a speed Gideon didn't expect, bringing around his gun arm and letting loose a shot that exploded in the rock by his head, the report bouncing off the cavern walls. He shouted something at the gathering in his own language, and the crowd moved forward toward Gideon.

"How many bullets, Gideon Smith?" cackled the old man. "Enough for all of them, eh?"

Gideon waved his gun and fired above their heads, the bullet pinging off the cavern roof.

"Please!" shouted the boy Gideon assumed was Chantico. "Please, they do not mean ill. They are under his control!"

Even had he wanted to kill them all, the old man was right. Gideon didn't have enough bullets. He saw Inez swing forward with her rapier, nicking the old man on his tissue-dry cheek, just as the mob fell on Gideon, dragging him from his perch. He swung the torch around, but there were too many of them, punching and kicking and hauling him toward the altar where Maria lay, still and quiet. *At least I'll die alongside her*, he thought crazily. *At least I found her*.

Through the melee he saw the old man wiping blood from his cheek, leveling his gun at Inez. "You shall die for that, bitch, and you, too, Chantico. You are a traitor to the Yaqui."

Someone wrestled the gun from Gideon's hand and he was dragged along the stony floor, flung forward and up until he rolled to Inez's feet. She tore off her mask and glared at him.

"Why did you follow me?" she hissed.

"I came to help," said Gideon.

"Now we all die," she said.

The old man had been passed Gideon's gun, and he pointed both of them at Inez, Gideon, and Chantico. Gideon thought, *If I get out of this alive, I swear I shall never again do anything without a proper plan*.

"Any last requests?" The old man grinned.

"Yes," said Gideon, indicating Maria. "She is my . . ."

The old man raised an eyebrow. "The thing I see in your eyes and your heart is true? You love a thing of metal and gears?"

Gideon looked him in the eye. "Yes. Yes, I do."

"And you would, what, have one last kiss?"

Nonplussed, the old man waved his pistols. Gideon bent forward and brushed a hair from Maria's face. He felt something bubbling up within him, as though he was going to laugh or cry, or perhaps both. He had found her, at last. Tears pricked his eyes. He had found her, and he had ruined it all again, just like he had when he took her to London and practically handed her to the monstrous Children of Heqet, just as he had when he climbed aboard the airship over London, leaving Maria in the hands of Louis Cockayne. He closed his eyes and leaned forward, and he touched his lips to hers.

Finally, finally, he kissed her.

++CONTACT IMMINENT. INITIATING PROBE++

++FUSION OF BRAIN/CLOCKWORK COMPONENTS TO
     ACHIEVE INDEPENDENT AUTOMOTIVE FORCE: 100
     PERCENT COMPLETE. HOST EMERGING FROM STASIS++

++READYING SIGNAL++

++PROBING CONTACT LEVELS++

++CONTACT DOPAMINE LEVELS: HIGH++

++CONTACT SEROTONIN LEVELS: HIGH++

++CONTACT OXYTOCIN LEVELS: HIGH++

++HOST DOPAMINE LEVELS: HIGH++

++HOST SEROTONIN LEVELS: HIGH++

++HOST OXYTOCIN LEVELS: HIGH++

++NECESSARY PARAMETERS ACHIEVED++

++SIGNAL TRANSMISSION: TRUE++

++HOST RECONFIGURED AND STASIS SUSPENDED++

++RECOVERY UNDERWAY. RECOVERY UNDERWAY. RECOVERY
     UNDERWAY++

And Maria kissed him back. At first he thought he was imagining the pressure on his lips, then he felt her tongue, warm and wet, push hesitantly at his teeth. Her hands were on him. He opened his eyes.

He looked straight into hers.

Gideon pulled back. "Maria!"

Her hand flew to her mouth, her artificial skin coloring at her cheeks, everything about her a testament to the genius of her creator, Hermann Einstein.

"Mr. Smith! Oh, my!" She pushed herself up on her elbows and looked around, blinking. "Mr. Smith? Where are we?"

"Texas." He helped her off the altar. "You have been unconscious for quite some time."

She looked around as Gideon drew her to him, feeling her body against his. Inez, her rapier extended, moved to Maria's other side and hissed, "Your moving reunion will have to wait, Señor Smith. We are in grave danger."

Behind them, Chantico whimpered, "I am sorry."

"And your sniveling apologies will have to wait also, idiot," said Inez over her shoulder. "Can't you do something useful, like call off your friends?"

The young Yaqui seemed drugged, or drunk, swaying toward them, muttering under their breath, their eyelids fluttering.

"Take her!" commanded the Old Man. "Take her to Steamtown!"

The Old Man leveled his gun at Gideon. "You first, boy, then the Spanish girl. Chantico, you may use the time it takes me to kill them to repent for your base betrayal."

"I see some things have not changed while I have been out of action," murmured Maria. "Men still underestimate me."

She reached forward and took hold of the pistol's barrel. The Old Man's eyes widened, and his finger tightened on the trigger. The gunshot was deafening in the hot cave, and the bullet ripped through Maria's tattered dress, lodging in her abdomen. She looked down and tutted, wresting the pistol easily from the Old Man.

"Who wants this? Gideon?"

He took it from her, one eyebrow raised, as she twisted slightly and dug into the folds of her dress with her forefinger and thumb. "Did no one tell you?" she said to the Old Man. "I am the clockwork girl." She smiled as she held up the snub bullet. "You cannot hurt me."

"You cannot kill them all!" shrieked the Old Man as the Yaqui advanced. "They shall overpower you!"

Gideon glanced at Chantico, then Inez. "Can we trust him?"

She nodded tightly, and he handed the gun to Chantico.

"I . . . cannot," he faltered. "Not against my people . . ."

"Kill them!" cried the Old Man. "Kill them all!"

Gideon, Maria, and Inez stood shoulder to shoulder, Chantico hiding behind them. The Yaqui were staggering toward them, arms outstretched. The Old Man shrieked again, "Kill them all!"

"No," rang out a stern, strong voice in heavily accented English. "There shall be no killing here today. Not on Yaqui land."

Another figure, an Indian, stood at the mouth of the tunnel, movement behind him. Gideon turned to Inez, but she gave him a shrug. Then Chantico groaned.

"My father," he said. "Now the trouble really begins."

The man emerged from the shadows, gazing down on them with proud dark eyes. He held up his hand at the young Yaqui and spoke rapidly in their language, which Gideon could not understand. He got the tone of it, though, as the Yaqui glanced guiltily at each other and began to shuffle their feet. Whatever spell they had seemed to be under evaporated at the strident tones of the older Indian.

"I am Noshi," he said, his arms folded, addressing Gideon. "I am one of the tribal elders." More men emerged behind Noshi, and he cast his gaze around the cavern, settling on Chantico. "My son. You bring shame on our tribe, skulking in the shadows with the Old Man."

"Silence, Noshi!" cackled the Old Man. "Your time has ended, eh? A new order is arising!"

Noshi stared gravely at the Old Man. "Quiet yourself, you foolish old *brujo*."

He withdrew his hand from within his robes and cast a leather bag to the floor. The Old Man gasped as it burst open, spilling coins across the stone.

"British guineas and shillings," said Noshi, looking around.

"Blood money from the Steamtown white men." He nodded at the Old Man. "We found it in his wigwam."

Chantico crouched and picked up a handful of coins. "British? Steamtown?" He looked up at the Old Man. "Where did you get this?"

The Old Man looked away. Noshi said, "He has been sneaking to Steamtown, selling secrets to the white man." He looked at Chantico. "Do you wonder why the Steamtowners knew where to find Ecatzin and the others with the trading party? Do you wonder why they knew there would be gold in their sacks? Ask *him*."

Chantico furiously threw the handful of coins at the Old Man. "You betrayed the tribe. And you would have taken Maria . . . not as an offering to free Quetzalcoatl, but to sell her?"

Suddenly the Old Man shrieked and plucked a torch from the wall. He swung it around and ran for the cave entrance. Gideon trained his gun on him, but Noshi raised a hand.

"Let him go. Those are your people at the abandoned mine, yes? You must come quickly."

"But he will be making for Steamtown!" said Gideon.

"And he will find it empty," said Noshi, "because Steamtown is on its way here."

21

LAST STAND AT THE MINE

"He did what?" asked Bent.

"Borrowed the rancher's horse, took a pistol from the armory, and headed off into the hills," said Rowena, intently watching a flickering dial on the liquefaction engine. "Do you think this being in the red is a good thing or a bad thing?"

"But why didn't you effing stop him?" demanded Bent.

Rowena looked up. "I am not Gideon's keeper, Aloysius. He does what he wants. My priority is getting the *Skylady III* back in the air."

Bent pulled a face and deftly rolled a cigarette from his pouch of tobacco. He turned to see Cockayne looking up at the airship. "Want a ciggie?"

Cockayne shook his head and patted his jacket pocket for a half-smoked cigar. He lit it from Bent's match and said, "How are the repairs coming, Rowena?"

"One cell fully inflated," she said. "Second well on its way. This liquefaction engine is a marvel. How does it work, again?"

Cockayne shrugged. "Don't ask me. Came with the 'stat when I won it in the card game."

Bent chuckled. "You really live on your wits, don't you, Cockayne?"

"Only way to survive, Bent. Where's Smith?"

Bent sighed. "Took off on a horse, apparently. Rowena didn't think to ask where he was going."

She gave him a pointed stare. Bent said, "Anyway, I'm sure he knows what he's doing. Any sign of this Indian yet, Cockayne?"

"No, and the Spanish girl's gone missing as well," said Cockayne thoughtfully. "Rowena? Is that a telescope?"

She nodded and passed him the brass cylinder. He focused it out east. Bent squinted into the distance. "What's that on the horizon? Dust storm or something?"

Cockayne passed him the telescope. "Something," he agreed. "Something beginning with Pinch."

⚡

"What do you mean, leaving?" demanded Rowena.

The ranchers had brought five horses with them, and Cockayne figured they weren't going to miss another one. He tightened the saddle and checked his guns. "I mean leaving, as in getting the hell out of here."

"Louis . . ."

"Don't *Louis* me, Rowena," he said firmly. "I've told Smith where they're keeping the damn dragon and we've found where Maria is. As far as I'm concerned, that's my side of the bargain done."

"So you're just going to abandon us?"

He sighed and turned to her. "Come with me. Hell, bring Bent, too. We don't owe these people anything."

She shook her head. "You're wrong, Louis. We owe them a chance at freedom. We owe them some protection."

"No, no, we don't. I saw five Steamcrawlers on their way over, and two dozen men on horseback. Thaddeus Pinch is out for revenge. He wants a poker up my ass, and God knows what he'll do to you for blowing up half of Steamtown. The man's insane, Rowena. I'm getting out, and I suggest you do the same."

"He still thinks you're a hero, you know," Rowena said quietly as Cockayne put his foot into the stirrup and hauled himself up onto the horse.

He frowned at her. "Who does?"

"Gideon. He knows what you're like; he's seen what you do. But he still believes, deep down, everything he used to read in the penny dreadfuls. He still thinks Louis Cockayne is the bold adventurer of the American plains, the great Yankee hero."

Cockayne shook his head vehemently. "Uh-uh, Rowena. Not my problem. If he's stupid enough to believe all that horseshit Lucian Trigger cooked up to add a bit of stardust to the nefarious deeds of his lover-boy, then that ain't my problem. I'm no hero."

"No," she said. "No, you're not."

He looked out east, where the long dust cloud was drawing closer. "They'll kill you, you know. If you're lucky."

"We won't go down without a fight. It might be our last stand, but we'll die with dignity," she said. "I have to say, I am disappointed in you, Louis."

"I'll remember that when I raise a glass to your memory," he said, spurring his stolen horse on and nosing it west, away from the advancing terror.

※

Bent stared numbly at her. "Gone? But he's the only one here who can handle a gun properly."

"My ass." Oswald P. Ackroyd snorted. "I can shoot a peanut off a steer's head at a hundred paces. And Albert's no slouch, either."

"Good," said Rowena. She looked at the others, the frightened faces of the fifty-four people who had been bundled into the hold of the *Skylady III*. "What do the rest of you want to do? These men who are coming here . . . they are not good men. And they are out for revenge. We've stolen what they see as their property—you people—and destroyed their town. They aren't coming for a quiet chat. Anyone who wants to leave can make a run for it. Anyone who wants to fight . . . I have weapons in the 'stat."

The young Scot, Hamish, put up a hand. "Can't we escape in your airship?"

Rowena shook her head. "She's not ready yet. We could

probably just about get airborne, but if they've brought their steam-cannon, we'd be sitting ducks."

Oscar stepped forward. "Then we fight. I can handle a gun."

"Me, too," said Hamish.

Slowly, hesitantly, the others raised their hands and nodded. Rowena smiled; the women were willing to fight as well. She said, "We'll get the children into the house, in the room without windows. Anything we can make barricades out of, drag it out front. Aloysius, Oscar, Hamish . . . and you, and you. Come with me. Let's get the guns."

"Is the Hotchkiss still bolted to the observation deck?" asked Bent.

Rowena nodded. He said, "Then that effer's mine." He nudged Oscar. "Dab hand with that bastard, I am."

Rowena looked out east. The Steamcrawlers were visible across the prairie now. They didn't have much time.

⁂

"You have a lot of work to do to make up for your stupidity," said Noshi gravely to the young tribesmen who had been hauled out of the cave by their fathers and uncles. "A *lot* of work. Dirty work."

There were horses waiting for them at the cave mouth, and Gideon stepped into the sunshine, gasping at the cool air. With each adventure underground, the grip his fear had on him grew a little looser. But that did not mean he would be seeking out subterranean endeavors again anytime soon.

As the Yaqui began to troop back to the settlement, Noshi held out his hand for Chantico to stop. He looked at his son, and then at Inez. "You are in love with my son?"

Inez met his impenetrable gaze. "Yes. Yes, I am. I have abandoned my family and friends in Uvalde. We are planning to set up a home at the abandoned mine near the canyon."

Noshi looked at Chantico. "Is this true?"

He nodded sheepishly. Noshi said to Inez, "You realize that my son is an idiot?"

She smiled. "Yes. Yes, I do. But I still love him. We cannot often choose the path our heart will follow."

"She is too good for you," Noshi told Chantico. "You are very lucky." He turned to another of the elders and rattled off a stream in the Yaqui language. Then he said to Gideon, "Your friends are at this mine?"

Gideon nodded. "And I must get back there. You said Steamtown is attacking?"

"They are on their way. Come. We will accompany you." He spoke again to the other elders. "And perhaps Chantico's foolish friends can atone for their mistake in allowing themselves to be seduced by the *brujo*."

In the shadows of a leafy mountain ash, Cockayne watched the passage of the Indians below him. So Gideon had found Maria. He felt something like pride swell in his chest. He was a good kid, that Gideon Smith. Louis Cockayne didn't often admit to actually liking anyone, but he couldn't help but feel a kinship with Gideon, that crazy fisherman from the ass-end of nowhere who had dragged himself out of the mud to walk with the greats. Cockayne smiled. He'd go far. He might just end up being the Hero of the Empire everyone said he was.

The horse whinnied and Cockayne laid a hand on its neck to calm it. He'd wait until the Yaqui had passed, and then he'd strike out west. He planned to go as far as the coast then try to get passage to Tijuana, see if he could get on an airship heading east. New York or Boston, maybe. He felt a sudden pang replace the pride in his breast. Gideon would take Maria down to the old mine. Steamtown would be there soon.

Still, not his problem.

Nothing was ever Louis Cockayne's problem. He didn't *do* problems. He'd lived on his wits for his whole adult life, and that generally did not include giving a shit. If you started to care, you ended up dead. That was the Louis Cockayne way. As soon as you started to feel yourself get soft, it was time to dig the spurs in, move on.

His horse scraped at the dust and shook its head. It was keen to be on the trail.

So why wasn't he digging his fucking spurs in, then?

Why wasn't he moving on?

The line of horses below him was passing by, and Gideon and Maria were almost hidden by a copse of thin trees. He'd done good, the kid had, to find her and get her back.

Yeah, for as long as it lasted, with Steamtown on the way.

West, west, he told himself. The fleshpots of Tijuana, a nice dirigible ride cross-country, then some time in Boston, among civilized folks. Maybe he could get a pot of money together, hit the gambling dens, build it up enough to buy a part-share in a little 'stat. Set himself up in business, maybe cross Rowena's path again. He smiled at the thought of Rowena. He'd always been too goddamn soft on her. Then he remembered his last words to her.

I'll remember that when I raise a glass to your memory.

Ah, Rowena Fanshawe was no damsel in distress. She could handle a gun better than half the men he knew. And she had Gideon, and Maria, and Bent on her side, and . . . and . . .

The column of Yaqui had almost passed by now. All he had to do was dig in his heels, point his horse in the opposite direction, and get the hell out of this sorry mess. Leave the heroes and the assholes to it. Louis held tight to the reins, keeping the horse's nose up.

Wouldn't it be a thing, though, a tiny voice said inside of him. *Wouldn't it be a thing, to be one of the good guys for a change? Wouldn't it be a thing to wear a white hat for a spell? Make things right? Hell, say sorry for some of the shit you've done?*

Wouldn't it be a thing to go down there and help?

He forced a smile. "Fuck that," he said, slapping the horse's neck and letting it have its head. It began to canter along the dusty hillside for maybe a dozen steps before he pulled it up sharply.

He sighed. Ah, who the hell was he kidding?

He dug his heels into the flanks of the horse and nosed it in the opposite direction, after the column of Yaqui horses, waving his arm and shouting, "Gideon! Gideon! Wait up!"

"It's Cockayne!" said Gideon as the rider galloped toward them.

"Mr. Cockayne," said Maria. "Gideon. I remember. He stole me away from you. When I was flying Apep, I was . . . subsumed. But I remember. He *stole* me."

"Gideon! Wait up!" called Cockayne, pulling on the reins and bringing his horse to a stop alongside. He looked at Maria. "You found her!"

"Yes, Mr. Cockayne, he found me," said Maria, bringing back her arm and letting her fist fly into Cockayne's chin.

Cockayne tumbled off the horse into the dust. "Ow," he said. "Well, I guess I deserved that. Can that be the last time anyone punches me, though?"

Gideon raised an eyebrow. Cockayne was being awfully . . . *friendly*. He said, "We need to get back to the old mine. Noshi says Steamtown is on their way." He paused. "Where are *you* going?"

"To find you," said Cockayne, nodding his head enthusiastically as he climbed back into the saddle. "Listen, Steamtown is coming, but that means . . ." He looked at Maria. "That means the dragon's practically unguarded. That's what we came for, right?"

Gideon looked at Maria, then back to Cockayne. He was right. That was the mission. "But what about the others . . . ?"

"Rowena's got it in hand," said Cockayne. "Look, if she can hold them off for a while . . . maybe we could get to the Alamo in a couple of hours, maybe three, and get that goddamn dragon back here to help out."

"I do not understand what you are planning," said Noshi, "but you can have my three fastest horses."

"We will go to the mine to help the defense," said Inez,

pulling her cowl back over her hair. "La Chupacabras will not allow Steamtown anywhere near her home."

"Is this important?" asked Chantico, handing over the cloth bag.

Gideon took it from him and glanced inside. The golden apple and the other artifacts that powered Apep. "Yes. Yes, it is, thank you." He looked at Maria. "Your key is here also . . . do you need . . . ?"

She shook her head. "Gideon, I must speak to you. Something happened while I was flying the dragon. I feel . . . different. As though my human brain and my clockwork body work in concert, not as separate things. I feel whole. I do not need winding. But I do not understand why."

"Later," said Cockayne. "We need to move now, while we have the element of surprise."

Gideon nodded. "Yes. You're right. And you can take us to this Alamo?"

Cockayne grinned and nodded. "Follow me, Smith. Follow me."

Then he let loose a wild whoop, raised his hat into the air, and spurred his horse on. Gideon and Maria took a moment to exchange a glance and a smile then followed.

"No one shoot until I give the signal," said Rowena. "There might be a chance we can talk them round before anyone has to get hurt."

Bent snorted from the observation deck, where he was crouched behind the Hotchkiss. "I say we take the first effing chance we get, Rowena."

They had torn down tree branches and dragged out broken furniture to fashion a makeshift stockade across the front of the stone house. It wouldn't even stop a bicycle, thought Rowena, but it was more of a psychological barrier than a physical one. It gave them something to crouch behind with their guns, offered some measure of shelter. She looked around. A

few people were praying. Others looked out at the approaching horses and armored tracked vehicles. A few looked at
their feet, perhaps wondering whether they might not have
been better off handed over into slavery.

A hush fell over them. Rowena held a pistol in each hand
and stood, one boot on the barricade in front of her.

They were here.

※

The tracked Steamcrawlers rumbled to a halt a hundred yards
out, the horsemen pulling up beside them in a long line. There
were steam-cannons mounted on two of the Steamcrawlers;
Rowena had been right not to take the *Skylady III* up, she
thought. The hatch on the lead Steamcrawler clanked and
lifted, and she finally got her first eyeful of Thaddeus Pinch.

His metal limbs were steaming angrily from the joints, his
jaw glinting in the sun. He wore a wide-brimmed hat, his eyes
two pinpricks in its shadow. In his metal claw he held a rifle.

"You know me," he rasped, spittle flying into the dry dust.
"You all know me, or you should. My name is Thaddeus Pinch.
I'm the King of Steamtown." He grinned, blood pulsing at the
joints at his chin. "You can call me the angel of death."

"You're not wanted here, Pinch," called Rowena evenly.
"You boys just turn around and go back home."

"British?" said Pinch. "You friends with Mr. Gideon Smith?
I owe him. Big time. He here?"

She shook her head. "Looks like you've had a wasted
journey."

Pinch pointed his rifle at the *Skylady III*. "Whose ship is
that? I got a word I want to have with the owner. Small matter
of busting up my fucking town."

Rowena hesitated a moment, then said, "She's mine."

Pinch spat. "Yours? Then you're responsible?" He waved
his good hand. "And these'll be my missing workers."

"These will be free people," called Rowena. "Who are
you doing business with in New York, Pinch? Who's dealing
human lives for coal?"

"None of your fucking business, bitch," shouted Pinch. He raised his rifle and took sight along its length. "Now how about you hand over what's rightfully mine. I want my slaves, and I want my bride. Where's Maria?"

Rowena raised her own pistols. "Maria's not here. These people are free men and women, Pinch. And they're going to stay that way."

"Your funeral, sweetheart."

A shot rang out and Rowena tensed, but it was Pinch who leaped like a scalded cat as the bullet pinged off the hide of the Steamcrawler. She turned to find a figure standing behind her, clad in leather and furs despite the heat, leaning on a long-barreled rifle.

"And who are you?" she said, raising an eyebrow. She hadn't heard anyone approach.

The stranger put a finger to his weather-creased forehead. "I do not go by a name, ma'am."

"Well, if you don't know your name, I'm taking it that you just fired that bullet. Would I be presumptuous in thinking you're on our side?"

※

The stranger turned narrowed eyes on Pinch. "I had to be sure. Had to be sure it was all going to work out."

"Sure *what* was going to work out?"

He waved his guns. "This. All these different folks, black and white, from all corners of the world. All together here in one place."

"And has it worked?"

The stranger gave a thin smile. "It has the potential to."

"You! Nameless!" shouted Pinch. "You got no business here. This ain't your battle."

"I sent a message with one of your boys," said the stranger Rowena now realized was the Nameless. "Perhaps you didn't get it. Told him to tell you that this place was off-limits, that it's under my protection. I'm guessing you've got the message now."

"That was then," said Pinch. "Things've changed. This bitch blew up half of Steamtown. Cockayne roasted my deputy. Those are my fucking slaves."

"Then I guess this is my battle after all," said the Nameless.

"Now?" shouted Bent from the observation deck of the *Skylady III*.

Rowena nodded. "Now, Aloysius!"

"Have at you, you effing bastard!" he yelled, and the Hotchkiss roared.

The dirt in front of the nearest Steamcrawler exploded, one track spinning off the wheels. The occupants poured out, heading for shelter behind the other vehicles. Bent looked over the gun. "Eff me," he said quietly.

Pinch sat down heavily on his vehicle. "Oh, you've done it now. Spirit or no fucking spirit, you people are—" His voice trailed off as he looked up and beyond the crowd. "What the shit?"

Rowena looked behind her, at the ridge that rose up beyond the creek. There was a figure there, dressed in black, masked and holding up a rapier.

"La Chupacabras!" she cried. The girl? Inez?

Then, rising behind her, wave after wave of whooping, hollering Indians, two dozen of them pouring over the ridge and down across the shallow water toward them.

Rowena ducked down as both sides started firing. Inez galloped up, dismounting in the shadow of the house. Rowena called, "Where's Gideon?"

"He's gone, with Cockayne and Maria."

So Louis had made good at last. "Where?"

"The Alamo."

She turned around as a bullet impacted in the stone wall. Despite the Yaqui, they were still outgunned. She couldn't put all these lives at risk. "Pinch," she called over the racket. "Pinch! Stop shooting."

He held up his hand and the Steamtowners paused. "You ready to give up?"

"Maria's not here," she shouted. "Gideon has found her and gone. There's no point you being here anymore."

Pinch shook his head. "I still need to pay you back for . . ." He paused. "Wait." He turned to his crony, the one wearing the sheriff's badge. "The fucker's gone to get the goddamn dragon."

Pinch turned to Rowena. "I'll be back for you." Then he waved his hand, turned his small army around, and had them gallop and roll back the way they came.

The Nameless stood at her side, watching them go. "You may have sacrificed your friends, you know."

"Maybe. But how many lives have been saved here? Gideon will understand. He's very big on the greater good and all that." She shaded her eyes and watched the retreating Steamtowners. "I just hope he got a good start on them."

22

The Battle of the Alamo

From a small copse of trees on a hill they watched the activity around the crumbling white stone church. There was a long, low building to the rear—dormitories for the missionaries who had first set up the abandoned mission—and the area was enclosed by a wooden palisade fence. In the dusty plaza before the mission was a wide tarpaulin staked to the ground, the unmistakable shape of Apep beneath it.

"I reckon there'll be thirty, maybe thirty-five men," said Cockayne. "I was hoping more might have fled Steamtown since Rowena shot it up and Pinch hauled off to the old mine."

Far beyond, to the south, they could see the pall of smoke that hung over Steamtown. Gideon hoped that the slaves and women forced to work in the brothels had been able to escape. Pinch's hellish little town was dead, more or less. But if he got his hands on Maria and was able to fly the dragon, there was no guessing what fresh terror he would be able to work.

Gideon looked at Cockayne. "What do you think we should do?"

Cockayne turned to Maria. "You surprised me. You can ride a horse. Do you think you can shoot?"

"I didn't know I could ride until I did it," she said. "I summoned some hidden memory . . . Annie Crook's, I suppose. Perhaps she went riding in Ireland in her youth."

It was little things like this that brought Gideon up short, reminded him that Maria was not a flesh-and-blood woman, but the clockwork creation of the genius Hermann Einstein. She was an automaton with the brain of poor old Annie Crook, the tragic London shopgirl who had dared to love a prince and been murdered by the Crown—by his own employers, he reminded himself bitterly—for the good of the nation. Cockayne reached into his saddlebag and handed her a revolver.

"Let's hope Annie Crook learned to shoot as well as ride," he said.

"Surely you can't be expecting Maria to fight as well?" said Gideon.

Cockayne raised an eyebrow. "This ain't London high society, Smith. We don't pack the ladies off to do needlework while the men do the important stuff. Unless Maria has any objections?"

She spun the chamber on the revolver and twirled the gun on her index finger, slapping it into her palm and taking aim with it rested in the crook of her other arm. Cockayne grinned, and Maria said, "None at all."

"Maybe we should wait until dark," suggested Gideon. "We could sneak in and—"

"And have our asses handed to us on a plate," said Cockayne. "Look, Smith, as soon as Pinch realizes we're not at the mine he'll be hauling his little army right back here to defend his property. We've walked into the lion's den. We don't have the luxury of waiting for nightfall, of formulating plans, of sneaking around. Pinch'll be on our asses soon, and we want to be airborne in the dragon by then or we've lost."

"So . . . ?"

Cockayne drew both pistols. "Blaze of glory, Smith. It's all or nothing, win or lose, black or white. We go down there and we take back our dragon, or we die trying."

Gideon gazed down the hill. "But it's suicide. . . ."

"Not if we win."

Gideon looked at Maria. He'd only just found her, and now he was going to risk losing her again? "What do you think?"

She smiled. "Blaze of glory, I believe Mr. Cockayne said."

Cockayne laughed richly. "All right. Let's make for the gate. Try to stick together."

With that, he dug his heels into his horse's flanks and whooped loudly as it began to gallop down the hill. Maria and

Gideon exchanged a glance, and she smiled and spurred her horse on also.

"Blaze of glory!" yelled Gideon, and followed them down the hill.

The mood in the Alamo was not good. Bernard Osterman had been put in nominal charge of the mission and given responsibility for looking after the brass dragon. It was a queer-looking thing, and he'd never have believed it could take to the air if he hadn't seen it himself before it crashed in the desert. There were thirty-two men at the Alamo apart from Osterman, and there were already rumblings of dissent and even mutiny. Mr. Pinch had gone off on some crazy mission and had taken most of the Steamtown men with him. Meanwhile, San Antonio had practically burned to the ground overnight; they'd watched the flames licking the dark sky, seen the groups of men and women—in twos and threes at first, larger mobs later—breaking out of the dormitories and making their bids for freedom. There was no one to stop them, though Osterman had ordered his men to at least try to shoot the packs of escaping slaves that passed anywhere near the Alamo.

Yesterday he'd had forty-seven men. Fifteen had absconded in the small hours. The rest wanted to know how they were going to get paid, what they were going to eat, and if anyone was stopping the whores escaping. There wasn't much left of Steamtown now, and that included loyalty; most of the men who had settled there had been drifters, criminals, murderers, and if the things that kept them in San Antonio—money, vittles, women, gambling, and the iron rule of Thaddeus Pinch—were now gone, then there wasn't much to keep them faithful.

Osterman stared at the dragon under the tarpaulin. Crazy thing. And it had caused all this trouble. If he were Pinch, he'd be ruing the day he'd ever set eyes on the thing. It had burned Steamtown to the ground without even flapping a wing.

"Mr. Osterman?"

He looked up at one of the young bucks. If he was asking about money, or food, or women, Osterman swore he'd—but no. The kid had news.

"Riders, sir. Three of 'em. Heading this way."

"Three?" said Osterman. Didn't sound much like an invading force. "Maybe it's a message from Mr. Pinch. Maybe he's won and he's on his way back."

"You want us to open the gate?"

Osterman shrugged. Maybe it was supplies. "Keep guns on them, but yeah, open the gate."

✠

"They're letting us in!" shouted Gideon.

"Then they're fucking idiots!" called Cockayne. "Okay, I've seen this place. When the gate opens the dragon will be right in front of us, staked down into the dirt. We're going to go straight through the plaza to the old church, around the dragon."

"Around it?" said Gideon. "Why not straight to it?"

"They must think we're from Pinch or something, but they're pretty quickly going to realize we're not. We'll have a tiny window of opportunity, Smith, and it won't be enough to get the dragon fired up. Go right to the wall, get off your horse, and get behind it. Then follow me."

They were two hundred yards away now, and the gate was fully open. There must have been some kind of walkway along the wooden palisade, because Gideon counted maybe ten men with rifles trained on them. He shouted to Cockayne, "Armed men. Should we . . . ?"

"Yeah," said Cockayne, then started firing. "*¡No rendirse, muchachos!*" he yelled. "Blaze of goddamn glory!"

✠

Too late, Osterman realized he'd fucked up badly. Of the ten men on the palisade, six were tumbling, dead, to the dusty ground. And he'd only counted six shots. Whoever the riders were, they didn't waste bullets.

"Shoot, you assholes!" he screamed at the remaining four. He turned around, looking for help. The kid who'd come to him was looking frightened, as though he was going to piss himself. "Get to the long barracks, wake those lazy bastards up!"

The long barracks was where most of them slept when on Alamo guard duty. The mission itself was crumbling and mostly roofless, but it was still a church, and the Steamtown boys might have been the scum of the earth but none of them wanted to sleep there, so it was pretty much empty save for a few boxes of ammunition and supplies. Osterman stood before the mission and turned to face the gates, the dragon laid out before him. He checked his guns. Before he came to Steamtown he'd been a rifleman in the Boston Cavalry Division. They'd drummed him out for screwing the daughter of some Indian chief up near Canada. That was why he'd come to Steamtown, where they let a man take what he wanted and screw who he liked, whether they said yes or no or what. That was why he was going to do his job and defend the goddamn dragon.

The three riders breached the gate at the same time. He recognized one of them and quailed. Louis Cockayne. Best shot in Texas, they said. There was a man and a woman flanking him. Osterman swallowed and raised his gun. He was going to be the man to take down Louis Cockayne. Thaddeus Pinch would be kissing his boots for a year.

❧

"Shit!" said Cockayne as the bullet whizzed past his ear. Gideon glanced at him then picked off a shooter with a rifle who was taking aim to his right. They were inside the mission, but there were men converging on them from all sides, the air singing with the passage of hot bullets. He saw Maria's gun jerk, and another man crumpled. In front of them was the dragon, and behind it a man in a battered brown hat, his gun raised. Beyond him was their goal, the white Alamo church, a brown door set into a porch.

"He's mine," said Cockayne, and put a bullet into the shoulder of the man standing in front of the church, who sprawled backward into the dust. "Damn. Must be losing my touch." Cockayne veered off to the right around the dragon, Maria to the left.

Gideon felt his heart pounding. Blaze of glory. Why did he always feel so alive when he was closest to death? The huge brass snout of Apep was in front of him beneath a flapping corner of the tarpaulin. He dug his heels in and the horse leaped forward, high into the air and over the covered wings of the dragon. Gideon couldn't stop himself from letting out one of Cockayne's whoops as his horse thundered into the dust, skidding to a halt before the Alamo porch.

"Everyone off! Use your horses as cover!" ordered Cockayne.

Gideon slid to the ground just as two bullets slammed into his mount. He felt a sudden pang as it whinnied and began to topple.

"Door's locked," said Cockayne. "Maria? Can you use a bit of that muscle you decked me with?"

She nodded and put her delicate foot to the door, drew it back, and kicked it inward with a splintering of wood.

"Good girl," said Cockayne. "Everyone inside."

The shooting stopped for a moment as they tumbled in and Cockayne found an old pew to wedge against the door. Gideon looked around. The church was largely roofless, dust covering the altar and the broken pews. Whatever there had been in the way of gold or decorations had been looted; black Bibles lay like dead birds scattered across the floor. The sun was beating down to the center of the nave, but in the shadows by the door it was cool.

"Now what?" asked Gideon, breathing heavily. In his hand he clutched the cloth bag containing the artifacts that allowed the dragon to fly.

Cockayne wiped the back of his mouth with his shirt-sleeve and began to dig in his pockets for bullets. "*Now's* the time for you to come up with one of your clever plans," he said.

"Do you think Gideon got a good enough start on them?" asked Bent.

Rowena shrugged. It had been more than an hour since Pinch and the Steamtowners had set off in pursuit. "I don't know. I hope so."

"Do you think Pinch and the Steamtowners'll come back here to finish what they started?"

"Depends if they get the dragon. If they do, then we're in trouble."

They had escaped the confrontation with no deaths. That was something to be thankful for. And a change had come over Oscar, Hamish, and the others. They had worked together, and they had survived. They seemed to have shed the broken, beaten mien they had worn like masks. They no longer seemed frightened. They were all working together, sawing down trees, collecting food and water, creating a corral to keep Ackroyd's cattle in one place.

The Nameless was standing in the dust in front of the house, peering out into the prairie. He was an odd one. Rowena could quite believe what people said, that he was some kind of spirit or ghost. He seemed solid enough, but there was definitely something otherworldly about him.

She turned her attention to the Spanish girl, Inez, and her Indian lover. Chantico's people had gone back to their settlement with the promise that they would return if needed. Inez and Chantico seemed to be arguing.

Bent chuckled. "She's got him right where she wants him."

Inez glared at Chantico and stalked toward Rowena and Bent. "He is an idiot," she spat.

"But you love him," said Rowena.

Inez sighed. "Yes." She pulled at the top button of her black shirt. "He gave me this. I asked him where he got it. I thought it was an old Yaqui thing, but he said—"

Rowena stared at the red gem hanging on the golden chain. She said slowly, "Aloysius? Tell me that isn't . . ."

"Oh, eff," he said. "It is. It's the Faxmouth amulet."

Inez bit her lip. "It is important, yes?"

Rowena nodded. "Yes, it is very important. And it should be a long way from here." She thought for a moment then glanced back at the *Skylady III*.

Bent groaned.

⁂

Osterman's shoulder felt as though it were on fire. He held a handkerchief to it that quickly blossomed red with his blood. He dragged himself to his feet, his head spinning, and looked around. Seventeen dead. Shit. He looked at the church. Still, they were trapped now.

"Get two men on every corner of the church," he called weakly, spitting into the dust. "The rest of you, up front."

He was losing blood fast, and the edges of his vision were feathered with darkness. Someone passed him a tin cup of water, and he drank gratefully from it. It made him feel a little better, well enough to shout at the closed door of the church.

"Cockayne. There's nowhere to go now. You better just open that door and throw out your weapons, then come out with your hands up."

He felt the others gathering at his back. He turned to them, staggering slightly. They looked worried. A few of them nudged each other, then one of the younger men stepped forward.

"Mr. Osterman? We've been talking . . . we're not rightly happy with the idea of going up against Louis Cockayne."

"He's just a man," said Osterman, his throat suddenly dry. He looked around at the seventeen corpses. He said it louder. "He's just a man. We've all got a job to do, and by God we're going to do it."

"The boys, they've been wondering . . . what if Mr. Pinch doesn't come back? What if we're just doing this for . . . for no wages, nothing?"

Osterman didn't really have an answer for that. He looked beyond his remaining men, to the open gate and the desert beyond. His eyesight blurred again, then he realized there was dust rising from the hills, a line of dust and sand. He staggered, holding on to the kid for support. He said, "It's all right." Then he slumped to the ground.

※

Cockayne peered over the lip of the window, through the slats of the busted shutter, his back to the wall and his freshly re-loaded pistols ready.

"What's happening?" asked Gideon.

"Nothing," said Cockayne. "The guy I got in the shoulder looks like the boss. I think the others aren't keen to go up against us." He smiled tightly. "Glad to see I've still got it."

"Where did you learn to shoot like that?" asked Gideon.

"Lifetime on the plains, I suppose. Started off shooting rats on my daddy's farm in Connecticut."

"Can you teach me? I mean, I've done firearms training, but—"

Cockayne grinned. "Sure I can, Smith. Soon as we get out of here we're going for a long, cold beer, and I'll teach you to shoot the balls off a horsefly from fifty feet."

"I think I would quite like to learn how to improve my own aim," said Maria.

"You, too, Miss Maria," said Cockayne. "Hell, maybe we should even show Bent how to tell one end of a—" He paused. "Shit."

"What's happening?" said Gideon.

The smile dropped from Cockayne's face. "We got company."

※

Thaddeus Pinch climbed stiffly from the Steamcrawler and stepped down onto the plaza in front of the Alamo. His dragon was untouched, but there were a dozen and a half bodies scattered about. Looked like he'd gotten there none too soon. Most of the Steamcrawlers had blown gaskets, and the horses had been ridden into the ground, but it had been worth it.

The idiot he'd left in charge—Osterman, that was it, German name, he'd never liked Germans, no fun in 'em—was bleeding from his shoulder and trying to stand up. Pinch marched over to him, exhausts pumping out steam from his leg and arm joints, and looked down.

"What the fuck happened?"

"Cockayne," said Osterman dreamily.

"Where is he?"

"In the church."

"With Smith? And the clockwork girl?"

Osterman nodded, his eyes flickering. "We opened the gate. Thought they was riders from you."

"Dickwad," said Pinch, and shot Osterman in the head. It was no less than he'd do for a dog or horse that was injured so badly. It was a kindness. He limped past the dragon to the doors of the old church and coughed, spitting phlegm into the dust.

"Ain't no sanctuary in those church walls, Louis," he called. "You're back on my turf now, so you might as well do as you're told." He waited for a response, but there was none. He continued, "We can do this one of two ways, Louis. Either you three come out of there with your hands on your heads, and we sit down and talk all civilized-like, or we come in there to get you. Either way, I'm getting my hands on your little clockwork girl, and my dragon's gonna fly. You understand?"

He squinted and waved his good hand for the muttering behind him to stop while he listened for Cockayne's answer. He saw the smallest movement at one of the windows, then a voice called out.

"Fuck you."

Pinch pulled back his jaw in his grotesque parody of a smile. "I was hoping you were gonna say that."

23

BLAZE OF GLORY

"What are we going to do?" asked Gideon.

Cockayne continued to peer through the broken window shutter. He said, "Hey, ain't you supposed to be the Hero of the Empire?"

"Don't get irritable," said Gideon.

Cockayne took a deep breath. "Sorry. The threat of impending death tends to do that to a man." He turned away from the window. "The goddamn dragon is so close I can practically touch it."

Gideon took Cockayne's place at the window. "If only we could stage some kind of diversion, take Pinch's attention away from Apep so Maria could get onboard."

"How long will it take to get that bird in the sky?" asked Cockayne.

"Once the artifacts are in place on the dashboard, I think I have full control over Apep," said Maria. "Perhaps only minutes from then, though I have always been somewhat *indisposed* when I have been at one with the dragon."

"Mmm," said Cockayne. "Now's the time you want to see Bent come blundering into the place, or Rowena shooting everything up. . . ." He paused, staring at the dust motes dancing in the shafts of sunlight slicing through the broken timbers of the church roof.

"What?" asked Gideon. "Cockayne, do you have an idea?"

Cockayne stood and squinted down his arm at his pearl-handled revolvers, flipping open the chambers with his thumbs and rotating them, each one the snug home to a shining bullet. He spun the guns on his fingers and slid them home into his holsters. Patting his pockets, he located a cigarette and a match, which he struck on his belt buckle and touched to the end of the tobacco. His face was briefly illuminated under the shadow of his hat, then it fell into darkness again, save for his shining eyes.

"Yeah," he said. "I've got an idea."

※

"No, no, absolutely not," said Gideon.

"It does seem like madness, Mr. Cockayne," said Maria.

"Yeah, crazy like a fox, that's me," said Cockayne. "Now, to save time, let's say you've tried to change my mind and it hasn't worked. You understand what you've got to do?"

Gideon sighed heavily then nodded. "You sure you can do this?"

"Hey," he said, smiling crookedly. "I'm Louis goddamn Cockayne."

He went to the door and opened it a crack. Gideon heard a volley of clicks as every gun in the courtyard was turned on them. He felt sick.

"Thaddeus," called Cockayne. "I'm coming out. Make sure your boys keep their trigger fingers under control."

Cockayne turned, touched the brim of his hat, and winked at Gideon. Then he let himself out and pulled the door shut behind him. Gideon ran to the window as Maria stationed herself behind the door, armed with half a pew. If anyone tried to come in, they'd get the full weight of her clockwork might for their troubles.

"What's happening?" she asked.

Gideon peered through the window. "Nothing, yet. They haven't shot him, which is a good start."

※

"Glad to see you've seen sense, Louis," said Pinch as Cockayne stopped and took a long drag on his cigarette. "But . . . where are your friends?"

Cockayne tossed his cigarette to the dust and ground it under his heel, spurs jangling. "Want to talk, Thaddeus. Got a bit of a proposal for you."

Pinch nodded. "Talking's good, Louis. And I like proposals. Deals. It's just . . . well, folks who make proposals generally got something to bargain with. Way I see it, Louis, you've kind of already cashed in your chips."

Cockayne regarded him coolly. He said, "You were always a fast gun, Thaddeus. Leastways, before you started with all the . . ." He waved his hand up and down. "All this machinery."

Pinch laughed. It wasn't a pleasant sound. "I know you, Louis Cockayne. You believe the bullshit they say about you. You believe you're the fastest gun between here and Japville. And yeah, before that coyote took my arm off, I'd have planted a bullet between your eyes before you'd even thought about touching your guns." He paused. "Where's this going, Louis? What's your proposal?"

Cockayne smiled. "Me and you, Thaddeus. Mano a mano. Let's see who's the fastest. You win, you get the girl. I win, we walk out of here."

Pinch waved his metal arm. "You got me at something of a disadvantage, Louis."

Cockayne waved his left hand. "I'll fight southpaw."

Pinch grinned with his metal jaw. "You serious?"

Cockayne shrugged. "Levels the field somewhat. What do you say?"

Pinch ruminated. "You win, you don't get the dragon. You just walk out, right?"

Cockayne said, "If you like, but why worry about it? If I win, Thaddeus, you'll be dead."

Pinch rubbed his jaw. "Still can't say as I like the odds much, Louis. But say you had as much of a handicap as me . . . that might be better."

"What are you suggesting, Thaddeus?"

He grinned. "You wear a blindfold, Louis. You shoot left-handed, and you wear a blindfold. Those are my terms."

✸

"Surely he isn't going to agree to that," said Gideon, horrified.

"He does tend to go on about what a fine gunman he is," said Maria.

"Even so . . ." He looked at her. "Do you think it's possible?"

"Let us hope so," she said quietly.

※

Cockayne lit himself another cigarette and walked over to the far side of the dragon, putting the church behind him and to his right. Pinch's men followed, as he hoped they would, and formed two groups to either side of the two men. This, too, was what he was banking on. With Pinch's men putting their backs to the dragon, it meant more opportunity for Smith and Maria to get out of the mission and get Apep in the air.

He just hoped they did it sooner rather than later. He also hoped they hadn't swallowed Cockayne's bullshit, just as much as he hoped Pinch had swallowed it all. He was a god-awful shot with his left hand, and he'd be about as much use blindfolded as a nun in a poker game. The plan was that as soon as Pinch's men lined up, Gideon and Maria would get the hell over to the dragon while Louis ran for cover in the confusion. As Pinch called for a blindfold and took up his position in the dusty courtyard, Cockayne began to have a bad feeling about it. He sucked hard on his cigarette as one of Pinch's cronies pulled an old strip of linen tight over his eyes.

His older brother Rick had been shot in a gunfight in Lomax Gulch, a one-horse town that had no right to claim the life of a Cockayne. Rick had been a faster gun than Louis, but for some reason he had fumbled his draw against some weasel-faced little asshole with an eye on the main prize. His childhood friend Ralph had brought his hat and gun belt back to the Connecticut farm, full of remorse and apologies as he handed them over to the weeping Mrs. Cockayne. They'd buried Rick out west, of course. Ma Cockayne had asked if he'd had any final words.

"Yes, ma'am," said Ralph, wringing his hat. "He lived a little while after he got shot; the doctor couldn't do anything for him. But he had time to tell me . . . he said the minute he stood out there in the main street of Lomax Gulch, he knew. Knew he wasn't going to make the draw. He said he supposed all gunmen knew when they weren't going to make it."

Louis Cockayne didn't know if that was true or just gunslinger bullshit that Rick and Ralph had liked to impress the ladies with in the saloon bars of dusty, one-street towns. All he knew was that he didn't have that unflinching certainty himself, even as he was blindfolded, even as his ears strained to pick out the steam exhalations of Pinch's modified body parts. All he knew was that he was going to try his goddamn best to come out of this alive.

Maybe that was Louis Cockayne bullshit overriding gunslinger lore.

He hoped to fuck that Gideon was already on his way to the dragon as Pinch said, "We've taken your right-hand gun, Louis. Gonna get a countdown from ten—can any of you fucking idiots actually count, by the way?—then you go for your gun. I'm right in front of you, Louis. I won't move. I promise."

Louis could almost see the grotesque grin. "That's a relief," he said. "Okay, Pinch. Whenever you're ready."

※

"Ten," came a voice from Cockayne's left. He felt his palm itch and his fingers flex. *Wrong hand, asshole,* he told himself. *The left. The left.*

※

"Nine." Gideon eased open the door. Pinch had put three men on the dragon, but they were all looking toward the imminent gunfight, their guns held loosely by their sides.

※

"Eight." *You don't need your eyes,* Cockayne told himself. *You've shot a gun, what, every day of your life since you were eight years old? That's thirty years. Even if you only shot once a day, that's more than ten thousand fucking times you fired a gun, Louis. You don't need your eyes.*

※

"Seven." Gideon eased himself out of the doorway, willing himself to fade into the white stone wall of the church. Maria held his hand tightly, and he slowly drew her to the open door. Quiet, quiet, quiet. He dared to look at her, and their eyes locked. *Please don't let me die here*, he thought, *not now that I've found her*. This was what it had all been for. Ever since he had found Maria in Einstein's house, then lost her again what felt like a dozen times over, he had fought to be reunited with her. The mere touch of her hand was like one of the fizzing electric connections in the tumbledown Einstein house, coursing through his body. So this was what it felt like. This was love.

"We can do this," he whispered. "Together, we can do this."

"Yes," she murmured back, her eyes never leaving his. "Together we can do *anything*."

※

"Sev—uh, I done that. Six." From his boot heels, which were planted in the dust, to his hat brim, which divided the tender warm breeze that flowed over his face, was six feet and two inches of space, space into which Louis Cockayne compressed the world around him, folding the distance between him and his mark so that Pinch's foul visage was up close in a halo of brilliant sunshine. Cockayne just had to bring up his gun and blow that stupid metal jaw right off his fucking face.

※

"Five." The courtyard was perhaps three hundred feet wide by fifty feet deep. Aside from the men watching silently as Pinch and Cockayne faced each other across the gulf of dust and sand, and the bodies of the fallen men, and the dragon staked beneath the sun-bleached tarpaulin, there was nothing. Nothing save for the single bone-dry twig that had conspired to be under Gideon's boot and that rent asunder with a crack thunderous enough to wake the dead.

※

"Four." Cockayne had focused every sound, every breath, every shuffling foot, into a pinprick that he locked away into a corner of his mind that he wasn't planning on using for the next two minutes. Then a snapping *something* shattered the lock, and every breath came like a snorting bull, every footstep like a flamenco dancer's heels beating out a tattoo on a saloon stage.

"Three." Slowly, minutely, as though time had stalled and everyone was swimming through Lyle's Golden Syrup, heads began to turn toward them. Gideon felt Maria's grip tighten on his hand, and his heart sank. The dragon's tail was within reach. But not close enough. As though in a dream, he felt Maria let go of him and bring up her gun.

"Two." Cockayne's head was filled with crackling and sparking, his concentration shattered. He didn't know whether he should be reaching for his gun or dragging off his blindfold and making a run for it. There was only the deafening sound of the snapping twig jarring against the measured rhythms he had sorted into an endlessly repeating pattern, the countdown from Pinch's crony, the sound of his own breathing, the steady beat of his heart. The snapping twig, and something else.

"One—uh, Mr. Pinch?" It was the final trumpet, the heavenly hosts come to take Louis Cockayne away to his final rest. A sustained note that began to break up into . . . yes, into a tune. A melody. Perhaps Pinch had shot already, perhaps Louis was behind the curve, perhaps he was already dead and he didn't yet know it. Or perhaps . . . he reached up and ripped the blindfold from his face.

The tail of Apep, as thick as a tree trunk, snaked out from under the tarpaulin, the layered brass scales shining in the sunlight. It was almost as though the dormant metal beast sensed Maria's proximity and shuddered slightly at the presence of its pilot. Gideon had no idea whether it was science or sorcery that put the dragon in the air, or if he'd know the difference between them anyway.

"Gideon . . ."

Maria had heard it, too. They'd all heard it. The horn, or trumpet or . . . or bugle. Gideon's heart suddenly soared. There, flowing over the hill toward the gates, was a dusty blue river of men on horseback, flying the Union Flag. He squinted into the sun as the men approached. It was Captain Humbert, from the garrison, he was sure. And alongside him, in leather and denim? Surely that was Jeb Hart.

All the Steamtowners were running to the gate to see what was going on, turning their guns away from Louis Cockayne, away from the dragon. They might just get away with this. Gideon glanced over at Cockayne and raised his hand in a tentative signal, his forefinger curled to his thumb, the other fingers standing to attention.

Cockayne glared at Gideon. *Go*, he mouthed. Get the goddamn dragon. He threw the blindfold away and pulled out his gun, transferring it to his itching right hand. It was only the cavalry heading over the hill. He allowed himself a smile. "All bets are off," he murmured. "I guess that's our royal flush."

Pinch seemed to hear him. Maybe he had steam-powered ears as well. The king of suddenly nothing very much dragged his eyes away from the approaching cavalry, even as his men began to open fire from the palisade. He turned to face Cockayne, his face contorted in fury. Cockayne hadn't thought Pinch could look any uglier. He guessed he was wrong.

"You know what beats a royal flush, Louis?" he said quietly, though strangely Cockayne heard every word over the din. "A gun."

A shiver ran down Louis's body from head to toe. His hand seemed to be made of stone as he tried to drag the gun up. He felt . . . he felt like he'd never felt before. Scared and frozen and oddly serene, all at the same time.

Maybe it wasn't gunslinger bullshit after all. Maybe Ralph had been right about his brother Rick.

Maybe, just maybe, when it was your time, you knew.

His heartbeat roared like a thunderstorm in his head, and he watched almost impassively the journey of the bullet that exploded from Pinch's gun.

※

"No!" yelled Gideon. Pinch's gun had barked, once, and Cockayne had tumbled forward, clutching his stomach. Gideon looked at Maria, who urged him onward with her eyes. She was at the dragon's head now, tearing the tarpaulin off its brass crocodilian head. Its eyes were two portholes, one shattered to nothingness weeks ago by the Fleet Air Arm over Biggin Hill.

"Get in," Gideon ordered. "I'll be one minute."

It took less than a quarter of that to reach Cockayne and turn him on his back. The sky was fuzzy with gun smoke, and Humbert's men were fighting their way through the palisade gates, making short work of the Steamtown rabble. Pinch was standing where he had been when he shot Cockayne, looking at his gun almost in puzzlement, as though he couldn't quite believe what he'd just done.

"Louis," said Gideon. Cockayne was bleeding heavily from his stomach. He opened one eye and grinned.

Blood poured from his mouth.

"It's all right, Louis," said Gideon gently. "The cavalry's here."

"Good old cavalry," said Louis, then coughed, more blood bubbling up from his mouth, frothing at his mustache. "Blaze of glory, eh, Gideon? Now go. Go get your dragon."

"We did it," said Gideon. "You did it. Just hold on. They'll get help. They've got a covered wagon."

Cockayne shook his head. Behind Gideon, he heard Maria shouting. He was dimly aware of Pinch, on the edge of his vision, stalking away from them. Toward the dragon. "It's too late, Gideon. He got me. Don't let all this have been for nothing. The dragon . . ."

Gideon felt tears sting at his eyes. "No. No, Louis. You said you were going to teach me how to shoot."

Cockayne shook his head, his eyelids fluttering. "You don't need me, Gideon. You're what they say you are."

Gideon strangled a sob. He *did* need Louis Cockayne. Louis Cockayne was a pirate and a thief and a self-serving bastard, but . . . Gideon couldn't bear to see another one of his friends die. No one had told him it would be like this. No one had said everybody would die.

"You're the Hero of the Empire, Gideon," whispered Cockayne. "I taught you all I know, kid. Time you stood on your own two feet. Don't be a follower anymore. Be your own man." He coughed again, more blood oozing between his cracked lips. "Remember what I said, a lifetime ago? Be prepared . . ."

Gideon nodded, tears clouding his eyes. "And if you can't be prepared . . ."

"Be lucky," finished Cockayne, suddenly becoming heavier in Gideon's arms. "I can see the corn waving in the breeze." Cockayne opened his eyes again and focused on him. "Be lucky, Gideon."

Then he was gone.

※

"Gideon!" He looked up at the sound of Maria's voice. She was letting off shots at Pinch, who was stalking toward her. Why wasn't she in the dragon? She could have had it in the air by now.

"Get in," he screamed, laying Cockayne down and sprinting toward her. "Get in Apep, get it airborne!"

She shook her head tightly at him, firing her last bullet at Pinch then tossing the gun away. She climbed through the broken eye porthole into the cockpit just as Gideon leaped onto the tarpaulin-covered wing, dodging a ricocheting bullet from Pinch's gun, then threw himself along the cantilevered neck and over the head, swinging himself around to join Maria.

He had not been inside the cockpit before, and he didn't have the luxury of more than a cursory glance around. There

was one seat, in wood and fragile animal hide, before a rudimentary dashboard. Snaking into the floor of the cockpit was
a thick, flexible metal hose. Gideon held it up, but Maria shook
her head. "I do not need to be connected directly to the dragon
anymore, Gideon. Not since . . . well, not since whatever happened, happened. I just need the artifacts."

The tarnished metal panel had indentations for all the artifacts that had been scattered across the globe until the dread
Children of Heqet had collected them all for the insane Dr.
John Reed. Each one was laid in its housing. The ring that
had sealed poor old Annie Crook's fate. The jeweled box, hidden beneath the cliffs in Sandsend, for which his father died.
The golden scarab, stolen from Castle Dracula, which had set
the vampire Countess Bathory on her quest for vengeance. The
small, crude funerary *shabti* figure, stolen from the British
Museum.

All there, in their places. All except . . .

"The amulet," groaned Gideon. "The ruby stone that
started it all in Faxmouth. I take it without it we can't . . . ?"

Maria shook her head tightly. Pinch was barely a dozen
feet from them now, a look of triumph in his eyes.

"It must have fallen from the bag on our journey," said
Gideon. "Or perhaps it was lost in the sands when you crashed."
He fumbled for his gun. "Pinch is here." He looked at her.
"Louis is dead."

Maria bit her lip. "I know."

He couldn't rely on Louis Cockayne now. Had been relying on him for too long, if the truth be known. He was Gideon
Smith, he was the Hero of the Empire, and it was time he
took matters into his own hands.

He raised his pistol and fired.

It clicked, dead, jammed.

He swore, just as a shadow fell across the Alamo. Gideon
craned his neck to look up, as did the battling Steamtowners
and the cavalry riders, as did Thaddeus Pinch.

Looming over the battlefield was the *Skylady III*.

24

THE GOD-KILLER

Chantico stood with his legs apart on the observation deck of the *Skylady III*, Inez holding him tight around his waist. He had at first refused to set foot on the 'stat, shaking his head maniacally and telling them that his totem animal was the coyote, not the eagle. Until Inez had given him a talking-to, of course. There was no doubt who wore the trousers in that relationship.

"Are you sure you can do this?" Rowena asked doubtfully.

"Chantico is the finest shot in his entire tribe," Inez said. "Of course he can do it."

They had sighted the Alamo just as the cavalry had streamed toward it, guns blazing. The brass dragon lay half-hidden under a tarpaulin, and Bent, his eye to the spyglass, had reported seeing Gideon on its snout.

"Perhaps we ought to just let the soldier boys sort it out," he'd said.

"The battle is not won yet," Rowena pointed out. "The dragon can turn the tide."

So Chantico, as Inez held him steady and the warm wind whipped his hair on the observation deck, took sight along the length of his arrow, the amulet in a small leather pouch tied just below the flint head.

"Put it to the left of the dragon's head," Rowena instructed. "And for God's sake, don't hit Gideon."

"I wonder where Cockayne is." said Bent.

"Probably hightailed it at the first opportunity," said Rowena. "Now quiet; give Chantico some space."

As the 'stat drifted as low over the Alamo as Rowena dared take it, fearing the steam-cannons that had almost finished her off before, Chantico took aim for painfully long moments then let loose the shaft.

Thaddeus Pinch watched the passage of the airship for a moment then turned back to the dragon. Gideon crawled out through the shattered eyehole. He would engage Pinch in hand-to-hand combat, if that was what it took. The cavalry were inside the Alamo, but the Steamtowners were fighting for their lives. If Gideon could just hold Pinch off long enough for Jeb Hart or Captain Humbert to take him down . . .

"It's over, boy," rasped Pinch. "You just give me what's mine, eh? The dragon and the girl."

"You don't have anything anymore, Pinch," said Gideon. "Your town's gone; your slaves have run away. You're right: It's over. But for you."

Pinch laughed unpleasantly, training his gun on Gideon. "Texas is a big place, Smith. There are other towns. I can start again. Especially with my dragon. Didn't I tell you I am as a god? Folks like you don't kill gods, Smith."

"I've exploded myths, Pinch. I reckon I can kill a god."

Pinch snarled, and his finger tightened on the trigger just as the arrow slammed into the dry earth a foot from the dragon's head.

Pinch blinked and looked around. Gideon saw the leather pouch swinging from the shaft, and he knew. He leaped for it and tore the pouch free.

"Maria!" he called, tossing the pouch to her through the open porthole. Pinch was at the dragon's snout now. Gideon reached down, took a handful of dry earth, and tossed it into Pinch's face, then clambered back on the dragon and slid into the cockpit. Maria had already emptied the amulet into her hand and placed it into its housing.

It began deep inside the dragon: a thrumming of hidden machinery, a turning of ancient gears, a rumbling of mechanical life. Gideon could only think of it as the dragon waking up. He looked at Maria. When she had first taken control of the dragon, she had been submerged beneath the creation that the Egyptian scientists—or sorcerers, he supposed—had fashioned, an homage to the Nile river god Apep. Remembering what Cockayne had told him, Gideon fumbled in the cloth sack for the last remaining artifact, the golden apple that John Reed had stolen from Shangri-La, the hidden valley high in the Himalayas. The golden apple conferred the gift of understanding and had allowed Cockayne to converse with Maria when she was deep within the ancient Egyptian persona of Apep.

She turned to him and smiled. "It's all right, Gideon. I told you something had happened. The artifact in my head that gives me life, it has . . . activated. It has brought together my clockwork body and my human brain. It has made me whole."

"More Egyptian magic?" he said as Maria arched her back and Apep's tail flexed, throwing the tarpaulin from it. She stretched her arms and the vast brass wings unfurled.

"No," she said. "I don't think so. I think the artifact is not Egyptian at all. It is . . ." She paused. "I'm not sure. Older, perhaps. More distant, possibly."

Gideon squinted through the porthole. Where was Pinch? Perhaps he had taken flight, now that the game was up. "Maria?" he asked. "Can we . . . can we fly?"

She smiled. "Hold on, Gideon. This is going to be somewhat thrilling."

※

As Rowena turned the *Skylady III* in a tight circle, Bent leaned forward as far as he dared on the observation deck. "Thar she blows!"

The dragon's brass scales shone in the fierce Texas sunshine. Suddenly, it was a living thing, lifting up its head and sinuous neck, pushing itself onto its strong hind legs. Bent gaped at it; he'd seen it before, but it still took his breath away. The vast wings flapped, sending up eddies of swirling dust.

The cacophony of gunfire slowed and quieted as every man, cavalry or Steamtowner, turned in awe to watch Apep wake from its slumber.

The dragon crouched and pushed upward, the wings sweeping back then forward in a smooth motion, dragging the impossible thing into the air. It hung there, its wings beating, for a long moment, then it began to rise, laboriously at first but with gathering speed until it whirled into the blue sky, swinging alongside the airship.

"Effing sky hog!" shouted Bent, shaking his fist, but then he was laughing, clapping Chantico on the back, kissing Inez on the cheek. The young lovers stared as though transfixed by a miracle. The last time Bent had seen the dragon, it had been threatening to destroy London. Now he could see what a thing of fearful beauty it really was. One's perspective on monsters always changed when the monsters were on one's own side. He shook his fist again, this time in triumph. "Go, Gideon! Go, Maria! Show 'em what that effer can do!"

"This is amazing!" yelled Gideon, half wanting to laugh, half terrified. The wind roared through the broken porthole, snatching his breath away. Maria sat back in the battered chair, her hands playing over the artifacts, bending Apep to her will like a virtuoso concert pianist.

"I am whole," she said again, sending the dragon banking far to the right, the Alamo spinning crazily in front of them. "I am in control."

Apep climbed, high into the sky, much higher than the *Skylady III,* which it quickly left behind. Gideon held on to the back of her seat. "Maria! How high can we go?"

"To the stars!" She laughed. "Will you come with me to the stars, Gideon?"

"I will go with you anywhere," he said quietly. "I love you, Maria."

She turned her head as the dragon soared higher, the pale blue deepening around them. "Come here."

He shuffled around to the seat, and she took his face in her hands and kissed him. She could do anything. They might swoon and tut in the parlors of London at her behavior, but she was not of that world. She was of this world, of the sky, of freedom.

"Gideon," she whispered. "I want you to . . ."

He stumbled and slid down the cockpit, and she straightened the dragon, looking out over the gently curving horizon. Her hands danced, and the dragon began to drift downward in a lazy spiral, its brass wings surfing the rising thermals.

"Maria?"

She placed a finger on his lips and began to tug his shirt from his trousers. Freedom. She could do anything. Her kid-leather skin felt on fire with his touch, and the gears and wheels at the V where her legs met meshed and ground most curiously with the wanting of him. Her hand slid down his torso until she could feel that he wanted her, too.

"Maria . . . ," said Gideon, breaking away.

"Hush," she commanded. She enjoyed being in control.

"Maria," he said again, his eyes widening. Then he pulled her toward him.

She had just time to say, "Gideon!" before the bullet slammed into the back of the seat. She turned to the instrument panel as Thaddeus Pinch, his metal hand clamped to the huge ornate nostril on Apep's snout, began to haul himself upright again, taking aim with his pistol.

"It's been a nice ride, Smith, but it's time for me to have what's due to me."

Pinch swung on Apep's nose, the wind buffeting him, his hair whipping his face. He hauled himself higher to get a better shot, his eyes blazing with triumph. Maria turned Apep into a tight roll, but Pinch grimly hung on, his metal arm unmovable, affixed tightly to the brass ridge of the nostril.

"You ain't gonna shake me off!" he yelled. "I'm taking my dragon and my queen. Say your prayers, Smith. But choose your god carefully. . . ."

Pinch dragged himself up on the nose, aiming his gun at Gideon. There was nowhere to go in the cramped cockpit, nowhere to hide.

"For I am the greater god!" roared Pinch.

"Maria . . . ," said Gideon.

She smiled, her hands playing over the artifacts. With a grinding of internal gears, the brass nose of the dragon began to rise, to separate from the lower jaw. Pinch swung alarmingly then secured his grip, losing his aim.

"This is a *dragon*, Mr. Pinch," she called. "Had you forgotten? This is Apep, who swallowed the sun god Ra whole. You think yourself a god, Mr. Pinch? Then meet the god-killer."

Too late, Pinch realized he was hanging in front of Apep's open maw. He cast one final, anguished look at Maria and Gideon, and then the dragon roared. A ball of yellow flame engulfed Pinch and burst in the blue sky, raining the ashes of the King of Steamtown over the hushed Alamo.

"The king is dead," said Gideon after a moment. "Let's finish what Rowena started, and wipe this misbegotten place off the face of the Earth."

The Old Man paused at the bar of the deserted saloon and helped himself to two swigs of whisky from the bottle abandoned on the flaking wooden surface. Over his shoulders he carried four bags, stuffed with money, gold, jewels, anything he could find. At first he'd been dismayed to find Steamtown abandoned, but once he thought about it, he decided it was a favorable outcome.

Thaddeus Pinch was a difficult man to deal with, and he would not have taken kindly to the news that the Old Man had *almost* brought him the clockwork girl. Now . . . well, whatever the reason that Steamtown was deserted, no one had thought to take their valuables with them. They were his for the taking. He would strike out east, perhaps, find another Yaqui tribe to insinuate himself into with his tales of ancient lore, find another warlord to do business with. It was a big place, what the white man called Texas. It was rife with opportunities.

The Old Man took another drink. He would have liked to see the brass dragon, though. Liked to have seen Quetzalcoatl. He hoped the old bird-god didn't take offense at him using his name for personal profit. The Old Man cackled. Perhaps he could use that story again to get him into the inner circle of some other tribe. The old gods were dead. This land belonged to those who seized their chances.

The first explosion rocked the saloon, plaster falling from the ceiling, tables shaking and overturning. The Old Man ran to the window as fast as he could, weighted down as he was with his booty. The general store three buildings down was aflame, debris littering the street. He frowned and looked to the sky.

Quetzalcoatl was bearing down on him, shining terribly in the sun: a savage, golden serpent, roaring its fire at Steamtown. The Old Man had just enough time to beg forgiveness from the gods—and to scream—before the saloon was engulfed.

The fight had gone out of the Steamtowners, and they meekly allowed the cavalry soldiers to tie their hands behind their backs and pile their weapons up on the dust. Every man watched as the brass dragon flapped over the Alamo, then alit in front of the old church. Ashes still rained down, and what was left of Steamtown was burning. Above the dragon, the *Skylady III* circled downward, Bent hanging over the edge of the observation deck, guiding Rowena to a space just outside the Alamo palisade.

It was over. He had recovered the dragon and rescued Maria, and Thaddeus Pinch was dead. Gideon Smith had won the day again.

Rowena ran through the palisade gates, Bent behind her. Behind them, Chantico and Inez hung back shyly. Rowena flung herself at Gideon as he climbed down from the dragon, wrapping her arms around him. "You did it. I'm so proud of you."

"I don't really feel like I did anything," Gideon said. He held her at arm's length. "Rowena . . . Louis is dead."

Pain crinkled her brow. "What happened?"

"He died saving us," said Maria, accepting Gideon's hand and climbing down from the dragon.

Rowena embraced Maria. "I am so glad that you are safe. We've been ever so worried."

"Hang on," said Bent, his hand on his side, gasping for breath. "I thought Cockayne was the effing villain? Now he's died a hero?"

"He was never a villain, not really," said Gideon. "He was just doing what he thought was expected of him, in a way. Had Louis not challenged Pinch to a duel, the Steamtowners would have finished us off. Pinch shot him in a most cowardly fashion."

"He lived by the sword," said Rowena. "It was inevitable he would die that way. You mustn't blame yourself, Gideon."

Maria squeaked as Bent picked her up and whirled her around. "And Miss Maria! Safe and sound!" He set her down and leaned on Apep's snout, rolling a cigarette. "So we got the dragon, we got Maria, and I'm presuming from that metal claw dangling from the dragon's nose that Pinch got his just effing desserts for his crimes." He broke into a wide smile. "You know what this means? It means mission accomplished. We can go home."

Gideon looked over to where the cavalry men were ordering the captured Steamtowners into lines. He saw Jeb Hart and waved at him. Bent took a long drag of his cigarette and said, "I suppose old Hart made good as well, in the end. We thought he'd effed off, and he was going to get help." Bent hawked noisily, to grimaces from Maria and Rowena, then spat into the sand. "God. Look at the color of that. Gin deficiency, that is."

Hart approached and took off his hat, nodding at them and looking curiously at Maria. Gideon said, "You got out of Steamtown safely, evidently."

Hart nodded. "I saw things go badly wrong in the brothel and decided that discretion was the better part of valor. Hightailed it back to the garrison."

"I thought there wasn't going to be any official involvement in this mission," said Gideon. "Governor Lyle talked about not wanting to antagonize the Texan warlords."

Hart grinned and nodded to the columns of fresh black smoke rising above Steamtown. "Reckon it's too late for that. Besides, when I got to the garrison a military dirigible had just landed." He coughed and indicated the covered wagon that the cavalry had brought with them. It was now being pulled by its four-horse team through the palisade gates.

Bent sniffed. "Here comes shit."

"What do you mean?" asked Gideon.

Bent shrugged. "I can feel it in my bones. Trouble's about to climb out of that effing wagon."

Gideon was about to say something when the canvas flaps were pulled back and a figure began to laboriously exit the wagon. It was only when he put his stovepipe hat on his head and turned around that Gideon realized who it was.

"Governor Lyle!"

"Mr. Smith!" said Lyle, already mopping his brow in the sun. He raised an eyebrow and wagged a finger in mock reproof at Rowena. "And Miss Fanshawe. I should have known you were up to mischief."

"Apologies, Governor—" she began, but he waved her away.

"What's done is done." He looked around, gazing at the dragon and then at Maria. "I see your mission was a success, Mr. Smith. And you have left Steamtown in, well, a bit of a state, to be frank."

Rowena raised a tentative hand. "That was largely my fault, Governor. Apologies. I hope it's not going to cause too many problems."

Lyle laughed. "You didn't particularly leave enough of Steamtown to cause problems. And you people aren't accountable; I am, but I had nothing to do with the attack on San Antonio. Captain Humbert and his men are here just to mop up."

"But what are *you* doing here, Governor?" asked Gideon. "You're a long way from New York."

Lyle smiled, almost apologetically. Bent murmured, "Here comes that trouble I was talking about."

"Yesterday a passenger airship came in from London, the same one that brings the mail. There was a letter for me." He reached into his jacket and withdrew a vellum envelope, sliding out its contents. He handed it over to Gideon and said, "You'll see it's signed by Mr. Gascoyne-Cecil."

It did indeed bear the signature of the Prime Minister, countersigned by Governor Lyle. Gideon scanned the rest of the letter and looked up. Bent had been right when he smelled trouble. "I'm afraid I don't understand, Governor."

"I have been in contact with London for some time regarding the situation with the Californian Meiji. The attack in the garden by the ninja that you yourself foiled was the last straw. I immediately contacted Whitehall, and they responded by return mail. Mr. Smith, the assassination attempt is being regarded as an act of war. I have been given carte blanche to take any action I see fit to protect British interests in America."

Gideon looked at the letter again. "But this says—"

Lyle smiled again, but not with much humor. He nodded and said, "Yes, Mr. Smith. I believe further attacks on New York and other British enclaves are imminent, and only what we might call a preemptive strike can safely defend our people. Mr. Smith, I am requisitioning you and your dragon, and we're going to Nyu Edo."

"No," said Gideon. "Absolutely not. Maria isn't some kind of . . . of war machine."

Lyle frowned. "Then what is she, Mr. Smith?"

She's the woman I love, Gideon wanted to say, no, to scream. He wanted to tell the world, to sing it from the rooftops. She was the woman he loved, and he'd moved heaven and hell to get her back. She was not Mr. Walsingham's war machine.

And he realized, so suddenly it dried out his mouth and made his head swim, that he was wrong. Was it the desire for a happy ending that had moved Walsingham to dispatch Gideon across the world to rescue Maria? Or was it merely that she and the brass dragon were invaluable assets, that a world-changing engine of destruction and its pilot simply could not be allowed to fall into the wrong hands?

Walsingham cared not a fig for Maria, only what was in her head. And he cared nothing for Gideon, did not believe in Gideon, not really. It had taken the distance Gideon had put between himself and London for him to see that now.

Gideon was just another soldier in the endless war fought to ensure Britannia ruled the waves. A highly decorated, much-publicized soldier, true, but just another resource. Mr. Gascoyne-Cecil might have signed that requisition order, but it would be Walsingham behind it, moving the pieces across the chessboard toward an endgame only he could see.

No, Gideon was not even a soldier. He was a machine, just as much as Maria—or at least a cog in Walsingham's unknowable, infernal device.

And the love a fisherman held for a clockwork girl amounted to nothing in all of that.

Lyle coughed. "Nyu Edo, Mr. Smith. We must strike now at the heart of the enemy. At *Britain's* enemy."

Gideon looked at Lyle, suddenly exhausted. "We're going nowhere, Governor. Not until we've buried our dead."

25

ACTS OF WAR

This was not, considered Gideon Smith, what he thought a life of adventure would be like.

As he wiped the sweat from his forehead with the back of his hand, he suddenly felt a longing for the life he had left behind. If he could turn back the clock, would he? If he could just go back to that night when the sea mist rolled in over Sandsend and stop his father Arthur from creeping out to take the *Cold Drake* fishing, only to die at the claws of the terrible Children of Heqet. Then he would never have met Bram Stoker, never have sought out Captain Lucian Trigger. Adventure would always simply be something he read about in the pages of *World Marvels & Wonders* and longed for from afar.

But he couldn't turn back time. It had all happened, and Gideon was—by royal appointment—the Hero of the Empire. The tales of Captain Trigger had been exposed as so many fancies and outright lies, and adventuring was not the pure, noble, tidy thing the penny dreadfuls claimed it to be.

He was standing up to his neck in the hole he had single-handedly dug in the dry dust, seven feet long. He tossed the spade out and climbed up over the lip, accepting Bent's out-stretched hand. The cavalrymen had wanted to help dig the grave, but Gideon had said no.

Louis Cockayne had died for him. Burying him was the very least he could do.

Rowena gave Gideon a canteen of water and he took a long draft as four of the soldiers laid Cockayne's body, wrapped in a Union Flag, into the hole. Captain Humbert raised an eyebrow at Gideon, who nodded, and they began to fill in the grave until there was just the slightest mound of earth displaced by the corpse of Louis Cockayne.

With the flat of his spade, Gideon drove a makeshift cross he had fashioned himself from two pieces of blasted wood from the stockade at the head of the mound, then laid down the shovel. He took out Cockayne's wallet from the back pocket of his ripped and dirty trousers. Inside was a faded photograph of a family group: stern-faced father, plump mother, three boys of varying heights. Cockayne smiled out from behind the shining eyes of the middle boy, aged just eight or nine. The thought of him as a child stabbed Gideon hard in his chest, brought prickling tears to his eyes. There was also a scrawled note in the wallet bearing the name of a farm in Connecticut.

"I'll have this sent back to his parents," said Gideon absently. "I'll write them a letter."

"What will you say?" asked Rowena.

"That Louis Cockayne died a hero." All heroes died, sooner or later. He wondered when it would be his turn.

"Someone should say something," said Bent.

Gideon blinked. They were all looking at him: Bent and Rowena, Governor Lyle, Jeb Hart, Captain Humbert and his soldiers.

"Me? I don't . . ."

"I think you should," said Maria softly. "He thought so much of you, you know."

Gideon smiled wryly. *Yes, maybe he did*, he thought. *And all this time I thought he hated me, considered me nothing but a country boy with ideas above my station*. He looked down at the photograph again, at the small boy who grew up to be Louis Cockayne.

We all start off as small boys with big ideas, he thought. *Yes, I owe this to Louis Cockayne*.

While he gathered his thoughts, one of the cavalrymen began to play a low, sonorous note on his bugle, and the assembled company took off their hats and cast their eyes down at the grave. As the "Last Post" faded, Gideon looked up at the wild blue sky that Louis Cockayne would never see again.

"I don't know if I believe in good and evil," said Gideon quietly. "My mother did; she was a churchgoer. My dad was a more . . . pragmatic man. He used to tell me that people weren't good or evil in themselves, but they sometimes did good things and evil things."

He paused, collecting his memories. "The first time I met Louis Cockayne, he was bringing a cargo of slaves back from Africa to Steamtown. He threatened to have my friends and me killed. Then he stole Maria from under my nose.

"The first words he spoke to me were when he asked me what I was doing, a boy from nowhere, walking with such great people. I thought him a pirate, a villain. But Louis was right. I was in the company of greatness. And he was among their number." Gideon smiled sadly again. "I just didn't know it at the time, and I don't think he did, either."

Gideon watched a tear roll down Rowena's face and fall to the parched earth at her feet. "He thought it was funny, all this *Hero of the Empire* business. He'd have called it a crock of shit or some such. Louis Cockayne looked after number one. But what he didn't realize . . ." Gideon felt something well inside of him, a great sob he had to strangle back. Maria put a hand on his shoulder, and he took hold of it fiercely. "What he didn't realize was that you only have to do good things once for it to cancel out all the bad. And Louis Cockayne did good when it counted most. He came back and he was a hero, and he was my friend. And that's all."

There was a long silence, broken eventually by the shuffling feet of Lyle. Now more than ever Gideon needed Cockayne's guidance. But Louis was gone for good, and Gideon couldn't rely on him any longer. He had to make the big, tough decisions himself. Gideon looked up and across the grave at Lyle. "Okay, Governor," he said wearily. "If it's really what must be done, let's go to war."

As the others moved away, Rowena stayed a moment, squatting down and running her fingers through the mound of dust.

"You were a bastard, Louis," she whispered. "A bastard and a rogue."

A breeze ruffled Rowena's hair. She smiled, imagining it to be the final, departing essence of Cockayne. *Couldn't shuffle off this mortal coil, huh, Louis? Not until you've heard me say it?*

Louis Cockayne was a bastard and a rogue. But he'd made good. Whether Rowena fully agreed with Gideon that Louis's final blaze of glory absolved him of all his other sins, she didn't quite know. All she knew for sure was that Louis Cockayne was one of the few men she really could call a friend. And, yes, more than that. She remembered the night in the *Yellow Rose*, as her 'stat had been called then, in the Alexandrian night that felt so long ago now, when she had only just met Gideon Smith. Yes, she'd lain with Cockayne; had before, too. Things were different for the 'stat pilots, they didn't follow the rules of polite society. You took your thrills where and when you could, because you never knew when your number would be up.

And now Louis Cockayne was gone. Another picture to stick up in the Union Hall chapel, another candle to light. Charles Collier, Louis Cockayne.

My soul is in the sky.

Rowena looked at where Gideon and Bent were talking in low tones. Why did all the men in her life have to leave? *Please let it not be Gideon next. I hope to fuck you taught him enough, Louis,* she thought.

The warm breeze caressed her again. *Say it*, it seemed to whisper.

She sighed and smiled sadly. "You were a bastard and a rogue, Louis Cockayne," she said. "But . . . I didn't hate you."

※

"We don't have to do what Lyle says," murmured Bent. "We can just tell him to eff off, you know. We were sent to bring back Maria and the dragon. We've done that."

Gideon looked over at Lyle, standing back a respectful distance with Jeb Hart and Captain Humbert. "He has a letter from the Prime Minister," he said flatly. "We have fresh orders. We're going to California."

Lyle, holding his stovepipe hat in his hands, took Gideon's glance as a signal to approach. "I thought, perhaps, Hart and I could travel in the airship. You will be accompanying, uh, Miss Maria in the dragon?"

Gideon looked at Rowena as she walked over from the fresh grave to join them. "You have no jurisdiction over Miss Fanshawe, Governor. She was employed to bring us to New York. She has already completed the task she was paid for."

"Done more than she was paid for, by all accounts," said Hart. "Heard you busted up Steamtown real good, Miss Fanshawe."

Rowena raised an eyebrow at him. "There was a reason for that. Governor Lyle, did you know someone in New York is selling your people into slavery?"

Lyle blinked at her. "Slavery? How so, Miss Fanshawe?"

She took out the manifest from her shirt pocket and handed it to him. "I took a job at North Beach. Secret cargo to Steamtown, in payment for a hold full of coal I was to bring back. Payment was fifty-four men, women, and children press-ganged from your streets, Governor."

Lyle rubbed his chin as he studied the sheet of paper. "This . . . this is shocking. These people were all from New York?"

"Kidnapped off the streets in some cases, tricked into bondage in others."

"But why?"

"For coal, Governor. Someone thought that fifty-four lives were fair payment for a 'stat full of coal to keep the fires burning in Manhattan."

"You'll look into this?" said Gideon. "Or do we need to come back to New York to sort it out ourselves?"

Lyle folded the paper and put it into his coat pocket. "No,

Mr. Smith, there's no need for that. Of course I'll look into it. This . . . horror must be investigated. I'll get on to it."

"At once?" asked Gideon.

"After we have dealt with the threat from the Meiji," said Lyle levelly. "The sooner we sort this out, the quicker I can get back to New York. As I said, perhaps the dirigible . . . ?"

"And as I said, Governor—" began Gideon, but Rowena put a hand on his arm.

"It's all right, Gideon," she said. "I want to see this out." She glanced at the sun. "If we have a following wind it will take us seven hours to reach Nyu Edo, and that's with the *Skylady III* flat out. If we want to get there before nightfall, then we should leave now. Otherwise in the morning."

"Nightfall would be perfect." Lyle smiled. "Element of surprise and all that."

Gideon frowned at him. "I take no pleasure in this, Governor. Had you not the backing of the British government I would not be allowing this attack on the Japanese."

"They started it," said Lyle, sounding to Gideon like a petulant child. "You were there yourself, Smith, when those ninjas attacked."

"Yes," said Gideon, scrutinizing Lyle. "So I was."

"And you remember I said the Japs were working on a weapon? Who's to say what they're planning with that. They could be getting ready to destroy New York even as we speak."

"What evidence do you have for this weapon, Lyle?" asked Bent. "And what sort of weapon could destroy a whole effing city?"

Lyle glanced at Hart, who had walked up with Captain Humbert to flank the Governor. "You know Jeb here does a bit of . . . reconnaissance work for me."

"Spying," said Bent.

Lyle shrugged. "If you like. He was raised in what used to be San Francisco; he knows the place well. Sometimes he goes back to visit the old homestead. Last time, he brought back news. The Japs are up to something, something big."

Gideon waited a moment. "What?"

Lyle pulled a pained face. "I can't say as I can really tell you, Mr. Smith. Classified information, and all that."

Gideon met Bent's eyes, then Rowena's. He sighed. "We have no choice. All right, Governor. Rowena will take you to Nyu Edo." He turned to Maria. "Can we fly this distance?"

She smiled. "I flew from London to America, Gideon."

Rowena said, "The dragon far outran the *Skylady III* when we were in Egypt. I'm not sure how that thing works, Maria, but I can't keep pace with you. Can you slow down enough to run alongside us?"

She nodded. Gideon said, "Then it's time. Let's get this done, and then we can all go home."

Gideon made himself as comfortable as possible in the cramped cockpit as Maria's hands played over the artifacts and the eldritch engines that powered Apep began to hum into life. He said, "You have everything you need for the journey?"

"All apart from one thing," she said, turning around in the seat. She reached out and grasped the front of Gideon's shirt, pulling him toward her, not for the first time surprising him with the strength in her metal joints. "This."

She placed her lips against his, warm lips that thrummed with life. Perhaps not a life that most people would consider conventional, but life nonetheless. And was there something else in her kiss? Love? Gideon felt it, too, felt invisible fingers probing his mind, grasping on to the sensations that threatened to flood him, to overwhelm him.

No. No, he would not turn back the clock, not for all the money in the Bank of England. Not even, he realized, to see Arthur Smith for one more moment. Life was what it was, and for good or ill there was no second chance. He kissed her back.

Maria gently pushed him away, planting a final, tender kiss on his lips, and turned back to the instrument panel, straightening her skirts. "When this is over, Gideon, I shall expect you to take me shopping for some new clothes. I simply cannot be seen in London in these rags."

"When this is over, Maria, I'll take you anywhere."

Then the huge metal wings of Apep began to flap and the dragon rose majestically into the blue sky as the *Skylady III*, freed from its moorings, bobbed up alongside them. Gideon peered through the broken porthole at Bent, waving from the observation deck, flanked by Chantico and Inez. He was giving the dragon a thumbs-up.

Gideon returned the gesture, then the airship and the dragon began to rise together, turning north and west, as the soldiers and captured Steamtowners below looked up, shielding their eyes against the sun and the magnificence of their passing.

There was a storeroom at the back of Serizawa's laboratory where no one but he ever went. He'd laid down some tatami matting and hung some floating world prints on the walls. He'd also secreted a few of Michi's toys in his duffel bag at home and brought them to work—including her headless doll, Kashira, which she had wailed about losing. No matter; they were reunited now. The storeroom was quite homey, he thought.

Akiko, of course, had other ideas. "You are crazy, Haruki. How long are we expected to stay here?"

"Just until the danger has passed."

She folded her arms while Michi sat down on one of the mats. "I'm sleeping here, Mummy."

"What about school?" hissed Akiko. "Her friends? We are supposed to just abandon our life?"

"Not abandon. Just put on hold." He took hold of her shoulders. "It might only be a few days. And I will be working right in the laboratory."

She shrugged him off. "I wish you would tell me what this supposed *danger* is, Haruki."

The images of the slaughter on the island passed through

Serizawa's mind, and he pushed them away. "I am working on a solution. But Nyu Edo is in terrible peril," he whispered. He turned to Michi and squatted down. "You will like living here? Just for a . . . a holiday?"

"It will be fun!" she said.

"And you can be quiet when Daddy tells you to? Daddy's boss, Mr. Morioka, he can be fierce!"

Serizawa thrust out his bottom jaw and frowned, making a growling noise. Michi laughed delightedly. "Your boss is a monster?"

"There are no monsters," said Akiko firmly, glaring at Serizawa. "You want to give her nightmares?"

No, he wanted to say. *I do not want to give our daughter nightmares. But there are monsters.* Instead he said, "So it is agreed, then? You will stay here for now?"

"For now," sighed Akiko.

"Good. Then I must go to work."

"Haruki," said Akiko, her voice softer. "You are driving yourself into the ground. We came here to the Californian Meiji to start a new life away from your father. Not so you could kill yourself trying to escape his shadow."

Serizawa smiled sadly at his wife. "My father casts a very long shadow."

After a moment's pause, Serizawa decided to lock the door to his laboratory. There was a bathroom in there, and he had left Akiko and Michi some basic food that would last until later. The facility on the hills overlooking Nyu Edo was busier than it normally would be so late in the afternoon, and he had to be careful that his family was not discovered. Science Officer Morioka had little enough patience with Serizawa as it was.

He made his way along the corridors to the main hangar, bustling with people and overseen from his glass office by Morioka, who nodded curtly from his desk when Serizawa slid back the doors and entered. Akiko was quite correct, of course; Serizawa was fighting to escape the shadow of his father. And it was people such as Science Officer Morioka who perpetuated the myth that it was somehow all his father's fault that they had been forced to flee Japan and come to start a new shogunate in America in the first place. There were those who said that the Emperor Kōmei should rightly be dead by now, and that his son Mutsuhito would have taken his rightful place as the progressive ruler of the old country instead of taking his supporters across the sea to found a new dynasty twenty-three years ago.

And yes, Serizawa supposed that Kōmei should be dead. There were few who survived smallpox. But then, not everyone had the benefit of Serizawa's father as their court scientist. The senior Serizawa had contrived a contraption that was quite miraculous, a network of pipes and pumps that, each evening, flushed the emperor's body with fresh blood, ejecting the diseased liquid. There was nothing that could stop each fresh infusion becoming contaminated with smallpox, but the new blood every night ensured that the emperor, though pitted and scarred with pockmarks, continued to survive.

They did not call him the Blood Emperor for nothing. And there was no shortage of willing volunteers who sacrificed their own blood every day in tribute to their beloved emperor.

Or so people said.

Serizawa, of course, being young and idealistic and forward looking, had been as appalled as anyone by his father's work, which was why he had made the pilgrimage with his young wife to the new world. And that was why the Serizawa name must be remembered for reasons other than his father's work. That was why he had to succeed.

As the doors slid closed behind him, Serizawa looked up to behold his work.

Project: Jinzouningen.

Even now, it took his breath away. Oh yes, they would remember Serizawa.

※

"Where are we going?"

"For a little walk, Prickly Pear," said Akiko. Curse Haruki

for locking them in! She would have harsh words with him later. She stuck her tongue out and closed one eye as she maneuvered the hairpin into the lock chamber.

"Daddy told us to stay here," said Michi uncertainly.

"Daddy is not the boss of this family; you will learn that," said Akiko as there was a satisfying click from the lock. She had read how to do this in one of the English novels that sometimes made their way over from the British East Coast. She hadn't been sure it would work, but evidently Haruki wasn't the only one in the family with technical know-how.

There was a white coat, of the type worn by Serizawa when he was working, hanging in the laboratory, and Akiko pulled it on over her kimono. Then she took Michi firmly by the hand and stepped out into the corridor. A blank-faced man pushing a trolley loaded with gears and springs nodded apologetically to her as he steered out of the way, and Akiko fell in behind him, glancing at the notices painted on the walls. They pointed to numbered rooms, occasionally bathrooms and canteens. Most people they passed either ignored them or gave them the merest cursory glance; everyone seemed very preoccupied. Perhaps this danger of Haruki's was something serious, after all.

The largest flow of people seemed to be in the direction of signs indicating a hangar of some description, so Akiko fell in with them. If anyone thought the presence of a small child was unusual, no one voiced it. Eventually they came to a tall set of sliding doors, guarded by two men in pale cotton all-in-one suits in the Western style.

"Mummy," whispered Michi. "They have *guns*."

The guards glanced at each other and frowned at the sight of Akiko and Michi. One held out his hand. "Identification papers, please."

There was a tap at the screen and the other guard turned to slide it back, allowing a scientist to exit as he pored over script on a long scroll. Beyond him, Akiko saw the unmistakable form of her husband.

"Haruki!" she called, but his name died on her lips as she saw what was beyond him, towering over the swarming men in the huge hangar.

Serizawa pinched his nose tightly. The engineers had shored up the knees on Jinzouningen with steel plates riveted to either side of the joint, as he had instructed. But the stress reports were still showing undue pressure. Science Officer Morioka tapped the wooden board on which were clipped the latest figures.

"Why, Serizawa, why? Why will this not work?"

He looked up at Jinzouningen. It stood forty feet tall, a skeleton made of the strongest bamboo shipped in from the old country, the steel plates fashioned in the style of a samurai's armor hiding the pistons and gears that powered the mechanical man from the steam furnace hidden in its bowels.

"It will work," Serizawa insisted. "It's as ready as it ever will be."

But all the same, he looked at the numbers with dismay. Those stress points were just too . . .

"Haruki!"

Serizawa turned in astonishment as Akiko and Michi pushed past the guards. He heard the intake of breath from Morioka; too late now. He bent down and caught Michi in his arms.

"Haruki . . . ," said Akiko, never taking her eyes from Jinzouningen. "*This* is what you have been working on . . . ?"

"It is like a giant Kashira," said Michi happily. "Did you copy my doll, Daddy?"

He smiled, then stopped and stared at her. "What did you say, Prickly Pear?"

"Kashira," she said. "My doll. I found it in our new room."

"Of course," he said. He handed Michi to Akiko. "Of course."

He had been too fixated on making Jinzouningen look like what it was meant to be—a mechanical man. The head was where the cockpit was situated, but of course . . . it was making the giant too unstable. He tapped his forehead, thinking swiftly, then hailed the nearest engineer.

"Take the head off!"

The man looked doubtfully at Morioka, who frowned at Serizawa.

"Take the head off!" Serizawa called again. "We don't have enough time to make a pretty job of it, but we can sling the cockpit in the stomach cavity, just above the furnace. It will be terribly hot, but it will make the thing a good deal more stable."

Morioka nodded curtly, and Serizawa gave Akiko and Michi a huge kiss each, dancing delightedly on the spot. Michi clapped her hands.

Then Morioka held up his hand as the noise began: a long, low, mournful note that drifted in through the open windows high in the hangar walls.

"What is that?" asked Akiko.

Serizawa felt the color drain from his face. It was the alarm, the one he had hoped never to hear.

"We're under attack," he said.

Morioka waved at the guards. "Get the pilots here, now!"

Serizawa looked at Jinzouningen. The engineers had already removed the helmeted head and were installing the cockpit in the belly of the mechanical man. He said, "There isn't time to get the pilots familiarized with the new setup."

Morioka stared at him. "What do you mean? That we should just stand by when we are so close? Let Nyu Edo be destroyed?"

"They have only ever worked the cockpit from above," said Serizawa swiftly. "The perspectives will have changed. I haven't even had all the links hooked up completely. Only I know the shortcuts. Only I know how to work Jinzouningen."

Akiko was shaking her head. "Haruki, if you mean what I think you mean . . . then no."

"I have to," he said. "I have to pilot Jinzouningen."

Morioka bowed stiffly. "Then may the spirits guide you,

Serizawa, for the price of failure is high." He rose and looked Serizawa in the eye. "For all of us."

As the klaxon wailed, Serizawa embraced his wife and child then set off at a run toward his giant mechanical man.

26

Jinzouningen vs. Apep

"What the *fuck* is that?" asked Lyle, leaning forward on the polished dashboard of the *Skylady III*'s bridge and peering into the gathering dusk.

"I couldn't have put it better myself, and I really effing mean that," said Bent, at his side. He turned to Rowena. "Have you ever seen anything like it?"

They had approached Nyu Edo from the east after traveling north from the remnants of Steamtown, making even better time than Rowena had promised. The city proper still lay out of sight, between the wooded hills that rose up on the outskirts of the Californian Meiji and the sunset-glittering sea beyond. The land was wild but showed the ceaseless activity of the Japanese, whole swathes of woodland razed for building and industry. There, on the hills, squatted a cluster of low brick buildings, with one tall tower, perhaps fifty feet or more, rising up from the center. It was beside this tower—one side opened up by way of tall sliding doors—that the focus of their attention was standing.

Rowena shook her head. "It looks like a giant samurai. With no head."

"Is this the secret weapon you were talking about?" Bent asked Lyle.

Rowena caught the look that passed between Lyle and Hart. A look that said this monstrous metal creature was as much news to them as it was to the rest. Lyle recovered quickly and said, "I suppose it must be." He looked at Bent. "You were asking what sort of thing could destroy a city, Mr. Bent. I reckon we're looking at it."

Rowena glanced out to starboard, where the brass dragon

was keeping pace with the 'stat, its majestic metal wings catching the golden rays of the sinking sun. Was Apep equal to this giant? Who knew what it could do? She called over her shoulder for Chantico and Inez.

"Gideon and Maria might need some help," she said. "Aloysius, can you take everyone who can handle a gun down to the armory and break out the biggest artillery we have?"

Lyle had a self-congratulatory air that she didn't like one bit. She glanced at the letter from London that he had left on the dashboard. Something about it niggled at her. She was sure it was genuine, that the Prime Minister had indeed given the order for Gideon to be deployed to Nyu Edo. But all the same . . .

She pushed the thought away. Apep was peeling away from them, flying high to get a better look at the giant from above. The enemy was standing stock-still, as though it were nothing more than a gigantic sculpture. Rowena had to grudgingly admit that Lyle had been right when he said the Japanese had a devastating weapon up their sleeves, even if he seemed a little . . . opportunistic about the whole thing. Soon it would be time to see just what the monster could do.

As she slowed the *Skylady III* to better get into position with the observation deck facing the monster, she did pause to wonder why, if it was bent on the destruction of British interests in the east, the metal man seemed to be facing out to sea and the sun sinking in the west.

※

The furnace had only been fired up for minutes, but it was already hellishly hot in the makeshift cockpit. The engineers had torn out one of the armor plates from the belly of Jinzouningen to allow Serizawa an unfettered view, but there had been no time to install a windshield, so the warm breeze of the Nyu Edo evening caressed him, offering some relief from the heat below. A forest of levers was arrayed before the leather sling that served as his seat. He pulled at them in turn, flexing the steel muscles of the mechanical man. As he bent the knees of

Jinzouningen and straightened again, he heard the protesting shriek of the over-tensioned joints. Relocating the cockpit had done much to alter the center of gravity—he sent a silent prayer of thanks to his Prickly Pear—but Jinzouningen was still unsteady on his feet. Serizawa raised the right arm, the wheels and pistons protesting and whirring above his head. The sight lines of the guns were based on a head-mounted cockpit; he would essentially be firing blind. The wrist-mounted guns were of his own design, each one surrounded by a cartridge "bracelet" containing more than three hundred bullets.

He hoped it would be enough.

Below him, Nyu Edo was eerily still save for the constant sonorous note of the alarm horn. The citizens had been herded off to makeshift shelters or ordered to stay indoors. Nyu Edo had a small standing army that was poorly equipped; though trade with the old country was brisk, Japan would not countenance selling weapons to the Californian Meiji, and neither Britain nor Spain trusted the fledgling state enough to offer guns and ammunition. The factories in Nyu Edo had produced third-rate copies of the few revolvers and rifles that had come their way, but they were notoriously inefficient and unreliable. There were the few samurai families who had made the journey across the sea to join the Meiji, of course, but that amounted to a handful of old men with swords and arrows.

Which was why Nyu Edo relied upon the genius of Haruki Serizawa to save the day in the event of the darkness that now befell them.

He swallowed and began to prepare Jinzouningen to walk down the hill toward the bay.

The alarm's wail suddenly faded away.

And a most unexpected shadow fell across Serizawa.

* * *

"Good God," said Gideon, leaning over Maria's shoulder as Apep spiraled away from the *Skylady III* and soared up over the collection of buildings, the metal giant below them. "What do you think it is?"

"Our enemy, by all accounts," said Maria, her hands playing over the instrument panel. "Perhaps the more pertinent question should be, what can it *do*?"

Ahead of them, down the hill, the city of Nyu Edo nestled by the sea. Its ordered streets were lined with low wooden houses, a mixture of styles that were both recognizably Western and exotically foreign. Pagoda roofs with carefully raked gravel paths snaked between them. Half a dozen boats bobbed in the shallows of the harbor. There were no people that Gideon could see.

Suddenly the giant moved, turning with exaggerated, stiff movements on the grassy hill to face their approach. It raised its right arm as though pointing accusingly at them.

"A mechanical man," said Gideon wonderingly. "It must be forty feet tall. Can we bring it down?"

Maria shrugged and cast her hands in an intricate pattern over the artifacts. Gideon held on as Apep banked sharply, descending low until its feathery shadow skimmed the ravaged woodland, and coming in straight and fast at the giant. The crocodilian maw opened with a grinding of gears, and Maria let loose a short burst of fireballs, generated by unknown means deep within Apep's brass body; whether ancient science or eldritch magic, Gideon was unsure. The fireballs engulfed the giant and it staggered backward, its arm still raised. But it remained on its wide metal feet, and the outstretched arm suddenly spat at them with a staccato roar.

Maria pulled the dragon up as the bullets began to impact upon its brass hide. None penetrated, though Gideon felt Apep shudder with each true hit. He smiled as Maria righted the dragon. "Well, if that's the best it's got . . ."

"Gideon . . ."

He looked down at the patch of wetness spreading across Maria's torso. "You were hit!"

She shook her head. "No, not me. A bullet must have punctured the underside of the dragon. Gideon, I *felt* it."

Her right arm was moving stiffly and jerkily, and oil and water leaked from beneath her sleeve. "And this is where the dragon was hit on the wing." She looked at him. "Gideon, whatever change has been wrought in the artifact in my head, it has somehow linked me more closely to Apep than I could have imagined. We are more as one than ever before. Which means . . ."

Gideon looked out the porthole at the giant. "Which means if Apep is damaged badly, you could . . . you could *die*?"

Maria smiled tightly. "Then we had better bring the mechanical man down first."

Serizawa's first thought was that the bamboo skeleton might have been a mistake. Although it was as hard as iron, he had not considered that it was still wood, still flammable. As he battered at the smoldering sections of the rib cage within which he was suspended, he also thought that Jinzouningen had not been created with battling a fire-breathing flying serpent in mind. So perhaps he should stop chiding himself and start thinking about surviving.

The thing that was attacking him was definitely a machine, piloted by human beings. The whys and wherefores of it could be debated later. Now he had to bring it down so that he could get on with the task at hand. An airship was circling some distance away. Evidently this was a concerted attack force on Nyu Edo. The fools. There might be nothing left for them to invade if he did not turn Jinzouningen back toward the sea.

Brass and steel the flying dragon might be, but it was not impervious, he learned not long after its opening salvo of fireballs. He had ducked behind the steel panel in front of him as the fireballs exploded, adding to the already unbearable heat from the coal furnace below. The fire was causing all kinds of problems with the rivet joints—Serizawa made a mental note to look at that in future, then another one to concentrate on surviving so there *was* a future—but the line to the guns was still working fine, and he let go with a ten-second round of bullets. The dragon had kept coming but shuddered at his onslaught. Perhaps he had a chance if he could concentrate his fire for long enough to cause some real damage. As the dragon began to fly low at him for another burst of fire, Serizawa brought up the left arm to double his firepower. If only he had some proper sight lines to follow. He pushed both levers down, hard.

Nothing happened. Both guns had jammed.

"It isn't firing," said Gideon. "Let loose the fireballs."

"We need to get closer," said Maria. "They'll just bounce off. We need to do some real damage to whatever is controlling it."

The giant stood with both arms outstretched, and then it moved, more quickly than Gideon would have guessed, and reached for one of the handful of tall redwood trees that grew sparsely among the stumps of its many former neighbors. Gideon said, "If it thinks it can hide in the trees that is to our advantage, yes? We can set that little copse on fire, cause it more damage?"

"It isn't hiding," said Maria.

The mechanical man took hold of a wide trunk in both hands and began to sway it, tearing it up by the roots from the dry earth. Then it turned its upper torso, its feet still planted on the hillside, and swung the tree trunk at them. Maria pulled Apep up fast, the dragon rocking as the branches of the tree clipped the underside of the flexible tail. Maria winced.

"Are you all right?"

"Yes," she said. "I won't tell you where that hurt me."

There was a huge crack, this time from behind them, and something whistled past the dragon. Gideon craned to look around. "It's Aloysius, with that bloody gun on the *Skylady III*. They're going to have us down if they're not careful."

Apep banked around again for another run. "It's a fast

learner, whatever it is. Can such a thing exist, a mechanical giant, with independent thought?"

Maria didn't look at him. "I exist, Gideon. Am I so very different?"

"I didn't mean—" he began, then shouted, "Maria!"

�

"Can't you get any closer?" shouted Bent, waving smoke away from the barrel of the Hotchkiss. The dirigible was bucking and swaying, and he couldn't get a decent bead on the mechanical man.

He heard a reply but couldn't make it out. "What? What?"

Hart appeared on the observation deck. "Miss Fanshawe says to hold your fire. You nearly hit the dragon that last time."

"If she'd keep this bloody thing still . . . ," said Bent.

"She says the crosswinds are too fierce here, and we need to stay out of reach of the Jap guns. Also, the dragon's whipping around too much. Leave it, Mr. Bent; we're causing more harm than good."

Bent sighed and leaned on the Hotchkiss. "That's the story of my life." He gave a salute, though he knew those in the dragon wouldn't see it. "Best of luck, Gideon and Maria, looks like it's all down to you."

✦

Serizawa cast the tree trunk away from him. Jinzouningen was becoming more fluid in its movements the more he exercised its steel joints and bamboo frame. He had almost gotten lucky and brought down the dragon with the trunk; he doubted whoever was inside the creature would make the same mistake twice. He squinted at the tangle of pipes and hoses above him. What had happened to the guns? He risked a tentative touch on the hydraulic connection; it was red-hot. Perhaps they had just overheated. The dragon was coming around again. Serizawa raised Jinzouningen's arms and hauled both levers down hard. This time the guns ratcheted into life, the force knocking the giant backward, causing him to toggle the leg levers frantically to keep his balance.

When Serizawa looked up the dragon was skimming downward toward the trees, its wings immobile. At the last moment it raised its long snout and rolled off to the left, the vast wings flapping into life. He had hurt it. He just had to do better.

As another hail of bullets thudded into the underside of Apep, Maria slumped forward, the dragon spinning away over the trees. Gideon was now beginning to get seriously worried. He had put too much faith in the invulnerability of the dragon. Just, he supposed, as he put too much faith in everything. Perhaps he should have taken a leaf out of Bent's book: Trust no one and nothing other than yourself.

But that way, surely, lay only loneliness. And after traveling the world in pursuit of Maria, he was not about to resign himself to *that*. Nor was he going to allow her to die here in the service of the British government.

"Did you see?" he asked as Maria recovered, bringing Apep around for another run at the metal giant. "There is a man in there, operating it from its belly. If we can take him out . . ."

"Then the thing will fall." She nodded. She was moving with studied, deliberate motions, as though she had to concentrate more and more effort on keeping her facade of humanity complete. He could hear the cogs and wheels grinding within her when she moved. The giant had already caused her serious damage. They could not afford to allow another salvo to hit.

She steadied Apep and the wings began to beat, bringing the dragon in low over the darkening land, the giant waiting for them with its arms outstretched.

Akiko held Michi close as they peered from behind the tall, open door of the tower at the battle unfolding on the hillside. Science Officer Morioka stood alongside them, his arms folded across his chest. Around them, men in overalls began to lug guns and small wheeled cannons out of the hangar.

"You are finally going to send men to help my husband?" said Akiko.

Morioka glared at her. "These men are going down to the town."

She gaped. "What? But that . . . that thing is going to destroy his machine! It will kill him!"

Morioka turned back to the battle. "Quite possibly. Jinzouningen was not created to fight this metal flying beast. It was not designed for such a conflict."

"Then what is it for?" said Akiko. "Haruki spoke of danger threatening Nyu Edo . . . what danger could be worse than this?"

"You will see," said Morioka. "Your husband has failed us."

"My daddy is going to save us!" said Michi angrily, pouting from within the folds of her mother's laboratory coat. "You don't say those things about my daddy!"

"Hush," said Akiko.

Morioka looked down at Michi as though she were something unpleasant he had stepped in. He shrugged. "It is true. He has failed us and damned us all."

As Akiko turned to watch the soldiers heading down the hill toward the town, she felt her child break out of her grasp. "Michi!" she cried as her daughter ran across the apron toward where Haruki was facing off against the dragon. "Michi, come back!"

Serizawa was in trouble. The leg joints of Jinzouningen had completely seized up, rendering him immobile. The dragon's fireballs must have burned out the hydraulic pumps. And the furnace below him was getting so hot he thought he might black out. Sweat ran down his forehead and into his eyes, but he had to keep both hands on the levers that controlled the giant's guns. The dragon was coming at him, low and fast. One more volley of fireballs and he would be lost. He had to make his next shots count. He would go for the head. Sweat blurred his vision, but not so much that he did not see the tiny figure hurtling out of the hangar, waving and jumping at him.

His heart sank to his boots.

Michi.

⁂

"I am about to fire," said Maria shakily. "Gideon, I do not feel too well. . . ."

"We can do it," said Gideon. "You can do it. We're almost there, Maria. You can . . . wait!"

He did not believe what he was seeing at first, but the dot on the hillside quickly resolved itself into the unmistakable form of a tiny child, tearing toward the giant, a woman in a kimono and a flapping white coat giving chase.

There is a man in there, operating it from its belly. If we can take him out . . .

What had he been thinking? There was a man in there. A *man* in there.

"His daughter," said Gideon, and abruptly the warm California evening faded to be replaced by the cool night of Sandsend, the cockpit of Apep transforming around him into the cottage of Yorkshire stone that perched on the hillside, facing the iron-gray sea. He looked out not on the mysterious city of Nyu Edo, the forty-foot mechanical man about to spit death at them, but at the moonlit ridges of the waves that gently broke on the beach of his home.

He was filled with the ache of loss, the memory of wondering what had happened to his father, lost in the mysteries of the ocean. He was consumed by the rage he had felt when he learned of Arthur Smith's terrible end at the claws of the Children of Heqet.

There was a man in that machine.

"No," he said. "Not at the pilot."

Maria paused, and glanced around at him. "What?"

Gideon thought fast. "Shoot around the thing's feet. Can you do that?"

Maria shrugged, and her hands played over the artifacts. Apep opened its maw and roared, and Maria put the dragon into a tight barrel roll, aiming a quick burst of fire around the soft hillside on which the mechanical man was perched.

It opened fire with its arm guns, but it was too late. Maria had undermined the ground it stood on, and the burning earth began to slide and give way. Apep pulled upward, avoiding the volley of bullets, as the giant, seemingly unable to regain its footing, began to topple.

From above, Gideon watched the giant collapse in a cloud of dust. The woman held the child back some distance away. The man inside might still be dead, but he would have more chance than if they'd boiled him alive.

"Maria, take us down," he said wearily.

She nodded, the dragon descending in a lazy spiral, then keeled forward, her head hitting the dashboard as Apep plummeted the last twenty feet and crashed into the hillside.

27

THE PRICE OF FAILURE

Governor Lyle was dancing a merry jig on the observation deck of the *Skylady III*, waving his stovepipe hat like a maniac as Rowena brought the 'stat in to land as close to the crashed Apep as possible. Springing the hatch on the dragon's cockpit, Gideon waved to show that he was all right but also that he needed assistance, then he gathered Maria up in his arms.

The impact of Apep into the hillside had been minimal and Gideon and Maria had been cushioned within the cockpit, so they were unharmed from the crash. But whatever mysterious relationship existed between the clockwork girl and the brass dragon had caused Maria very real and—to Gideon's eyes—very serious harm. There were tiny tears in the smooth leather skin that covered her metal frame, as though it had been ripped open by minuscule bullets. They exposed the lie of Maria's humanity, revealing pipes and gears and leaking tubes within her soft, perfect—yet ultimately inhuman—skin.

Yet, thought Gideon as he stepped down from Apep, casting a glance at the crumpled, smoking remains of the mechanical giant, appearances could be deceiving. He had met more than one man of flesh and blood whose humanity was barely a tenth that of his beloved Maria's.

And here was one now.

"Mr. Smith, Mr. Smith! A tremendous effort!" panted Lyle as he waddled over from the *Skylady III,* where Rowena, Chantico, and Inez were mooring the anchor ropes to rocks and trees. "Whatever the hell that thing was, it was no match for our dragon." He gazed admiringly at Apep, curled on the hillside. "What a magnificent beast."

Gideon ignored him and laid Maria down on a bed of soft grass. Her eyelids flickered, as though she was asleep and lost in wretched dreams, and that gave him some measure of hope. Her body was clockwork, but her brain was human. As long as that endured, then surely she would be all right . . . ? His hands came away from her slick with thin oil and clear viscous fluid from the torn pipes and tubes that snaked within her. But how much of the machinery was necessary to keep the brain alive and active? He knew so little about her inner workings, really. Despite himself, he smiled. Bent would say that any man felt the same about any woman.

"Gideon?" It was Rowena, approaching with Bent and the others. Lyle, at last sensing that something was wrong, was hanging back with Jeb Hart. Gideon looked up at her. "It's Maria . . . something's wrong."

"You did effing phenomenally up there, lad," said Bent, brandishing his notebook. "What happened? Did she take a hit?"

"I'm not sure. . . ."

Maria's eyes flickered again, and she looked briefly at Gideon, smiling. "I feel so very . . . far away . . . ," she said softly.

"Hang on," he said. "We'll get you fixed up."

"Um, Gideon," said Bent. "Look."

From the tangle of steel and bamboo a man was emerging, helped by the woman Gideon had seen rushing across the hillside. The tiny child, who had been standing some distance away, ran to join them. The pilot was alive, then.

"He was operating that thing?" asked Bent.

"Gideon," said Rowena urgently. "Listen, I need to speak to you." She lowered her voice. "It's about Lyle, that letter from London."

He held up his hand. "It'll have to wait a moment, Rowena." He straightened as the man, supported by the woman

Gideon could only assume was his wife, limped away from the fallen giant, toward them. He hailed them. "Hello. My name is Gideon Smith. We are from London."

"What are you doing?" hissed Lyle, coming up behind them with Jeb Hart. "You're fraternizing with the goddamn enemy!"

The woman scowled at them, and the man held up a placatory hand. He said in halting English, "I am Haruki Serizawa of the Californian Meiji. This is my wife, Akiko, and my daughter, Michi."

"How lovely," said Bent. "Gideon, weren't you trying to kill each other five minutes ago?"

"Your weapon is destroyed, Mr. Serizawa," said Gideon. "I hope you will accept defeat and cease your hostilities toward British interests on the East Coast."

Serizawa blinked. "Hostilities? If there have been such things, I have been no part of them. Nor has Jinzouningen."

"Jinzouningen?"

He cast his arm backward. "My creation. It was a weapon of defense, Smith-san."

"For God's sake, Smith, finish him off!" said Lyle. "Or take him prisoner at the very least!"

"Serizawa!"

"What now?" said Bent as a tall figure began to hurry toward them from the tall hangar.

"Science Officer Morioka," sighed Serizawa. "My superior."

The frowning Japanese man stalked to Serizawa and cast his gaze around the others. "British. I will speak in English so the aggressors realize what they have done. They have destroyed Jinzouningen. They have damned us." He shook his head. "You have failed, Serizawa. I suppose it was too much to ask that you might be equal to your father."

"I could hardly have prepared for this . . . ," he said. "Jinzouningen was not designed to tackle a . . . a flying dragon."

"We aren't the aggressors," protested Gideon. "You are!"

Morioka ignored him. Instead he said to Serizawa, "I told

you that the price of failure would be high. You leave me no choice."

The older man moved aside his laboratory coat to reveal a short, flat-bladed sword, which he drew and presented, the blade on the palm of his hand, to Serizawa. "Take the tantō."

Akiko looked at him, horrified. "You cannot mean . . . seppuku?"

"What is going on here?" asked Gideon as Serizawa wearily took the blade.

"I have failed. I must commit seppuku."

Akiko covered her daughter's ears with her hands. "He means he must disembowel himself. Here, in front of Michi. In front of me."

"That's effing barbaric," said Bent. "Can't you just tell him to eff off?"

Serizawa smiled. "I think I can, but I will be banished from Nyu Edo. My wife and child—"

"Your wife and child will follow you to the ends of the Earth!" said Akiko angrily. She took the short blade from Serizawa and flung it away from her into the brush. "There is your answer, Science Officer Morioka. Better we renounce the Californian Meiji and Nyu Edo than this."

Morioka stared impassively at her. "There is no return from this course of action. You will be disgraced."

Akiko spat at him. "We left Japan to start a new life here. But we are shackled to the old ways. What is the point? We might as well have stayed."

Morioka said nothing but turned on his heel and stalked back toward the hangar. Akiko and Serizawa exchanged a glance. "Well," he said. "I suppose that is that."

Gideon put up his hands. "Wait. I have no idea what is going on here but . . . look, who do I see? Who is in charge in Nyu Edo?" He looked desperately at Bent, then Lyle. "This is supposed to be a bloody war, isn't it?" He turned back to Serizawa. "You said this metal man of yours was a defense. A defense against what?"

The alarm wail began to sound again in the deserted town below. Bent tugged Gideon's sleeve until he turned to face him, then he pointed wordlessly down to the harbor.

"Yes," said Serizawa. "A defense against *that*."

Against all the odds, she had survived. The first three days had been the worst, her stomach groaning and rumbling with hunger, the muscles in her legs seizing up with the effort of propelling herself forward through the waves, her backbone aching from holding her head above the salty water. Then something had come swimming around, circling her at a distance, closing in, its dark fin slicing through the water, its mouth widening to display rows of pin-sharp teeth.

It didn't last five minutes. Her hunger sated, her dominance of this new, wet world assured, she roared into the sky and pushed on, her claws eventually scrabbling on soft sand, pulling her up to a deserted, tiny island where she collapsed in the surf and slept.

There was no food on the island, but there was a supply of fresh rainwater, pooled in a tiny lagoon fringed with trees. It gave her the impetus to move on, barely hesitating as she waded out until her feet no longer felt the shore and she began to swim again.

Thus her days and nights rolled into one, and she began to forget why she was doing what she was doing. She was ready to succumb to the waves and the predators that circled, warily, around her, when she came upon a bigger island. This one wasn't empty. Tiny figures pointed and swarmed as she clambered up on the rocks, and she remembered. Remembered the ones who had invaded her home, the ones who had stolen that which was most precious.

She fed well, though she sensed these were not the creatures that had raided her nest. No matter, they were enough alike. But her hunger for vengeance was not sated, and she knew that there must be more of the two-legged creatures out there somewhere.

And there were. Dusk was heavy over the calm sea as she sighted the huge bulge of land that stretched, dizzyingly, as far as she could see. She had thought her island and the surrounding iron-gray ocean the extent of the world.

She had been wrong. As the first creatures on their tiny boats beheld her with astonishment then sped for the land, an eerie wail began to sound over the city. It was like the death song of an injured beast.

The feeding would be good in this place, and she would finally have her revenge.

"That's it, isn't it?" said Gideon flatly. "The thing from the island."

"Unless you're on speaking terms with any other tyrannosaurs, then I'd hazard a guess that it probably is." Bent nodded, never taking his eyes from the beast that lumbered out of the shallows, threw its enormous, green-scaled head back, and roared, shaking the very hillside they stood upon.

"That is what Jinzouningen was designed for," said Serizawa bitterly. "There is an island . . . we know it only as sector thirty-one. It is closer to California but officially in Japanese waters. It is top secret. Impenetrable."

"Not anymore," said Bent.

"I'm very much afraid that is our fault," said Gideon. "We went to this sector thirty-one on a rescue mission. We had no idea . . ." He looked at Bent. "But can it have followed us? Really?"

"I don't think it's after us specifically, but close," said Bent. "I didn't tell you because I didn't think much of it at the time, but when we were leaving the island I went to look for the head on the ship—I damn near shat myself when that thing came running out of the trees. Though I suppose that's a little more information than you need. Anyway, I saw old Professor Rubicon skulking around in the engine room, so I thought I'd see what he was up to. He was stashing something by the furnace. I had a quick look after he'd gone, but I thought it was just, you know, scientific samples and all that."

"What was it, Aloysius?" asked Gideon, wishing he'd get to the point.

"It was an egg, Gideon. What I now reckon was an effing tyrannosaur egg. And Mummy ain't happy, not one bit."

"Only the Japanese and Californian Meiji officials know the island as sector thirty-one," said Serizawa, looking down the hillside at the dinosaur with what looked to Gideon to be something that approached admiration. "Children and those who like old tales call it Monster Island."

"And we have destroyed your only defense," said Gideon. He felt sick.

"Still," said Bent. "They've gone and dumped you, haven't they, Serizawa? No skin off your nose what happens to them."

"But what about my class?" asked Michi, held tightly in her mother's arms. "I don't want it to eat my teacher."

"She is right, Haruki," said Akiko. "There are innocent people down there."

Serizawa nodded. He said to Gideon, "They have banished us, true. But . . ." He glanced at Lyle, who was staring with a mixture of horror and fascination at the beast loping up and down the harbor in the gathering gloom. "Those in power do many things that the ordinary people would not necessarily countenance."

Gideon took his point. "Quite. Is there anything we can do . . . ?"

"You have a rather marvelous brass dragon, Smith-san." Serizawa nodded. "Perhaps . . . ?"

"Maria!" said Gideon. He bent beside her. She seemed unconscious, though the machinery within her still hummed and throbbed.

"She is the pilot?" guessed Serizawa. "She requires a doctor?"

"An effing mechanic, more like." Bent chuckled. "She's clockwork, you see. Not a real woman."

Serizawa, with the help of his wife, crouched beside Gideon. "Clockwork? An automaton? How fascinating . . ."

"There's a bit more to it than that," sniffed Gideon. "But Mr. Bent is right; I'm not wholly sure what has happened but there appears to be some kind of damage to her internal workings."

Serizawa smiled. "Then you are incredibly lucky that I am here. I am the finest scientist in the Californian Meiji. Possibly even the whole of America!"

As Gideon began to tell Serizawa all he knew about Maria, Bent sidled over to the young woman. Pretty little thing. He'd always liked 'em a bit exotic. Put him in mind of the folk in Limehouse, London's Chinatown, a little, but different. . . . The thought sent a familiar tickle to the base of his skull, the one that was like an alarm bell telling him he should be sniffing around this particular thing or that particular thing. Then he remembered his notebook, jammed into his pocket.

"Here, Akiko, is it?" he asked.

She frowned at him then nodded. "That is correct, Bent-san. Can I be of assistance?"

"I reckon you probably can." He smiled, showing the stumps and gaps in his wide mouth. "Back in New York I took a drawing of a bit of Japanese writing. It awfully puts me in mind of something. Wondered if you could take a look, maybe translate it for me? I must say, your English is effing—I mean, wonderfully, erm, good."

She inclined her head. "Thank you. We occasionally trade with caravans of wagons from the east; I like to read English books."

"Oh, I'm something of an author myself," said Bent, withdrawing his notebook. "You ever get *World Marvels & Wonders*? It's a particularly high-quality publication in London. I write the adventures of our Gideon Smith up for it. He's something of a hero, you see."

She surveyed the wreckage of the mechanical man and cocked an ear to the roar of the dinosaur that had now begun to nose through the fragile pagoda roofs of the houses nearest the harbor. Someone screamed distantly, and Akiko covered the child's ears with her hands. "I suppose that's a matter of perspective," she said.

"Yes, well," said Bent, and jabbed a thumb at Lyle. "Like your hubby said, them as is in charge don't always have people's best interests at heart, even their own. Like your fellow with the sword. I mean to say, I've had some fierce bosses, but I've never been asked to disembowel myself before." He paused. "Well, there was the time I was told to take my pen and shove it—anyway, that's by the by. This writing I was telling you about . . . ?"

Akiko glanced down at Bent's notebook. "I can see your mistake, Bent-san. It is similar to Japanese, but I believe that is actually a Chinese pictogram."

Bent frowned. "Chinese? But it was a tattoo on the neck of one of those Japanese assassins—what did Lyle call 'em? Ninjas. On the neck of one of the ninjas that attacked him back in New York . . ."

Then he realized where he had seen the symbol before, why it was so familiar. It had only been that year, in March or April, when there had been all those murders in Limehouse, over that shipment of opium that had gone missing from the docks. The Chinese criminal gangs, the tongs. This was the mark the toughest of them wore as tattoos, just like the assassin in New York.

The mark of the dragon tong.

"Then he wasn't Japanese at all," Bent said slowly. He cast a surreptitious glance at Lyle, who was glowering at him. Bent swallowed drily. He needed to speak to Gideon.

"Remarkable," Serizawa said. "A human brain and a body of clockwork? Truly remarkable."

"But can you help her?" asked Gideon.

Serizawa shrugged. "I can try. Do you have any tools and instruments?"

"Plenty on the *Skylady III*, and room to work," said Rowena. She wiped her hands on a rag and put her tools into her bag. "We took a couple of stray bullets in the gondola and near the helium cells. I've been patching the old girl up." She dropped her voice. "But, Gideon, I really need to speak to you."

"And me," said Bent.

Gideon pinched his nose. "Seriously, can this wait?" He turned to Serizawa. "Do what you can. I beg of you. She is very special to me."

Akiko shook her husband's shoulder. "Haruki. I don't think there will be time. The monster is going berserk. It will destroy Nyu Edo."

Gideon stood straight. "We will help." He turned to Rowena, and beyond her to Inez and Chantico, who were hanging back near the 'stat, watching everything with interest. "Are you two up for a little excitement?"

Inez waved her sword. "Yes, Señor Smith. And we have something that might help!"

Rowena said, "Aloysius half blew up one of Pinch's Steamcrawlers. We loaded it up into the hold, and I think Chantico and Inez might have patched it up enough to work."

Gideon smiled. "Perfect! We'll take the Steamcrawler down to the town and try to hold off the dinosaur while Serizawa works on Maria. If she recovers quickly enough, she can fly Apep down to finish the job."

Gideon heard a strangled yelp from Bent. The thought of more danger, undoubtedly. Conversely, Gideon felt his heart race at the prospect. It was as if with each new adventure he began to believe, just a little bit more, what they said about him. Perhaps, after all, he really was the Hero of the—

"You have all got to be fucking joking, of course," said the voice of Edward Lyle. "Pardon my French, ladies."

Gideon turned to see Bent, wild-eyed and red-faced, floundering against Lyle, who had his arm around the journalist's throat. In his other hand he held a stubby Derringer pistol, which was pointing right at Bent's head.

"I think we all need to calm down and get a bit of perspective here," said Lyle. "Nobody is going anywhere, is that understood?"

28

Seize the Day

Before Gideon even knew what he was doing, he had drawn from his belt the pearl-handled revolver that had until recently belonged to Louis Cockayne. He brought it up in a fluid movement until he held it with his arm outstretched, one eye closed and the other sizing up the sweating head of Edward Lyle along the sights.

"I'm not sure what you're doing, Governor," he said evenly. "But please release Mr. Bent."

"Just getting your attention, Smith," said Lyle, but he kept the gun at Bent's head; the journalist held up his hands to show the governor that he wasn't going to make any sudden moves.

"Again: Release Bent, then we'll talk."

Lyle looked jumpy, his eyes wide. He said, "You've pulled a gun on the Governor of New York, Smith. What the hell do you think *you're* doing?"

Gideon heard a click to his right and risked a glance. Jeb Hart had his own gun out, pointing at Gideon. Lyle smiled and seemed to relax somewhat.

"Good work, Jeb. Keep your gun on him." Lyle pushed the barrel of his Derringer into Bent's temple. "And just so we keep this nice and neat from here on in, the next person who draws a weapon ensures the fat boy buys the farm."

"Hey, now!" protested Bent. "I'm not fat, I'm big boned."

There was a moment's silence, punctuated only by the roar of the tyrannosaur in Nyu Edo below.

"Governor," said Gideon. "Please. Allow Serizawa to work on Maria. Let me go and put right what I've done before the monster slaughters everyone."

Lyle smiled crookedly. "Isn't that exactly what we want, Smith? We came here as a war party, after all. The best thing is, we don't even have to lift a finger. We can just stand by and let that crazy beast destroy Nyu Edo for us. I'm not even asking you and your freak clockwork girl to do anything anymore, Smith. All I want you to do is nothing, like a good little hero."

Gideon kept the gun on Lyle, at the same time asking himself, *What the hell are you doing? Are you really going to shoot the Governor of New York?*

Maybe I am, he thought. Maybe I have to.

"Governor . . . ," he said. "Think about your wife. And your son. If I have to do this, I will. Think about them."

Bent nodded enthusiastically. "Yes, Lyle. Cora? Clara! Clara and little Alfie! Think about them!"

"Shut up," said Lyle. "Shut the fuck up."

Hart coughed. "Clara and Alfie? They're dead."

"Shut the fuck up!" screamed Lyle.

Gideon frowned. "Dead?"

"Yes, they're dead!" said Lyle, pushing the barrel of the gun harder into Bent's temple. "Back in 'eighty-seven, we had a winter like we'd never seen. We couldn't cope. Couldn't keep the fires burning. I lost them both to pneumonia. Swore the lights would never go out in New York again, Smith. And they won't. Hart, shoot him."

Gideon turned his head slightly, not taking his eyes off Lyle, and said to Hart, "You're going to do that?"

Lyle laughed. "Jeb Hart does exactly what I tell him to, and right now I'm telling him that if you don't put your goddamn gun on to the ground, he's going to blow your head off."

There was another roar, seemingly closer. The dinosaur must be making its way up the hilly streets of Nyu Edo. Serizawa's daughter, Michi, began to quietly cry.

"The thing is," said Jeb Hart casually, "that's not *strictly* true, Governor."

Lyle blinked. "What?"

"I mostly do what you say, so long as it chimes with the needs of the people who actually pay my wages."

"And who might they be?" said Lyle, his concentration slipping. Gideon squinted along the barrel of his gun again. He could take Lyle out now, with one shot . . . but ultimately, the governor was right. Gideon couldn't start shooting up servants of the Crown. Not without reason.

Hart grinned. "You could say me and Mr. Smith have the same boss."

Gideon couldn't help but turn his head toward the man pointing the gun at him. "Are you talking about Walsin—"

Hart raised the forefinger of his free hand to his lips. "Hush now, Smith. Too much information is a bad thing, yeah?"

"You're lying," said Gideon.

Hart shook his head. "Did you really think the mission to reclaim the brass dragon would be left to you and Bent? I've been working for the Crown for years, keeping a low profile, traveling across America and gathering information, helping out where and when needed. I was your backup, Smith."

Bent winced as Lyle pressed the gun harder into his head. "So, what?" said the governor. "You're on his side now? Then why the hell are you still pointing a gun at him?"

Hart shrugged. "Because you're the Governor of New York, and you have been given approval by the Prime Minister to stage a retaliatory strike against Nyu Edo. Gideon Smith is disobeying your direct command. So, no, Governor Lyle, I'm still on your side."

"Then shoot the asshole," spat Lyle.

"Wait!" said Bent. "Hart, hold on!"

"Shoot Smith!" said Lyle, his voice rising tremulously.

Hart raised one eyebrow. "Hold it, Governor. What've you got to say, Bent?"

Bent swallowed, his eyes swiveling around to try to look at the gun at his head. "Are you going to shoot me if you don't like what I say?"

"Probably," said Lyle.

Bent took a deep breath, and locked eyes with Jeb Hart. "The whole thing's a crock of effing shit. The Prime Minister has been conned. There was no attack on Lyle, was there, Governor? Those ninja weren't Japanese at all. That tattoo on the assassin's neck, it was from the dragon tong. Chinese gangsters. You've got a Chinatown in New York, haven't you? I don't know how you roped in four of 'em to attack you on a suicide mission . . ."

A cloud passed over Lyle's face, then he shrugged. "Sing Sing prison's full of tong crooks who'll cut any kind of deal to get out of jail. So I massaged the truth a little. It's only a matter of time before the Japs make a move for real."

"But that's not all, is it?" said Rowena. Gideon arched an eyebrow in her direction. His friends seemed to have been uncovering all manner of secrets. Perhaps he should have been taking more notice of them.

She walked into Gideon's sight line and withdrew a folded piece of paper from inside her shirt. She held it up. "This is the letter from the Prime Minister."

"You going to tell me that it's fake?" asked Gideon.

"No," said Rowena. "I think it probably is Mr. Gascoyne-Cecil's signature. It was Governor Lyle's mark that interested me more."

"Maybe I'll sign you an autograph later," said Lyle. "When I'm Governor of Nyu Edo as well." He seemed to suddenly lose patience. "Come on, Smith, put your gun down. I'm gonna count to five."

"The thing is," Rowena continued, "I'd already seen your signature before, but I didn't know it then. I saw it on the manifest for the coal run to Steamtown that's in your pocket. For which the payment was people, stolen from the streets. That was you, Lyle. You said you'd do anything to keep the lights on in New York City. And that includes trading lives."

Gideon stared at Lyle, filled with loathing. Was this what power did to a man? Stripped him of his humanity?

"Why?" he asked. "You fake an assassination attempt on

your own life, cook up some story that the Japanese are working on a weapon that can destroy cities . . . why? Why did you want war with the Californian Meiji?"

Rowena tucked the damning paper back in her shirt. "Lyle and Hart looked as surprised as anyone when we saw Serizawa's metal man." She looked curiously at Jeb. "What did you really discover in California, if it wasn't a weapon?"

"I think I can answer that," said Serizawa. He dug into a pocket in his laboratory coat. "My daughter went on a trip with her school into the hills, not very far from here. She brought this back."

He held up a tiny thing between his thumb and forefinger. It glistened in the dying light.

Gideon said, "Gold. This was all about gold?"

"Old Lyle did say it takes a lot of effing money to run a city like New York," said Bent. "And he ain't getting much help from London. So he decided to go to effing war with the Japanese for the gold that Jeb Hart told him was in the hills. But he couldn't just go straight in and take the gold; he needed a reason for war. So he cooked up this ninja attack using Chinese criminals from his own prisons, made up this whole bullshit story about a weapon the Japs were making to attack New York—a weapon we've just destroyed, which was actually a defense against bloody monsters, by the way—and conned us hook, line, and sinker to do his dirty work for him. And on the side he was selling off the flotsam and jetsam of his city to those buggers in Steamtown until he could get his hands on the gold."

"That's it," said Lyle. "Hart, take that gun off Smith or shoot the hell out of him."

"Yes, Jeb," said Gideon, locking eyes with Lyle. "Are you going to take this gun off me? Or shoot me? Or maybe you're going to stop protecting a corrupt criminal who needs to be summarily stripped of his role as Governor of New York and returned to London for trial."

There was a heartbeat, then two, then three. Jeb Hart

sighed and said, "Gideon, I'm sorry. Lyle is still the Governor of New York, and he's got more stripes than you. I have to follow orders."

Lyle roared with triumph, holding his Derringer above his head and firing into the air. Gideon heard Hart spin the cylinder in the gun that was just a few feet from his head. Was this how it ended? Shot by one of his own compatriots over the criminal deeds of a British governor? Was this really how *wrong* the world was?

"Oops," said Hart. Gideon turned his head a fraction, just in time to see six shiny bullets fall from the chambers in the open cylinder and plummet to the dust. "Gosh, that was darned clumsy of me. Looks like I'm fresh out of bullets."

Lyle's cry of triumph turned to a roar of fury at Hart's betrayal. Eyes blazing, he strengthened his grip around Bent's neck and brought the gun down, his finger already tightening on the trigger as he thrust the Derringer to Bent's temple.

But Gideon was quicker. In the elongated second that followed, he considered that this was how it must feel for Maria to be at one with a piece of machinery. In her case it was Apep the brass dragon; for him, right at that moment in time, it was Louis Cockayne's gun. He felt the pearl-inlaid handle, slick with the sweat from his palm, as though it were an extension of his hand. The curve of the trigger sat so snugly against the crook of his forefinger that their atoms mingled, even the very thought of bringing the trigger back acting to move it before the pressure of physical movement did so with satisfying fluidity. The hammer whispered down, oiled to the point that friction was completely nullified: a perfect, pure movement that was almost not of the physical plane.

And as the hammer struck home with explosive finality, Gideon could have sworn that somewhere in the spaces between each orchestrated movement, Louis Cockayne urged him on.

Be prepared.

And if you can't be prepared . . .

Be lucky.

He couldn't claim preparation, though perhaps Jeb Hart could. And it wasn't so much luck as opportunism. The bullet found its mark, right in Edward Lyle's forehead. It wasn't clean, but it was quick. Lyle jerked backward, his Derringer flying out of his hand, Bent lunging forward to escape the spray of blood, bone, and brains that geysered out of the gaping black-red cavern where Lyle's face used to be.

Perhaps Gideon was finally doing what Louis Cockayne had said he should. Perhaps he was finally being his own man. Maybe, just maybe, he could start writing his own rules for what Rowena called the heroes club.

Be prepared.

And if you can't be prepared . . .

Be lucky.

And if you can't be lucky . . .

Seize the day.

There was a stunned silence as time twanged back into shape. Lyle sprawled in the dust, a widening pool of blood pouring from the back of his head. Gideon pulled Cockayne's gun back to his face, breathing in the cordite, and blew the wisp of gun smoke from the barrel.

"Carpe di-effing-em," he said.

"Jesus Christ," croaked Bent, on all fours and rubbing his jowly neck. "Jesus effing Christ." He looked up. "You saved my life, Gideon. The effer was going to do for me."

Rowena bent down by Lyle. "He's dead, for sure."

Bent hauled himself to his feet and patted his pockets for his tobacco. "Heh, he might have served up a good turkey, but you cooked his goose well and effing proper, Gideon."

Gideon turned to Jeb Hart. He said, "Thank you."

Hart pulled a bent cigar from his shirt pocket and lit it with a match he struck on his belt buckle. "You just bought yourself a hill of shit, Smith." He grinned. "Glad I could be of service."

"Then we'd better get our stories straight before I go back

to London," said Gideon. "Rowena? I'm sorry. You were trying to tell me about Lyle and the slaves. And Aloysius, too. I
should have listened. Made time to listen. It won't happen
again. Being my own man doesn't mean I have to do everything on my own. I understand that."

"Smith-san?" said Serizawa hesitantly.

Gideon nodded, holstering Louis's—*his*—pistol. "Yes. Mr.
Serizawa, I would appreciate it if you would start doing what
you can for Maria immediately." He looked over to the *Skylady
III*. "Inez? Chantico? There was mention of a Steamcrawler in
the hold?"

Chantico waved excitedly, and Inez raised her slim sword,
dragging her cowl over her head and crying joyously, "La
Chupacabras!"

Gideon allowed himself a thin smile. "Then let's go and
bag us a Tyrannosaurus rex."

The Steamcrawler chugged down the ramp from the *Skylady
III*'s hold, Inez at the wheel. The armored cover of the vehicle
was missing, and it seemed to Gideon that it was pumping out
a lot more steam exhaust than a healthy engine should, but he
had to admit that they had done a bang-up job repairing the
metal tracks. There were two guns—now exposed by the missing carapace—at the front and rear of the cockpit, each fed by a
ribbon of ammunition. Whether they would have enough firepower to bring down the tyrannosaur remained to be seen.

Inez, who insisted on wearing the black cowl, an ensemble
to which she had added a black, narrow-brimmed hat with a
chain of silver buckles around the crown, smiled. "Chantico repaired the track. Who knew he had an aptitude for things like
that? Perhaps he is not so much of an idiot after all."

Chantico scowled at her but glowed with pride at the mor-
sel of praise she had thrown him. Bent murmured, "He's going to have his work cut out with that one, mark my words."

Gideon checked the guns Rowena had brought him from
the small armory on the 'stat and began to pass them to

Chantico to store in the Steamcrawler. It had been agreed
that Gideon, Chantico, and Inez would take the vehicle into
the Nyu Edo streets and tackle the dinosaur. Jeb Hart, by
tacit agreement of them all, had done quite enough; if anyone
was going to get into trouble with Walsingham for rank dissent, they decided, it might as well just be Gideon.

Or, as Bent had said, considering the prone body of Edward Lyle, "Might as well be hanged for a sheep as a lamb."

It was properly dusk now, and below in Nyu Edo glass balls
strung together along the hilly streets began to glow into life.

"They were my invention," said Serizawa proudly. "Fully
automated. At this time each evening, gas begins to flow into
each globe and is lit by a sparking flint."

"They'll help us track the beast." Gideon nodded, watching patches of the city plunge into darkness, strip by strip, as
the dinosaur crashed through the chains of lights.

"'Ere, Gideon, before you go," said Bent, plucking his
sleeve and taking him to one side. "I just wanted a word."

"Quickly, Aloysius," said Gideon, but not unkindly.

Bent nodded. "I just wanted to say . . . look, you saved my
life back there, Gideon. I really thought Lyle was going to kill
me. But I know you. . . . I know what you must be feeling."

"Yes," said Gideon. And Bent was right. Gideon had shot
the Governor of New York, and he accepted all the attendant
trouble that was going to blow in with that. But more to the
point, he had shot a man, in cold blood, right in the head.
Eventually he said, "Captain Trigger once said to me that a
hero is only as brave as other men, but just for five minutes
more." He smiled crookedly. "It didn't feel a very brave thing,
what I did."

"That's a good thing," said Bent. "The minute you stop
feeling terrible about killing a man, you're no longer a hero.
You're a villain. You're going to have to make tough choices in
your job, Gideon, and I don't envy you one bit. But I think
you made the right one there. If you hadn't shot Lyle, he'd

have shot me. And God knows how many would have died down there."

"Speaking of which," said Gideon. "Inez? Are we ready to go?"

"Just feeding the furnace," she called back. "Two minutes."

Gideon took the opportunity to quickly climb aboard the *Skylady III*. He found Serizawa in the galley, where Maria lay, naked, on the main worktable. Gideon averted his eyes as Akiko and Michi watched from the side.

"I am sorry I had to shoot that man in front of your daughter," said Gideon to Akiko.

She shrugged wearily. "I suppose now that we are cast out into the lawless land we must get used to that sort of thing."

"There is a place, quite far from here," said Gideon. "A new community of people like yourselves. We could perhaps take you there?"

Akiko smiled. "We will need friends. Thank you." She looked at her husband and squeezed her daughter tightly. "Our little Pathway. I told you she was well named." Gideon turned to Serizawa, who was standing, his fingers steepled under his chin, staring at Maria. Unlike Gideon, who regarded Maria as a woman, it was clear Serizawa saw her through an engineer's eyes, as a particularly complex puzzle.

"Here," said Gideon, and placed his hands on either side of Maria's navel. How he had longed to take her in his arms, to touch her. But not like this. He massaged her stomach until, just as she had shown him on their very first meeting, her torso parted with the slightest click, doors opening on tiny hinges to display her clockwork innards.

"Fascinating," breathed Serizawa. "I can see that there are hydraulic pipes that have been severed, and one or two cogs have been smashed. . . ."

"You can fix her?" said Gideon.

"She is very special to you," said Serizawa. "Important."

"Yes," said Gideon. "She is very special. To me as well as to the country."

Serizawa nodded. "Then I will fix her."

"Gideon!" called Inez from outside. "We are ready!"

The little girl, Michi, broke free of her mother's arms and walked over to Gideon, her face serious.

"Can you stop the monster, please?" she asked in perfect English.

Gideon squatted down and ruffled her black hair.

"Yes," he said. "That's what I do."

29

SISTERHOOD

 "Are you sure you want to do this?" asked Gideon. The Steamcrawler was rumbling and shuddering, perched on the crest of a compacted-sand track that led down a steep hill from the complex of warehouses and laboratories toward Nyu Edo.

Inez opened her mouth to answer, but Chantico got there before her. "Yes," he said. "We both had a good look at this machine on the flight over. We think we know how to make it go."

Inez nodded. "Chantico is right. It needs a lot of coal to feed the furnace and someone to steer it."

Gideon sat in the rear of the cockpit, by the two guns that were mounted on the steel carapace. "I didn't mean that," he said. "You are putting yourselves in grave danger. This is not your fight."

"It isn't your fight, either," said Inez. "You are British. The Japanese are your enemies, yes?"

Gideon shrugged. "Not really. Not my enemies personally. Besides, it is my fight. I destroyed their only defense against the tyrannosaur. If people die down there, it will be my fault."

"This land . . . ," said Chantico haltingly. He swallowed and tried again. "The Nameless, he said . . . he said this land is injured. Fractured. It needs healing. I think this is a way for us to help."

Gideon nodded. "You are both very brave. You have my thanks."

From below, there was a roar. The sky was dark now, and the black patches among the lamp-lit streets marked the progress of the dinosaur. Gideon said, "We should go."

Chantico climbed into the space beneath Gideon's perch. There was coal in the open furnace, already burning with fierce heat. The Steamcrawler pulled against the brakes that held fast its steerable wheels at the front and its long tracks that ran the rest of the length of the vehicle. Inez sat in the sprung driver's seat and surveyed the leather-covered steering wheel and the array of levers.

"I think this is the brake—" she began, and the Steamcrawler jerked forward, the tracks spitting dust into a huge cloud behind them, and then began to roll down the hill with a speed that tore Gideon's breath from his throat.

Inez raised her gloved fist high above her head, her black hair flowing from beneath her cowl. "La Chupacabras!" she called, as Gideon's stomach flipped and the Steamcrawler tore into Nyu Edo.

Nyu Edo was all hills, and Gideon was exhausted from holding on to the edge of the cockpit by the time the Steamcrawler had swept at a speed unimaginable for such a heavy metal vehicle down one and up another. Inez whooped and hollered as she dragged the machine around corners, its tracks skidding on the roads. Once the rear of the Steamcrawler smashed into a column holding up a string of gas lamps, and they came crashing down behind them. A small shrine in the middle of the road was plowed through, the stone statuary grinding under their tracks, making Gideon fear they were going to be upended. Periodically, Chantico raised his sweating face from the furnace to gulp fresh air and glance fearfully at the erratic route Inez was taking through the town.

Once they were in the town, which was eerily devoid of life, it was more difficult to track the tyrannosaur. Gideon begged Inez to stop the Steamcrawler; she did so by hauling on the brake lever, causing the vehicle to skid outward, rear first, into a fence bordering a block of small wooden houses with pagoda roofs.

Trying to push away the chugging of the steam engine, Gideon clambered up onto the metal shell of the Steamcrawler, listening to the night. A roar suddenly split the air, close enough to make Gideon throw his hands to his ears. Ahead of them was a patch of darkness between two large houses. Gideon held up his hands for quiet, peering into the blackness, just as a small group of men came running from the far right.

The first of them glanced with puzzlement at the Steam-crawler but urged the rest on. Gideon counted a dozen, all wearing black armor composed of metal scales and plates, joined together by rivets and lengths of silk. They had metal plate helmets with broad neck guards and carried long swords. Gideon searched his memory and came up with a name for the weapon: katana.

"Samurai," he said quietly. He had read of them—in *World Marvels & Wonders*, of course—but never thought to see them.

Inez stared at the backs of the men as they jogged in formation into the dark street. "They have only swords?"

"The samurai are fearsome warriors," said Gideon. "But even so . . ."

There was a volley of shouts from the alley, then a terrible, high-pitched scream. The first of the samurai came running out, eyes wide and shining with terror, followed by two more. There was a rhythmic beat of thunder, or an earthquake that shook Nyu Edo, the Steamcrawler rattling as it bounced upon the dry, compacted earth.

Then the beast stepped out of the shadows. It let the rag-doll shape of a decapitated samurai fall from its jaws, and roared.

"My God," breathed Inez. "I had no idea. . . ."

Gideon stared at it. It seemed even more magnificent here among the incongruous roads and streets of civilization than it had in the jungle of the lost island, as thought it had suddenly become the head of a whole new food chain and knew it. The dinosaur threw back its head and roared again, shaking the glass out of the windows of the houses all around them. Then it bent forward, creating a straight line from the tip of its nose to the end of its tail, and turned its huge head—as big as their Steamcrawler—to one side, regarding them curiously.

"Inez," Gideon said softly, calmly. She ignored him, trans-fixed. "Inez."

"Yes?" she whispered.

The tyrannosaur sniffed the air, its yellow eyes staring un-blinkingly at them.

"Does this thing go backward?"

The dinosaur took a step toward them, crushing the corpse of the samurai and barely noticing. It straightened, towering above the pagoda roofs, then bent forward sharply, its gore-dripping jaws widening.

"I think so," she murmured.

"The guns," said Gideon. "They are facing backward. I need you to go back as quickly as you can and turn the Steam-crawler around. Can you do that?"

Inez nodded. The tyrannosaur took another tentative step and lowered its head. It was barely twenty feet from them. Gideon felt its warm, fetid breath wash over him.

"Quietly . . . slowly . . . ," he said.

Chantico popped up his head. "Why have we stopped? What's the—"

The tyrannosaur's eyes flickered at the sudden movement, and it reared backward.

"Now!" shouted Gideon.

Inez slammed one of the levers, and the Steamcrawler lurched . . . forward, taking them another five feet closer to the dinosaur.

"Backward!" shrieked Gideon, pushing Chantico's head back below. "Shovel coal, for God's sake!"

The tyrannosaur roared straight at them as Inez found the right lever and the Steamcrawler began, painfully slowly but with gathering speed, to reverse back up the road they had come down. The dinosaur watched them, almost quizzically, for a moment then put its head down and began to follow in huge, thunderous strides.

As the Steamcrawler picked up speed, Gideon drew the pearl-handled revolvers and began firing at the beast. He winced as the bullets pinged off its scaly hide. "We need to turn, Inez!" he shouted. "I need the bigger guns!"

Inez suddenly yanked the steering wheel, and the Steam-crawler veered to the left, Gideon ducking low as the rear of the vehicle slammed into the fragile wooden frame of a house. Inez pulled forward and turned up the hill as the dinosaur came within feet of them, its glistening maw opening wide. Gideon began to empty the bullets from the gun mounted at the back of the Steamcrawler.

Stung by the bullets, the beast faltered and slowed, glowering at them then redoubling its pace. Gideon fired a whole belt of bullets, most of them bouncing off the thing's hide but several finding a home in its softer underside, as evidenced by the dinosaur's anguished howls and the holes oozing with black ichor that peppered its belly.

But still it came. The gun clicking emptily, Gideon switched to the other one. "Perhaps we can lead it out of the town," he shouted over his shoulder.

"We'll lose speed on the hills," called Inez. "What about down toward the sea?"

"Whatever you—" began Gideon, but the breath was knocked from him as Inez swung the Steamcrawler hard to the left and then, incredibly, pulled on the brake lever.

"What are you doing?" he screamed. They had put another thirty feet between themselves and the tyrannosaur, but the gap was closing fast.

"Señor Smith . . . ," said Inez, and he chanced a turn. There, ahead of them in the road, was a woman, her eyes tightly closed, her kimono torn and muddied. She sheltered three tiny children within her thin arms.

Gideon swore and began to pull at the trigger of the gun.

The tyrannosaur was evidently a quick learner because it came in low and fast, snarling, the moon glinting off its green, scaly hide, its soft underbelly close to the ground, its feet pounding the road.

For a moment its eyes met Gideon's, and it hissed, as though recognizing him.

Finally, its gaze seemed to say. *Finally, after all this time. I have found you.*

"I'm sorry if Rubicon stole your baby," he murmured. "But it's you or me. And I'd rather it was you."

As the dinosaur powered toward Gideon, he took aim along the Steamcrawler's gun barrel. If he could hit it in the eye, pierce the brain . . .

"Come on, Louis, if you were ever going to make my aim true . . ."

He pulled the trigger.

Nothing happened.

The belt was empty, or the gun had jammed.

The tyrannosaur roared in triumph, its gaping mouth wet and red as it bore down on Gideon, just as the first of a volley of fireballs exploded around the beast's head.

Maria turned Apep into a steep climb after letting loose the first series of fireballs at the dinosaur, rolling up and over to come in for a second wave. The monster had reared away from the vehicle, and Maria's heart—or what passed for it—leaped as she saw Gideon in the gloom, staring up at her with astonishment. She laid another series of fireballs around the feet of the tyrannosaur and it turned with a roar, snapping in her direction with its jaws before lowering its head and moving away from the Steamcrawler.

Maria had come to awareness to find Serizawa wiping oil and lubricant from his hands in the hold of the *Skylady III*, watching her with interest as she stirred and sat up straight.

"You are a wondrous creation," he said. "I have reconnected some pipes that had been severed and tightened a single flywheel. But your body . . . it seemed to be repairing itself even as I worked." He shook his head. "I have never seen anything like you."

"There is nothing like me," she said, turning her back to him and fastening her dress. "Where is Gideon?"

Rowena had rushed into the hold. "Maria, thank God! Are you able to fly the dragon? I think Gideon needs some help down there."

Maria pursued the tyrannosaur through the streets of Nyu Edo, guiding it north with a carpet of fireballs. She had already decided not to kill the dinosaur if it had not killed Gideon.

Bent had told her, as she climbed into the dragon's cockpit, that the tyrannosaur was a mother, in search of its stolen egg. Maria had no right to kill it, not if she could help it. So she had decided, from high in the sky above Nyu Edo, to nudge it toward the vast forest that she could see to the far north of the town. Let it find its own way. Let others hunt it, if they dared. It was a magnificent beast, a marvel of nature. Who was to say it had no place in the world?

Perhaps those people would say the same thing about her.

So she herded the tyrannosaur out of the limits of Nyu Edo, across the hills to the start of the tall redwood trees, and she gave it a smile and a little wave as she pulled Apep up and over the forest that stretched north as far as she could see.

"Have your freedom," she said softly. "Consider it a gift from one wondrous creation to another."

※

"What do you mean, you didn't kill it? We could have been eating effing tyrannosaur chops for a week!" said Bent.

"Hush, Aloysius," said Gideon. He put his arm around Maria as they sat together in the light from their campfire in the hills, the *Skylady III* tethered nearby, Apep slumbering beside the 'stat. "I understand why she did it."

"Well, I wish someone would effing explain it to me," said Bent. "Who's to say that thing's not going to come back and chow down on Nyu Edo? What was the point of it all?"

"It will probably die," said Inez, staring at the flames. "Señor Smith made several good hits to the beast."

"She won't come back, anyway," said Maria. "She was just looking for her place in the world, I suppose."

Bent sniffed. "The symbolism doesn't escape me. All I'm saying is it would have made better copy if you'd brought the thing down, that's all."

Gideon smiled. "Not everything happens so you can write your stories, Aloysius."

"Then what the eff am I doing here?" he said, but he gave Maria a wink. "You think this is my natural environment? Sitting here in the bloody hills of California, waiting for something that should have been dead sixty-five million years ago to wander up the hill and eat me whole?"

Maria raised an eyebrow. "Eat you whole, Mr. Bent? Are you sure?"

Bent scowled at her. "You saying I'm fat, Miss Maria?"

Rowena laughed as she brought out a tray. "Gin and sausages, Aloysius. This will cheer you up."

Bent patted his stomach. "I'd better leave the old spicy sausage alone, if everyone thinks I'm fat." He paused then made a grab for the bottle of gin. "Although I daresay a few shots wouldn't hurt."

Jeb Hart accepted a glass of gin from Rowena and turned to Gideon. "I must say, Smith, you have a rather . . . unorthodox way of getting things done. But you do get results, I'll give you that."

Gideon nodded. "I suppose I'll be in all kinds of trouble when I get back to London."

Jeb shrugged. "Edward Lyle caught a stray bullet from the Japanese mechanical man. It was all very unfortunate."

Gideon stared at him. "That's what you're going to say?"

"I suggest you do, too. Just so we all stay out of trouble."

"But why?"

Jeb smiled. "Because you're one of the good guys, Gideon Smith." He drained his glass and stood up. "Well, I'm going to saddle up and get off. I'll ride through the night until I get to Tijuana, then beg a place on an airship to New York." He grinned. "It's been a real pleasure working with you guys. But tell me when you're next in America, so I can make sure I take a long vacation somewhere very far away."

They decided to pack up the camp and head overnight to Texas. With the departure of the tyrannosaur, activity had returned to Nyu Edo. A cautious party of uniformed Japanese soldiers had been dispatched to poke over the remains of the destroyed Jinzouningen, but they were roundly ignoring the *Skylady III* on the hillside. Gideon, Hart, and Bent had buried Lyle in a rough grave before Jeb Hart departed, taking his personal effects to deliver back to New York. Rowena wanted to get airborne as soon as possible, before the soldiers of the Californian Meiji decided they wanted to investigate the 'stat and its passengers a little more closely.

"What's to stop it coming back? The dinosaur?" asked Bent.

Gideon looked into the distant, dark hills. "Who knows? Perhaps Maria should have killed it, after all."

Rowena shook her head. "I understand why she didn't. It wasn't the monster's fault. It was protecting its baby, or trying to."

"Never had you down as the maternal type," chuckled Bent.

She shrugged. "I'm not—" she said, meaning to add *yet*, but Gideon laughed, also.

"I can't imagine you like that, Rowena. Babies and marriage and that sort of life. I don't see you like that at all."

She looked at him for a long moment. *No*, she thought. *You don't see me like that at all, do you?*

"I suppose you could say the same for Lyle," said Bent. "Protecting his baby, I mean. And his wife." He shook his head. "You can sort of see what that would do to a man, losing them when he's the one who's supposed to keep the city running. You can sort of see why he went over the effing edge."

"Once, maybe," said Gideon. "Perhaps that was his driving force for keeping the fires on in New York, whatever the cost. But he went too far. Greed and power finished him."

"Actually," said Bent, "I think it was *you* that finished him. But I know what you mean."

"They'll cope in Nyu Edo," said Rowena. "They'll learn to defend the city if the beast ever comes back." She stared thoughtfully across the hills. "I hope it doesn't. I hope they don't kill it. Everything deserves a chance."

"They'll have to learn to defend themselves anyway," said Bent. "Once word gets out about all that gold in the hills . . ." He glanced around. "I don't suppose it's worth us having a little dig, is it . . . ?"

"You're right," said Rowena. "A secret like that won't stay secret for long. Nyu Edo will have its hands full if there's a gold rush over this way."

"Did we do the right thing?" asked Gideon. "Stopping Lyle, I mean. He had a mandate from the British government. Maybe we should have let him have his war with Japan. We're British, after all, aren't we?"

Bent shook his head. "It wasn't right, Gideon, we all know that. If you go to war for the right reasons, fair enough, though I'm more of an effing lover than a fighter myself. But Lyle lied through his arse about the Japanese, made them out to be warmongering savages, just so he could come in and wipe them out for their gold. That's not right, however you cut it."

Bent farted, long and low, and wrinkled his nose. "And *that's* not right however you cut it, either."

Rowena thought this an excellent opportunity to excuse herself and give the *Skylady III* a once-over before they took off. She stood on the bridge, checking the instruments. They could get back to the old mine, no problem, but she wanted to fill the balloon as tight as possible with helium, and make sure the framework was patched up right, before attempting to cross the Atlantic in the airship.

There was a slight movement behind her, and she turned to

see Maria, rubbing her hair with a towel. She had finally shed the ragged dress she had been wearing since London and exchanged it for a pair of Rowena's jodhpurs and a white shirt. Every time Rowena saw Maria, it took a little while longer to remember she was not human. Standing there on the bridge, drying her hair, she looked for all the world like any normal girl. Any normal, breathtakingly *beautiful* girl, Rowena corrected herself.

"Thank you for use of the bathroom," said Maria.

Rowena nodded. "Hey, us girls gotta stick together."

Maria's smile of gratitude almost broke Rowena's heart. The clockwork girl said, "I don't think they understand why I didn't kill the monster. Do you?"

"I think I do," said Rowena. "Sisterhood."

Maria nodded excitedly. "It must sound insane. But I felt a . . . a kinship with the beast. It did what any mother would do, any woman." Maria tilted her head. "I envy you. It must be wonderful to have the . . . what do you call it? Brethren?"

"Esteemed Brethren of International Airshipmen," said Rowena. "Ah, they're just a bunch of flyboys who drink too much and tell increasingly taller tales. It isn't that much fun." She paused. "You fly. Perhaps you could join."

"Or perhaps we could form our own . . . what did you say? Sisterhood?"

Rowena smiled. "That sounds like a capital idea."

Maria gave Rowena a hug. "Then at least we'll always have each other," she said, and departed to help the others load the Steamcrawler up into the hold.

Rowena watched her go. "Yes," she murmured to herself. "We'll always have each other. But only you have Gideon Smith."

30

FREEDOM

Gideon looked out over the old mine from the cockpit of Apep, as the *Skylady III* beside them spiraled around to land on the dry prairie. He was amazed at what the new settlers had done so far: Three log houses were already practically finished, and more rose from foundations. Ackroyd's cattle were contained within a wide corral, and Gideon could see a stream of people carrying buckets of water from the creek. Below them stood a lone man, his face hidden by the brim of his hat, waiting for them to land. The one they called the Nameless.

At the sight of the brass dragon, everyone stopped and stared, drifting toward them as Maria brought Apep down, its flapping wings stirring up a dust cloud. Rowena dropped the anchors on the *Skylady III* and brought the 'stat down beside them. The Nameless waved at them, puffing on his clay pipe. As Gideon climbed down from Apep and helped Maria onto the ground, he called, "Job done?"

Gideon nodded and walked over to him. "My name is Gideon Smith," he said.

The Nameless nodded. "I know."

"Thank you for helping Rowena hold off the Steamtowners while we went for the dragon. And thank you for looking after Maria."

The Nameless appraised Maria for a moment. "So you *are* alive, then?"

She smiled. "After a fashion."

"I know how that feels," said the Nameless.

Bent huffed up. "Bang-up job you chaps have done here," he said, looking around. "Two questions: Have you built a bloody outhouse yet? I'm dying for a shit, and Rowena won't let me go on the airship because last time I stunk the place up for four hours."

The Nameless smiled. "We've one over yonder. You said two questions?"

"Gin," said Bent. "For God's sake tell me you have some. I appear to have drunk the *Skylady* dry."

"We've got whisky, Mr. Bent. Will that suffice?"

"Suppose it'll have to," said Bent. "Oh, and there's one more question, Mr. Nameless, which you can be thinking about while I'm on the throne."

The Nameless raised an eyebrow. "Oh?"

"Yes," said Bent. "We've killed the villains, lost a friend, saved the girl, and gotten back our stolen dragon. We've freed the slaves and nearly gone to effing war. But one mystery remains. Just who the eff *are* you?"

Later, when the sun had gone down, the fledgling township settled into its new rhythm of eating around campfires dotted around the territory, the people helping themselves from great pots of beef stew and beans. Gideon carried a bowl back to a fire bordered by log benches, joining Bent, Rowena, and the Nameless. Inez and Chantico had gone to see the Yaqui and Noshi. The disparate people who found themselves among this strange new gathering would retire to sleep in the existing log cabins or the stone-built mine house, said the Nameless. They would rise early to start work on building more cabins, creating irrigation ditches from the river to the planned crop areas, chopping down trees, and casting around for stone and other resources.

"They're staying, then?" asked Rowena. "All of them?"

The Nameless nodded. "They've got nowhere else to go."

"What are you going to call this place?" said Bent. "Misfit City?"

The Nameless gazed into the fire. "Freedom. That's what we agreed. It's a town called Freedom."

"Good to have a name," said Bent, slurping the gravy noisily from his bowl. "How about you? Can't *really* be called the Nameless."

The Nameless put his empty bowl down and lit his cigar from the licking flames of the campfire. After a long moment he said, "No, I suppose I can't. That's what other men call me. I did have a name once . . . but I can't remember. Can't remember anything before April eighteenth, seventeen seventy-five."

"You're in damn fine shape for a hundred-and-fifteen-year-old," sniffed Bent.

"I'm older than that," said the Nameless. "I think I was forty years old in seventeen seventy-five."

"April eighteenth," said Gideon. "That's when the British marched into Lexington and Concord and put down the rebellion."

The Nameless nodded. "When Gideon, the great British mystery man, stopped Paul Revere from spreading the word that the redcoats were coming." He looked at Gideon. "Your namesake."

"I'd never thought about it before I came to America," said Gideon brusquely. "My mother was a churchgoer. Named me for the man chosen by God to free the people."

"The judge of the Hebrews," said the Nameless. "His name means 'the destroyer,' you know."

"You a rebel, then, Nameless?" said Bent. "Given you don't remember anything before the revolution?"

He puffed on his cigar. "Not sure what I was. Not sure what I am now, to be honest. All I recall is that I woke up on April nineteenth, seventeen seventy-five, with my head hurting like crazy. And something was wrong."

"Wrong?" said Gideon.

The Nameless looked at the glowing tip of his cigar. "I can't really explain it. It was like . . . like the land was in pain, and I could hear its scream, and that forced everything else out of my head. It was like something had happened that shouldn't have happened, that things weren't supposed to happen the way they did."

"The *land* was in pain?" asked Gideon. "What do you mean?"

"America," said the Nameless. "America was in pain. Like it was just about to be birthed, and . . . then it wasn't. Like something was lost that shouldn't have been. And in its pain, it chose me. Chose me to live forever, to find what was lost. So I started looking."

"Did you find it?" asked Bent.

"Didn't know what I was looking for. So I started traveling around America, to see if I could chance upon it. And all I saw was British at one end, Spanish at the other, then the Japanese, the Indians caught in the middle. And people were fighting over this bit and trying to buy or sell the other, and gaining a mile here for their own borders, losing ten miles there." He paused, looking out into the night and, thought Gideon, beyond the darkness, down the years. "And all the while, America kept screaming in my head."

Gideon caught Bent staring at the Nameless, and the journalist said, "That's possibly the biggest load of codswallop I've heard in my life." The Nameless raised an eyebrow. "But I say that every time I hear a new load of codswallop, and since I started hanging around with Smith here, it all turns out to be effing true." He shook his head. "So America thought something was wrong, and picked you to put it right. What now?"

The Nameless smiled thinly. "Since I came here, the screaming's stopped."

"You're free?" asked Gideon.

"I'm free." The Nameless nodded. *"And as he journeyed, it came to pass that he drew nigh unto Damascus: and suddenly there shone round about him a light out of heaven."*

"Then this is what you've been looking for. This is what you wanted," said Gideon.

"I think maybe this is what America wanted. Maybe it

doesn't mind people from all over the world coming here, so long as they can get on, work together. Maybe that's what America is all about, *should* be all about. Maybe that's its destiny after all."

Bent looked around, at the campfires. "This? They've got skyscrapers in New York, Nameless. They've got the heads of rebels in pickle jars in Boston. You think a few runaway slaves and some cowpokes are going to challenge that?"

"Everything has to have a beginning; 'tis the order of things," said the Nameless.

Bent shook his head. "You sure talk funny, you know."

The Nameless smiled. "Hark at yourself, Mr. Bent, if you don't mind me saying so."

Bent sniffed. "I do, as a matter of fact. And you've got to have a name. That's the order of things. Man's got to have a name."

The Nameless shrugged. Bent said, "That bollocks from earlier, all this *light out of heaven*. Acts 9:3, if my schooling serves."

"I have read the Bible. I have read many books in my time. I do not aspire to holiness, but it seemed to have a certain fit."

"Paul's conversion on the road to Damascus," said Bent thoughtfully. "Paul's as good a name as any."

The Nameless smiled again. "If it be your will."

Bent put out his hand. "It does, Paul. Everybody's got to have an effing name, after all. Stick it there."

The Nameless shook his hand. "Paul it is, then, Mr. Bent, at least to you." He paused thoughtfully. "I don't find it displeasing."

✦

The next morning, Rowena announced that she'd pumped more helium into the cells of the *Skylady III* and made the necessary repairs. "She should get us back to London."

Bent, yawning and scratching his crotch and enjoying a breakfast whisky, glared at her through one eye. "*Should?* Can't you be a bit more positive than that?"

Rowena laughed. "Where's your sense of adventure, Aloysius?"

"Think I crapped it out when Lyle had that gun to my head," he said. "What about you, Gideon? You flying in the airship or cozying up in the dragon?"

Gideon glanced at Maria. "With Maria, I think. It's taken me so long to find her, I'm not letting her out of my sight again."

"Just you and me then, Rowena," said Bent, belching and putting an arm around her. "Unless we're taking any waifs and strays back to London. What about you, Paul? Now your work here is done and all that?"

The Nameless was watching the liquefaction engine as it sucked the raw helium out of the mine shaft and transformed the element in its bowels into working lifting gas. "No," he said. "There's plenty to do. Steamtown is gone, but there are plenty of warlords like Thaddeus Pinch. Freedom will need my guns."

A horse approached, ridden by Inez with Chantico clinging to her waist. She brought it to a halt and slid from the saddle. "And the sword of La Chupacabras," she said.

"You're staying, then?" asked Gideon.

"Of course! We found it first!" said Inez.

Maria embraced the Spanish girl. "Thank you for looking after me while I was . . . unconscious," she said.

"It is good to see you back in the land of the living," said Inez. She looked around at the work progressing in the morning sun, the cabins rising from their foundations. "So much to do. But we have secured a treaty with Chantico's tribe—they will trade with us, and help protect us should we come to the attention of aggressors." She turned back to the others. "Tomorrow we ride to Uvalde, and I will secure a similar treaty with my stepfather."

"Sounds like you've got it all sorted out," said Bent. "But at the end of the day, Paul, you're just a big farm. If you want to grow, you're going to need some effing money. Steamtown had the coal and the whores. What have you got?"

"Perhaps something better," said Inez slowly, her eyes narrow. "This gas . . . this helium . . . it is the only thing that makes your airships fly?"

"Well, there are other gases," said Rowena. "Hydrogen, for one. But that's highly flammable." She paused. "My God."

"What?" asked Gideon.

"They're sitting on a huge source of helium," said Rowena excitedly. "Do you know how rare that is and expensive it is to extract?"

"They could make their own airships?" asked Bent.

"Or maybe we could sell it to others," said Inez. "The British, the Spanish, the Japanese . . . they will pay good money for helium, yes?"

"You'll need to extract and bottle it," said Rowena with a frown.

The Nameless coughed. "This gadget of yours . . ."

"The liquefaction engine?" said Rowena. She paused then smiled. "It's yours."

"Then I guess we got something better than coal or whores, Mr. Bent," said the Nameless. "It looks like Freedom is in business."

"Coal I can take or leave," muttered Bent. "But I'll have nothing said about whores." Then he let loose a long fart.

※

"Ready?" asked Maria.

Gideon waved once more from the snout of Apep and slid through the broken window. He had assembled a makeshift chair of cushions behind Maria's seat and stocked the cockpit with provisions. It was going to be a long, uncomfortable journey back to London, but he didn't care as long as he was with Maria.

They had decided that London wasn't ready to see Apep in all its glory again, so soon after the Battle of London, so they had timed their arrival to coincide with night in England. They planned to make landfall on the Cornish coast and await word from Whitehall.

"Ready," Gideon said.

Maria turned to him as the vast wings of Apep began to flap and the dragon started to rise from the dust. "Thank you for coming for me, Gideon."

"I could do nothing less." He paused. Louis Cockayne's words came back to him. *Sometimes bravery's just about having the gonads to stick your head above the parapet and say, "Hey, I'm different. And I don't give a rat's ass."*

"But what happens when we get back to London?" she asked.

Yes, indeed. What was to happen when they returned to London? He had spent so long hoping against hope that he would find Maria, but he had never given much thought to what would happen when they were finally reunited. Where was she to live? She had nowhere, save for Einstein's tumble-down house, and she was not going back *there*. What would Mr. Walsingham be expecting with regards to the dragon? Would he be expecting to spirit Maria away to have his scientists and engineers conduct experiments, turn her into the weapon he evidently wanted her to be? And what of Gideon, and his feelings for her? Were they even allowed?

Hey, I'm different, he said deep inside. His words spiraled out into the brilliant blue sky, where he fervently hoped Louis Cockayne would, somewhere, somehow, reach out and snatch them off the warm summer breeze like dandelion clocks.

And I don't give a rat's ass.

Seize the day.

Carpe di-effing-em.

"I love you, Maria," he said out loud. "With all my heart, and forever."

"And I love you, too, Gideon, with whatever is inside me that passes for a heart. But also with my head, for that is truly human, and it is there that I know I will love you forever."

"Then let's make for London," said Gideon, "and hope that forever doesn't come too soon."

They kissed, and the dragon rose into the blue sky, the sun bouncing off its brass hide as they headed east.

※

"Follow that dragon!" said Bent, waving at the gathered population of Freedom below as the untethered *Skylady III* began to ascend, Rowena wrestling the wheel to point the 'stat toward home. He couldn't wait to see London again; he could almost smell the stink of the Thames and feel the polluted air washing over his face. Gin, sausages, and the love of a good woman who didn't charge too much money. Never let it be said that Aloysius Bent didn't learn from his experiences; now, as before, he knew that slavery in all its forms, whether that of men forced down mines or women made to work in brothels, was villainy incarnate. But things were different in London. The whores there were happy, and well fed, and earned their money through honest (well, honest-ish) toil. And wasn't he Aloysius Bent, official chronicler of the adventures of the Hero of the Empire? He was practically doing them a favor, bestowing his presence upon them.

He waved until Freedom disappeared in the haze then joined Rowena on the bridge, the outline of Apep ahead of them in the blue sky. He didn't fancy that much, living in a pioneer town, not knowing where your next bottle of gin or comfortable crap was coming from. He liked his home comforts, did Aloysius Bent.

"Think they'll make a success of it?" he asked.

Rowena gazed at the distant horizon for a while then said, "Of course they will. They're in love."

Bent had been talking about Freedom, but looking at Rowena's glistening eyes he thought it best, against everything right and natural, to keep his trap shut. Just this once.

※

London was enjoying a late bloom of summer, the final burst of clear skies, warm sunshine, and a pleasant breeze blowing off the Thames, just the faintest nip in the air to herald the onset of the coming autumn. Gideon looked at the pleasure boats on the river and the 'stats nosing lazily across the blue sky, wishing he were out there drinking in the rays of the sun.

Mr. Walsingham coughed, and Gideon returned his attention to him. It was cool in Walsingham's office, the smell of beeswax almost overpowering. At least he had Maria at his side, and Bent at the other, picking his nose and inspecting the booty on the end of his quick-bitten fingernail.

Walsingham placed the sheet of paper he had been reading on the blotter of his neat and ordered mahogany desk. He steepled his fingers and looked from one person to another, his gaze eventually settling on Gideon.

"Well," he said.

Gideon waited.

"Welcome home, all of you. And you have succeeded in your mission. You have recovered Maria and the brass dragon. Well done."

"And where is the dragon now?" asked Gideon. They had landed in Cornwall in the dead of night after circling high above the clouds while the *Skylady III* signaled to the Fleet Air Arm base at Falmouth with the codes that Walsingham had given her before they departed.

"Safe," said Walsingham. "Our scientists are examining it as we speak."

"Safe where?" asked Maria.

Walsingham raised an eyebrow. "Just safe. But fear not, Miss Maria. Your work with the dragon is far from over. By your own admission, *changes* occurred within you during your American sojourn. You have become more independent. Whether that is because of your continued association with the dragon or despite it, we need to find out. As Gideon's old friend Charles Darwin would have it, you are evolving, Maria. Tests must be carried out. We shall be requiring your presence . . ."

"Maria goes nowhere without me!" said Gideon.

Walsingham sighed. "Oh, Mr. Smith, do not be tiresome. You think we allowed you to embark upon this enterprise purely so that you could be reunited with your true love?

The brass dragon is a weapon, Mr. Smith. Miss Maria is, whether you like it or not, inextricably a part of that. Tests must be carried out. Miss Maria must be a part of that. No harm will come to her, you can be assured of that."

"We can be assured of nothing," said Gideon. "Perhaps I am tiresome because what you do not overtly lie about, you omit. For example, why didn't you tell us about Jeb Hart? Why let us believe we were the only ones responsible for the rescue?"

Walsingham raised an eyebrow at Gideon's tone but said nothing, simply spreading his hands. "It is always wise to have a contingency plan, should things go wrong."

"Nothing went wrong," said Gideon.

Walsingham's already thin lips tightened. "I wouldn't be quite so . . . positive, Mr. Smith." He picked up the sheet of typed paper again. "Edward Lyle, the Governor of New York, dead. Louis Cockayne, whom I have employed in the past, dead. San Antonio destroyed in a flagrant act of aggression. Orders to engage with the enemy in Nyu Edo blatantly disregarded." He looked up at them. "Aiding and abetting the creation of a breakaway community whose interests are in direct competition with those of British America."

Gideon began to count off on his fingers. "Louis Cockayne died a hero, protecting Maria and me and enabling us to secure the dragon. We did, in fact, engage with the Japanese, but the reason for attacking them was proved to be utterly fraudulent. San Antonio, or Steamtown, was a viper pit of villainy where men and women were enslaved in the basest manner imaginable. The town of Freedom would have been established whether we were there or not. And Edward Lyle . . ."

"Edward Lyle died when he was hit by a stray bullet fired by the mechanical man created by the Japanese," finished Walsingham, laying down the paper. "Yes, I have read Mr. Hart's report."

Gideon breathed a silent thank you to Jeb Hart. Walsingham sat back in his leather chair. "Still, as I said, you have succeeded in your mission. You have returned our assets to British soil."

"Maria is not an asset," said Gideon, taking her hand in his. "She is my—" He looked at her, then back at Walsingham, defiantly. "She is my sweetheart."

"How terribly Bohemian," said Walsingham. He looked at Gideon for a long moment. "You, too, have . . . *changed*, Mr. Smith. Could it be that Maria is not the only one *evolving*? Not the only one experiencing increasing *independence*?"

"Perhaps I'm becoming my own man at last, Mr. Walsingham."

Walsingham frowned. "But I thought you were *our* man, Mr. Smith. By royal appointment."

Gideon leaned forward. "Mr. Walsingham, God knows just how many fingers you have in how many pies, but please let me clear one thing up: You pay our wages, but you don't own us."

He heard Bent snort in surprise beside him but didn't look over. He continued, "We have done as we were instructed, Mr. Walsingham. Now we are going to take a rest, have some time to recuperate. I trust that sits well with you."

Walsingham seemed faintly amused. He inclined his head. "Of course. If you do decide to leave the country for any reason at all, Mr. Smith, you will keep me informed, won't you?"

"Naturally," said Gideon, standing. Bent and Maria rose beside him.

"The Empire will call upon you when it needs you," said Walsingham. "Good day, Mr. Smith, and once again . . . well done. All of you."

Across London, in the Union Hall of the Esteemed Brethren of International Airshipmen, located in an ornate stone building on the edge of Highgate Aerodrome, court was in session. Or had been for some hours; Rowena waited impatiently in the wood-paneled corridor outside a closed wooden door, wondering if Gideon's debriefing had been more convivial than hers.

As soon as she had returned to London, a message was

sent to the offices of Fanshawe Aeronautical Endeavors. Miss Fanshawe had been commissioned to take one cargo to San Antonio and bring back another; the brief had not been fulfilled. There might be a case of maladministration to answer.

The panel of Brethren officials had heard her evidence—or as much as she'd dared give them, given the nature of the last few days—and had retired to consider their verdict. She had been waiting in the corridor for an hour, aching to get out into the sun, desperate to fly, even if it was just to take the *Skylady III* on a test flight to make sure the repairs to the balloon she had effected before her return were holding.

The door opened, and the clerk, a young man with a serious face and greased-down hair, nodded at her to enter.

She took her position before the panel of three men, all former airmen. Her peers. Her people. Her Brethren.

The chairman peered over his half-moon spectacles at her. "Miss Fanshawe. The panel has come to a decision."

She smiled at them and nodded. It was all a formality. Even the Belle of the Airways had to show she was accountable.

The chairman said, "We have heard your evidence about the job that was assigned to you at North Beach in New York. We consider that there were severe lapses in Brethren rules in even allowing this cargo to be taken. Accepting cargos for transport without allowing the captain of any vessel full disclosure is simply not acceptable according to the Brethren code. We accept that you had a desire to travel to San Antonio for your own reasons related to your, ah, extracurricular work on behalf of the British Crown. You ultimately proved pivotal in bringing to the fore a hidden and illegal trade in human beings. For that you are to be commended."

Rowena nodded. "Thank you. I—"

The chairman held up his hand. "*However* . . . although the whole enterprise was flawed from start to finish, you agreed as a member of the Esteemed Brethren of International Airshipmen to take on a cargo with the express understanding that you did not tamper with the documentation relating to said cargo. By your own admission you opened the cargo manifest when you were strictly forbidden from doing so."

"But—"

The chairman glared at her. "Miss Fanshawe. The word of the Brethren is their bond. Any lapse in honesty or integrity reflects on the whole organization. Whatever the rights and wrongs of the situation, you gave your word and you broke it."

"Then I am to be punished," said Rowena numbly.

The chairman nodded. "It is the decision of this panel that your membership in the Brethren shall be held in abeyance for the period of one year from today's date. During that time you may carry on your business but not under the auspices of the Brethren, and you must inform any and all clients before you take business that you are not Brethren at the present time."

Rowena stared at him. "This is my livelihood . . ."

He smiled. "Come, Miss Fanshawe. You are the Belle of the Airways. You were given the Conspicuous Gallantry Medal by Queen Victoria herself. Surely you will find enough lucrative adventures to fill your time until your punishment is at an end."

The chairman and the panel nodded and rose, leaving her alone in the room. "And this is the thanks I get," she said. Did they think adventuring actually *paid*? Conspicuous Gallantry Medal, indeed. She wondered, as she sighed and left the Union Hall, how much they'd give her for it at the pawnbroker.

Outside on Whitehall in the sunshine, Bent laughed long and hard and clapped Gideon on the shoulder. " 'You pay our wages, but you don't own us?' Now where have I heard that one before?"

"Here's another one you might know. 'We're going to have sleep, and lots of it, with ale and gin at regular intervals.' "

Bent cackled as Gideon took Maria's hand in his. She squeezed his, and he squeezed back then impulsively leaned over and kissed her on the cheek.

"Shall we take a steam-cab back to Grosvenor Square?" asked Bent.

"Oh, can we walk?" asked Maria, pirouetting and laughing, the wind from the river blowing her hair behind her. "It's such a lovely day, and the weather will turn soon. I haven't seen London look so beautiful for a long time."

"It's nothing compared to you, dearest Maria," said Gideon.

Bent mimed a vomiting motion with his stubby fingers in his mouth. "You might steal all my best lines, Smith, but I can see I'm going to have to teach you how to speak to a lady properly. And you can learn to effing cuss right, as well. Now come on, it might be a lovely day, but there's ale in them barrels that's not going to drink itself. I said we'd meet Rowena in the Audley Hotel after her Brethren meeting. And it's your round, I believe, Gideon . . . ?"

From his window, Walsingham watched the three of them walk arm in arm along the bank of the Thames. They had earned their break. He looked back at the neat pile of buff folders on his desk. There was plenty of time, and enough to keep them busy. For now, at least. After that . . . what was it Gideon Smith had said? Ah, yes. He had many fingers, and many, many pies.

Three Months Later

It was turning colder, much colder than it had ever been on the island, and she could feel herself slowing down, her blood running more sluggishly. But she was still fast enough and big enough that the black-furred beast that had bared its teeth and growled at her, standing upright on its back legs and batting its paws at her when she'd interrupted its attempt to scoop fish out of the bubbling stream, had offered little real resistance. The hunting was good in this place, and the animal would make a satisfying meal.

The wounds on her belly from the spitting sticks of the hairless creatures had healed, leaving her yellow underside crisscrossed with scars. She had resolved to keep away from such animals in the future, and none had ventured deep into the forest of soaring trees that stretched right up the coast of this vast new land she now called home.

Taking the beast in her mighty jaws, she began to thunder back through the forest. She shouldn't be here, she knew, perhaps shouldn't be anywhere in this world. But she was here, and she was alive, and she had to survive.

She felt a pang in her chest for her mate, whom she knew she would never see again. She could not conceive of going back into the vast ocean, could not think that she would ever see her island, or her mate, again. But life would go on.

Before she had left, he had filled her with eggs, barely a couple of months since her last clutch. She had known, as she fled into the forest of tall trees that shielded her from the hot sun, that something was happening inside her. It was only a week or two later that she had found herself clearing a space on the forest floor and lying down to ease out the eggs, seven in all.

Just like on the island, there was nothing bigger than her here, nothing to threaten her babies. Two had not hatched, and one had not survived longer than a day. But that left her four strong babies, two like her and two like her mate. They were tiny, still, no bigger than half of one of the hairless beasts that had attacked her, but they were growing stronger by the day. They chirped and growled as she nosed into the clearing and dropped the dead animal in the middle of the nest, the four of them falling on it hungrily, nipping at each other to get around its still-warm flesh, burying their teeth into its furry hide.

She watched, proudly, as they ate. Soon they would be big and strong, and she would teach them to hunt. Then they would leave to strike out on their own in the forest. They would pair up, if they survived, and have babies of their own, and she would be the head of a grand dynasty that would rule the forest.

And woe betide any of the hairless beasts who ventured into her domain.

As her babies ate, she thought, as she often did, of the egg that had been stolen from her, and she paused to wonder if by some miracle it had survived and hatched, and if it was out there somewhere, in this world that was so much bigger than she had ever imagined.

She threw back her head and roared, and the vast trees shook, and the tiny, feathered creatures flew, squawking, from the branches, and the furred beasts of the forest quaked and hid in their burrows. The land was huge, unending. She had never felt so free in all her life.

Snow blew against the window, the sky beyond pitch-black save for the pale corona of the nearby gas lamp on the street outside. Perhaps it was going to be a white Christmas. Emily Dawson paused to rub a stubborn smudge from the glass and glanced out at the rapidly falling flakes. Just the main laboratory to clean, then she could be away for the weekend. She moved away from the window and stood before the tall double doors, smoothing down her apron. She always left the laboratory for last. She hated it in there, hated the way the beast regarded her with its yellow eyes. She was sure an intelligence lurked behind those eyes that seemed to be sizing her up, appraising her. She couldn't understand why Professor Rubicon gave the thing houseroom.

He called it his "baby," which she thought an affront to nature and God. Still, Stanford Rubicon was a good employer, better than any she had worked for before. She had kept house—well, laboratory—for him these past three years—even while he was lost on that remote island—and he had always paid her well, on time, and never troubled her like some of the other girls said their masters did, especially in drink. She wasn't sure that Professor Rubicon had any interest in ladies at all; his work was everything to him, and he often jovially said that if science wasn't quite his wife, then it was certainly his mistress. She blushed whenever he spoke that way, and he always roared with laughter. Still, life with the Professor of Adventure was never boring. He always had some tale to tell of his expeditions to the far-flung corners of the world, some knickknack or trophy to show off. He had a home, of course, somewhere in Holborn, but he spent most of his time either at the Empirical Geographic Club on Threadneedle Street, where he was currently holding court, no doubt still regaling his companions with tales of being shipwrecked in the lost land of monsters, or his discoveries here, in his laboratory in the warren of streets just off Bishopsgate. Very often she would come in during the morning to find him snoring gently in a chair in his study, or slumped over a scattered pile of stones or ancient tiles in his laboratory, the thing in the cage mewling like a cat, waiting to be fed the chunks of raw meat she was obliged to bring in every day for its breakfast. The monster ate well, better than most within a square mile of the laboratory.

Taking a deep breath, Emily pulled open the doors and picked up her basket of polish and dusters. The laboratory would only need a cursory wipe-down, and then she could be off, away from the beady eyes of the beast until Monday morning, the pay Professor Rubicon had left for her in the kitchen safely tucked into her apron pocket. She poked her head around the door, took one look at the laboratory, and screamed.

※

The laboratory had been wrecked, benches overturned, books and glass phials scattered across the pale carpet. The gas lamps burned dully in their sconces, illuminating a vivid burgundy stain across the floor. Emily's first, mad thought was that someone had spilled a decanter of wine, but then she saw the door to the cage that dominated the room swinging open on its hinges.

The cage was empty. The beast was not inside.

Emily backed up against the door, casting fearful glances around the room. The monster—she corrected herself, as Professor Rubicon did every time she used that word—the tyrannosaur was not in the laboratory. It was as tall as a man now, and there was nowhere it could be hiding. And the doors to the laboratory had been closed. Unless the beast really was as intelligent as she had feared, and it had let itself out of the room and then closed the door . . . but no. One of the three windows that looked on to the dark alley running alongside the building was open, the curtains billowing inward, snow dancing through the gap. Two three-toed footprints, as big as dinner plates, led from the bloodstain toward the window.

Someone had been in here, an intruder. They had released the beast and . . . what? Been killed by it? But there was no corpse, unless the thing had eaten it whole. Safe to say that the intruder was someone who had not been as badly injured as the blood suggested, then, or perhaps there had been a second intruder who had helped their stricken colleague out through the window.

Emily ran over and peered into the alley. It was one story

up, low enough for a man—and a dinosaur?—to leap down. The snow below was disturbed, as though a fight had taken place, and there was more blood. Emily paled. The tyrannosaur was loose in London.

Emily ran to the study and began to search for a telephone directory or a notebook that might hold the number for Professor Rubicon's club. She could find nothing. Should she alert the constabulary? She bit her lip. She should tell the professor first. It couldn't be helped; she was going to have to walk. She took one more look out of the window before closing it. Who was to say the beast wasn't lurking out there, nearby, waiting to bite her head off?

But it couldn't be helped. She had to tell Professor Rubicon that his dinosaur had escaped.

Emily hurried through the snow, past the tavern that spilled out warmth and men on to the track churned to slush and mud by the horse carriages and steam-cabs. She pulled her shawl tight around her, to ward off the biting wind, the falling snow, and the catcalls from the drunkards.

"Over here, love. Penny to see your titties."

Emily kept her face down and almost ran past, but a thick hand grabbed her shoulder, a whiskery face breathing beer and a rotten stench at her. "Two pennies for a fuck, eh, love? I'll be quick."

"I'm not that sort of girl," she muttered, shaking him off. The others laughed as the man staggered back and said, "Every woman is that sort of girl, for the right price."

"You should give her one anyway, Harry," cajoled one of his friends.

"Think I will."

Emily uttered a small scream and began actually to run, casting a glance over her shoulder as the man staggered after her, fumbling with his trousers. She ran blindly, turning a corner and getting a dozen yards into pitch-blackness before she realized she had fled into an alley piled high with stinking refuse that rustled with rats, or worse.

She paused to look back. He had not followed her. But should she continue into the darkness, or retrace her steps to where he might be waiting? As she bit her lip, undecided, there came a noise beside her, something bigger than a rat. She jumped and turned to see a dark figure, something glinting in its hand. There was the faintest glow from a window high in the wall behind her, and the figure stepped into the slight pool of light. It was a man, clothed head to toe in black. He wore some kind of mask that covered the top half of his head, leaving his mouth and nose, and a neat mustache the only things visible save for eyeholes in his cowl.

The man was weeping.

He said something in a language she didn't understand.

"You've lost what?" she asked. "Lost yon toe? What do you—?"

At first she imagined a snowflake had kissed her forehead below her hairline, until a curtain of blood crept down to obscure her vision, and she saw the stranger's right hand whip to his side, the blade he held flashing in the dull light. With a sick, thudding heart, she knew.

Jack the Ripper.

It was the last thought she had.